Enigma Books

Also published by Enigma Books

Hitler's Table Talk: 1941–1944
In Stalin's Secret Service
Hitler and Mussolini: The Secret Meetings
The Jews in Fascist Italy: A History
The Man Behind the Rosenbergs
Roosevelt and Hopkins: An Intimate History
Diary 1937–1943 (Galeazzo Ciano)
Secret Affairs: FDR, Cordell Hull, and Sumner Welles
Hitler and His Generals: Military Conferences 1942–1945
Stalin and the Jews: The Red Book
The Secret Front: Nazi Political Espionage
Fighting the Nazis: French Intelligence and Counterintelligence
A Death in Washington: Walter G. Krivitsky and the Stalin Terror
The Battle of the Casbah: Terrorism and Counterterrorism in Algeria 1955–1957
Hitler's Second Book: The Unpublished Sequel to *Mein Kampf*
At Napoleon's Side in Russia: The Classic Eyewitness Account
The Atlantic Wall: Hitler's Defenses for D-Day
Double Lives: Stalin, Willi Münzenberg and the Seduction of the Intellectuals
France and the Nazi Threat: The Collapse of French Diplomacy 1932–1939
Mussolini: The Secrets of His Death
Mortal Crimes: Soviet Penetration of the Manhattan Project
Top Nazi: Karl Wolff—The Man Between Hitler and Himmler
Empire on the Adriatic: Mussolini's Conquest of Yugoslavia
The Origins of the War of 1914 (3-volume set)
Hitler's Foreign Policy: 1933–1939—The Road to World War II
The Origins of Fascist Ideology 1918–1925
Max Corvo: OSS Italy 1942–1945
Hitler's Contract: The Secret History of the Italian Edition of *Mein Kampf*
Secret Intelligence and the Holocaust
Israel at High Noon
Balkan Inferno: Betrayal, War, and Intervention, 1990–2005
Calculated Risk: World War II Memoirs of General Mark Clark
The Murder of Maxim Gorky
The Kravchenko Case: One Man's War On Stalin
Operation Neptune
Paris Weekend
Shattered Sky
Hitler's Gift to France
The Mafia and the Allies
The Nazi Party, 1919-1945: A Complete History
Encyclopedia of Cold War Espionage, Spies, and Secret Operations
The Cicero Spy Affair
A Crate of Vodka

NOC
The First Iraq War: Britain's Mesopotamian Campaign, 1914-1918
Becoming Winston Churchill
Hitler's Intelligence Chief: Walter Schellenberg
Salazar: A Political Biography
The Italian Brothers
Nazi Palestine
Code Name: Kalistrat
Pax Romana
The De Valera Deception
Lenin and His Comrades
Working with Napoleon
The Decision to Drop the Atomic Bomb
Target Hitler
Truman, MacArthur and the Korean War
Working with Napoleon
The Parsifal Pursuit
The Eichmann Trial Diary
American Police: A History
Cold Angel
Alphabet of Masks
The Gemini Agenda
Stalin's Man in Canada
Hunting Down the Jews
Mussolini Warlord
Election Year 1968

Paul G. Ritchie

Deadly Sleep

A Scientific Spy Thriller

Enigma Books

Published in the United States by

Enigma Books
New York, NY
www.enigmabooks.com

First Edition

ISBN 978-1-936274-45-1
e-ISBN 978-1-936274-46-8

Printed in the United States of America

Library of Congress Cataloging-in-Publication Data Available

Deadly Sleep

Prologue

Tongues of fire began to lick at the corner of the house. The flames gradually heated the rain gutter and then, as if following a route that had been laid out for them, rapidly spread to the lowest planks of the side wall, beneath the window. From there, the fire entered the house, spreading beneath the floorboards. In the bedroom, the planks of the hardwood floor started creaking and groaning, emitting a dense smoke that wafted over the bed and out the half-open window. From the farthest corner of the large yard, Skol, the Labrador retriever, yelped and snarled, hackles raised and front paws rigidly splayed. On the other side of the house, the windows in the living room were already gleaming with a blinding yellow light that increased in intensity by steps, as the fire fed off new sources of fuel. In a corner, the potted fichus curled up over its vase, as if it were trying to conserve air. On the mantelpiece, the heat had already scorched and wrinkled the photograph of poor Jim, who had been carried off by a malignant tumor years and years ago. Across from the fireplace, the bonfire that was consuming the Chippendale sofa was slowly melting the plastic of the old Mazinga action toy that Stevie, feeling nostalgic, had pulled out of the attic that morning before he headed back to college. Julia hadn't had the heart to put it back yet.

When the television set exploded with a sharp sharp boom, followed by the tinkling of falling glass, Skol started running frantically in a circle, barking furiously. In the bedroom the flames were starting to leap up into the sheets. They climbed up the quilt that Julia had stitched with her girlfriends before she got married; they licked at her motionless foot. On the far side of the house, the crackling floor finally gave way, and the outside wall of the house folded over onto it with a roar, kicking the flames even higher. With a yelp, Skol turned and jumped over the hedge, galloping headlong toward the waves. In her bed, stretched out on her side, Julia Sweig went on sleeping.

From high atop the hill, a man looked down and watched the fire take over the town of Massapequod. Aside from the sound of a few barking dogs, the flames, moving from house to house, appeared to be the only living thing in the small town. The man could hear bottles bursting inside the bar where he'd spent some time earlier chatting with the pool players. Across from the bar, the shop run by that old lunatic woman with her obsessions about jams and jellies was already a seething inferno. He noticed to his astonishment that even some of the playground equipment had burst into flames. Earlier that afternoon he'd helped a mother brush the sand off a little boy who had tripped and fallen while playing ball. Together he and the woman had smiled to comfort the weeping toddler. He'd explained to the mother that he loved little kids and she had smiled back at him encouragingly.

He took one last satisfied look at the burning houses. His work here was done. He waved to the truck: they could leave now.

Massapequod, Maine, Tuesday, October 29, morning

The sheriff got slowly out of his car and leaned on the door. He took off his hat and looked around open-mouthed. Everything was black and gray. The entire town of Massapequod was either as black as coal or ash-gray. In front of him a metal shop sign dangled, black and gold, half-melted, suspended from what remained of the charred wooden wall. The plate glass window had exploded, as had the jars that were on display behind it: the sidewalk in front of the shop was a sea of broken glass, immersed in a sticky tar-black goo. The sheriff squinted to see better.

"That's Miss Sullivan's jam, isn't it?"

"Yes, sir, it looks like jam. Or like it used to be jam, anyway."

The man who had answered him was a young uniformed officer, as slender and wide-awake as the sheriff was big, fat, and just now, dazed.

The officer, Paul Jackson, had awakened the sheriff a little over an hour before. Both of them stood staring across the street: the bar was just a black hole. The second stories of the houses had collapsed onto the ground floors, creating heaps of rubble that spilled out onto the street. All up and down that street, nothing remained standing but a section of wall here and there and a few blackened phone poles. The flames had consumed that wooden town. The parked cars were just shells of twisted steel. The air was redolent with the acrid scent of burnt plastic car seats. Fifty feet down the street, a fire truck was parked in the middle of the street. Men in firefighting suits wandered among the skeletal houses, but the fire hoses were still rolled up on the truck: there was nothing left to put out. The sheriff started to walk over to a car, but he stopped short. A dense wave of heat already told him that it was scorching hot.

"What the hell happened here?"

"Everything burned up, sir."

"Well, hell, I can see that for myself. What I mean to say is, how could it happen? Where is everyone? What's become of them? Who turned in the alarm?

Jackson was a methodical guy. So, unhurriedly, he began answering the questions in order. Starting from the end.

"We got the alarm from a cod-fishing boat. The fisherman were sailing past offshore and..."

"Cod, huh? Well, that's good." The sheriff glanced out to sea. "They said there was no more cod, but the cod's back after all. It's nice to know there're boats out there pulling in cod again, like when I was a little kid."

Jackson cleared his throat. "Well, they're not actually fishing cod. The government pays them to check how many fish are still out there and to do some experiments in repopulation and restocking. Any cod they catch they throw back. They're a little embarrassed about that and they prefer to say they're cod fishermen. Anyway, about four in the morning, before the sun came up, they saw a fire on shore and called it in over the radio."

"You had the night shift, is that right?"

"Yes, sir. I called the fire department and then I hurried over."

The sheriff seemed doubtful.

"You had to call the fire department?"

"Yes, sir. There's a fire station here, in 24-hour contact with the city fire department, but apparently no one called them."

The sheriff and the police officer looked down the road at the same time, toward the fire house. The garage door had collapsed. Through the gap the outline of the fire truck was visible. It had been charred by flames, probably when the gas tank exploded.

The sheriff grunted.

"Where is everybody? Where'd they get to?"

Jackson hesitated briefly.

"Eh, they're all here, sir. I don't think anyone left the town."

The sheriff looked at him again, open-mouthed.

"Come on," said Jackson.

They walked into what had once been the bar. Slumped over the countertop was the body of someone who had once worked as the bartender there, but who was now nothing but a charred torso, studded with chunks of the liquor bottles that had exploded behind him.

"Poor Stennis," the sheriff murmured. He made his way through the still-smoking boards and furniture, until he reached the pool room. Stretched out on the pool table was an unrecognizable body. One arm had detached from the body and had fallen to the floor. The other arm still clutched what remained of a pool cue.

The sheriff stammered:

"This just can't be. It's like they didn't even notice they were burning!"

"Exactly, sir. That's just what I thought. Look at this."

Jackson pointed to what had been the common wall with the house next to the bar. On the other side of the wall was what must have been the living room. In the middle of the rubble and detritus and the smoking remains of the bedroom furniture that had rained down from above when the ceiling burned through, you could see the ghost in black and gray of a peaceful evening at home. In front of the shattered television set, a charred corpse sat in an armchair. Another body was stretched out on the sofa, half melted on the plastic slipcover. The sheriff leaned against the wall, feeling an overwhelming urge to vomit. Jackson looked at him sympathetically:

"Do you want some water, sir? I've got a canteen in the car."

"I'd take something stronger than water, if you've got it."

Jackson hesitated for a moment, then pulled a half-empty flask of whiskey out of the back pocket of his trousers. The sheriff didn't seem to find any fault with that. He grabbed the flask and took two long slugs.

"Thanks," he said, and nothing more.

"Whiskey strikes me as a damned good idea, Jack." Behind them, the silhouette of the fire chief came into view. He was wearing his fire hat, his fire gear, and a depressed expression. He reached his hand out toward the flask.

"I've never seen anything like this."

He shook his head: "I must have said the same damned thing at least ten times in the past ten minutes."

"Got any ideas what happened?" the sheriff asked.

"Absolutely not."

"It's the same everywhere," he added, pointing into the bar. "It's as if everyone stopped dead right in the middle of whatever they were doing and just let the fire burn them up."

He spat on the ground.

"There are people who just lay there and sizzled on their bedsprings and there are other people who just let a glass of Coke melt in their hands. At the fire station everything is so badly charred that I can't tell if anyone even tried to do anything or not."

"What do you think, Brett? Do you think they tried to raise the alarm?"

The fire chief shook his head.

"Look, there's one thing I'm ready to make a bet on." He pointed to a stump of a power pole, charred and blackened: "You see that pole? Well, the fire went out on its own. No one lifted a hand to stop the flames, even by pissing on them."

They were back out in the middle of the street. The sheriff looked along the street that ran gently downhill toward the harbor. In the other direction, uphill, he could see the silhouette of a child's slide, crumpled and folded over upon itself, next to the skeletal structures of a group of houses. "When the election was held here, I got 80 votes out of 120 voters. The rest were children," said the sheriff, speaking to no one in particular.

Jackson jerked a thumb behind him.

"At the town limits on the way in, I saw a sign, pretty badly charred. It says: Massapequod, population 160."

"That's right, more or less. How could it be that nobody noticed what was happening? What about the dogs? They must have been barking, right?"

"They probably were, sir. But they ran away. I took a look around and I saw five or six dogs lurking in the trees."

The sheriff sighed: "We'd better get forensics down here."

"Have you alerted the governor's office?" he asked Jackson

"Yes, sir. They're waiting for a report, urgently."

"I'll bet the FBI is going to want to get involved."

Jackson looked up at the sky. It was a clear, sunny day. The sound of a helicopter filed the air.

"Yes, sir. They've already called ahead. I think that's them now."

New York City, FBI field office, Tuesday October 29, noon

The report appeared halfway through the midday news broadcast. The footage was scanty, all of it shot at a considerable distance. From a hilltop vantage point, the video feed showed a panorama of a blackened, charred town. The police had ordered reporters to stay away from all houses. The forensics team was still at work on what was now a vast crime scene. The police had also prohibited film crews from overflying the town by helicopter, without further explanation. There were no survivors to interview, so there wasn't much to add to the brief clips of the disaster. The anchorwoman simply reported that a strange fire, of as yet unknown origin or cause, had charred the entire village of Massapequod, Maine, and that the town's 166 inhabitants had perished in the flames.

"Probably just as well, for now," muttered O'Malley, as he switched off the television.

Time hadn't cut Jamie O'Malley any special deals. Twenty years earlier, his rumpled world-weary features and his equally rumpled suits, the perennial shadows under his eyes, and his spare taut physique made him something of a tall, dark, and smoldering object of fascination to the eyes of his female college classmates and, later on, to his female colleagues at the FBI. Now he was pushing fifty and his rumpled face only highlighted his sagging features, especially his cheekbones and jawline, while the red and yellow veins in the whites of his eyes testified to his problems with digestion, the shadows under his eyes had turned into bags, his clothing just looked threadbare and shabby, and his spare taut physique had become gaunt and withered. He was a beanpole of a man, too skinny, with the first onset of hip arthritis. To make things worse, he was a die-hard smoker. These days, that meant that part of his brain was constantly busy calculating how much longer he'd have to wait before he could leave the office for a cigarette. The result was usually: too long, for his tastes. What with his involuntary abstinence and a sour stomach, O'Malley was a grouchy, irascible guy. Two failed marriages and countless failed relationships were reliable testimony to the fact that women don't like dysfunctional personalities. Neither do coworkers, when it comes to that. O'Malley knew that his team considered him an intolerable boss.

Not that he really gave a damn. He looked around at his team. Jill— tall, chilly, lithe, impeccably groomed, her raven-black hair pulled back in a bun, a string of beads around her neck, and a simple sweater over a black sheath dress that did little to conceal what O'Malley considered the finest ass in the whole department. He'd be happy to hop into bed with her but, frankly, he figured she was out of his league. Meg was a blonde with softer curves under her loose, shapeless tracksuits. But she was tough and determined, a genuine steamroller when it came to investigations and interrogations. In the right conditions, O'Malley thought, she'd be available, but he wasn't sure he wanted her. Then there was Larramee: black, hardbodied, very self-confident, and pretty sure he was going to take O'Malley's job. All of them in their early thirties, in excellent health, with degrees from Ivy League universities. All three of them could run, fight, and even shoot better than he could. They were a little slower at thinking, that was true. But in the shitty situation they were facing right now, that was a source of moral satisfaction he would gladly have done without.

"Is Stefan still there?" asked O'Malley. Stefan Pierkowski, also known as "the librarian" or "four-eyes," was the fourth member of the team. His sector was "documentation and analysis."

"Yeah," Larramee replied, "he says he remembers something, but he can't seem to find it."

"It's three in the afternoon, we've been on this case for eight hours, and he takes the first four hours to remember that there might something he ought to remember, and the second four hours to not remember it?" O'Malley snapped. Larramee shrugged.

O'Malley strode over to the wall. Dangling loosely from his suspenders, his trousers gapped around the waistline, suggesting they had once fit more snugly. Pinned to the wall with a thumbtack was a Google Earth map of a stretch of the Maine coastline. Inside a red circle was a small bay, with a few rows of houses along the water. It was the same map that filled the screen of the PC that Jill was balancing on her knees. In fact, she had printed it out from her laptop.

"Okay, let's summarize what we know. There's this village—Massapequod? What a fucking name, goddamn it to Hell."

"That's apparently exactly what God has just done," Meg noted wryly.

"Don't bust my balls. Okay, where was I? Massapequod. At four o'clock, this morning a boatload of cod fishermen..."

"There are no cod fishermen there," Larramee broke in. "Cod is completely fished out off the Maine coast, they told me. All they're doing now is monitoring the cod repopulation..."

"Can you stop interrupting me with bullshit, goddamn it! These fucking whalers—or whatever it is they were fishing for—think they spotted a fire onshore but instead of going in to check, they just phone it in to the local sheriff."

"Well," Larramee spoke again, "they told us they thought that'd be faster. And it didn't look like much of a fire to them."

"That's right, because it was dying down by then. Anyway, it takes the sheriff's office an hour to get to the town..."

"From the city, you have to drive up and over a mountain. It's a narrow, winding road..."

O'Malley snorted in annoyance.

"Whatever, it takes them an hour. When they get there, it's all over, the fire's out."

"Everything's burnt up that can burn," Jill pointed out.

"All right," O'Malley resumed, "so far you and Larramee have cost us one jet and one helicopter. Why don't you go back over the details a second time for Meg and me."

"All right," Larramee said. "Everything was charred and smoking. The fire chief said that the fire burnt out by itself. Nobody even tried to put it out."

"No fire alarms, no calls for help?"

"Nope, neither one. They just burned in silence."

"What about the people in this town over here, on the other side of the promontory? They're just a stone's throw away. Didn't anyone notice anything?"

O'Malley was pointing to a village on the shores of the adjoining bay.

"No," Jill chimed in. "Someone told us they smelled smoke, stuck their head out the window, didn't see anything worrisome, and went back to bed."

"I wouldn't want them for neighbors," said O'Malley. "No one made it out alive, then?"

"No one," Larramee took up the story again. "Just the dogs. The people lay there burning. Wherever they were."

Jill closed her eyes and turned to face the wall.

O'Malley pulled a lighter out of his pocket and clicked it into flame. He looked into the fire, brought it close to his face, and recoiled immediately when it burned him.

"One hundred sixty-six people sleeping, and none of them noticed they were on fire."

"No, that's not it," Jill spoke up. "We explored that point. Lots of them weren't in bed sleeping at all. It looks like they fell asleep, on the spot, while doing something else. Playing pool, watching TV."

O'Malley looked at her approvingly.

"Exactly, and that's a crucial point. They seem to have dropped into *cataleptic trances, trances so deep that they didn't realize they were on fire. So, what conclusions have you drawn*, you and Jill? Let's go over this again."

"They were drugged."

"That's right, Jesus, Joseph, and Mary! Drugged, and it must have been a damned powerful narcotic."

"I'm not sure I'd want to take that sleeping pill," murmured Meg.

"Well, neither did they, you can bet on it," O'Malley resumed.

"All right then, a narcotic is what we're dealing with. But how was it administered? By pill? No way. Injection? Why would everyone in the village take an injection? Someone going house to house with a cloth soaked in chloroform? Come on. And you told me that the autopsies don't reveal anything."

"The bodies are too badly charred for an autopsy," Larramee explained.

"Right, right," O'Malley resumed. "So, like we decided a couple of hours ago, this narcotic must have been in suspension, in the air. And we haven't been able to get past that point since the two of you got back, damn it. The big problem is identifying the fuckers who released this narcotic. First of all, though, we have to figure out what kind of narcotic we're dealing with. What the fuck is Stefan up to?"

He rushed over to his desk and punched the intercom:

"Stefan, damn it! You making any progress?"

A triumphant voice answered him from the speaker on his desk:

"I've got it, boss! I found it! I had a vague memory of something, but I couldn't pin it down. The report wound up in the Cosmetics file."

"Cosmetics?"

"Yeah, that's right. Cosmetics. You know how these things go."

Stefan snickered.

FBI field office, New York, NY, Tuesday October 29, afternoon

O'Malley had an unhappy look on his face. Gillespie was a true ball-buster, the kind of guy who took an endless amount of time to examine the front and back as well as the top and bottom of any issue. Sometimes that could be a good quality, but right now the important thing was to take action immediately. Still, you can't pick your bosses.

"Umm, let me see if I've got this right," Gillespie was saying. They were all arrayed around him: O'Malley, Larramee, Jill, Meg, and Stefan, sitting variously on the chairs, armchairs, and the sofa of the large office of the deputy director of the FBI.

"So you're telling me that the only possible explanation for what happened at Massapequod is that a powerful narcotic was released into the air? That theory would look fanciful at best if it weren't for this... Matterre-Faquet?"

"Yes, sir, Stefan spoke up. "Pierre-André Matterre-Faquet, a Frenchman."

"A Frenchman?"

"Yes, sir, he's a French citizen. He has a position at Stony BrookUniversity, on Long Island. He's been there for two years. Before that, he was in France."

"So Prof. Matterre-Faquet comes to America, stays here for two years, and then comes up with this sleeping-pill...bomb?"

"Well, according to our report, that's not exactly how he put it."

"What does he say now?"

"We're looking for him, Steve," O'Malley broke in.

"Well, you'd better find him, Jamie," Gillespie said quietly. He turned to Stefan again:

"Since all we have is this report, exactly what does it say?"

"Last week Professor Matterre-Faquet delivered a lecture at Stony Brook University presenting the results of his research. He announced that he had succeeded in producing a molecule that is completely odorless and which, if rubbed on the skin, can produce a sudden state of sleep in anyone who inhales it. The interesting thing, sir, is that the state of sleep can last up to six hours."

"And you're saying that someone rubbed this molecule on the skin of 160 residents of a small town in Maine?"

"No, Steve," O'Malley broke in. "You rub it on the skin and that releases it into the air. But it could be released into the air in a thousand other ways. Someone must have arranged for quite a few of these little molecules to evaporate into the air of Massapequod."

"And just how did they get it to evaporate? Any ideas?"

"We're not sure, but we do have a theory. Larramee?"

Larramee held up a transparent plastic bag. Inside it were two pieces of curved glass, attached to molten masses of metal and plastic.

"Forensics sent us this. Probably, there were lots of others but the fire destroyed them completely, or else they haven't been found yet.

From the shape of the glass they would appear to be small vials, and they might very well have contained the narcotic..."

"Any traces?"

"On the glass? No, it evaporated completely. Anyway, these chunks of plastic and metal might be timers, to open the vials."

"Timers? The kind that can be triggered by cell phone?"

"Exactly, sir," said Larramee. "Probably, someone stood up on the hill, set off the timer, and waited for the narcotics to take effect."

"And then he went down and set fire to the houses. Wearing a gas mask, right?"

"It seems likely, sir. But he needn't have gone down the hill. On top of the hill, we found tire tracks, from a truck, possibly a small tank truck, that backed up and turned around on the grass. We think they might have poured kerosene down the slope and then simply set fire to it."

Gillespie felt a chill run down his spine.

"A river of fire running down the hill."

"That's right," said O'Malley. "A liquid wall of fire that ignited all the houses on Main Street. From there, the wind pushed the fire through the rest of the town. Everything's made of wood."

"And you're saying these molecules could have had the effect that we saw here? A village full of people sleeping right through the horrible experience of being burned to death?"

"From the report," O'Malley replied, "we have no indication that Matterre-Faquet ever tested the use of the molecule in large quantities. It's possible that Massapequod was just the first test run. But whoever used it knew what they were doing when they set fire to that wave of kerosene."

"Are you sure about the kerosene?"

"Yeah, the fire department found traces of it everywhere. On the telephone poles, and on the walls of the houses."

"And was Matterre-Faquet the only one who possessed this mole-cule?"

"Yes, as far as we know."

"So, you're saying he gave some to whoever burnt Massapequod?"

"That's our first theory. Though I can't see why he would announce it beforehand at a public conference."

"Let's find him, Jamie," said Gillespie, with the instincts of a squad leader. Then he shook his head.

"I still can't believe it. So the molecule can have this effect?"

"Apparently, yes it can. Jill talked to the people from NIH. Jill?"

The young woman sat up straight on the sofa.

"They're preparing a detailed report, sir. In any case, the people at the lab say that if the numbers are the same as the ones that Matterre-Faquet mentioned at his conference, then the answer is yes."

She picked up the sheet of paper she had laid on her knees.

"Now then. Matterre-Faquet says that the molecule has a molecular weight of about 330 and an equilibrium constant with the olfactory receptors on the order of from 10 to minus 13 molar."

Gillespie waved one hand impatiently.

"Okay, okay. So?"

"The gist of what that means," said Jill, this time without consulting the sheet of paper, "is that, if you diffuse two pounds of these molecules at an elevation of 60 feet above ground level, you can put everyone within range to sleep, for six hours, over a surface area of 50 square miles, both outdoors and inside the buildings. In the winter, when the central heating is on, outside air is pulled into the houses and the narcotic can function undisturbed."

Gillespie whistled softly.

"My God, it really is a bomb." Then he turned to O'Malley, with a look of reproof.

"But what about us? When Matterre-Faquet delivered his lecture, weren't we paying attention? Didn't anyone put two and two together?"

"The report didn't mention anything in particular," Stefan said defensively. "It didn't emphasize anything. I don't read them all, they come in by the dozen. I read the headings and, if it looks interesting, I download the file. All this one said was: 'Olfactory effects of chemically extracted molecules and their consequences.' Plus, it was archived in the Cosmetics section and, frankly, I don't pay a lot of attention to that department."

"Cosmetics?" Gillespie was glaring at them furiously. "Just who was the idiot who submitted this report?"

Stefan was about to speak, but O'Malley beat him to the punch. "In France Matterre-Faquet worked chiefly with perfumes and cosmetics and the report begins with an explanation of what he had done previously. But that's not the point, Steve. Ten years ago, Larramee would have attended Matterre-Faquet's lecture. Or Jill. Or Meg. Or in any case, one of our agents, someone who is accustomed to thinking in terms of national security. But, as you know all too well, ever since they've cut our funding we've been using part-timers: students, professors, ordinary people. And so the report sort of got..."

"Rajiv Rasumarian," Stefan suddenly blurted out.

"Rasumarian? Is he Indian?" asked Gillespie.

"He was born in India, but he's an American citizen," Stefan explained. "He graduated from Stony Brook and now he works there. He's an entomologist."

"An entomologist, a guy who studies insects, you understand?" O'Malley exclaimed. "Now why would we hire an entomologist for this kind of work?"

Stefan was about to speak, but the phone on Gillespie's desk rang, and he hesitated.

"Bartsch?" Gillespie spoke into the receiver. "Sure, put him through."

"Yeah, Jerry," he said a minute later. "Yeah, we know about that... Yes, we've figured that out." He glanced rapidly at Jill.

"Yes, Matterre-Faquet.... Oh, no, I didn't know that."

A faint smile appeared briefly on his lips.

"That's too bad... Well, we're all looking for him... Sure, of course, if we do I'll let you know... Good luck," he ended the conversation.

"That was Bartsch, at the Pentagon," he said, looking at O'Malley in particular, but speaking to everyone in the room. "He says they had Matterre-Faquet in custody but they... ah... let him get away. They're going to get him now."

"We've got to find him first!" hissed O'Malley. All five of them lunged out of the office. Before he'd gone very far, O'Malley felt Stefan's hand on his shoulder. He stopped and turned around.

"Chief," Stefan said, "I was about to say this, but I didn't have time. I... actually I spoke with Rajiv."

"And?"

"He says that he hadn't understood how important Matterre-Faquet's molecules could be."

"So we can see."

"But his report wasn't entitled 'Olfactory Effects etc.' It was head-lined 'Chemical Extracts That Put People to Sleep'."

"Ah..."

"Which would have caught our attention in a completely different manner. The other title was assigned in this office. And he didn't classify it for Cosmetics; it was marked for Chemistry."

"Hmmm," O'Malley stopped to think. "First thing we do is find Matterre-Faquet. Then we're going to have to look into this a little more thoroughly," he decided.

Between Long Island and Connecticut, Friday, October 25, morning

In the days following the seminar, Dr. Pierre-André Matterre-Faquet had surprised his colleagues with an unaccustomed and apathetic form of distant behavior. They assumed that the strain of the seminar had simply consumed all his psychic and physical energy. Actually, he was worried about the future. At the end of the conference, on the previous Monday, he had been surprised to see her in the audience. They'd known each other for years. They first met at a conference on Cosmetic Chemistry and Social Behavior, in London, when he still worked in France and his family inheritance was still to come. Back then he was forced to chase after the funding and the favor of the major French scent companies, and he was forced to disguise his research into the psychological impact of olfactory signals as cosmetics.

Their relationship had been a blend of profound intellectual respect and burning physical lust. Susan was probably the real reason he had come to the United States but his male pride had prevented him from confessing that fact even to himself. And here the two of them had just hovered awkwardly. She knew that she loved him deeply but she was un-willing to face up to it unless he admitted it first. He loved her just as deeply but was unwilling to say so. And so the passion that united them had failed to find a solid foundation in an honest emotional exchange. Gradually the fear of what they felt had become stronger than the warmth of the love that should have joined them. They drifted apart and lost touch with one another. Now what did he want from her? He loved her catlike walk, her dark luminous skin, her ironical smile, typical of beautiful women from Jamaica. He'd been caught off guard when Susan, with her intensely British accent, said to him:

"Oh, Doctor Matterre-Faquet, you are quite the mother-fucker, aren't you?"

That had been her lead-in to what she wanted to tell him. Susan Sheffield was a professor of sociology at Yale, but her real unstated role was to serve as a head-hunter and talent-scout for one of the most powerful and respected universities on earth. As they sipped wine, she had complimented him for a discovery that, scientific importance aside, had an economic potential that no university could safely ignore: a sleeping pill that you can simply apply to your skin, instead of taking it in pill form, thus circumventing all the possible side-effects for the digestive tract. Thatwould sell like hotcakes, she thought to herself. Therefore, Dr. Mother-Fucker, what would you say about popping up to Yale, to see whether there might not be a full professorship available for him? In other words, with that discovery, the time was ripe to submit his name as a candidate.

In response to his quizzical gaze, she assured him that she could organize three or four interviews at Yale. Pierre-André sat there open-mouthed. While his brain was wrapping itself around the idea, however, he had felt a wave of warmth that had nothing to do with academia at all. Otherwise, there would have been no reason for the impulse that made him say: "Let's go up together on Friday."

Maybe she'd been thinking the same thing, because she didn't seem to be surprised in the least. And she'd immediately asked him: "Shall we take the whole weekend?" And she'd subtly suggested that he swing by and pick her up at her house, at Oyster Bay, on Friday morning. That way they could spend the weekend together, traveling over the roads they'd explored a few years earlier, and then go to Yale the following Monday.

He'd nodded with a smile.

"Shall we take the old road?" she had asked him, raising a glass in her cocoa-colored hand, as if she were toasting to something.

He'd nodded a second time.

And so Friday morning had been filled with hope and expectations. He'd dressed appropriately for hikes in the woods, with sturdy running shoes, a silk scarf, a Missoni sweater, and a suede jacket. In a small valise he'd packed a dark-blue suit, a white dress shirt, and a tie, to wear at Yale the following Monday. After breakfast he decided that he should probably take a sample of his extract with him to Yale. He left his house in Cold Spring Harbor and went to Stony Brook. As usual, he parked his Acura in his reserved parking spot (another privilege that annoyed certain colleagues no end) and arrived in his office after Rachel Goldstein had already distributed the mail and the internal correspondence. Rachel was always around, a genuine second pair of eyes and ears for Professor Benjamin Safar, the department head.

Every chief of an organization needed a spy to keep an eye on his employees, and Rachel was the officially sanctioned spy. But she was skillful enough to succeed in penetrating the psyche and the professional and personal secrets of the employees, even though they knew full well that Rachel was in fact acting as a spy for the department head. Of course, that morning Rachel Goldstein was not the person that Pierre-André would have chosen to see chatting with the beige-jumpsuit-clad staff of the cleaning service, right in front of the large refrigerator in Konstantinos Papadopoulos's laboratory, when he came in to get a sample of his extract.

It was the kind of thing that drove him crazy. He had put two half-gallon bottles of his extract in the lab refrigerator of his Greek friend and colleague, in part because that refrigerator was an ideal place to store volatile and flammable substances, and his extract was dissolved in an ethyl alcohol solution. The real reason he used Konstantinos's refrigerator was that it made it less likely that his nosier colleagues might have access to his samples, and there were more than a few of them who would have been eager to know more about Matterre-Faquet's mysterious extracts.

He knew that he could trust Papadopoulos, a leader in the field of neurophysiology, whom he was constantly trying to persuade to move into the field of the biochemestry of the transmission of olfactory signals, but now two other people had seen him rummage around in the refrigerator, and you didn't have to be a Nobel laureate to understand what the devil was hidden in that refrigerator.

He had stood there for a moment in a state of perplexed hesitation, then he'd scratched his chin, muttered a few words, and wound up with an:

"Et puis, merde!"

and he'd concealed a half-gallon bottle under his lab coat and gone back to his own laboratory. There, he sat down at one of the laminar flow and exhaust fume hoods, and proceeded to pipette twenty milliliters of his extract into a plastic vial and then, after sealing both vial and flagon, he'd slipped the vial into his pocket. Then he'd slipped the half-gallon bottle back under his lab coat and put it back into the refrigerator in Papadopoulos's laboratory.

With a false smile of friendliness at Rachel Goldstein and a bad-humored grunt at the rest of the world, he had walked toward his Acura. To calm his nerves he decided to listen to a Mozart flute concerto, driving at exactly 55 mph along Old Nichols Road, and then along the Smithtown Bypass and the Northern Parkway all the way to State Route 106.

Mozart had restored his good mood and he arrived in Oyster Bay on time. With a tweed skirt, a pair of sunglasses, and a lovely smile, Susan was ready. He found her cleaning her car's windshield, which had been the target overnight of a spray of seagull shit.

State University of New York at Stony Brook, NY, Friday, October 25, just before midnight

Midnight. While Pierre-André Matterre-Faquet was sleeping the sleep of the just in a hotel in Connecticut, his arms draped loosely over the blanket and his legs intertwined with the legs of Susan Sheffield, the cleaning service van pulled into the parking lot outside of the building that housed the biology laboratories of the State University of New York at Stony Brook. In a noisy flurry of activity, punctuated by shouts and laughter, men and women in beige overalls were pushing wheeled trashcans, picking up brooms and scrub brushes, wringing out rags, and arranging boxes and bottles of chemical products for the antistatic cleaning of the floors of the biology labs. Everything was designed to ensure that microorganisms could not escape and contaminate the environment, possibly in an irreparable manner.

The night security guard was reading a newspaper article about the thousand and one ways to help children get ready for Halloween. Two men in beige overalls stood by the van talking. One was short, energetic, and skinny, with an alert Latin-American face. The other man, tall and very fat, was clearly uncomfortable in a jumpsuit that was too tight for him. He looked dull but determined. The enormous hand of the fat man almost entirely concealed a large wad of cash.

"Are you sure about what you saw the other day?" The tall man's tone of voice was arrogant, with a heavy Brooklyn accent.

"*Si, señor, sin duda, seguro.*"

"Okay. Get moving."

"But..."

"Don't get me mad, punk! I didn't come all the way out here for nothing. Unless you want me to take back the money, along with four or five of your fingers, take me to the refrigerator. I'll take care of everything else. With all this confusion, nobody'll notice a thing." The fat man grabbed the little man by the shoulder with an iron grip and practically lifted him off the ground. The young Latino was too dignified to start whining or kicking. And he had learned to pay attention to the fat man and other men like him. He headed for the stairs. Upstairs, the small man took a few seconds to get his bearings and find the corridor that led to Konstantinos's laboratory. The fat man was impatient and he urged him on with a sharp slap to the nape of his neck. The little man grumbled, "*Señor,* with all these posters and all this equipment, *no se entiende nada, ¿entiende?*" Then he identified the freezer with temperatures of 80 degrees below zero, covered with pictures of the Acropolis in Athens. His face lit up and he said: "*¡Para allá para allá, a la derecha!*"

The man from Brooklyn opened the refrigerator next to the freezer, the one with signs stating that it was safe for the storage of flammable substances, and identified a half-gallon metal bottle, and pulled it out. He pulled a black plastic trash bag out of the pocket of his overalls and slipped the bottle into it. He looked around, noticed a trash bag already full of rubbish, put the trash bag with the bottle in it inside it, and threw it over his shoulder and started down the stairs.

The night watchman saw yet another black plastic trash bag go by and plunged back into his newspaper, eager to find out if zombies or witches were more fashionable this year. Turns out that this year mythological monsters were the people's choice. Harpies and sirens, mermaids, centaurs, and fauns were the most fashionable identities this year.

He thought about his own daughter: how could you put a fish tail on the legs of a little girl who wants to do nothing but run around with little boys and jump rope?

Once he was outside the door, the fat man opened the trash bag, pulled out the other trash bag with the metal bottle, gave the bag with the rubbish in it to the skinny guy, dismissing him with a wave of his hand. He headed toward a nondescript light brown Chevrolet, parked at the far end of the parking lot. When he got to the driver's side window, the fat man pulled the large bottle out of the trash can and extended it to the driver.

The driver took the bottle and carefully set it down on the passenger seat. Then he turned back to the fat man.

"Hey, Little Joe, you know that you're gaining weight? That jumpsuit's pretty tight on you."

"Fuck you."

The driver snickered. Then he furrowed his brow, put all five fingers of his right hand together in a sort of cone and, moving them back and forth with a quizzical gesture asked: "And where's the rest of the stuff?"

"And how do you know that there's any left?"

"I don't know for sure, but I *expect*there to be some left over, capeesh?"

A hotel in Connecticut, Saturday, October 26, morning

There were still plenty of green leaves on the late-October trees when, in the luminous morning of a still early Indian summer, Pierre-André Matterre-Faquet and Susan Sheffield woke up and decided to stay in bed, to extend the warmth of the first night they had spent together in far too long. They looked out of the window and saw the emerald, ruby, gold, brown, and orange leaves standing out against the dark blue of the western sky. They had breakfast in their room, then they showered together. The soft white towels, the slow process of getting dressed together, stopping frequently for a sweet embrace or a tender kiss—it all expressed the magical state of psychological well-being that characterizes the morning after an unexpected night together that, after all, they both realized, they had expected for years.

Susan was radiant and Pierre-André, who was usually so rigid and constrained, was distinctly relaxed. He even managed to be funny, tossing out a few stupid jokes and offering naïve compliments to the dark-skinned woman who had spent the night with him, and who seemed to be promising even sunnier days to come.

When they got over to Susan's car, they found a small knot of men wearing sunglasses and the uniforms of the US Navy and, clearly, waiting for them.

The signs of happy relaxation vanished from Pierre-André's face. He looked at Susan with the pained expression of someone who is suddenly filled with a horrible sense of doubt, but he detected signs of fear in her and chose to keep his mouth shut.

While the little group fanned out into a subtle outflanking maneuver, the one who seemed to be in charge, blond and tan the way only sailors seem to be, walked toward then and introduced himself.

"Ms. Sheffield, Professor Matterre-Faquet, I'm honored to meet you. I'm Commander Ralph Randall, U.S. Navy. Your seminar the other day at Stony Brook was deeply appreciated for its true worth..."

Pierre-André Matterre-Faquet turned pale and bit his lip. He glared angrily at Susan, but under the strict self-control that his family had inculcated in him, he said nothing more than:

"Perhaps I should rethink things and conclude that all this is your doing..."

Commander Randall hastened to correct the misunderstanding: "I hope there's no mistake about this. We know that Ms. Sheffield had suggested you travel with her to Yale to meet the heads of the university. What Ms. Sheffield could not have known and in fact does not yet know, is that the Department of Defense would prefer that you work for the U.S. Navy rather than for Yale University." The officer went on quickly. "As you probably know, the Department of Defense can exercise a right of first refusal... an option, in other words, on any scientific research done in the United States."

Even through the dark skin that she had inherited from her Jamaican forebears, a red flush of anger appeared on Susan's face: "What are you saying? What right of first refusal do you think you have? This is a clear abuse of power! Another example of arrogant military oppresssion!"

The officer grimaced in a way that was eloquent of boredom rather than irritation. He had invoked the Pentagon's legal privileges, more than anything else out of a respect for formal procedure, as his commanders had suggested he do, in the hope of avoiding awkward public scenes. But they had also told him not to waste any time. He briskly brought the discussion to an end:

"Ms. Sheffield, we have the highest respect for your rights, as well as those of Doctor Matterre-Faquet. But the professor is expected urgently in Washington. My orders are very clear."

Susan tried another approach: "But why can't he go to Washington after visiting Yale? If he wants to speak with the university first why can't he do that? Then he'd come to Washington." The officer replied patiently: "As I told you, he's expected in Washington with the greatest urgency." They had suggested another possible fall-back argument: "For that matter, we're quite sure that your university is fully aware of the importance of the needs of our national defense. And I'm sure that you will discover, if you'd care to investigate, that Yale will be happy to cooperate with us."

Susan set her lips grimly. She didn't need to phone the school to have a clear idea of just how carefully Yale, like other universities, cultivated its relations with the Pentagon and catered to whims of one of the biggest sources of funding for scientific research. The officer was completely right. If asked, the university would probably be willing to send another car to take Pierre-André anywhere the generals asked. She looked at the man she now knew she was in love with and whom these officers were taking away from her. Pierre-André looked irritated and disappointed, but he seemed to understand the situation clearly. The Pentagon might have acted in a highhanded and offensive manner, with this rude act of force that bordered on kidnapping, but it wasn't uncommon for them to demand that a scientist work for them, nor was it illogical. He didn't understand what they wanted from him, nor why they were in such a hurry. But in the end, resistance would have been not only pointless but ridiculous. Actually, the thing that scared him most might have been the risk of being ridiculous.

Susan let herself be taken by the arm and steered away, delicately but firmly, and she gave Pierre-André one last sad glance.

"Call me right away, as soon as you can," she murmured to him.

"I'll see you again soon," he assured her, as he walked toward a massive black automobile. One of the men was holding the rear door open for him and, once he was seated inside, got in next to him. Another man got in on the other side. A third man got behind the wheel, started the engine, and pulled out quickly, heading for I-95.

Commander Randall stood at Susan's side as they watched the car move away. Then he politely asked her whether she intended to head back to Yale. Susan shook her head. "No, I'm going home." The officer extended his hand: "I'm very sorry for the situation that has arisen. But don't worry. You'll have him back in a couple of days." Commander Ralph Randall turned and headed for a dark blue sedan, bearing the insignia of the U.S. Navy. The sedan moved off toward I-95 as well.

In the first car, Matterre-Faquet continued to be seized by an icy wave of fury. At first, he had reacted with anger against those who smashed the delicate enchantment of his new discovery of Susan by tearing him away from her. Soon, that anger was replaced by the chilling disappointment of seeing the ambitions he had nurtured for a post in one of the world's most respected universities suddenly frozen into a limbo of uncertainty. That was followed by bafflement as to the reasons that might have led the Pentagon to requisition the services of an expert on cosmetics, a scientist who had simply invented a better way to get to sleep. But now, above all, he felt ridiculous and humiliated. He understood how helpless he was, and for a man as proud as he was, this was the hardest insult to take.

Newark Airport, Saturday, October 26, noon

The unsightly squared-off Japanese car pulled up alongside the departures sidewalk at Newark terminal and the couple inside the cockpit locked in an endless kiss that seemed designed to intermingle the internal organs of the two lovebirds. After a long string of seconds,

seconds that seemed like minutes to the policewoman who was directing traffic, the car door swung open, but the two of them went back at it, tongue-in-mouth, in a farewell that was starting to look longer than the flight that was to follow. Moving her short legs, the policewoman started walking slowly over to the Japanese car, but before long an El Al steward stepped out, pulled a suitcase off the back seat, looked at the policewoman, and smiled. At the wheel of the squared-off car was a girl who was just too skinny, with hair that was just too long, with eyeglasses that were just too transparent, and a mouth that was just too wide, whose lips barely managed to conceal jutting incisors, a mousey smile, and bike racer's gloves. She waggled the five fingers of her right hand in a sentimental bye-bye wave. The El Al steward kissed his fingers, blew the kiss toward the Japanese car, and melted into the variegated crowd that was congealing outside the revolving doors of the terminal, and then headed toward the boarding area.

Driving through the traffic that was taking her back to New York, and barely avoiding collisions with thirty-ton semitrailers hurtling toward the George Washington Bridge at more than 70 mph all along the way, Rachel Goldstein thought fondly about the last few days, these last, fabulous, glorious days of autumn, in which she had been able to see once again what she had decided was the man of her dreams.

Her lucky chance had been the seminar held by Pierre-André Matterre-Faquet. After the applause that had greeted his closing remarks and the end of the conference, a burst of applause that was only slightly more intense than the basic minimum level demanded by good academic manners, she had waded into the small crowd in order to procure a glass of wine. Having also procured the small regulation chunk of cheese that was standard issue on these occasions, in which the chief objective is to entertain the participants in the seminar in order to facilitate the exchange of opinions, scientific information, proposals of cooperation, and various gossip, she had exchanged a few timid and innocuous remarks about the quality of the wine, which Professor Matterre-Faquet had shipped specially from his family château, in the Bordeaux region. When she had seen the crowd break up into small clusters of people conversing animatedly, it had been easy to slip away toward the laboratories, without anyone noticing. She knew particularly well how to pretend she had nothing in particular to do, when she was checking to make sure that students, technicians, and post-docs in the department of Plant Physiology were at work rather than wasting time on the phone. She was just as expert at pretending to have something specific to do when in fact she wanted to do something quite different. She slalomed adroitly around the freezer in order to avoid running into the Texan post-doc who was passionately kissing Konstantinos's assistant, a chesty blonde from Arkansas; the Texan post-doc had slid his hands up the Arkansan assistant's skirt and was groping her ass cheeks. With a grimace of disgust, Rachel Goldstein ignored them and walked into her office.

Stretched out in the darkness on an anatomically designed office chair, she pulled out a cell phone from her purse/bag, something a hippie, or a liberated woman, might carry, punched a single button, and pressed it to her ear.

After a couple of minutes (she knew that she would have to wait at least 125 seconds before she should expect an answer) someone answered and she uttered the phrase that she'd learned by heart:

"Hello? Jeremiah no longer weeps."

The answer was equally conventional:

"Really? Then what does Baruch write?"

"Hello, yes it's me, I'm sorry to bother you, you must have been asleep, where you are it's two or three in the morning isn't it? Yes of course....certainly, otherwise I wouldn't have woken you up.....listen, there's a scientist here who's discovered...."

The noise of a low-flying airplane, probably heading for MacArthur Airport in Islip, drowned out the rest of what she said. She was only too happy to have the noise: it was an extra guarantee that the phone call would remain secret.

"...so I assumed you might find that interesting. For the south-western territories, of course."

The direct consequences of that phone call that she had made were still warm in her memory, and perhaps even on the seats of her car, that horrible uncomfortable square automobile. As she was trying to steer over into the right lane in order to get onto the highway ramp that would take her to the Lincoln Tunnel, she realized that, while it had been a lucky break for her love life, that phone call had also put into motion something much bigger and much more momentous. Whatever it was, it dwarfed her own diminutive stature and the puny size of her automobile. Both she and the car weren't much taller than one of the tires of the thunderously roaring semitrailer in the next lane. The huge truck threatened to crush her every time it swerved ever so slightly into her lane. Who could say what freight it was transporting, and where it was headed? The semitrailer, whose mudflaps were rattling and clattering with a deafening din, was to her mind the very image of blind, ineluctable fate, indifferent to human misery, callous destiny which would decide, or might even have already decided, what the outcome of her love affair and the mission would be. Having finally solved the logistical problem of swerving across the truck's onrushing trajectory without actually entering into physical contact with the bruiser, she steered toward the right side of the toll plaza, aimed at one of the booths marked Lincoln Tunnel, and dove back into her thoughts as she drove on, eager to prolong the impression that she was still with him.

She knew that, the minute the phone call was over, the person at the other end of the line had already begun making all necessary arrangements to leave Tel Aviv, as soon as possible and without his departure attracting undue attention. He had therefore been obliged to conclude a number of undertakings, none of which she knew about although she guessed that they were tricky, sensitive, and important, so that he could be free for an entire weekend and catch the first plane available to New York. His profession allowed him to hop on a plane without giving explanations to anyone. For that matter, he was vigorous, muscular, and bronzed (for an instant, his image appeared in her mind's eye and she couldn't keep from shivering in delight) and was therefore a sort of latter-day Agent 007, powerful, decisive, and even a little cruel, free of any sort of moral scruples, and not so much because he was in the service of the higher interests of national security, but because, like some sort of Archangel Gabriel, he had been selected, as he'd explained to her, to perform justified missions, missions that were blessed by God's own benediction.

Uriel Silberzahn, to tell the truth, tended to look cautiously over his shoulder even when he was alone. He lived the unhappy life of a man who is convinced that he has both power and powerful enemies. For instance, he assumed that even if no one is trying to follow you, it's a good idea to cover your tracks.

After his plane landed in Newark, he took a taxi to Secaucus, New Jersey, and from there a bus to the Port Authority terminal on Eighth Avenue in Manhattan. He left the terminal and wandered aimlessly around the West Side of Manhattan, along the streets lined with Broadway theaters. He found an inexpensive hotel, not particularly clean but with two different exits. Then he walked south to Penn Station, looking over his shoulder as he walked, changing the side of the street he walked on at each intersection, stopping to buy a bag of hot roasted chestnuts or to look into the shop windows of drug stores or other shops along Eighth Avenue. He caught a Long Island Rail Road train to Huntington Station, where he changed trains and then got off at Kings Park. In the large lot that during the week was filled with the cars of commuters traveling to New York City, Uriel was all alone, the way he wanted to be. But it was cold. Maybe because Long Island sticks out into the ocean, here the last warm breath of Indian summer, in late October, offered nothing more than a chilly sun that set early. The wind out of Long Island Sound, the stretch of salt water that separates Long Island from Connecticut, whipped over the deserted parking lot, driving torn pages of discarded newspapers before it, along with rattling empty beer cans that emitted sounds of sadness.

The railroad timetable was posted in a small cabin that offered no protection from the bitter wind and the waiting room—if an insanely optimistic person with a vivid imagination were to choose to call the small space with four glass walls containing a few notably uncomfortable seats by that name—was locked. He waited for half an hour out in the cold, because he preferred not to take a seat at the bar in the pub on the far side of Main Street. He was tired and chilled, so far away from the warm sun of Tel Aviv. He caught the next train for Stony Brook, and arrived long after sunset. It was nighttime by now, and both in the streets of the expensive suburbs and in the parking lots of the train stations, Long Island lacks street lights that offer even a minimally acceptable illumination. He found the darkness disconcerting. He flipped open his cell phone, pushed a button, and waited a couple of minutes.

"Hello? Jeremiah no longer weeps."

"Really? Then what does Baruch write?"

"Yes, it's me....this morning....exhausted, cold......can you come pick me up?"

Rachel Goldstein drove her square, black, Japanese car with all-wheel drive, an automobile that would be nondescript if it were only a little less ugly. She too, with her mousey smile, would have passed unobserved if she'd only make a little extra effort. But for Uriel, the thing that made Rachel a priceless treasure was what she did—not what she was. When she pulled into the Stony Brook train station, a light freezing drizzle was falling and the Israeli, in his light raincoat, was sliding into a state of hypothermia.

"Darling, are you crazy? You're going to damage your health, sweetheart, you have to take care of yourself..."

If he had felt a little better, Uriel would have snickered. Instead he just burst out into a hoarse complaint:

"Oh, I like that! I think you have a pretty good idea of how dangerous the work I do can be to my health..."

Her mousey smile lit up with shy modesty:

"Yes, of course, darling, but at least I can try to protect you from the rain and the cold. But what are we going to do now?"

"Well, let's go get the material, and then I have to head back."

"When is your return flight?"

"Tomorrow at noon."

"But darling, we can't simply go to the university, just like that, and pull the stuff out of the refrigerator. It's too late, the guards would see that I'm not alone in the department, that is to say..."

"What do you mean?"

"I mean that we can't, I can't afford to be seen at night, with a stranger, in the laboratories, the night before Dr. Matterre-Faquet discovers that he's missing a one-gallon bottle from his refrigerator!"

"All right then give me your keys and your badge..."

"Are you crazy? That'd be worse, it would leave indelible evidence in the electronic security system... why didn't you call me before coming? I could have arranged to get a little for you."

"Which would mean running the risk of causing an accident and ruining our plan? Let's think it over. If we can't take the sample that he has in the refrigerator, does the Frenchman have any more?"

"I think he does, but I don't know where he keeps it."

It looked like they'd wound up in a blind alley. Uriel certainly hadn't set out to build that mirage of true love only to discover that there was nothing in it for him. He raised his voice: "There has to be a way. Find it!"

"Oh, of course, what a fool I am. He was supposed to go to New Haven with a lady, to talk about his new discovery, in fact. I think I have her address somewhere, in my Blackberry...here it is! Maybe she knows something...let's go, she lives in Oyster Bay, not more than an hour's drive from here."

Night had fallen, the good citizens had pulled down their blinds for the night. They'd had their dinner, they were watching television, some of them might even be asleep already. Uriel and Rachel did not feel the pangs of hunger. Rachel could think of nothing but Uriel, while Uriel could think of nothing but the sample of Matterre-Faquet's formula. Both of them were wholly and completely satisfied in material and spiritual terms.

Once they got to Oyster Bay, it wasn't hard to identify the house.

They parked far away from the isolated street light that spread a squalidyellow light over the lawns covered with dead leaves.

They approached the house in the darkness. In order to impress his companion, Uriel showed off his strength and agility and did a standing high jump, straight into the air, vaulting impeccably over the gate in the white vinyl fence which must have been a good six feet high. The gate might even have been unlocked, for that matter, as they usually are in the back yards of the houses in wealthy suburban neighborhoods.

Rachel hid in the bushes and felt the stinging cold of the dry branches and the dead leaves that were poking her underneath her skirt. Silent as a cat, Uriel moved across the courtyard toward the kitchen door; there was a large swinging flap to let pets in and out. The inside of the house was pitch black. He kneeled down and studied the pet door. It looked reasonably big, even for someone his size. He tried to get through but inside, at the last minute, something kept him from standing up completely. He pulled back and the little door fell into place behind him, with a flip-flap sound that echoed in the night.

No one called out "who's that?" No one shouted. No one hurried downstairs. There was no one at home. Uriel slipped a credit card between the door jamb and the kitchen door and easily walked in. He heard a meow and then felt the cat rubbing between his ankles. He walked in and checked to make sure that no one was in the house to deal with. A quick inspection showed him that whoever lived in that house had no safes, secret drawers, or even the desire or need to make objects or information secure. Uriel left the house, followed by the cat which wandered out into the yard. The square black Japanese car headed south at high speed, in order to reach busier streets where, if necessary, they could elude pursuit and get back to Stony Brook to complete the mission.

Certainly, they had to find a way of getting into the laboratories and stealing the material from the refrigerator without being noticed.

Rachel furrowed her brow as she thought. She knew that Uriel would never agree to leave empty-handed, and failing to get him what he asked for meant losing him once and for all. Still, the only solution that occurred to her was too dangerous: it would be too easy to be caught: if not immediately, later. The laboratories were rife with electronic door locks. Uriel would leave, she would remain behind. Finally, she set her mind at rest: "Here's what let's do. There's a tree next to the window of my office. You climb up and if you give it a good solid kick, you ought to be able to get the window open. As for getting out, I can't say. Anyway, I'll help you. Inside, you'll have to take care of things yourself. The important thing is that you absolutely must not be seen."

Uriel laughed shortly:

"Don't worry about it. That's my specialty."

The Pentagon, Washington, DC, Saturday, October 26, afternoon

That day at the Pentagon was interminable and Pierre-André Matterre-Faquet—who, on general principle, hated the military and soldiers, which is what his father had been—suffered through every second of it. Everything seemed to repeat itself in an unchanging cycle:

they made a proposal, he rejected it, they argued to bring him around, he rebutted, they made an offer, he said no again, but that no somehow, apparently, never managed to become definitive. The scientist was convinced that, under normal conditions, he would easily have managed to be firm and persuasive. But the truth was that he still hadn't recovered from his initial shock. He had finally figured out why the Pentagon was so interested in his work. But he refused to acknowledge that the innocuous sedative, upon which he had placed so much of his personal ambition, could be the deadly combat weapon that they were presenting to him now.

If prepared properly, they had told him over and over again, his molecule could be useful in countless circumstances, it could save thousands of lives, both American and other, it could spell the end of Middle Eastern terrorism.

And each of the high officers spangled with silver and gold stars, Navy admirals, and generals of the Army, the Air Force, and the Marines had concluded by telling him that, if he allowed them to consult his laboratory notebooks, they could help him to obtain American citizenship rapidly, as well as a source of considerable income for a very long time.

Pierre-Andre Matterre-Faquet had done his best to be reasonable and courteous. He had politely shown that he completely understood their point of view. But he felt duty-bound to emphasize that, because his father had been a career soldier, he had a deep and abiding aversion to the use of science for military objectives. Actually, he went on, he had always wondered whether these applications were acceptable to ordinary people's consciences. He would certainly have been guilt-ridden, deeply and intolerably, if even a single innocent human being was forced to suffer because of the way that one of his scientific discoveries had been utilized, if it were different from the objectives that he had set out for himself.

"It wouldn't be the first time," he pointed out, "that a scientist and his discoveries were held hostage by weapons and politics.

"When I was working with this molecule," he said, "all I had in mind was something that, on a small scale, could help each of us, increasing the level of everyday well-being. People's normal, happy, peaceful day-to-day life. Something to help people to sleep better. An innocuous remedy to fight insomnia. It never dawned on me that it could become a weapon. I don't like weapons. Call me a pacifist if you like. I have only contempt for weapons. I think that they are a heavy toll that we pay to the worst aspects of our past as a species. If I'd ever thought that it could become a weapon...I...I would have given up my research."

The officers across from him were seated along a bow-shaped table, while he was seated in the only chair on his side of the same table. More than a meeting, it looked like a trial. It created the worst possible atmosphere, as one of the generals later pointed out bitterly to the officer in charge of logistics, to persuade a foreign scientist who was relatively indifferent to the call of patriotism, especially a scientist who came from France, the land most likely to produce ball-busters. Bart Siegel, a Marine general, realized this immediately, and up till then for the most part he'd kept his mouth shut. Now he weighed in, with the most conciliatory tone of voice he could muster. It fell to this man with icy-cold eyes, gaunt cheekbones, and a square jaw, a man who looked more like a pitiless pirate than a philosopher of science, to attempt a conversation about the great subjects of ethics and war.

"You have a one-directional idea of weapons," said Siegel. "You see them as tools of death and destruction. But often weapons serve—not always, but often—as a way of preventing death and destruction. It depends on us and on the weapons. Yours is in fact one of these."

"Don't call it a weapon!" Matterre-Faquet interrupted with an angry convulsion. "It's not a weapon. It never was, until you started thinking about it. And don't give me that old line about the importance of deterrence."

"No. But let me offer a concrete example, a case very much like the kind of thing I deal with on a daily basis. Imagine a commando operation. We need to come down on a guerrilla lair, let's say to liberate a hostage, a politician or a journalist, that they're holding captive. What would we do, the way things stand now? A group of our special operations soldiers would move in and attack, with a heavy volume of firepower, while helicopters rain down missiles from above. It's very likely that in the hideout—let's say it's a village in the jungle—there are old men, women, children, and other prisoners. Lots of innocent people. But now we can't make any distinctions. The mission has to succeed and we have no time to waste. So we shoot indiscriminately, without paying any attention to who we kill, because of the immense pressure. How many innocent lives are lost?"

Siegel paused. Matterre-Faquet gulped uncomfortably.

"Now just imagine that we possess your narcotic. We release it into the air from a helicopter flying over the theater of operations. That is to say, we put it into action and then we arrive. Everyone's asleep and we can liberate our hostage, without touching a hair on anyone's head."

"Yes, I can imagine it. And wouldn't you take the opportunity to cut the throats of a number of sleeping guerrilla fighters?"

"You're not fair if you think we'd cut someone's throat without a second thought. Anyway, it would let us spare the women and children."

Matterre-Faquet shook his head.

"That's not what I've devoted my life to."

John Pendlemore was the general with the largest number of stars on his shoulders. From the beginning, he had led the discussion.

"Mr. Matterre-Faquet," he said, stumbling over the pronunciation of the surname, "for us, national security is a sacred and important matter. Just like science is for you. And now, let me repeat, if you were to work with us that would make it possible for us to make resources and funds available to you for research, including research that has nothing to do with this..."

Matterre-Faquet interrupted him, banging his fist on the armrest of his chair.

"It's not a matter of money!" he shouted. He was clearly taking it too far now. His heart was racing. He tried to catch his breath. He was horrified at what he was about to say, but he said it without arrogance.

"I was born into a venerable family. I am wealthy. It's not a matter of money, can you get that through your heads? This is about science, MY science. I'm paying out of my own pockets to do this science, the way I like it. I want to do it myself, even if I have to wash the test tubes and retorts myself, every night. And I want to do with it—and get out of it—what I want. I didn't cross the Atlantic Ocean to help you solve your strategic problems."

Pendlemore sighed. His sigh was like a signal that the meeting was over. Many of the officers relaxed as they sat back in their chairs, with a gloomy expression.

"Yes, I understand,' said Pendlemore. "Okay. But please, give it a little more thought. You could receive all the logistical and scientific support you'd ever need, for the rest of your life."

After a moment of silence he added:

"In a university, in the institute of your choice."

Matterre-Faquet had calmed down. He saw that Pendlemore was chatting with the two generals sitting near him. One of the generals got up and left the room. The scientist realized that he had allowed himself to be carried away by his temperament and his stubbornness. Almost all of his answers had been guided by instinct. He didn't want to hand over his invention to the Pentagon, but he wasn't sure of how the Pentagon might react. Still, he knew that soldiers usually found a way around things: wasn't it von Clausewitz who said that war is a continuation of politics by other means?

"I hope you'll forgive me if I reacted in a somewhat...impetuous manner. But you must understand I was....nonplussed... surprised... I never thought of my invention in that light. It's all so... new. I need to think it over. General, you're quite right. Please give me a few days to reflect."

"Of course, Professor, of course. We hope that you are able to think and that you come to the... right decision."

Pendlemore stood up. All the others stood up. An admiral leaned forward and whispered:

"Now a couple of Navy men will take you back to Long Island: you'll be home before midnight."

Two Navy petty officers led by a midshipman were waiting for him at the door Matterre-Faquet could hardly avoid shaking hands with the four generals and the admiral. He couldn't fail to notice, all the same, the nod of the head exchanged between the midshipman and the admiral.

Between Washington and Brooklyn, Saturday, October 26, evening

As he walked toward the automobile, Matterre-Faquet had the feeling he was in the same situation as a buccaneer he'd read about once who was told that he was a free man but who was still being marched to the gallows. He could easily get back to Long Island on his own. All he needed was a taxi to the train station. So he had no illusions about the real meaning of that escort. It was clear that the two petty officers would arrange to delay him, while the midshipman rummaged through his office in search of notes and other material documenting his discovery. The generals had most certainly not been taken in by the promises he'd made at the end of the meeting. If he continued to refuse to cooperate, they certainly hoped to take what they could get and move forward without his help.

Luckily the three sailors were young, and Pierre-André was sufficiently full of adrenaline from the day to formulate a plan. He had plenty of time to put that plan into action.

Once they were in the car, he introduced himself, asked the name and rank of each of his escorts, and started talking about boats and sailing. He told stories about sailors with a woman in every port and how a good sleeping pill can encourage an intense and versatile love life. Soon, they were on a first-name basis, exchanging slaps on the back. When Pierre-André suggested stopping, as he said, "for a rapid exchange of fluids with the environment," they all burst into laughter. At the filling station, the midshipman ordered the two petty officers to stay in the car while he walked the professor to the restrooms since, as he pointed out, he had the same problem. Of course, it was really to keep an eye on him, but that was exactly what the scientist had hoped.

When the car stopped in the parking lot, the midshipman jumped out to keep an eye on things. Pierre-André took a deep breath and opened the vial with the twenty grams of extract that he had planned to take to Yale, with Susan, to demonstrate its efficacy. He poured half of it between the rear seats. Then he calmly got out of the car, slammed the door, and started off briskly to catch up with the midshipman who was waiting for him a few yards ahead.

In the restroom, Professor Matterre-Faquet asked somewhat stiffly if he could have a little privacy. As he expected, the midshipman stood guard outside the door, walking up and down. There was a gap of fifteen inches between the bottom of the stall door and the floor, and the officer, as he paced back and forth, could see Matterre-Faquet's feet.

At a certain point the scientist jumped up and stood on the rim of the toilet. No longer seeing his feet, the midshipman first began to call his name, and then to pound his fists against the door of the stall, and finally ordered him to step back out of the stall. In vain. Impulsively, the officer bent down to put his head into the opening under the door. That was the moment that Pierre-André was waiting for. He pressed the other half of the vial into his nostril and, while the midshipman was slumping to the ground, he walked out of the bathroom free as a bird, holding his breath, and taking mental note of just how quickly the sedative had acted. He pretended to adjust his belt but, luckily, there was no one else in sight. He let the bathroom door close behind him, he crossed the room, slaloming between children eating hamburgers and mothers chasing after them, calling their names. He stopped in front of the pizza counter where they were giving kids masks of the rotting dead and snickering skeletons.

It only took a couple of minutes. He heard a voice:

"Hey, there's a sailor out cold on the floor in there!"

He saw a janitor come running. He heard the voice again.

"He must be drunk, like all sailors, but what is he doing here, so far from the port of Baltimore?"

"We don't sell alcohol here," said the janitor, walking into the restrooms. "He must have brought it with him."

Pierre-André sighed happily: it was a small dose, it wouldn't last long, and an accusation of drunkenness was exactly what he was hoping for. Probably the police would be called and they'd make sure the sailors were prevented from driving off after him. He stepped out into the cool air with a sense of relief.

In the parking lot he decided to abandon the suitcase with a change of clothes that he'd planned to wear at Yale. He walked up to a truck driver and asked if he'd give him a ride to New York. The truck driver was a taciturn guy, but he liked jazz. He had an i-Pod full of Billie Holiday and Ella Fitzgerald. It was a cold, starry night, and the truck roared north through Maryland, carrying a load of trees to be used as pilings at the South Ferry terminal where boats leave for the Statue of Liberty. Matterre-Faquet could finally relax.

He needed to think of what the Pentagon's next moves would be, what he should do with his invention, which by now was perhaps useless, indeed harmful, in terms of the ambitions that the soldiers had stolen from him. But he was too tired to deal with the anguish of plans and decisions. His adrenaline was tapped out. The minute he got in the truck, he put his hand in his pocket. He felt his cell phone, and he felt like calling Susan. He realized that could be dangerous, and he switched it off. He even thought about removing the battery but he was so tired that he couldn't seem to focus. He'd even lost his grip and could barely coordinate his fingers. He couldn't get the battery out. In the meanwhile he'd started thinking about Susan. He kept on thinking about Susan.

He realized that he was deliberately doing everything possible to keep from thinking about the Pentagon and the sedative. He went on lulling himself with memories of his time with Susan.

As the truck roared north along Interstate 95, he saw the moon rising into the night sky on his right, and he thought that right now he should have been with her, in a nice restaurant in Providence or Boston, talking nonsense, smelling her perfume, wooing her.

The interior of the truck cabin was fairly well soundproofed. The laboring motor added a note of peace to the saxophone-like wailing ofBillie Holiday's voice. The night was black. The truck driver drank can after can of coke, slowly, in silence.

Pierre-André thought back to his night of love in the hotel in Connecticut. He compared it to the night of two or three years earlier. He could see the same passion, the same ecstasy, the same violence. Susan knew how to excite his libido well beyond any imaginable limit. But this time there was something more.

But then the troops had landed.

"And now we're watching the championship match of Pentagon against Pierre-André Matterre-Faquet," he said to himself.

The faces of the generals in the conference room in Washington appeared before his face. And, finally, rocked to sleep by the truck's roar, he drifted off.

Headquarters of the Direction Générale de la Securité Extérieure, Paris, France, Sunday, October 27, morning

The office of the three-star general in charge of external security looked more like a luxurious and exclusive drawing room in the sixteenth arrondissement thanthe operative headquarters of a center for counterespionage working on overseas operations, overwhelmed with terrorist threats, and obliged to lend discreet muscle to the various French diplomats, scientists, artists, and businessmen working in every corner of the planet.

The Persian rug that covered the oakwood floor did nothing to muffle the strangled shout of the man behind the desk.

"What?" the general was saying, as he stood up and then fell heavily back into his chair. The cup of café-crème on his desk teetered perilously and the glasses in the bar made out of a Louis XV nightstand near the chair tinkled loudly.

The woman across from him didn't blink an eye. She was petite, with slightly hunched shoulders, gray hair cut short, and minuscule eyeglasses with metal frames. At the corners of her mouth, her lips twisted slightly downward, in a perennial grimace of what looked like scorn for the world around her. She wore a gray suit with a pleated white bib in front. She looked like a governess embittered by the passing years. According to many observers, she had the most brilliant mind in the department.

"*Oui,mon Général*, we have specific information. We double checked. And we can confirm that a French scientist, who works in the United States, has made a discovery of primary importance in the field of tactical weapons, for the utilization of chemicals in a conventional war."

The general's jaw trembled, making his mustache quiver imperceptibly.

"In this specific case..." the woman resumed.

"Forget about that. Spare me the technical details. You know they make my head hurt. This is a political problem. What the hell is one of our scientists doing in America?"

"You see, *mon Général*, he worked for years, here in France, in the sector of biotechnology and such. Then he decided to move to America. As we speak, he's at the Pentagon having a meeting with officers from the American Navy."

"Again? Another brilliant scientist that we haven't been able to offer decent working conditions? What the fuck are they doing at the

Ministère de l'Éducation Nationale? What's his name?"

"He's an old acquaintance, *mon Général.* He's the scion of a venerable and noble family, Alsatians on his mother's side, Protestants and Gascons on his father's side... his father attended the Military Academy of Saint-Cyr with you, and...."

"*Putain!* Don't tell me that it's that hothead, that *gauchiste?*"

"Oui, *mon Général,* none other than him, Pierre-André Matterre-Faquet."

"Ah, *merde,* why do the good ones always have to be such pains in the ass? Bring him back to France. We'll find him a position at the École Polytechnique, at the Institut Pasteur, or wherever he wants to go. I'll make a call to the Ministère de l'Éducation Nationale. But bring him back to France."

"But how, *mon Général?*"

"He wants glory, otherwise he wouldn't have gone to America. We can't give him glory. But does he like money? Isn't he bored to death in America, surrounded by all those puritans who spend their lives watching young men dressed in pajamas hitting balls with a stick? Doesn't he miss the *vie francaise,* the pepper of our *parisiennes?* Get busy!"

The gray tailored suit under the gray hair stiffened to attention without the gray shoes making any noise.

"Keep money as the last resource, understood?" he added, hurriedly. "And let me know when you've got some results."

"Yessir, *mon Général.*"

The woman turned on her heel and walked quickly out the door. In the hallway, her step slowed. She stopped by one of the large floor-to-ceiling windows, and looked out at the garden below. Further on, the mansard roofs of Paris served as a backdrop that had inspired poets and painters, directors and American novelists. But her eyes saw nothing. She was thinking. Then she nodded to herself, and walked briskly off toward her office. Once again, she opened the dossier on Matterre-Faquet that lay on her desk, reading through it slowly. Then, she shut the file and took another one off the bookshelf behind her. She skimmed through this one quickly, nodding to herself as she did. She'd read it many times, and it never failed to amaze her.

She went to the bookcase, opened a small cabinet, and poured herself a drop of Pernod in a small glass. She clucked her tongue, closed the cabinet door, and went over to open another door, different from the one that looked out onto the hallway. "Claude?" she called.

The man who walked in was tall, skinny, and athletic-looking. He wore the uniform of a captain of the gendarmerie. *"Oui, madame?"*

"For that American project, I've decided to send Annick Delaporte."

"Annick? You said that this is a matter of the utmost importance."

"And so?"

"And so, Annick is an agent who is still a little...inexpert. Perhaps...maybe...in conjunction with someone else..."

"Are you joking? With Annick? Just try to imagine what a team that would be! And we can't afford to spend too much. We're already going to hear about the expense and get peppered with questions about why we aren't using the people that we already have in America. But we need people with special...skills. You say that Annick is inexpert. I've studied the operation, the characteristics of the subject of interest. For what we need, the girl," and she waved her hand at the file on her desk, "has just the right experience. I'd say, in fact, that she has a natural gift."

The captain cleared his throat. "Yes, but...you... because of that very same natural inclination...she is easily distracted."

"In this case, distraction happens to be the objective."

"And what if—how to put this—she gets lost along the way?"

"Nothing of the sort has ever happened, Claude. Don't be misled by idle gossip. Annick is no fool. In fact, she's a very effective agent." She pointed once again at the dossier on the table.

"How she attains her results," she added, with a faint sigh, "is her business."

"Of course, of course, *madame*," said the captain. "She has no lack of talent."

The woman looked at him for a moment with a quizzical air, but he immediately looked away.

"I've already described it as a natural gift, which she uses without losing sight of the objective. And men," this time her sigh was a little longer and more drawn-out, "just seem to stick to her. That's what counts in this case. Go tell her, now. She has to get moving immediately."

Tel Aviv, Sunday, October 27, noon

The room was white, the walls were bare. In a vase a dwarf palm tree was eking out an existence. Through the window sunlight poured in and it was possible to see the waves of the Mediterranean. Sitting in hard chairs around a low table on which perched a teapot with mint tea, four or five men were speaking in low voices.

"Agent Uriel Silberzahn has identified a material of vegetal origin capable of inducing a generalized cataleptic trance for six hours. With a kilogram you can put every human being to sleep over an area of 50 square miles."

"Mmm, interesting, interesting." The man had salt-and-pepper hair, large ears, and was in shirtsleeves, with baggy-kneed gray trousers. "Are you talking about the Silberzahn who works in the southwest territories?"

"Yes sir."

"Where is he, right now?"

"He's on his way back from a two-day trip to the United States, where he went to pick up a sample of that material, sir."

"Who exactly authorized that?"

"No one, sir. He says that there was no time, that he got the tip from a contact of his and that he wanted to verify whether or not the material actually existed."

"Bullshit. I don't like this disorderly way of operating."

Another man broke in. Young, with a khaki shirt, a yellow scarf around his neck, Ray-Ban sunglasses, and a dark blue yarmulke.

"You know that agent Silberzahn prefers solo operations, sir."

"Yes, I do, and I also know that I don't like it one bit. He's a tough agent, I know it. And I know that he's also terribly effective. Mossad ought to have more agents like him. But, sometimes… he pisses me off with his idea that he's on a mission from God with the task of acting out the holy scriptures…Well, what about this material?"

"He says that if we put men and women to sleep in the Southwest Territories, it would be extremely easy to take prisoners."

"Oh, he does, does he? Well, there's no question that Silberzahn can have even more imagination. Tell him to report here as soon as he gets back."

"He said that he was going directly to the Territories, so that he'd already be in position."

"Shit!" yelled the man with big ears, and dropped his cup of tea on the table, "would you kindly remind him that he's part of an organization!"

"Yes, sir, I certainly will, you can count on that. We'll do our best to intercept him..."

"We need to talk this over. In depth. And this material needs to be studied. In the meanwhile, please keep an eye on him."

The men stood up, but the one who seemed to have the greatest authority over the group remained seated, in silence. Then he looked up at them and said:

"And one more thing, gentleman, listen carefully. This meeting never took place, are we understood? Until we get our hands on the material, no one is to know about Silberzahn's initiative."

Long Island, NY, Sunday, October 27, dawn

Pierre André had no idea of what effect his escape from the restrooms in the highway rest area would cause in the collective psychology, nor did the truck driver when he dropped him off in Brooklyn. Matterre-Faquet would have preferred to be left at a service station, where he could be sure he'd find a pay phone so he could call a taxi. He was no expert on investigations and espionage, but he was pretty sure that a cell phone, if left on, could be tracked down easily. He'd turned it off the minute he escaped back at the rest area. But he didn't want to ask the taciturn truck driver for any more help. So when the truck left the Gowanus Expressway, took Third Avenue, and turned right on Ninth Street toward Prospect Park, he asked the driver to drop him off at the Park Slope subway station. There were no pay phones in the subway station, but was Methodist Hospital not far away. From there he called a cab that took him to Oyster Bay, where he was able to pick up the car he'd left parked outside of Susan's house.

He didn't live far away. Ambitious scientist that he was, when he arrived on Long Island he had chosen to live in Cold Spring Harbor, which many considered the Mecca of biology on the East Coast. When he finally parked in front of his house, between state route 25A and the shore, it was almost dawn.

He made himself a cup of very strong black coffee, then he took it to his enormous desk, beneath a large canvas that recalled the cuts of Lucio Fontana. There he began to carefully sift through all his scientific documents.

He used all the material concerning the pharmacognosy and the pharmacology of the perfume-sedative to light a cheery fire in his fireplace. He added some wood from a tree he'd cut down in his yard last year, which made a pleasant smell waft through the house. He wasn't worried about destroying invaluable information. He knew exactly how to reproduce his results, and his notes would be useful to others and superfluous to him. Even if he had needed them, he would have destroyed his notes in any case. He had no desire to offer his science to the military of any country.

He put on some music to keep himself awake as he waited for the fire to do its job completely. By now exhaustion was starting to sweep over him, but he resisted the urge to take a shower. He looked longingly at the enormous terrycloth towel that hung on the turquoise green tile wall of his bathroom. He would gladly have wrapped himself in it and then stretched out on the bed and forgotten everything that had happened in the last forty-eight hours. Instead, he decided to forego even changing his clothes. Unshaven, he left the house, got into his car, and headed for Stony Brook.

In the leaden dawn, the Connecticut coast was dark grey, and the sun was too dim to brighten it. Shielded behind a thick screen of clouds, the sun barely managed to emerge from the waves of the Atlantic Ocean.

The night guard, a tall and elderly African-American gentleman who looked as if he'd seen it all, with a handsome scar on his neck, wasn't surprised to see him in the lab so early: sometimes Dr. Matterre-Faquet behaved more like an ambitious post-doc hungry for glory and success than the professor, rich in money and experience, that he actually was.

He hurried to his office to get the three lab notebooks in which he'd transcribed all his scientific work over the past two years. Then he went to Papadopoulos's laboratory to take possession of the two large half-gallon bottles that contained the extract. He stood, breathless, in front of the open door of the refrigerator. They had to be where he'd left them on Friday morning, the last time that he'd handled them. But they weren't there anymore. What had happened?

Furious, he went back to his office. The phone rang. It was Susan.

The last few hours they'd spent together already seemed to belong to another world. The ironic, sweet, effervescent Susan of that night in Connecticut was also a thousand miles away. This Susan had a faint and anguished voice.

"Where are you? I woke up early, I had a terrible night, I saw that you took your car, are you back? I tried to reach you on your cell phone, but there was no answer. You weren't at home. I tried calling your office at the university because I didn't know where else to call. What are you doing there? What's happened?"

Pierre-André was no longer listening to her. His eyes were glued to the window. Two long black automobiles, with Navy insignia, were pulling into the parking lot. He slammed down the phone and ran for the stairs. He needed to get out of there as soon as possible and, if he could, unobserved.

At the wheel of his Acura, Pierre-André started talking to himself, something that he often did when he was under stress.

"Sure, but where am I going to go now?"

Of course, Albert Hancock's sloop was the closest, safest, easiest place he could go in all of Long Island, and if he was in luck, the Army and Navy and Air Forces and Marines didn't even know that Hancock was his friend.

"Where the hell is it docked?"

With one eye on his rear view mirror, another on the map of Long Island, and a third checking that the road ahead of him was free, Matterre-Faquet made sure that no one was following him along Old Nichols Road. Then he lightened his foot on the accelerator and relaxed as he pulled onto Montauk Highway, heading east. He hoped he could quickly find the marina where Albert Hancock had docked his sloop for the Halloween regattas.

Albert and Pierre-André had both been post-docs at the University of California at San Diego, he in plant biochemistry and Albert in semi-conductor physics. Albert had then gone on to found a company that made semiconductors in Silicon Valley, he'd made a lot of money, and now he was devoting himself to many earthly pleasures, which included sailing.

They hadn't seen each other for years. Then, two weeks earlier, they happened to run into one another in San Diego. Pierre-André had flown out to talk with a scientist at the Scripps Institute about certain details of his proposal for a research grant; he was applying for funding from the National Science Foundation for a post-doc. He spotted Albert by chance, aboard the *Star of India*, where he'd gone to drink a nostalgic glass of whiskey as he had done every week for two years during his own post-doctoral training in La Jolla. That evening Albert had told him he was planning to come to Long Island for the Halloween regattas. Hancock was pleased because he knew how chic and exclusive the Hamptons were, and this was a perfect opportunity to go there again.

Unlike the climate of eternal spring that reigns over southern California, that day the sky was gray and clouds heavy with rain hung over the Atlantic Ocean. A damp wind blew out of the south. The ocean was dark as ink, tall rollers moving in the distance.

Stony Brook, NY, Sunday, October 27, morning

As Dr. Matterre-Faquet was slipping out of his laboratory with the cunning and agility of a hardened cat burglar caught in the act by the owners returning home earlier than expected just as he is emptying the safe, six uniformed men, two officers and four enlisted men, were getting out of the two black automobiles of the US Navy and walking toward the entrance, where they were greeted by a night watchman who was more helpful than curious. At the sight of their uniforms, he snapped to attention and said, "I served the Navy on the *Saratoga* in Portugal in 1975, I can still serve the Navy in Stony Brook today." He stood there stiffly until the officer called out, "At ease." They went upstairs to the scientist's office.

Matterre-Faquet had run toward the stairs in the back of the building. He'd descended into the basement and from there he made his way to the fermenter rooms. There, he had checked to make sure that, tucked away among the barrels, demijohns, basins, Sharples centrifuges, ice crushing machines, electric pumps, and other equipment, the four two-and-a-half gallon drums that contained his extract were still there, well concealed because in fact they were hidden in plain view, and weren't concealed at all. Peering out a window in the large cellar room, he had watched the six officers leave their cars unguarded in the parking area and enter the laboratory building. That's when he'd sprinted across the lot in a way that would have stood him in good stead at the 200-meter finals at the Olympics and reached his Acura. In the meanwhile, the six Navy men had reached Matterre-Faquet's office, where the night watchman, who assured them that he had seen the doctor enter the building, stood flabbergasted at the sight of the wreckage of his desk, the disorderly papers and books, but not a sign of the French scientist. One of the officers said:

"Take the lab notebooks."

Noticing the quizzical inertia of his petty officers, the other officer decided that the poor young things probably didn't know a lab notebook from the personal diary of reluctant debutante, so he smiled and encouraged them:

"All right, take everything there is, books, dossiers, files, notebooks, scrap paper, correspondence, newspapers and scientific journals, and, of course, the computer, the CDs, the DVDs, and even the old floppy disks, you never know."

The four petty officers set to work and filled a dozen or so cardboard boxes in just half an hour. In the meanwhile, the two officers had explored the laboratory with their hands clasped behind their backs and the mistrustful air of those who know that, in a scientific laboratory, an apparently innocuous object could be a harbinger of death or serious accidents. Matterre-Faquet was already far way, but they were in no hurry. Ahead of them stretched the temporal eternity of the just mission they had to perform. *Novus ordo seclorum annuit coeptis*, are the words written on a one dollar bill. The new order of the centuries approves our undertakings. And therefore it was possible to take their time. They asked the night watchman to help them with one of those special machines used to lift and transport heavy objects. In a single trip, with that immense hydraulic hoist, the twelve big boxes were deposited next to the two black cars with dark blue banners decorated with golden anchors.

A home in New Jersey, Sunday, October 27, afternoon

The mansion was one of those elegant residential structures, built in recent years, of which so many have sprung up in central New Jersey. A closer look however would show that it was built more with brick than with wood, a fairly unusual thing on the east coast of the United States. The long fence that surrounded the tall elegant oak trees and the green meadow covered with multicolored leaves and the forsythia and hydrangea bushes was more than a simple hurricane fence. Moreover, it also surrounded the section of yard in front of the house, leaving only a single opening with a gate, controlling access to the gravel driveway and lined by a hedge of boxwood and butcher's broom. A circular section of ground around the house, at least a hundred feet in depth, was completely free of bushes, hedges, trees, and flowers. Only Kentucky bluegrass, which bent in the autumn wind, sketching moving figures the way that a sea breeze does on the water. A careful inspection would have revealed that in many ways this mansion showed many unsettling similarities to the fortified manor houses of the Middle Ages, manor houses that can still be found today in the British Isles, in southern France, and in Sicily.

Numerous elegant automobiles were parked on the driveway. In the living room of the house, six or seven men with crystal glasses filled with red wine in their hands were talking animatedly. The meeting had been scheduled long ago and the guests came from the four corners of America. They were supposed to talk about substantial interests, beginning with the national geography of the organization's casinos. To be precise, the minimum number of miles that had to separate each casino from the others. But an unexpected topic had arisen to monopolize the discussion. Now, one of the guests was doing his best to express a knotty concept, and he was massaging his testicles as he searched for the words that best matched his ideas.

"My great grandfather fought in the First World War. He said that the Germans used gases, uh...what were they called? oh, asphyxiant gases. We Italians used them too, in the War of Abyssinia. My grandfather told me that when the wind blew in the opposite direction, the gas killed our soldiers instead of the enemy, capeesh?"

"Those are blessed words you're speaking, my friend!" added another man, the fingers of his right hand compressed into a sort of cone shape.

"How long will it take us before we can master this... innovation? Isn't the secret of our success the fact that we make use of... well-tested techniques? Now the professors of management at Harvard Business School call them Standard Operating Procedures, but in other words, wiseguys, if you leave the old way for the new way, you never know what might happen, am I right?"

"Eh, sometimes proverbs can be misleading," replied the man who, until this point, had led the conversation. "And if the old path turns into a mule track that runs around in circles and, moreover, is full of potholes and you can't travel at anything but a snail's pace, isn't a superhighway better?"

"I have to say that I can't see all these potholes. And I'm not sure I see a superhighway for that matter," another one broke in. "But this stuff," he went on, "let me ask, do we have it in our possession?"

"Do you really think I'd be here talking to you about it, if we didn't have it safely in our hands? We've got it, we've got it," replied the one who didn't like proverbs.

"And where is it?"

"In a safe place, don't worry about that," was the chilly response, followed by:

"With all the respect that I have for you, you know that the point of this operation is to help the families..."

"Well, maybe not, maybe not," and a man who was vigorously scratching his neck with a hand under his shirt unknotted his tie, stood up, and said: "Help the families, sure, but sometimes mistakes are made, and that's not good, capeesh?"

"There won't be any mistakes, you can count on that. It's been planned out to the last detail."

"What kind of details are you talking about?"

The man made a vague gesture with his hand:

"Just leave that up to me. What I care about are the results that I'm going to bring you. This is an opportunity that the organization can't afford to miss. We need to create something new. Out there are Mexicans, Chinese, and Puerto Ricans who can't wait to shove us aside and take our place. They'd love to kick us out of the business. We need something that'll let us make a qualitative leap and put the competition far behind us. How do you think that can be done? Take a look around. The way everyone else does it. With technology."

Now, they were all talking at the same time.

"We could rob banks in the blink of an eye!"

"Much more than a few paltry bank robberies! Think of our import-export business: we could open up a highway right through customs, direct from the Middle East to New England."

"I'd say that this is much more important than that. This whole issue of technology is real. Everyone's talking about it, everyone's making money off it. So why should we be kept out of it? If we have one, let's use it and see what happens. Times change, and we need to change with them."

They weren't all in perfect agreement.

"It's one thing to ride a donkey, it's another matter entirely to ride a tiger."

"Why a tiger?" broke in the man who didn't like stock phrases and clichés. "Let's call it a horse, a fast and powerful stallion. Which will take us far and fast. I'm sure of it, but you'll see too, in time. Soon. Like I told you before, what I'm suggesting here is an experiment. The results will astonish you. But the ones who will really be surprised are the ones outside of this room." He waved his hand in a sweeping gesture: "Everyone else." He let the words sink into the minds of his audience.

"You'll see that, after this experiment, nothing will be the same as before. The organization will be much more powerful. Feared. And it can make more demands."

He paused. And then, eventually, he said:

"Problems like the ones we had with the casinos, things we were so worried about when we first got here, this afternoon? You'll see: they'll solve themselves." The crowd murmured quietly. Then, silence. The man who had talked longer than anyone else considered that to be a yes. He spoke to the eldest of those present: "Do you think you should ask the opinion of our... our... out there?" and he nodded, as if to indicate somewhere far away.

"Of course, we could always ask," was the response. "But only after we've got a more complete opinion, right? You understand this? It's better if we have the whole situation laid out clearly."

The Hamptons, Long Island, NY, Sunday, October 27, late afternoon

Finding out where the devil a boat that's going to take part in the Halloween regattas is moored is no easy matter, even if you know what marina it's docked in. It's even more difficult when you don't even know what marina the boat is docked in and when, moreover, you don't want to talk to the Coast Guard or use your cell phone, to make sure that the armed forces can't track you down.

Thank heavens, everyone seemed to know everything about these regattas, the last big event before the end of the tourist season in the Hamptons, and the invisible and fine-grained organization allowed him to find out not only what marina but the slip number of the *Sexy Diode*, Albert Hancock's sloop.

When he got to the dock, it was almost dark. Albert was putting on a handsome white-and-blue sweater, to ward off nighttime temperatures that were much cooler than the seasonal lows of San Diego.

Emerging from his sweater, Albert saw Pierre-André in the opening of the hatchway. He stood there for a moment looking at him and then he said:

"What an honor! I see that for once you've kept your promise and you've come to visit me."

The Hamptons, Monday, October 28, daytime

The next day the sun was shining over the Atlantic Ocean. Hancock and Matterre-Faquet emerged from the hatch of the sailboat and headed for the nearest Starbuck's to start the day with a giant cup of coffee, three croissants, and a newspaper. The evening before Hancock had learned the essentials and the details. For now, Pierre-André was in no impending danger. Concealed on the yacht, it would take a couple of days before anyone, searching the island with a fine-toothed comb, could associate the names of the *Sexy Diode* and Matterre-Faquet. Pierre-André wound up lulling himself into the psychological illusion that the worst was over. They set sail around eleven in the morning. They heeled into a few strong winds and did some jibing. The *Sexy Diode* was a sweet-sailing ship. Albert sat in the bowsprit, with the main brace between his legs, while Pierre-André handled the helm. Then it was Pierre-André's turn to face the waves, hauling on the jib, braced in like a skydiver, hooked to the stanchion with a stainless steel snap-hook. They tried reefing the mainsail, then they hoisted the spinnaker. In other words, they did all the things you'd need to do in a regatta. They returned to dock before sunset.

They took a leisurely shower and then slipped into more comfortable and elegant clothing. Albert loaned Pierre-André a pair of clean socks, as well as a handsome mariner's sweater, soft and warm. They got a bite to eat and then they headed for the marina clubhouse.

The Hamptons, Monday, October 28, night

Albert and Pierre-André had spent the night drinking beer and whiskey in the marina clubhouse. After spending the night in Manhattan, Annick had spent the whole day driving the length of Long Island, dressed as a woman just leaving her teens and with plenty of time on her hands. No one answered at the house in Cold Harbor and when the security guard at Stony Brook told her that Professor Matterre-Faquet had suddenly vanished and that a crew from the Navy had come looking for him, Annick concluded that the scientist had gone to ground and was hiding. If that was the case, Matterre-Faquet wasn't stupid and he was unlikely to pick any of the more obvious hiding places. Annick began by discarding the house of the Jamaican professor with whom Matterre-Faquet had had a relationship. Almost everybody knew about them, so the men from the Pentagon would have gone to look for her there as well. The same applied to the homes of his other colleagues.

In the dossier that Josiane had given her, there was a mention of Matterre-Faquet's friendship with a certain Albert Hancock, a Californian who manufactured semiconductors and was a fanatic about sailing. Moreover, it stated that in the Hamptons, at the far end of Long Island, there were a series of regattas being held in which Hancock was expected to participate. The DGSE carefully monitored the activities of French people of any particular interest. Annick tried to put herself in Matterre-Faquet's shoes and decided that, if it had been up to her, Hancock would have struck her as the safest hiding place. The Americans, for that matter, hadn't shown any interest in the French scientist and therefore it was unlikely that they knew anything about Hancock. She decided to start there. If she came up empty, she'd just cover Long Island in the opposite direction, in an attempt to flush the scientist out of hiding.

She started from the most obvious place, on an evening of various regattas: the clubhouse of the marina. Before entering, she took a look at the photographs of Matterre-Faquet and Hancock that Josiane had given her. The minute she was inside, she knew that her instincts had steered her right. Hancock and the scientist were sitting at the bar and, in case she'd had any doubts, the light French accent of one of the two men made them disappear as if by magic.

But the men had just stood up and were about to leave the clubhouse and vanish into the night, before she had a chance to hook up with them. Suddenly a wave of frustration and paralysis swept over her, as if she lacked some vital connection between body and brain. But Annick was no ordinary young woman: a black pageboy haircut, huge gray eyes flecked with gold and fringed with long silky lashes, slim hips sheathed in a tight-fitting dress, breasts that swelled within her snug cashmere cardigan, which was sufficiently light to reveal a proud absence of brassiere—it all added up to a picture that was hard for anyone to miss. In fact, Albert stopped when he came even with her and, impulsively, at the sight of her distraught expression, he asked: "Are you all right? Do you need help?" Annick regained her self-control and flashed him a smile. The blend of her fragile distress and that provocative smile proved irresistible and Annick knew that very well. "We're willing to do anything we can," Matterre-Faquet smiled in turn.

The girl mumbled something incomprehensible about having lost or forgotten who knows what and neither of the two men really cared what it might have been. She walked with them toward the exit and, on the steps down to the parking lot, she'd already agreed to drink a cup of coffee with them on board Albert's yacht and maybe even to polish off the bottle of Laphroaig that was stowed in the galley.

They walked together along the jetty, admiring the moored sailboats and breathing in the salt air of the Atlantic Ocean.

"Are you foreigners?" she asked. "Such courtesy is an uncommon experience on this island."

"I'm French," said Matterre-Faquet, "and I don't think I'm alone here, am I?"

The girl laughed, explained that her name was Annick Delaporte and that in fact she was from Paris. Then she asked the two men what their names were. She noted that Matterre-Faquet's name was, in fact, very long and very French, while Albert's name was as American as the whoosh and the crack of a baseball bat. Annick and Pierre-André stepped down into the cabin, loudly complaining about the unmistakable mark of their homeland that emerged whenever they opened their mouths to speak a foreign language. They took off their shoes, stretched out on the pillows of the sofas, and started talking nonsense.

All three of them laughed loud and long. The two men asked her what would happen if, instead of a university professor and a manufacturer, she had met a muscular, tattooed weightlifter with long hair and pierced ears and tongue. Of course, the muscular, tattooed weightlifter with long hair and pierced ears and tongue would be incapable of stringing two sentences together. And Annick replied that words aren't everything and that muscular, tattooed weightlifters can have their good points, too.

The night was cold. The moon was setting in the western sky. In the tight quarters of the sloop's cabin, it was difficult to move.

When Annick turned to give Pierre-André a goodnight kiss, Albert was just moving forward to shake hands at the end of the evening. As she turned, his hand hit her back and unintentionally he shoved her into Pierre-André's arms. Could she have overreacted and tipped forward on purpose? Or was it that he had failed to understand her enthusiasm? She felt the heat of his face, her feet slipped on the wooden floor, damp from the evening dew, and Pierre-André couldn't keep her from falling.

Albert took a step forward and caught her, helping her to get back on her feet, but by this time her tight skirt had hiked itself up her thighs. She needed support and she wound up leaning on him. He felt her slender body against him and couldn't resist the temptation to place his hands on her hips. Pierre-André finished his goodnight kiss, but she insisted on a second one, on the other cheek, and then she shoved her derriere against Albert. Her skirt was still hiked up on her thighs. While Pierre-André was turning his face from one cheek to the other, she seized his lower lip with her teeth and then kissed him deeply, as she waggled her bottom against Albert, who finally began to get excited and glued his body against hers.

The situation could easily have become awkward, but Albert turned off the lights and the cabin was plunged into darkness.

Albert slipped a hand under her skirt and left it there, but no negative signals seemed to emanate from the young woman. And so he moved his hand up to her damp crotch. Pierre-André was lost in a dream, their tongues dueled an ancient and unfailingly new duel while he caressed her breasts and she wrapped her arms around his neck, dragging him into a furiously passionate kiss.

Albert no longer hesitated. He slipped his hand inside her panties, stroked her pubic hair trimmed Brazilian style, fondled her *mons veneris*, slithered one of his fingers between her labia, felt the moisture, the anxious aperture between her upper thighs, the pulse of her arteries.

Annick felt the imperceptible caress and a quivering convulsion ensued, while Pierre-André explored her nipples and whispered sweet nothings into her ear. At this point, she was the mistress of his cock, and she unzipped his pants. In the cold of the night, Pierre-André shivered slightly in anguish when his free nude penis felt the ocean wind, but she bent forward, pressed her ass cheeks against Albert, and let her tongue run the length of Pierre-André's member, only to begin titillating the tip of it with her fleshy lips.

Albert was losing control. He tore off the panties, unzipped his pants, and hesitantly tried to get closer to her. Annick shifted her legs slightly, pushed her vagina closer to Albert's member. Annick vibrated in the darkness, her mouth filled with one throbbing penis, her vagina eagerly accommodating another.

There was a long moment of silence. Pierre-André had both hands on Annick's head, holding her steady, while she worked with her tongue on the most sensitive zones and pressed her ass against Albert, to achieve the deepest possible penetration, to stimulate her G spot beyond her wildest dreams, until she spun completely out of control.

When Albert began pushing, Annick felt her muscles relax: her body opened up to this new adventure and her satisfied femininity found confirmation in the turgid virility that was filling her mouth right down to the back of her throat.

Pierre-André came first, filling Annick's mouth with viscous love. Annick felt the intense psychological pleasure of having given an orgasm, then she concentrated on herself, swinging her hips, panting, groaning, breathing in rhythm with her motion, drooling. Albert did his best to hold out as long as he could, then he came too, in a salvo of successive contractions. Annick touched herself, caressing her clitoris, while her pubic and iliac muscles and her sphincter contracted and relaxed, contracted and relaxed and contracted and relaxed, until she slumped over on the sofa, exhausted and satiated.

All three of them fell silent, their eyes closed, Pierre-André near Annick on the sofa, Albert in an armchair. Annick was savoring the moment, as were Pierre-André and Albert, at least at first. But the two men began to feel vaguely embarrassed by what had just happened. The first to react was Albert. He started straightening up, putting pencils away, stacking sea charts, and stowing navigational instruments and goniometers, which had been thrown into disarray by the unexpected threesome.

One unwritten rule of maritime etiquette is that the guests help to clean up in the cockpit. So Annick and Pierre-André got up and took care of some of the less esoteric matters, such as washing glasses and putting away sheets and blankets. No one spoke. Annick organized shirts, undershirts, underwear, and socks, while Pierre-André folded towels and sheets.

The young woman found her way to the shower and slipped inside. When she got back, not even Albert's oversized bathrobe could make her look silly. Albert had poured her a generous glass of Laphroaig. She was exhausted. For her it was more or less five in the morning. Her body was sweetly relaxed, but she couldn't stop now. Annick was a disciplined agent and she had a mission to perform. Madame knew which horses to put her money on.

Annick looked at the two men.

She felt sure that he had them in the palm of her hand.

She decided to show her cards.

"They want you to come back to France, Dr. Matterre-Faquet."

The two men stared at her in astonishment. She lit a cigarette and went on:

"I've been looking for you all day, but you are very good at hide-and-seek, aren't you?"

Pierre-André looked at Albert, Albert looked at Pierre-André, and both of them looked at Annick.

She went on: "Well, a biotechnology star and a guru of semiconductors, don't you think that the DGSE ought to keep an eye on you?"

Pierre-André was even more astonished now:

"The DGSE? The Direction Générale de la Securité Extérieure? The French espionage service?"

"Of course. Usually we keep just one eye on all the things you do, so to speak, without any particular focus, but sometimes we step in as your guardian angels when you run the risk of causing diplomatic incidents, or worse. And now, here you are, in America, hiding out in a sailboat, with the CIA, the FBI, Mossad, and who knows who else, maybe even the Mafia, chasing after you."

"The CIA? Mossad? What do they have to do with this? I knew about the Pentagon. What do they want from me?"

"When you come up with an invention like yours, you have to assume that a lot of people are going to be interested, you know. They want your narcotic."

"It's not a narcotic, it's a sedative," Matterre-Faquet shot back in a flat voice. "And the DGSE? Even the French?"

"Even our compatriots, professor," Annick nodded.

"But, everything that happened before? Was that all..."

Annick shrugged. "You don't turn down such an attractive invitation. There are some good fringe benefits to this line of work. You meet some interesting people. When we get back to France, we can talk it over."

"To France? You want me to go back to France? Don't you realize that the reason I left is that it's impossible for me to even think of going back there? Can you seriously imagine seeing me back there with those bastards, people who ruined my life because I was trying to achieve some form of success, people who hate me now because I'm successful?"

"Doctor Matterre-Faquet, I don't give a damn, and the DGSE doesn't give a fuck *royale*, about what your French colleagues might think of you. The problem is that you've made an important discovery and there's strong risk that this discovery may fall into the hands of a foreign power or a criminal gang, or even terrorists..."

"Annick, you're a very attractive and sensuous woman and if I could, I'd take you away with me, to Baja California, and I'd make you very happy. But don't think for a minute that I can tell lies to myself, at least not lies that I'm capable of believing. I left because there's no room, in France, for a biotechnology company unless you're willing to tug your forelock and bend down in adoration of the academic Mafia. I didn't do it then and I don't intend to start now."

Annick smiled, and her pretty, inviting lips allowed her gleaming white teeth to make her radiant smile even prettier, adding seductive power to her tanned face.

"Of course, neither the ANVAR, nor the CNRS, nor the universities have helped you. But you did what you wanted and the government and the Direction de la Surveillance du Territoire let you act as you liked. They let you do exactly what you chose, didn't they?"

She lit another cigarette, exhaled a cloud of dense blue smoke, and went on:

"But in this case, hell, you've created a weapon... we can't let you wander around like any ordinary tourist..."

Hancock had followed the pingpong match between Annick and Pierre-André up until that moment. But he knew his friend's positions and he could guess the line of argument that the girl would follow. He was a pragmatic man. He was also curious to understand what the next step would be.

"So what do you suggest?" he asked Annick.

"Well, Doctor Matterre-Faquet and I would be picked up by a Panther helicopter in, let's say, two hours. The helicopter would set us down on the deck of a French Navy frigate that's cruising off Nantucket. You, Albert, could happily finish your regattas and, without a word to anyone, go back to your life in California, even though, I admit, we'd have to continue to keep an eye on you."

Matterre-Faquet's face was purple. The nightmare of going back to France, turning his back on everything he'd done in the past several years, drowned out even Annick's references to the CIA and Mossad. He couldn't think of anything else.

"No, no, absolutely out of the question. Not with those idiots. I have no confidence in the intelligence service. They'll wind up doing something incredibly stupid, as usual."

He made a gesture with his hand, as if to brush away an annoying thought and he focused on another problem that was bothering him. "Anyway, I couldn't just vanish like that. No one knows where the bulk of my preparation is hidden, ten gallons of extract, and I'm still waiting to find out whether it's toxic or not. Really, if you want to help me, if you want to defuse that—what do you call it?—that weapon, you have to help me get my hands on it without anyone else being able to know. Because they've stolen two half-gallon bottles from me already, and I'd very much like to know the name of the bastard who stole it from me and what he's planning to do with it."

FBI field office, New York, NY, Tuesday, October 29, evening.

O'Malley put out his cigarette on the railing of the fire escape. The chief, in the face of the hail of pressure arriving from all directions, had decided to make public the conclusions to which the Bureau had come by now on Massapequod, and the first television news reports were about to air. He went back into the hall. He didn't want to be sitting with everybody else when he finally saw how the press was going to serve up the news and so, instead of going back to his office, he stopped in what everybody called "the boiler room," a room with a trapezoidal plan with stiff wicker chairs, a refrigerator from the Seventies, two coffee machines, a wobbly coffee table, and four flat-screen TVs, tuned to various news networks. As he expected, there was no one inside.

Naturally, Massapequod led the news reports. CNN headlined the story "Killer Sleep," while Fox News headlined it "The Narcotic That Kills." They'd been quick to jump to conclusions, thought O'Malley. He decided to watch Fox News, assuming they'd paint the most lurid picture.

The report opened with footage of Massapequod. Unlike the footage from that morning, when they had only been able to film from up on the hill, the videocameras had been allowed to enter the small town. But only at nightfall, and so Massapequod was shown to the rest of America in the harsh glare of spotlights. The effect of the contrast between the brightly lit flat images and the deep wells of shadow behind them was even darker   and more unsettling. O'Malley had listened to Jill and Larramee's accounts and he had looked at a few photographs. But now that the images were flowing past him, as if in slow motion, they made his flesh crawl. The firetruck in the garage, the bar burnt to a charred black cave, furniture and everyday objects devastated and consumed by the pitiless flames, the playground slide twisted into a grotesque spiderweb. O'Malley had a cramp in the pit of his stomach. Luckily, the police had carted away all the corpses by the time the news cameras were rolling. Unfortunately, no one had explained that to the sheriff who was now droning into the microphones about bodies left to sizzle on the bedsprings and stumps and fragments of corpses scattered across the pavement and the dirt.

"They were burned to death without ever waking up" the sheriff concluded, with a still incredulous expression on his face. "Shit," said O'Malley in a loud voice, "isn't it horrible enough already?"

The feed went back to the newsanchor in the studio, to address the most obvious question: what happened?

An anchorwoman with straw-blonde hair and a twisted mouth explained that, according to the FBI, a narcotic had been nebulized into the air, putting the unfortunate inhabitants of Massapequod into an instantaneous, deep sleep. This narcotic, the anchorwoman went on, was of unknown origin and makeup. Nothing about the French scientist: the FBI hadn't said anything about Matterre-Faquet's role in all this. "But it won't take them long to get to it," O'Malley concluded. They had to lay their hands on the scientist, before pictures of him began to circulate and some group of wingnuts beat them to it.

Fox News, in any case, had no doubts about who was behind the massacre in the small Maine village and the danger that was threatening the nation. The anchorwoman brought up the word terrorism:

The nation, she explained, had once again fallenvictim to a treacherous, ferocious, and cowardly attack from internal and external enemies. Powerful and invisible enemies, enemies who might look like your next-door neighbor, and enemies that were especially dangerous now that Halloween was coming and everyone would be wearing a mask, thus making it easier for those who wished to spread the toxic substance from hiding and perhaps even set fire to houses.

On that basis, it took a politician from Georgia to suggest the best way to behave now: the only way to safeguard our country and our families, said the senator, was to form armed vigilante squads that could aid the police in every county, both in carrying out investigations and in apprehending the criminals. The Harvard egghead who was interviewed immediately afterward ventured into a long, hypothetical socio-psychological analysis of the perpetrator. He warned the television audience to distinguish carefully between facts and interpretations of facts and even wound up forgetting to talk about Massapequod entirely. It was hard to understand what he'd actually said. "People," O'Malley concluded, "will only remember what the senator said."

Wednesday, October 30

Burt Paxton needed to empty his bladder. He'd rocketed at top speed past the last service station for fifty miles like an idiot and now he knew he wouldn't make it to the next one. The road was narrow and he needed a clearing to stop his big pickup truck for even a short time. There was one, a few hundred yards ahead. He pulled his truck over between the road and a hurricane fence, behind which he could see lights in the windows of a farmhouse and the dark silhouettes of what he assumed were a barn and a silo. He parked the truck and stepped over to the fence, with his back turned to the house. He heard a horse whinny.

At last, he unzipped his trousers. With a sigh, he began to relax. Suddenly he saw a flash of light and almost simultaneously, he heard a sharp crack, like a wooden stick hitting a tin can. A bullet whistled past his head. He was so surprised he stopped peeing. He turned to look at the house.

From one of the second-story windows, a woman was pointing a flashlight at him. "There he is, next to the pickup. It's the one from that news show," he heard the woman scream. Next to her, a kneeling man was trying to draw a bead on him with a rifle. He heard another gunshot and a bullet bounced off the side of the truck.

He hit the ground, right in the middle of the puddle that he'd just created in the gravel. He turned around, trying frantically to stuff his junk back in his trousers, and wound up pissing in his pants. He heard another, more muffled-sounding shot. He looked back at the house again. Now the porch was lit up and the light almost extended to him. Standing in front of the door was a young man with a double-barreled shotgun. "I see him, Paw."

Slithering as fast as he could go, Burt Paxton made his way around the front of the pickup truck. He half-stood up to open the door and slid into the driver's seat. He started the truck and, tires screeching, swerved back onto the road. At the last minute he remembered to bend low over the steering wheel. The young man had reached the fence and had fired again. He heard the rear window shatter and he accelerated toward Tuscaloosa. Only a few miles later did he realize that there was a round hole in the middle of the windshield.

Beirut, Wednesday, October 30, afternoon

For three full days, Uriel Silberzahn relied on every excuse imaginable to avoid finding himself face-to-face with his superior officers. He had obeyed the order to stay out of Gaza, not because he was particularly obedient, but because he expected a bitter dispute within Mossad concerning the utilization of Matterre-Faquet's big bottle of perfume / narcotic. In fact he assumed that, if the hawks won out and they decided to make use of it, he would return to Tel Aviv with a hero's welcome, while on the other hand, if the doves were victorious, he could go to the Palestinians on his own time.

But now he was thinking about a woman.

He had seen her in the alleyway behind the mosque, standing next to the hooded man that he knew was Ahmed Batik. He had come to Beirut because of Batik in the first place. Before Rachel phoned him, his mission had been to identify his contacts and then kill him. Upon his return from New York, he had gone immediately to Beirut, both because he was determined to conclude his missions, especially when that meant killing a Palestinian, and because the mission struck him as a good excuse for staying clear of Tel Aviv entirely, so that he wasn't forced to hand over to his superior officers the large bottle with all its fascinating possibilities.

But now the thing that was filling his mind was that image of Fatimah. This was not the first time that they had crossed paths. That firm, confident determined demeanor, as the mistress of her own destiny that she was, was what drove him to the verge of fury, when he considered that it was people like her who made it hard for him to complete his mission of taking back his own land. In the days that followed, he noticed that Fatimah no longer appeared at Batik's side. He knew that she was much more than a bodyguard. Instead she was an influential assistant, a spokesperson, as well as a right-hand woman. From his contacts, he knew that the woman was in Gaza, on Batik's behalf, to attend a rare summit meeting between Hamas and Fatah. She'd be back soon. To strike her, to humiliate her, he thought with a shiver of anticipation, would be a political statement.

He decided to abandon the strict confines of his mission for a while. But he couldn't even remotely perceive that violating the confines of his mission could be considered an act of injustice.

On other occasions, he had had the distinct sensation that he was the reincarnation of Joshua, returned to earth as a twenty-first century leader. But it was Fatimah who had intervened between his "trumpets of Jericho" and the defenses of the city that he hoped to annihilate. His fanatical faith had given him the moral justification for the many horrible acts he had committed. A psychoanalyst might have concluded that it was his mother, who had conceived and borne him shortly before her own menopause, and who was therefore much older than him, who was the source of this conviction of his that he was a divine creature. A psychiatrist would have noticed that he had a certain degree of difficulty relating to women who were comfortable with their own sexuality. His colleagues knew that Uriel Silberzahn was better versed in the use of brute force than he was in the tender skirmishing of seduction, and that he was more inclined to commit bold acts of violence than to appreciate the erotic pleasure of the unpredictable outcome of such skirmishes.

With a laugh, his colleagues said that Uriel knew the book of Deuteronomy by heart and when he went into combat, he followed the letter of the divine commandment, solely to satisfy his sexual desires:

"But if the city does not make peace with you, but makes war with you, you shall besiege it.

HaShem shall deliver it into your hand, and you shall smite all its males by the blade of the sword.

Only the women may you plunder for yourselves..."

The Hamptons, Long Island, NY, Wednesday, October 30, evening.

Albert and Pierre-André had spent the previous day and a good part of today sailing off Long Island, heeling over on the eastern end of the island, between Montauk and Orient Point. Sailing demands silence, and it was welcome. They didn't want to talk about their night with Annick, and they had decided, despite her protests, not to take her with them: there was a palpable wave of embarrassment and unease between the two friends. In order to allow Albert to get as familiar as possible with the waters, the lighthouses, and the rocks along the coasts of Long Island, they had decided to spend the night offshore, anchored in Gardiners Bay, where they would be sheltered from the ocean winds.

They returned in the early afternoon, wet, cold, and hungry, and they moored the *Sexy Diode* before hurrying to get piping hot showers. Toward evening they wound up in an Irish pub, where they ate fish and chips and drank Guinness. There were twenty deafening television sets that mostly transmitted pictures of football players with gladiator's helmets, shoulders as broad as refrigerators, and slender legs sheathed in tight white pants, who thundered against one another and piled up in a heap in the middle of the field. Other screens showed video clips of singers or talk shows.

At eight o'clock the bartender turned on a television screen that was off to one side from the others, right next to the bar. It was time for the Long Island News evening broadcast and that's what caught the attention of everyone in the bar.

The report that led the evening newscast on the Long Island News was devoted to a little harbor town in Maine called Massapequod. The village had been devastated by fire: millions of dollars worth of damages, the entire village charred, and an atrocious death for all 166 inhabitants. It was a quick summary of the story. Long Island News was clearly delivering a capsule presentation of other reports already broadcast on earlier editions, but Hancock and Matterre-Faquet, who knew nothing about it, were staring at the TV, eyes wide open in astonishment and horror. While the scientist and his friend Albert were making an intimate acquaintance with Annick, the little port town in Maine had experienced hell on earth. The police of York County, Maine had found the residents and the firemen burned where they stood, sat, or lay, as if they'd been unaware of the roaring flames that were burning their houses, built of wood, that lined the bay. The police, the sheriff, and the FBI were investigating the powerful narcotic that had been atomized into the air over the village, causing all the inhabitants to fall asleep and sending them to their deaths. Pierre-André's breath caught in his throat.

There was a new development, Long Island News reported. Someone had phoned in to a TV station in Maryland, explaining that in a highway reststop three Navy men had been found in a deep sleep, two in a car and one in a restroom, in conditions very similar to those of the inhabitants of Massapequod. At first it was assumed that they had passed out in a drunken stupor but when the press peppered the Pentagon with questions, the spokesperson had been forced to admit that the three sailors had in fact been drugged. By connecting the two facts— and this was the core of the explosive new information—it had been possible to identify the person who was responsible for the narcotic: a French scientist who worked at Stony Brook University, named Pierre-André Matterre-Faquet. The pronunciation was badly bungled until the name was incomprehensible, but his name was written clearly, in big letters, on the screen. Pierre-André's hands were trembling, clammy drops of sweat slid down his forehead. There was even a picture of him, luckily taken from a considerable distance, from a graduation ceremony. It would be hard to identify him from that photograph.

Pierre-André's brain had ceased to function. He kept swallowing a bitter taste in his mouth, looking around without actually seeing anything. In the end he managed to focus on Hancock. His friend had reacted quicker than him. He was looking around to see if anyone had recognized Pierre-André. But most of the customers had gone back to starting into their beer or were chatting idly. Albert stood up hurriedly: "Let's get out of here," he said.

Washington, DC, Wednesday, October 30, evening

The tablecloth was linen, there were teardrop crystal chandeliers, the service in the restaurant at the high end of a small back lane in Georgetown was impeccable. And the crème de la crème of Washington filled the place every evening. He decided that politics was a burdensome line of work, but that he was happy to keep working in that field, as long as they would let him. He had dreamed of becoming the Speaker of the House of Representatives from the very first day he came to Congress, twenty years earlier. And if that meant subjecting himself to dinners like this one, well, he was willing to tolerate another hundred of them. The tragedy of Massapequod had been hypnotizing the country and its institutions for two days now, but he knew very well that, underneath the drama and the tension, the river of politics kept on flowing, with its deadlines and its demands. He took another half-hearted bite of steak, decided not to finish, and picked at the potatoes. He relaxed into the back of his chair, sipping from a last glass of California wine. He was ready for the coffee. He allowed the conversation to flow around him. His assistant Jennifer was excellent at keeping alive meaningless chitchat. What mattered had already been said. If the man across the table from him wished to put a large chunk of cash into his next election campaign, which would be long and challenging, well he was most welcome to do so. All he asked in return were some tweaks to the bill on industrial wastes. He wasn't the only one to ask for those changes and, probably, he told himself, they would be incorporated into the draft in any case.

A cup of coffee had been brought to the table along with the check. He took care to pay his share of the check to the last penny, to avoid any appearance of impropriety. He stood up, as did the others, to leave. He waved to a few of his colleagues, but he stopped to exchange a few pleasantries with that viper Bixby. He knew perfectly that he was preparing to filibuster the budget bill, but he wanted to show that he wasn't worried in the slightest. A little further on, he saw a Washington *Post* reporter signaling to him. That was Burbank, who had just published a particularly venomous profile of him, but those were the rules of the game and he could hardly hold it against him. The reporter stood up and came over.

"Is it true," he asked, "that you're discussing whether or not to support Greene's reelection campaign?"

"No," he answered tersely.

"Does that mean you won't support him?"

"That means we're not discussing it."

The coat check girl ceremoniously handed him his raincoat. As he was putting it on, he felt something odd. As if there was something in the pocket. He slipped in his hand and felt an envelope. He was careful not to pull it out. Outside of the restaurant, he said an unruffled goodnight to one and all. In the car, he pulled out the envelope and took a quick look inside. It was a white envelope, addressed to the President of the United States. As soon as he got home, he tore the envelope open. Inside was a sheet of paper. He read it by the front hall light and could feel the blood drain from his face. He dropped the raincoat on the floor and went into his office. At his desk, he reread the letter three times, with furrowed brow and moving his lips as if he were reading aloud.

He picked up the phone and called his old friend and colleague, who was now the White House chief of staff. He cut short the greetings and the objections about the lateness of the hour.

"I need to speak to the President."

"Well, let me see what his schedule looks like."

"Not tomorrow. Right now."

"You know he goes to bed early. And tomorrow is the press conference."

"It has to do with Massapequod. There's a new development he's not going to like."

There was a moment of silence on the other end of the line.

"Okay. I'll go alert him. Stop by my office when you get here."

Thursday, October 31

There are plenty of paranoid Americans who consider Halloween to be the day that pedophiles lurk in the bushes, and they forbid their children to walk around the neighborhood dressed as witches and skeletons to trick or treat for hard candies and chocolates. Even though it's statistically proven that Halloween is actually the day of the year with the lowest incidence of child abuse, precisely because the children are out walking in groups and a pedophile would be forced to act in front of numerous witnesses, many adults insist on accompanying their children as they go out trick-or-treating, and so the children have much less fun. This Halloween took place under the bad star of the mysterious narcotic, and it wasn't only isolated neurotic adults, but virtual armies of parents armed with shotguns, hunting rifles, and even assault rifles (modestly described as collector's items) patrolled the street corners of the various neighborhoods of Long Island, from Manhasset and Merrick and Hauppauge to Commack and Babylon and Islip, from Cold Spring Harbor and Huntington to Wyandanch and Ronkonkoma.

The children were terrified.

FBI field office, New York, NY, Thursday, October 31, dawn.

Gillespie was pale as a sheet. O'Malley hitched his trousers up around his waist and sat down across from him.

"The chief," said Gillespie, "just got back from an emergency meeting at the White House."

"With this," he added, pointing to a sheet of paper lying on his desk. "The Speaker of the House found it in the pocket of his raincoat after he left a restaurant. In an envelope addressed to the President of the United States."

"This is a fax, naturally. Top secret," he added.

"It's a computer print out," said O'Malley, before he began reading.

"Obviously," Gillespie answered. "We can determine the make and model of the printer, but I don't think that will be very useful. Read it."

O'Malley's gaze immediately ran down to the signature at the bottom of the page.

"The families? Is this from the Mafia?"

" Read it," Gillespie said again.

The letter was short and almost brutal.

"You've seen that we can cause serious pain," it began. "But we think that it's possible to come to an arrangement." A series of demands followed. The first was for licenses to be issued for six casinos, listed in detail, scattered across the country. Then came a request for a series of convicts, currently in solitary confinement, to be moved to low security prisons. Eight Mafia capos, all convicted in the last four years. Last of all, the letter demanded the suspension of all monitoring of the flow of money between certain Caribbean island and the United States, for twelve hours.

"A license to launder," O'Malley muttered.

"It's time to talk," the letter concluded. "If you show a sign of interest, we'll let you know what the next step is."

"An extortion letter, old school, in the best tradition," O'Malley murmured. He suddenly jerked his head up and looked at Gillespie:

"They want to negotiate with the president."

"Jamie. We've got to flush them out of hiding and get the narcotic away from them. Immediately. You're the one who knows the most about Massapequod and you've spent your life chasing the Mafia. You're the right person." O'Malley wasn't sure how happy he should be.

A marina in the Hamptons, Long Island, NY, Thursday, October 31, morning

It had rained all night long, all over the island.

The rain seemed eternal, it was chilly and drab, and it seemed cursed, the kind of rain you'd expect in Dante's Inferno. Perfect weather for Pierre-André's anguish. Turn himself in? Go into hiding? Return to France? Annick would soon come around again. Albert had recommended he accept the DGSE offer; that would solve all his problems at one fell swoop. But Pierre-André shook his head.

"No," he replied, "behind this whole story of Massapequod are the two bottles of narcotic that someone stole out of Papadopoulos's refrigerator, don't you see? And then there are the drums I hid in Stony Brook. I can't go."

When they opened the hatch just a crack, Pierre-André and Albert noticed that the security guards at the marina, instead of lying around drinking beer and reading *Sports Illustrated*, had split up into two little groups and, armed with target-shooting rifles, they were patrolling the pier and the pontoons at a cadenced step, as if they were enlisted men in the Military Police busy keeping soldiers away from off-limits areas.

"Pretty soon," Pierre-André observed grimly, "they'll have pictures of me too."

"You have to disappear," Albert pointed out.

"Where do you want me to go? I don't know where to go, damn it. You're the only friend I can trust. I could stay here, on your boat."

"Are you kidding? It's amazing to me that they haven't burst in here, guns leveled, on my boat! Look, I'm not worried about myself. I can always claim that, what with the regattas, I never got a chance to see the TV news. But sooner or later, I can guarantee that they'll come nosing around here. Trust me."

"So what should I do?"

"You have to get out of here. Get moving. And fast. Keep moving, before they can track you down. No cell phones. No credit cards, and that's important. No ATMs. They'd identify you in a heartbeat. How much money do you have?"

Pierre-André looked in his wallet. He had exactly 215 dollars. "You wouldn't last two days," Albert noted coldly. "I'll take care of it. You can't go to the bank, but I can. There's a branch of my bank, not far from here. I'll go see if they'll cash a check."

He was about to leave, but he stopped a moment to think.

"I'll take your Acura. You need to get rid of it fast. Otherwise it's like traveling around with a spotlight and a sign on your back saying: arrest me. I'll leave it a certain distance from here, and let's just hope someone steals it and takes it who-knows-where. Then I'll take a cab to a car rental place and I'll rent you a car in my name. But you can't keep it for long. They'll work their way back to me pretty quick, and then it'll be no different."

Pierre-André envied his friend's clear-minded view of things.

"Thanks, Albert. You're doing a lot for me."

"Don't mention it. By the way..." He turned around and fished a Halloween mask out of a drawer. "If you absolutely have to leave the boat, put this on." He looked at it a little closer. The mask was a grinning death's head: "My God, all we need now is for them to catch you wearing this. Try to stay inside if you can," he added. And he left.

He was back a few hours later driving a nondescript Chevrolet. As soon as he entered the cockpit, he pulled out a wad of cash, in small bills. "This is 2,000 dollars. That should get you by for a little while."

"You'll see, this problem won't last all that long," said Pierre-André in a hopeful voice.

Albert shrugged his shoulders. "I'll leave you my cell phone too, but only use it for an absolute emergency. I repeat. They're going to work back to me soon." Then: "I have an idea," he announced.

"Well?"

"Find yourself a whore, an escort, a call girl, someone like that, in other words. The phone booths are full of addresses. Go to her house and stay as long as you can. For the money, we'll find a solution, you'll see."

Pierre-André looked at him with a new light in his eyes. He had no intention of telling Albert about Julie, the call girl in Mineola that he'd been seeing on a regular basis for the past several months. But it struck him as a remarkably good solution. There was already a special and well established understanding between the two of them, and he got along with Julie in a way that went well beyond ordinary casual interactions between prostitute and client. He knew that Julie didn't read the newspaper or watch television news. She only watched old movies and the occasional music video. She probably didn't know anything about what had happened. It would be expensive, but he was an old client, they were practically friends, he'd persuade her to take a check and maybe he could even postdate it and convince her to wait a couple of weeks before depositing it. He just needed a place where he could think without interruption. He stood up with a new sense of purpose. "That sounds like an excellent idea. Give me the car keys."

"They're in the car. Just give me a few minutes before you leave, to be safe. I'll go ahead and get myself some breakfast. You can leave the boat in about fifteen minutes."

New York, NY, Madison Avenue and East Forty-Seventh Street, Thursday, October 31, morning

The two men exchanged chilly greetings.

"Sit down, O'Malley. I was sure that it would be you who'd come."

"Let's say that I know the territory. And now, I'm in charge of emergencies and this is undoubtedly an emergency."

"Undoubtedly."

"Actually, Counselor, I didn't expect to come here."

The law office was spacious, lined with dark hardwood mouldings and wainscotings, with just a few books on the bookshelves. A secretary had greeted O'Malley at the front door, and he had glimpsed a couple of rooms, with no more than two or three young paralegals. Aaron Hankemann was a successful criminal lawyer, one of the best around. But instead of expanding his practice and becoming a legal services machine chewing up trials and defendants and spitting them out, he preferred to pick and choose among the cases he handled, focusing on the most spectacular and legally demanding ones. From a certain point of view, he was an aesthete of his profession. In that context, he had more than once defended accused members of the Mafia, and some of those cases were the result of trials that sprang out of investigations carried out by O'Malley, whose career had largely involved working in the FBI's anti-Mafia team. But no one would dare to call Hankemann a Mafia lawyer.

"After the letter," O'Malley went on, "we were expecting a phone call. But we were thinking of someone, how to put it, closer to the organization."

The lawyer shrugged his shoulders.

"I don't know why they contacted me. That doesn't strike me as important." Hankemann wasn't tall, but still he managed to be imposing. It was the result of a studied slowness of all his movements, a calm and confident tone of voice, and steel-gray eyes, just as the hair that framed his balding head was gray and thinning. When he spoke in court, his eyes moved constantly, underscoring his arguments and making his gaze even sharper and more piercing, when cross-examining or delivering a summation to the jurors.

Now, O'Malley noticed, the eyebrows were motionless and the forehead was furrowed. It didn't look at all like the usual Hankemann. The lawyer seemed uncomfortable.

O'Malley leaned forward in his chair.

"How does it feel, Counselor, to represent someone who slaughtered more than a hundred helpless innocent people?"

Hankemann sighed.

"I'm a lawyer, O'Malley. In my business I frequently find myself side-by-side with despicable criminals. Even though in that specific case they might be innocent. And, in our system, even despicable criminals have the right to be given an adequate defense."

"Just a minute, Counselor. This isn't a courtroom. Here, there is no doubt about guilt. You're about to negotiate on behalf of a band of admitted murderers."

Hankemann took umbrage.

"Negotiate? Who said anything about negotiating? If there was any negotiating to be done, you can be sure I would have refused to be involved. I would like to make one thing very clear in this business: my feelings and my emotions are no different from yours."

"I'm glad to hear that. Then what are we doing here?"

"We're here to prevent errors or misunderstandings like the one into which you just stumbled. It's not my job to negotiate. My job here is to make explicit and unmistakable, beyond any conceivable doubt, exactly what this letter means, what the choices and possible options are, and what the consequences would be. Even though the conditions are not ones that I particularly care for, this struck me as an important responsibility and, for that reason, I agreed to accept it." He paused briefly. "Now then," he resumed, "the letter makes certain demands, agreed? These are not negotiable. My clients expect them to be met without discussion. As you may have noticed, however, no specific deadlines are set."

"I did notice that."

"My clients believe, in any case, that matters can be expedited in a fairly efficient manner. Let's say, a couple of weeks, but what they want is an immediate signal. Ah, as for the blackout in monitoring the transfer of funds, naturally, they would like to have some advance notice as to the exact date, of course."

"Naturally. Through you, I would imagine."

"Yes, through me."

"And at what point in this process would they be willing to return the narcotic?"

Hankemann looked at him grimly.

"They have no intention of giving it back to you."

"They want to keep the gun held to our head?"

"That's correct."

O'Malley was starting to have a hard time keeping his temper in check.

"So what does that mean? That if we fail to do exactly what they ask, they'll burn another town, maybe a neighborhood with a thousand retirees in Florida?"

Hankemann looked straight at him.

"I'm afraid so. This was the most important thing I had to tell you. And I'm very worried."

"Hankemann, tell me who gave you this job."

The lawyer shook his head.

"Sorry, O'Malley. That wouldn't be right. You know the rules. You'll have to find that out for yourself."

O'Malley pounded his fist on the table in exasperation. He stood up: "Is that all?"

"That's all," the lawyer said with a note of chagrin. He stood up to walk the policeman to the door.

"Tell me something, O'Malley. Do you think there's any chance at all that these demands will be accepted?"

O'Malley swung around resentfully.

"You know the rules, Hankemann. I wouldn't tell you even if I knew. In any case, it's not my decision."

The lawyer bit his lip.

"It was a personal question. But you're right, of course. Still, it's my impression that we're in a blind alley here."

O'Malley reached out and grabbed the door handle. He turned around and said:

"It won't be easy to wash our hands of it."

"What are you doing, starting up with that again?"

"No, I'm not starting up again. It's just that I'm deeply frightened. But do me a favor and don't tell your clients that."

Hankemann nodded.

Long Island, NY, Thursday, October 31, morning

He pulled out onto the Montauk Highway. Pictures of him would start circulating soon, maybe even as early as that morning. Better photographs than the one he had seen, cruelly excellent likenesses. He needed to vanish, as Albert had said. He stopped in a shopping center and looked around for a pay phone. He knew Julie's phone number by heart. But he was about to be disappointed She didn't answer and her voice mail was full. He got back in the car and half an hour later tried again. This time she answered the phone. But what she told him wasn't what he had hoped to hear.

"Of course, honey, but not tonight, I'm super-busy, I'm going to a costume party...I'm going as a mermaid...drop by my house, that's right, in Mineola.... no, tomorrow's no good, I'm really sorry, you know, I have an invitation for a deep-sea fishing party, that way I can see the sailboats racing in the regattas, and the next day is Saturday, you know, I have a lot of dates... So come by on Sunday afternoon."

Pierre-André remained silent while she rattled off her agenda, but at the end he couldn't restrain himself: "There's no way you could make it any earlier?"

"Darling, what a sweetheart you are! You do know how to make a woman feel desired! All right, let's try Sunday morning, but call first, don't forget. I don't want you to come all the way over and find an empty house. You remember where I live, don't you?"

Pierre-André remembered clearly, naturally. But now the problem was how to get through three days, and perhaps longer, exposed to the eyes of the world, without being recognized.

He'd have to look for a disguise of some kind. No question. But a false mustache wasn't going to solve the problem. He stopped to think. Everyone that knew him remembered him (and the photographs testified to the fact) with long dark hair and salt-and-pepper sideburns. They expected to seek and find a French university professor of noble birth, impeccably dressed with European style and quality, a fairly unusual thing in the United States, even on the East Coast. His suede jacket, Lanvin shirt, ascot around the neck, and sporty Ferragamo loafers, the clothing he wore when he was heading out for a weekend in Connecticut with Susan, would be dead giveaways. Even in his sportier version, in the sailing clothes that Albert had lent him, he looked in fact just like a well-to-do gentleman attending the regattas. He had to substitute a different image. He needed to project the idea of a completely different man, starting with a radical overhaul of the social class. That shouldn't be all that difficult. He looked around. There was a hardware store, where he bought a pair of scissors and an electric razor. He got back in the car, heading east. He left the Montauk Highway, took the Southern Parkway, turned off onto Route 109, and just south of Farmingdale airport he noticed an out-of-the-way motel. This, he knew, was the moment in which he was most vulnerable. He was still Professor Matterre-Faquet. He could do nothing but hope that those damned photographs weren't in circulation yet. He could just imagine them on TV, on the web, and in the papers. He thought to himself, with a shiver, they might even post them in the LIRR stations. When he walked in to the motel office and stood at the counter, his heart started racing. The proprietor was looking at him with a perplexed look. But he immediately realized that the owner's bafflement had nothing to do with Professor Matterre-Faquet. Quite simply, that wasn't a motel where clients usually checked in alone. He smiled, muttered something, paid, and went to his room. He needed to avoid making that kind of mistake ever again. Luckily, this was one of those motels where you park your car right in front of the room door and he wouldn't need to talk to the proprietor again.

In the motel room, he laid out a newspaper on the dresser in front of the mirror and started cutting long locks of hair with a pair of scissors. When he realized that he couldn't cut any closer with the scissors, he picked up the electric razor. As he ran the buzzing razor over his head, his thoughts began to wander. He had been caught off guard by Massapequod. The discussion at the Pentagon had given him some warning about the use to which his molecule could be put, but in his mind it had always been nothing more than a harmless sedative, something you rub into your skin. A mild sedative, something you take in small doses, so as to spare the digestive tract by avoiding oral ingestion entirely. He had used it differently at the service plaza, and to a certain extent the result had been a complete piece of luck. But Massapequod was something on an entirely different scale. An entire village rendered helpless, put to sleep, by making his molecule evaporate, and he didn't even know how it had been done. When he had done his experiments, he'd never thought of such a vast and massive application. Was it even possible? He ran through the characteristics of the molecule in his mind.

Basically, the calculations were simple.

And so were the results.

A small and volatile molecule, like all perfume molecules, has a very large coefficient of diffusion, which is to say that it can travel long distances in a short time. For that matter, dogs, which have very keen senses of smell, can tell when their master is returning home because their master's odor-bearing molecules reach their nose when their master is still a quarter mile away. That is, if on a windless evening you were to put lots of vials containing the molecule here and there, and then made them explode, you could "fill" the air space over a small town with the molecules in a matter of minutes. If you had a great deal of the material, perhaps dissolved in ethanol, then you could fly over a larger area at low altitude and put everyone who lives there to sleep, by spraying it from a small airplane or a helicopter.

Yes, the effects could be the same as what had happened at Massapequod. How could he have been so blind as not to see it?

He looked at himself in the mirror. The results were disastrous. Clumps of hair, invulnerable to each new swipe of the razor, tufted out in all directions. His head looked like a wheat field that had been devastated by a tornado. He put his jacket back on, climbed into the car, and headed for Farmingdale. There was a barber shop in a little alley behind Conklin Street.

The risk of being recognized had only increased with every passing hour, but he couldn't think of any alternatives. He tossed the scissors into one rubbish bin, along with the newspaper in which he'd wrapped up all the hair. He tossed the razor into another trash can. When he walked into the barber shop the barber looked at him in astonishment, baffled by the clash between his elegant clothing, unusual in that neighborhood, and his ravaged head. Matterre-Faquet smiled and spread his arms wide, helplessly: "My daughter," he said

"Your daughter?"

"Yes, she decided that she wanted to be a hairdresser, she was looking for guinea pigs, and I was stupid enough to agree to be an experimental subject."

"You shouldn't let little kids do everything they want to do," the barber commented in a scolding tone.

"Well, she's not really a little kid," Matterre-Faquet replied with another smile. "Anyway, she's an only child, you know, and..."

"Well, you can tell her for me that she might not really have the gift."

"Okay, maybe it's better that way. In any case, for right now, I think the only solution is to shave it all off. I say we go for the bald look."

"Shave your head completely? Don't you think that's going a little too far? It looks to me like you have a nice head of hair. If you can hold out for another week or two, we can give you a short haircut, but it would still be a haircut."

"You think I can walk around looking like this for two weeks? No, no, no, let's cut it all off. After all, the nice thing about hair is that it grows back, right?"

He dropped into the barber's chair. "Let's go bald," he said.

The barber shrugged his shoulders. "Whatever you say," he said and pulled out an electric razor identical to the one that the scientist had used at the motel.

It didn't take long. When the barber was done, Matterre-Faquet looked at himself in the mirror. His cranium was as smooth as a cue ball. He had a hard time recognizing himself. He heaved a sigh of relief. As the barber was counting the money he'd given him, he warned him: "You'll catch cold like that. A couple of blocks up you can at least buy yourself a nice woolen watch cap."

Two blocks away was an Army Navy Surplus Store. Matterre-Faquet walked in, picked up the first woolen watch cap he found, and started looking around. In his mind, he started to see an image of the new Pierre-André.

"Some friends invited me to go hunting with them," he explained to the young man behind the counter who was looking at his suede jacket. "But I don't want to spend a fortune buying hunting equipment and clothing that I'm only likely to use once."

"Well, you came to the right place," the young man assured him. He led him over to a heap of high-top hiking shoes. These were Marine combat boots. "They're as waterproof as rubber boots, but they're much more comfortable, durable, and warm," he guaranteed.

Matterre-Faquet tried on two or three different boots, and found the right size. He also bought a few pair of thick warm socks and some T-shirts. Finally, he asked for a warm coat. The young man came back with a padded army combat jacket, which even came with collar badges. He showed him a pair of camo trousers, which probably really were useful for hunting. But Matterre-Faquet didn't want to look too much like a veteran, say someone who was just home from Iraq. He decided to buy a duffel bag and nothing more. He put his suede jacket and the rest of his purchases into the duffel bag. With his combat jacket and the woolen watch up pulled down over his forehead, Matterre-Faquet got back in his car and head north, along Route 110. He stopped at another shopping center. In a shop, he bought a pair of faded chinos and a black sweatshirt. Then, with a full duffel bag, he stopped at a vending machine and bought a couple of chocolate bars. He got back in the car, drove to Huntington Station, and walked into a McDonald's crowded with kids already dressed in their Halloween costumes, and ordered a burger. Then he slipped into a bar for a beer.

At the bar, a tall gangly blond man, with a prominent nose and glasses, was speaking loudly to the bartender and a couple of customers, explained that the time had come to take action and get control of the situation.

"You know, I have a dozen or so rifles," he was saying. "And I have an AK-47, the good old Kalashnikov, and an M-60, same as what I had when I was in the army. Sooner or later, I'm going to buy myself a heavy machine gun, a serious one, with a tripod. Oh, and I also have—and here he started counting on the fingers of one hand—a Colt, two Lugers, and a Beretta 9 mm." He shrugged modestly. "I collect weapons, that's all, I keep them because I like them. But they're all perfectly functional, you could use them tonight." He stopped to take a long gulp from his beer goblet. "I'm a good citizen. In the evening, I always walk around my neighborhood with my dog and my Beretta in my back pocket, to make sure everything's calm and quietin my neighborhood." He smiled broadly. "Well, you have no idea of the things I see. I almost always find parked cars with teenagers inside. What do you think they're doing? They're doing drugs, that's what. I turn on my flashlight, I shine the light into the inside of the car, and I explain to them clearly, and calmly, that if they want to take drugs, they're welcome to do so, but not around here. Ditto, if I find some of these modern little girls in the car, with the fire down below. If they want to have sexual intercourse like a bunch of animals, well then, out of here, do it somewhere else." The man finished his beer and set his empty glass down on the bar. He looked up and down the bar, looking at the other men. "But now, it's even worse, people, it's not a problem of public morals anymore. You never know what might happen, but did you see on television? If they put you to sleep and they burn a whole village, they could put a whole town to sleep and burn it too. Even here, even us."

A tall brawny man with a leather jacket agreed vigorously. "Of course, Christ, here we're all at risk, us and our families. Once, the only danger was poisoned candy, but now, tonight, they could put a sedative in your trick and treat candy, and then who can save you?"

Up till now, Matterre-Faquet had given only vague consideration to what might be the mass reaction to the tragedy of Massapequod. Now he was confronted with it, face-to-face. He put his empty beer glass down on the bar in front of him with a shiver. The blond man was talking again. "All right, then, who wants to come over to my house, tonight, in Huntington, and form a team to watch out for our children? I'll provide the weapons." He looked around and locked eyes with Matterre-Faquet, a few yards away from him: "You. You want to come?"

His last gulp of beer went down the wrong way. Coughing and spluttering, he answered that he agreed it was a great idea, but he was just passing through.

"Hey, wait a minute, what's that accent?" said the blond man. "Where do you come from?"

Matterre-Faquet felt faint. "Montreal. Montreal," he finally managed to say. He had pronounced the first Montreal in French style, the second one in English style.

"Of course! How stupid of me!" The blond man flashed a big smile, took a step toward Matterre-Faquet, and slapped him vigorously on the back. "A Canuck!"

"Hey, Frank," he went on, turning to speak to the bartender, "another beer for me and my new Canuck friend."

In the bar, the discussion went on. "Where do you live?" someone asked the blond man.

"Cider Road, near the shipyards."

"Where the King Kullen is? When do you want us to show up there?"

Another man, who looked like a prosperous white collar worker, spoke up:

"Of course, we'll put out teenagers standing guard at every street corner, and then us adults, in groups of two, with weapons, can walk around in the dark, ready to jump anyone who looks suspicious. Let's meet at seven o'clock tonight on Cider Road."

"Give me the numbers of your cell phones," said the blond man.

Matterre-Faquet walked out without attracting notice, hopped in his car, and headed south again.

FBI field office, New York, NY, Thursday, October 31, afternoon

O'Malley shuddered and laid the sheets of the latest news bulletin down on his desk. It hadn't been possible to keep the story of Matterre-Faquet and the narcotic released into the air out of the news. At Atlanta, in many neighborhoods, both poor and wealthy, they'd closed off roads and created check points. Chicago's O'Hare Airport was shut down for more than two hours, because of a bottle that someone found in a corner, and which was later revealed to contain nothing more than cheap beer. Other airports were on the verge of being paralyzed for similar reasons. In New York, the mayor had tripled the police officers on duty in the subways, but that hadn't been sufficient to prevent brawls and disorders. Every stranger was an enemy, every act could be suspicious. Paranoia was rising and the country was on the verge of paralysis.

He stood up, left his office, and walked down the hall to the door that gave onto the fire escape. There, perched in the open air, he smoked a cigarette, thinking about what he'd just read in the news bulletin and what Hankemann had told him just a few hours ago. He, James O'Malley, and all of America were walking on the razor's edge. When he got back to his office, from the hallway he saw a woman sitting across from his desk. Klara Siebers, CIA. Of all the people to find in his office, it had to be her. Long legs in a pair of close-fitting black pants, a pinstripe jacket, a white blouse open at the neck. As he drew closer, he noticed that her blonde hair was cut short, unusually short: practically a Marine buzz cut. The light, chilly eyes that watched him walk in were the same as ever. "An icy beauty," someone might say. "As icy and painful as a Finnish sauna: there's the icy river, but also the blistering steam," O'Malley responded to his own thought.

He walked around the desk and collapsed into his chair. "No hello kisses on the cheek?" she asked.

"Maybe later, if you've earned it."

"You know, they're mine by right."

It was a wisecrack, and not a bad beginning, but O'Malley had been in a bad mood for awhile now.

"Of all people they decide to send you."

"At Langley, Jeff's in charge of this case."

"And you're his gal Friday, aren't you?"

"I guess you could say that."

"Gal Friday, eh?"

"Jamie...don't get started again..."

"Okay. And just what is it that you and Jeff want to tell me?"

"We have to lay out a playing field, Jamie. Decide who plays what position."

O'Malley grunted.

"I didn't know that you'd come all this way just to talk about sports."

He paused:

"Listen, I need a cup of coffee. You want some?"

"No, thanks."

"Well, let me go get a cup. I'll be right back."

When he got to the coffee machine, he met Purvis, the head of the fugitive section, who had just walked past his door.

"Who's the superbabe in your office?"

"My wife."

"Oops. Sorry. I didn't even know you were married."

"No sweat. In fact, I'm not married. We're divorced. And she's a complete bitch."

"They're all bitches."

O'Malley no longer felt like having a cup of coffee, and he came back empty-handed. They'd been married for two whole years, his second marriage: the first year was wonderful, the second year was intolerable. Now, two more years had passed. She looked him carefully up and down.

"You smoked a cigarette, didn't you?" she said.

"Yes, I did. How do you know?"

"I can smell it on your breath from here."

"Still sensitive, eh?"

"You smoked me like a herring for two whole years."

"Are you trying to tell me that you left because you wanted to get away from the secondary smoke?"

"Well, that was part of it. At the beginning, the little things are just little. Then, as time goes by, they become mountains. Have you ever heard of the straw that breaks the camel's back?"

O'Malley snorted.

"So what's breaking the camel's back over at the CIA? Since when have you become sports nuts? Are you rooting for the Giants or the Colts? Oh, of course, the Redskins."

"Well, first off, you need to know that we're not the only team involved in this."

"The Russians?"

"No, the French."

"The French? Aren't they allies of ours?"

"Sure, but Matterre-Faquet is a French citizen. They consider him to be their property and they want to get him back. Before we can get our hands on him. We believe that they've sent an agent here to intercept him."

"Who else?"

"Well, the Israelis."

"The Israelis? Aren't they allies of ours too?"

"The Israelis always do whatever the fuck they want to do. They might primarily be interested in getting their hands on the narcotic."

O'Malley raised his eyebrows.

"To use it?" he asked

"Of course. They have plenty of opportunities. You do realize what a powerful weapon it could be, right? All you'd need is some junky old helicopter to spray it into the air, over Gaza, for instance, at sunset, the one time of the day when the wind isn't blowing."

"I don't have a hard time imagining that. At the Pentagon they were drooling at the mere idea."

"At the Pentagon they're furious about the whole thing. For that matter, they're the ones who let him slip through their fingers."

"Speaking of the Pentagon, are you still sleeping with that faggot from the State Department?"

"He's no faggot, Jamie. Believe me. I know what I'm talking about."

Now, it was O'Malley who was looking at her. He watched her breasts pressing against her blouse. He could still remember those long Scandinavian tits, with their large pink nipples. He wondered if they still stood up the way they used to. He shook his head. He had to keep part of his brain from buzzing away on the problem of how to get her into bed that evening. He managed to quell the thoughts. But it was too late. She knew him all too well. She flashed him an ironic smile.

"Your problem is you're obsessed with sex."

"Me, Klara? I seem to recall that both of us were, once. You didn't mind so much."

"Of course. But there are other things that can hold two people together."

"Like what? I'm not the one who didn't want children."

"What did you want? Did you want to lock me up in the house all day?"

They glared furiously at one another.

"You're such a loser, Jamie."

"What do you mean?"

"That you are the way you are and there's nothing you can do about it."

"If you're talking about that last night in the hotel, I'd like to remind you that I was drunk."

"You're never drunk, Jamie. Never. It's just that all you know how to do to the people who are close to you is insult them."

"I like things done right."

He saw her press her lips together and then relax in her chair.

"Stop," said Klara "We're not in court anymore. And let me remind you that our final divorce decree has already been issued." She looked at him hard for a second or two and then went on:

"We're all in big trouble here, Jamie. So, at least let's do this one right. Do I make myself clear? Matterre-Faquet is a major national security problem."

"What are you saying, that the Mafia extortion threat isn't a national security problem?"

"Of course it is, you poor fish. But don't pretend you can't understand what I'm telling you. I'm not using the phrase at random. When I say that other countries are involved and that Matterre-Faquet is a national security problem, I'm telling you that Matterre-Faquet is a CIA problem. Is that clear?"

O'Malley stopped to think.

"All these people that you're talking about know all about the letter and about the Mafia."

"They probably do, yes. But I don't think they give a damn about that. It's not their problem. They just want to get their hands on a sample so they can copy it."

"Well, as far as I can tell, right now they'll have to ask the Mafia for some."

"I believe they assume it'd be easier to make Matterre-Faquet give them the formula. That's why I told you that nobody else can get their hands on him. This is the number one priority on our agenda."

"Oh, really? I thought that the number one priority was the danger of handing over the entire country to the Mafia. This country's going to hell, Klara. Do you read the newspapers? And do you realize that that bastard of a French frog-eater is the only clue that we have for now that might lead us to whoever has the narcotic?"

"You're such a knucklehead, Jamie. Don't just look down at your own desk. Do you realize what that narcotic really is? You've seen what it can do. You know why the Pentagon wants it. Think of how it could be used in a theater of combat. Or behind the lines. Or anywhere else, with a surprise attack."

"Like at Massapequod."

"Exactly. Like at Massapequod. But there would be no need to set a fire. That narcotic means neutralizing any defense at all. The enemy attacks while the soldiers sleep. And they're peacefully murdered in their sleep, their throats are cut, one by one. No one could ever sleep again, Jamie. Generals and soldiers, civilians and heads of state. Do you see what that would mean? It's simpler than an atom bomb."

"But the French and the Israelis..."

"Of course, the French and the Israelis. But if we don't manage to catch him, Matterre-Faquet could give it to the Russians or the Chinese. Think of the President being summoned to Beijing to be told that either we hand over Taiwan or there's going to be trouble. It could even wind up in North Korean hands. We're walking around the mouth of a volcano, Jamie. Whoever has it would be confident that they could attack anyone they chose. Just think if the Indians or the Pakistanis got hold of it: who could stop a war from breaking out?"

"Anyway, right now the Mafia has it and they're already waging war on us right here at home."

Klara stopped to think.

"Right. Even though from what we know about Matterre-Faquet, it doesn't seem like the first thing he would do is go in cahoots with the Mafia, is it?"

"The problem is that we don't really know much about Matterre-Faquet at all."

"But do you think he gave it to the Mafia?"

O'Malley stiffened, defensively.

"It's a first theory, and we need to explore it."

"So before striking his deal with the Mafia, Matterre-Faquet decides to reveal everything in a public conference?"

"Maybe he made the deal afterward."

"Then why wouldn't he make a deal with the Pentagon too?"

"Look, Klara, I have a hard time believing all this crap about the pacifist scientist. It might very well be that he realized that if he started working with the Pentagon, he'd have a hundred eyes watching him night and day."

"Why, did he think that if he had that formula in his hands, he wasn't going to be watched day and night anyway? You think he's that naïve, Jamie?"

"Well, he knew what he'd gotten his hands on, didn't he? Look at how he took to his heels at the service plaza. Why should he have run away like that?"

Klara thought for a second, then shrugged.

"I don't know that and, right this second, I don't care about it. What I care about is catching him, before he can do any more damage."

"Whereas I, on the other hand, just have to figure out what he's done, even without catching him."

"Don't make things so complicated, Jamie. I don't want your bosses to trip you up. Let us do our work. We can catch him."

"Sure, from the way you describe it, you've already practically got him in the bag. What makes you think that you can do it?"

Klara flashed him a faint smile.

"Usually, we know exactly where the agents from other countries are in our country. And we have reason to believe that the French know where Matterre-Faquet is."

"Ah. I see."

"Anyway, Jamie, your bosses have already been informed of this change of plan. I just wanted to tell you about it in person."

O'Malley grimaced. Then for a while he tapped a ballpoint pen on the desktop.

"I see. Mighty nice of you," he finally said. "Really. Well, all the best, then."

"Is everything clear?"

"Of course. The Mafia is my business. But you guys want Matterre-Faquet."

"Don't worry. The minute we get him, you'll be able to talk to him."

"I can't wait. And the Pentagon wants the narcotic for itself."

"Exactly. Good job. It's easy to work with you, I'll say that much."

Klara stood up to go. She ran her hands over skirts of her jacket, as if to wipe sweat off them. She jerked her thumb behind her.

"While I was waiting, I got a look at your team. The babe dressed like a grande dame, who's constantly swishing her ass around, is that the one you're screwing?"

"Jill? No."

"Come on! Don't tell me you're screwing Brunhilde, the Valkyrie."

"Meg? No not her, either."

"Jamie, I don't recognize you anymore."

She turned around with a smile and walked out the door. Swinging her hips a little too much for a woman in her forties, O'Malley mused.

He let out a heavy sigh and dropped back into his chair. To hell with Klara! There was an idea that had been buzzing around in his head for the past few hours and now it was time to put it into practice. He called Stefan.

"Stefan, do you remember the Mafioso who spilled the beans during the Atlantic City trial?"

"Yeah. Vito Barrilà."

"Right. Nicknamed Vituzzo. Find out where he is now."

Brooklyn, NY, Thursday, October 31, Halloween afternoon

The man was getting dressed. He was massive, a refrigerator, a side of beef, tall, with a bull neck and the legs of a much shorter man. He put on a gray jacket over a blue dress shirt with a white collar. He had on a white-and-blue tie, with many white and blue checks of different sizes. The jacket couldn't fully conceal a bump on his back, possibly the result of an illegal weapon, which he needed in the performance of his duties. The house was filled with screams and laughter, with little kids dressed in fanciful costumes galloping down the hallways, bursting into the living room, jumping on the sofa, eating *chiacchiere* and *cannoli*.

A Merlin the Wizard was chasing after a zombie while a skeleton battled a vampire for possession of a handful of chocolates. He looked at the children lovingly. As he left his house, he gave his wife a peck on the cheek and said to her:

"Okay, I'll be away for a couple of days. Let the little ones have some fun, but tonight, after all the pagan things they're doing, make sure they say a prayer to the Virgin Mary, *capeesh*?

A motel on Route 109, Long Island, NY, Thursday October 31, evening

Stretched out on the bed eating chocolate, Matterre-Faquet couldn't help but hear the noise of the transient guests in the motel where he was staying. The giddy laughter of tipsy women, the deep voices of men out for a night with their local sex workers, the clatter of high heels worn by clumsy teenage girls, the roar of the turbocharged engines of cars driven by muscular tattooed young men. Despite the din, Pierre-André was rapt in thought, focusing on Papadopoulos's refrigerator and the two bottles that hadn't been there anymore. The narcotic of Massapequod couldn't have come from anywhere but there. But who could have taken it?

He could rule out Papadopoulos for starters. The jovial scientist was above all suspicion. Safar? The head of the department might very well have guessed where he kept his samples. But he couldn't imagine him being implicated in a cruel, pitiless plan like the one that resulted in Massapequod.

The relationship between the French scientist and the head of the department of Plant Physiology at Stony Brook wasn't a simple one. He had an intelligent face, he looked like a young Mel Brooks, he wore a yarmulke, and his name was Benjamin Safar. He was a man who was accustomed to dressing well, possibly a sartorial rival to Matterre-Faquet. The day of his seminar, he recalled, he'd worn a Donna Karan suit. He liked to challenge the French scientist, play a cat-and-mouse game with him. Often, he flattered him, telling him that everyone was grateful to him for his generosity. He never hesitated to call him legendary, and he insisted that everyone was happy for Matterre-Faquet to make use of their laboratories, because he brought prestige and soft money. But if he knew how to rub ointment into his back, it was because he was getting ready to hold a lighter to the hairs on his chest. The day of the seminar, for instance, he had attacked him, asking him point blank: "Why are you always so damned defensive?"

But Matterre-Faquet hadn't fallen into the trap. That was a typical politically correct expression, used to accuse someone of being aggressive. Just to answer it meant confessing that you had been aggressive, which was a serious confession, the Frenchman knew, in American intellectual circles. So he hadn't said anything, counting on the fact that, probably, Safar was in a hurry. A date, whether personal or professional, but in any case a date with a woman was clearly in the offing, because he was wearing a special eau de toilette, as he always did, for instance, when he was going to interview female candidates for research or post-doc positions. But Safar hadn't let go of the bone. "Your colleagues are sick of it," he explained, and not for the first time. "You're just too damned caustic sometimes."

"You know lots of things," he had continued, "you have a level of international experience that most people here lack, but you need to quit shoving your colleagues' noses in the shit when they get something wrong, especially in front of the students!" But Safar had saved the cruelest blow of all for the end.

"This is Stony Brook," he had said. "If you want to be so damned aggressive, why don't you go to Harvard?"

Safar knew that the thorn in Matterre-Faquet's was precisely the Ivy League, and he enjoyed crucifying him this way every time he had the chance, even on as crucial a day as the day of the seminar. And that wasn't all. Safar had dragged up the old story of the purchase of the inverse laminar flow and exhaust fume hoods with a supplementary charcoal filter, which were incredibly expensive.

Matterre-Faquet couldn't admit to him that if his extract evaporated outside of the inverse laminar flow hoods, he would fall asleep like an idiot... perhaps because of the action of the volatile substances of his extracts on his olfactory receptors. Still less did he want to attract the attention of those imbeciles, as he called them, to the potential action of those substances on people's central nervous system. Instead, he had simply answered that when you make a perfume extract, sometimes the smells can be unpleasant and the bitch in the laboratory next door like to bust his chops and complain about the smell. That's why he needed the inverse laminar flow and exhaust fume hoods with a double charcoal filter, to keep any gasses from escaping.

At that point, having manifested his power in full, Safar let him go, dismissing him with a "Have a good seminar" that had actually seemed quite sincere. For that matter, Safar was anything but a backstabber. He was a petty bureaucrat, that much was true, confined in a small university, possibly afflicted with envy. But he remained within the bounds of academic feuds. Still, he could say the same thing about his other colleagues, thought Matterre-Faquet, as he tossed and turned in his bed. They could all despise him for the arrogance he was incapable of repressing, they might envy him for his scientific CV, and even wish in their heart of hearts that his discoveries, including the discovery of this new molecule, might culminate in an embarrassing flop. But for them to take it from there to contriving a tragedy like what had happened in Massapequod, just for the sake of ruining his career, was not even remotely conceivable. None of them seemed capable of such a thing, or even anything close to it. Was it possible that someone might have contrived a prank to undermine him and had then, unawares, been manipulated by some power outside of Stony Brook? Perhaps, but who? In any case, he certainly couldn't set out to interrogate all his colleagues.

Still, the bottles had vanished from a refrigerator in the university. How could an outsider have known they were in Papadopoulos's laboratory? It remained true that there had been someone behind that refrigerator, the morning he left with Susan, in Papadopoulos's laboratory and that someone had certainly seen him fool around and come in and out with the bottles. That someone was Rachel, Safar's secretary. Now if the head of the department projected a jovial image, in the final analysis, Rachel was unquestionably a malevolent presence. Too skinny, her hair was too long, her eyeglasses were too transparent, and her mouth was too big. Everyone knew that she liked to spy on people and that she was also very good at it. And he also knew that she didn't much like him. When she met him, shortly before the seminar began, she had asked him, with her mousey smile: "Did you remember to bring the wine, Dr. Matterre-Faquet? Everyone says that, when it comes to fermentation, you are the best!" A cutting aside, a dumb joke, probably nothing more. But only an insensitive woman, embittered by loneliness, could have chosen the beginning of his first seminar, the most important moment of his short academic career at Stony Brook, to razz him. And Matterre-Faquet was mistrustful of women embittered by loneliness.

Rachel probably knew about the bottles. But who could a woman like that have told? A woman who seemed to have no life of her own, outside the walls of this department?

Matterre-Faquet heaved a long, exasperated sigh. Luckily, he was very tired. A short while later, he was finally asleep.

Friday, November 1

Janet Pallen swore at herself. She was moving from Ann Arbor to Kalamazoo, where Bob had just landed a new job. Her husband was driving the family car, with a U-Haul trailer hitched to it. He said that driving with a trailer was harder. So she had wound up driving the U-Haul truck, with the rest of the furniture. Bob had told her ten times to keep an eye on the gas gauge, because those monsters sucked incredible amounts of gas. But how could she have imagined that it would use up a full tank so much faster than the car? To make a long story short, the truck was out of gas. So Bob had unhitched the trailer and stayed behind on the road, to keep an eye on their possessions, while she drove off to find a gas station, to fill up a gas can.

She got out of the car, opened the trunk, pulled out the gas can, and went over to the pump. She started filling the gas can. "Hey, what are you doing over there?" shouted a man, getting back out of the car he'd just filled up. "Yeah, hey beautiful, what do you think you're going to do with that gas?" yelled a truck driver who was just leaving the fast food outlet. Janet looked around in bewilderment. A woman had stepped out of her car and was coming toward her: "Just look at her face! She doesn't know what to say!"

The woman walked right up to her and gave her a shove that knocked her into the gas pump. Rough hands grabbed the gas can and the hose away from her. The woman slapped her in the face. She felt a sharp pain in her shoulder, when someone hit her with a stick of some kind.

"Lock her in the bathroom! Call the police!" they shouted from the bar.

Bob found her, two hours later, half-suffocated, gagged and tied with duct tape, in a stall in the women's restroom. He had his hands full calming down two policemen, who were even more hysterical than all the others.

Between Long Island and Connecticut, November 1, morning

Now, he said, as soon as he was awake, the problem is to test out his disguise, without running too many risks. He looked in the mirror: with the combat boots, the sweatshirt, and the combat jacket, and his bald dome, he looked many years younger. He could be a veteran who had left the army after the war in Iraq. More likely, a truck driver, a plumber, a carpenter. Or better yet, one of those men, no longer young, who never found their place in life and drifted from one job to another, across the country, incapable of looking past next week or next month. Not a scientist who, until yesterday, had thought of a post at Yale.

First of all, he needed to get rid of the old clothing that he had stuffed into his duffel bag and that, sooner or later, might give him away.

He closed the door of the room behind him as he left and, taking care to stay out of the line of sight of the reception, he got into his car, drove up Route 110 to the Jericho Turnpike, turned right, and started driving along slowly in search of a dry cleaners. When he saw one, he parked, jumped out of the car, and emptied the bag full of clothing onto the counter—the suede jacket, the silk ascot, the Lanvin shirt, and Albert's yachting apparel—and asked how long it would be to clean them. The Korean who ran the dry cleaners felt the clothing, noticed the quality, and said that this was stuff that had to be dry cleaned. It wouldn't be ready before two days. Matterre-Faquet raised no objection. He gave a fake name, address, and phone number and left with his receipt. A few steps away from the door, he peeked at the small print. If he hadn't picked up his clothing two weeks from the initial date of consignment, the laundry could do with it as it pleased. When he bought that clothing, he had paid more than two thousand dollars. The Korean was unlikely to go to a lot of trouble to track down the rightful owner.

He got back in the car and headed for Port Jefferson, where he planned to take the ferry to Connecticut. The least dangerous place he could test out his disguise, without the risk of someone recognizing him by name and hurrying to call the FBI or the police, would be the hotel where he had spent the night with Susan just a few days ago. While he was parking the car, she had gone to the reception desk and registered under her own name. No one there would know what his name was.

Inevitably, sitting on the ferry during the crossing, he found himself thinking about Susan. It had been their first trip to Connecticut that had triggered the chemistry of their relationship. That time, they hadn't taken the ferry, they'd driven up overland from New York. That time it had been autumn too, that time she had driven the car, and that time they had the whole weekend ahead of them. Away they went, across Nassau County, across Queens, driving across suspension bridges, out-maneuvering semitrailers.

Then, as if by magic, the traffic that turns your mind into a shapeless gruel, the traffic that makes you feel like a helpless robot in a mechanical duel, thinned to a trickle.

They left the Interstate, and the road ran through fields and forests, in arabesques that took it first far from the coast, and then back to the water's edge.

Neither of them spoke. She was focused on driving, he was busy fooling around with the CD player. She had put on her glasses, she'd shifted her legs under her dress, and was beginning to hold the steering wheel a little more loosely.

The car was moving through alternating patches of sun and shadow. The music he had chosen was perfect for these stretches of open countryside.

He watched her, admiring her confidence.

She felt his eyes on her, pretended to ignore him, and whipped her hair.

Once again, admiring her elegance, he had smiled at her. In his mind, he had compared the mahogany color of her skin with the red and the gold of the autumn leaves. He had told her. She'd smiled and told him that she would never have taken him for such a male chauvinist. Then she had offered him a second chance. She'd asked him to check the road map to see if the GPS was working properly and if there was a better way to get to their destination.

He remembered that he'd plunged into the map and said nothing: only the melodic colors of the music and the harmonious hues of the leaves accompanied their thoughts.

He remembered perfectly that, at that moment, he'd felt embarrassed by her confidence. She was clearly studying him: she was examining his personality with what seemed like excessive curiosity for a purely professional analysis.

Thinking back on it, he realized that her feminine intuition had allowed her to understand his situation perfectly, and speaking in a low voice, she had said that maybe they could stop a little earlier. Reaching out to point to a place on the map, she had touched his hand. He'd pulled back.

The road ran along the Long Island Sound, white and blue on the sea, blue and white in the sky. Looking at the seagulls plunging into the waves, he had spoken to her about the age-old link between man and the sea. He had told her millennia-old stories of women who waited for their men to return from their travels, sailors, traders, and warriors, when life was lived to the rhythm of the waves.

She felt as if she was discovering a world that had been unknown to her, a new form of humanity, and she looked at him with a different kind of curiosity. At that point, she had spoken to him about her child-hood, the tropical island, the jungle, the ranch with the horses, the juicy tropical fruit, the childhood free of repression. She seemed to want to share intimate feelings, buried memories.

He had understood, he'd put a hand on her shoulder to emphasize a portion of what he was saying. This time, she had pulled back, shaking her shoulders, as if estranged.

Beneath her mahogany skin, she had blushed again, she had taken off her sunglasses, and she had put them into the hair on top of her head. A tremor ran through her right leg. She had removed her foot from the accelerator while she tried to uncramp her leg and recover her position. He had taken his hand off her shoulder, slowly, she had shivered and then looked at him.

The road ran along the beach, they could see pelicans skimming just a couple of feet above the waves, seagulls uttered their harsh cries.

They had stopped to get something warm to drink. It was sunset.

The golden sunlight contrasted with the dark blue of the eastern sky.

The autumn wind lifted her skirt.

He had looked at her and she had pretended to be a hapless nun being pursued by a randy satyr.

She had laughed, and he had reminded her that in antiquity all the natural phenomena, such as wind, lightning, and thunder, were con-sidered to be deities. Wind was especially mischievous.

She had smiled again.

They had sat down in a restaurant, looking at one another in silence.

That evening a few years earlier, they'd drunk mulled wine, without any desire to get back in the car.

The restaurant also offered hotel rooms.

They'd gone upstairs. She had seemed unsteady on her feet.

When they got to the room, he had taken her in his arms, to warm her.

She had responded to him, perhaps a little too quickly. He had breathed his warm breath into her ears. She shook her hair while he held her in his arms and searched for her mouth.

Feeling suddenly weak, she had tried to play with him, then she had turned her mouth to his and had felt her knees go weak.

Then he sat her down on the bed, and her skirt hiked up until it barely covered the tops of her thighs. He'd kissed her hands and her knees.

She had relaxed her tension, he had kissed the insides of her thighs, he'd reached her panties, he'd caressed them with his tongue, triggering an intimate and profound confusion within her.

She sprawled back on the bed as he caressed the inside of her thighs. She shivered and quaked and began stretching rhythmically, emittinghoarse moans, while her breathing became labored.

Pierre-André had lifted Susan into a paroxysm of pleasure. Her body was stretched like a taut bow, and she was panting as she approached her climax. But he stopped and then she was swept by a rapidfire sequence of contractions, which repeated themselves over and over again.

Pierre-André had given her time to recover, to catch her breath, to descend to a lower level of excitement, and then he had climbed on top of her to join his body with hers. She had taken him in and tensed up, she had wrapped her hands around the nape of his neck. While the two bodies lay motionless, spasmodically tensing, he had felt her gasp, he had withstood her scratches, he had survived her desperate, profound undersea kisses, he had watched her face contort into a grimace of intense pleasure, and he guessed that Susan was almost passing out, and he had felt her repeated contractions.

Pierre-André came to. He realized, to his embarrassment, that he had an erection, but also that the ferry had been tied up for several minutes and that nearly everyone was already ashore. He hurried to get his car, he drove ashore and checked the map to see how to get back to the hotel, not the one where they had stayed the first time, but the second time, a few days earlier, when the experience of the first trip had magically repeated itself, until the men from the Pentagon had so rudely interrupted it.

The hotel was a few miles from the port. Matterre-Faquet parked and walked to the reception desk. The clerk at the counter was the same person he'd said goodbye to when he walked out the door of the hotel that day and fell into the trap laid for him by Commander Randall and the entire United States Navy. He walked up to the counter, letting his heavy combat boots thud loudly on the wooden parquet floor. The reception desk was set in a delicate white bow window. This was a boutique hotel, the kind you can only find on the coast of New England. White wood on the walls and mouldings, dark wood on the floors, lace curtains at the windows and on the beds, armchairs upholstered in delicate light-colored patterns, discreet, efficient staff. The kind of place your friends are happy to recommend for your honeymoon. He walked up to the clerk with his stomach knotted into a cramp of apprehension. But there was not a glimmer of recognition in the man's gaze. In fact, the man was sizing up his combat boots, his fatigue jacket with the insignia of some airborne division, the cheap sweatshirt, the shaved head.

Matterre-Faquet asked for a room. With Susan, he'd taken a suite, but this was another matter entirely. The desk clerk took one last look at his sweatshirt, then pretended to concentrate on the hotel register. The examination didn't last very long and the result was exactly what the scientist had expected.

"I'm very sorry, sir," he said. "We don't have any vacancies. There are no vacancies for all of next week."

Matterre-Faquet felt happy.

"Well, thanks all the same," he said and did his best to resist the impulse to leap into the air and click his heels together in joy.

"Please come back and see us again, sir," the desk clerk said, without much conviction.

Matterre-Faquet got back in his car and went back to the port. Now he could deal with the photographs in the LIRR station.

Beirut, Friday, November 1, afternoon

The journey had been exhausting.

From Gaza to Beirut, by sea, at night.

She'd seen the glare of rockets and the bursting of bombs. She'd heard the roar of explosions devastating the city, and she'd heard the screams of innocent, terrified civilians.

At sunset she'd boarded the fishing trawler with its diesel engine, moored to a floating dock made dangerously slippery by kerosene and foul smelling from the seaweed rotting beneath it.

She'd spend the night holding on for dear life amidships, trying to find a clear space to brace her feet so she could keep her balance, on a deck cluttered with hawsers, cables, sheets, jerricans, halyards. All night long she was worried that she might trip and fall down a hatchway. The trip was punctuated by the sound of the bell for the changing of the watch, and the silence of the night was interrupted, from time to time, by the call of the helmsman.

The trip was uncomfortable, the fishing trawler rode high in the water, and the Khamsin, the wind that blows from the southwest driving the boat at speeds well above ten knots, kept the vessel off balance, yawing dangerously.

Wet with brine from the Mediterranean Sea, suffering from sea sickness, and with the burka, which she had worn to make herself virtually invisible, spattered with machine oil, fish blood, and mud, she finally managed to land in Beirut.

She stood for a long moment in the warm sunshine, enjoying its radiant heat, and noticed that her burka was releasing plumes of water vapor. Then she realized that there was a little shop that sold coffee. She asked a sailor to bring her a hot tea.

Walking on potholed asphalt streets, dragging her wheeled suitcase behind her, she had the sensation that the ground was swaying, a perpetuation of the pitching of the fishing trawler on open waters.

She caught a cab and asked the driver to take her to the hotel.

In the taxi she managed to get herself back into shape, she wiped her face dry, and felt warmth flood back into her body, the upper section of her legs. She took off the reeking burka, and was dressed in a blouse and a loose light skirt. She wrapped a scarf around her hair. The taxi driver showed no sign of surprise. It was common for Arab women to arrive in the cosmopolitan city of Beirut and liberate themselves from that prison of their femininity. The hotel was no longer a hotel: now it was a building with empty windows, with scars on the walls. Years ago, the concierge must have been a respected professional, and he welcomed her to the hotel with courteous cordiality.

She felt reassured and refreshed.

Still, she'd had to carry her own luggage up to her room. The elevator was empty, and she yearned for a male presence.

The hallway was long and empty, with a badly worn carpet. She walked past many doors. When she opened the door to her hotel room, she heard a noise, as if someone else were walking along beside her.

She shoved her suitcase in with one foot, and without turning around pulled the door shut behind her. That's when she felt a hand shove against her back. She tripped over the suitcase, lost her balance, and started falling forward, with her face plummeting straight toward the sharp corner of the table. A powerful hand kept her from falling, a strong arm lifted her up again, while the door slammed violently shut.

In the half-darkness of the hotel room she couldn't see what was happening to her. Breathless from astonishment and shock, she couldn't scream. Fear made her legs tremble, and fatigue made her feel unready to fight.

In the darkness she could smell his sweat, the man's poorly shaven cheeks were abrasive against her sunburnt, salt-roughened skin.

He lifted her skirt, ripped off her panties, but didn't touch her scarf. She felt a hollow space appear in her stomach, the way you feel when an airplane drops into an air pocket.

Her legs refused to hold her up. The man held her close to his body, and she felt his erection against her belly. The empty feeling moved from the pit of her stomach to her abdomen. A wound opened inside her while a strange warmth spread between her legs, down to her knees.

She was having a breakdown.

The man held her up, to the point that her feet no longer touched the ground, and held her close to him, his erect penis between her thighs.

With a reflexive act due to her rigorous professional training, she looked at his face closely and memorized his features.

Then she allowed him to push her body, now emptied of all strength, onto the floor and penetrate her.

The man fell on top of her, with all his weight atop her body, crushing her into the soft carpet.

He was aggressive, and all his movements were violent.

Then suddenly something lifted the heavy body off her and up into the air. A hoarse male voice reverberated in the semidarkness, followed by the sound of a powerful fist thudding into an open mouth, the crunch of snapping cartilage, drops of blood spattering her forehead, a furious voice accompanying an uppercut, the thump of a falling body, the noise of breaking glass, the hiccupping cry of a man taking a violent kick to the testicles from a husband rescuing his wife.

And a kick in the teeth, and then another kick, driving the senseless, bloody, obscene body out into the corridor.

Husband and wife left the hotel room and the hotel and disappeared into the teeming city.

Miami, Friday, November 1, afternoon

Muggy air greeted him when he left the airport. He had discarded the idea of spending the night in the airport hotel. He'd stayed there once before, and he remembered the small windowless room like a burial vault in a catacomb. He had no desire to see that place again. He set off on foot for the Marriott, a few hundred yards away. He tood a room, went up, and got on the phone immediately. After talking to a succession of orderlies, he was finally put in touch with the head nurse of the ward. She told him that the patient was undergoing treatment, and that he'd have to wait until tomorrow. O'Malley identified himself.

"Well, in any case, if you want to come tonight, don't show up before seven."

"At seven o'clock, then."

"Listen, you won't be able to talk long. But you'll be able to see that for yourself."

He hung up. He called Hertz and asked for a car to be brought to the hotel at six. He looked out the window. There was a pool downstairs. He decided to head down. Of course, he hadn't brought a bathing suit with him. In his formal suit, he was dying of heat. He found a beach chair under an umbrella. He took off his jacket, hung it over the back of a chair by the beach chair, loosened his tie, and sat down to take off his shoes and socks. He pulled out his iPad to take a look at the files he'd brought with him. He lit a cigarette. The desk clerk had told him that he was allowed to smoke by the pool, while it was of course forbidden to smoke in the rooms.

He took a look around. For a hotel close to the airport, there were actually a lot of people here. He identified a couple of airplane crews on layover. But what struck him was the sheer number of girls walking around: in the water, on the beach chairs, at the bar. Pureblooded young American women, Asian girls, a black woman. It looked like an ad for a Caribbean resort. Of course, he thought to himself: the girls who, any-where else, would have been clustering around the hotel bar, were at the pool here, where they had the added advantage of a generous display of the merchandise they were offering for sale.

O'Malley wasn't very surprised when, a couple of minutes later, he heard a rough voice whispering in his ear: "Would you happen to have a match, please?" The girl was leaning over him, so close he could smell her sweat.

To get the lighter out of his pocket, O'Malley had to turn onto one hip, pushing his shoulder into her breast. The girl didn't move.

"Silly me, I left my lighter in my room," she said. O'Malley clicked his lighter into flame and held it out to her. The girl slipped a long, thin cigarette between her fleshy lips and took a quick puff. Then she stood up, shaking her hair and, with the hair, her slender, soft body.

"I was dying for a smoke," she informed him.

"But my room is all the way on the other end of the hotel, very far away, on the top floor, at the end of a long hallway. Room number 422," she added, after a pause. O'Malley said nothing.

"From the way you're dressed, I knew you weren't here on vaca-tion," the girl went on. She was smoking hungrily, with long drags on the cigarette. Every time she exhaled, O'Malley saw the tip of her pink tongue darting between her lips. She's certainly intense when it comes to smoking, O'Malley decided.

"You have business in Miami?" she was asking him.

"Actually, I'm waiting to find out if I have to go to a funeral."

"Ah." The girl seemed slightly embarrassed. From the way she was sucking on it, the cigarette was already half burned.

"If you want, you can keep the lighter, I have another one in my pocket," said O'Malley.

"Oh, thanks, you're a sweetheart. You can come get it whenever you want," she added. She turned to go, swinging her hips on her high heels, and offering him a panoramic view of two firm butt cheeks, swinging high and proud.

O'Malley sighed, stretching back out on the beach chair. He closed his eyes. He know those files by heart. He could afford to take a rest.

The hospital was at the end of a long boulevard, lined by tall dark trees. He parked in front of a building with a classical style façade, punctuated by columns and capitals. Through the plate glass window of the reception area, however, he could see that the hospital was made up of pavilions scattered with gardens and benches.

"Wait here, someone will come to get you," said the young woman at the counter. A few minutes later, an orderly showed him the way to a small electric vehicle, like a golf cart. The orderly dropped him off at the largest and tallest pavilion. A nurse accompanied him upstairs on the elevator, to the third floor and then down a long corridor, to a room with a shut door.

O'Malley slipped into the room, doing his best to make as little noise as possible. But from the bed a pair of eyes were staring at him. Vito Barrilà, AKA Vituzzo, was practically unrecognizable. His cranium was perfectly smooth, his face was pale and puffy, without a trace of whiskers. An IV was running out of his arm. On the night table was a vase with some wilted flowers.

"Hey, Vituzzo, how you doing?" he said, walking quickly to take a seat in the chair standing next to the bed.

A slurred voice greeted him.

"Oh, that's a good one. O'Malley. Maybe I'm dead and you're just the first devil, come to torment me?"

Vito Barrilà had been the key prosecution witness in O'Malley's last and most important Mafia trial. He had never explained why he, an up-and-coming Mafioso, had decided to betray his colleagues in Atlantic City. Shortly after the trial it was discovered that he was dying of an inoperable tumor. O'Malley had always suspected that Vituzzo knew about the tumor all along: when he found out about, he decided to take revenge on fate, dragging his entire world down with him into the abyss.

"The doctors say you're responding well to treatment," O'Malley began. Vituzzo looked at him without interest.

"What they're trying to say is that the treatments aren't killing me. But they aren't killing the tumor either."

O'Malley did his best to sound cheerful.

"The witness protection program works, though. I had to go through three different checks to get to you," he lied

"You're wasting your money. No one wants to kill me. Everyone knows that I'm about to die and that I won't live long enough to testify again. They're happy to know that someone else is doing their job for them. And I'm sorry."

"About what?"

"That they don't come kill me. That they don't just kill me right away."

"Don't talk bullshit."

"What do you mean bullshit? Have you ever had the barrel of a pistol aimed at your forehead? You're sitting there, tied to a chair, helpless, and all you see is the barrel of that gun? You know that in one, or two, or maybe five seconds, that son of a bitch is going to pull the trigger and splatter your brains against the wall. Nothing can save you. So you sit there and you wait for him to shoot. You're already dead, you just don't know it yet. And you wait, you wait for the bullet. Are you going to hear the sound of the shot? Are you going to have time for a last thought? The only thing you can feel is a sharper and sharper cramp in your stomach. Okay, that's where I am right now, with the cramp in my stomach, and the pistol aiming at my forehead. And I just can't take the waiting."

The mumbling came to a halt. O'Malley didn't know what to say. "Vituzzo, I need your help," he finally said.

"Again? What for this time?"

"Have you heard what's happened?"

A flicker of curiosity appeared in his weary eyes.

"Well, I watch the TV news every so often."

"Then you know."

"What do I have to do with it? Charred children? Who was it, the Russians, the Chinese?"

"The CIA thinks otherwise."

"Then it must have been Al Qaeda. Terrorists, right?"

"Mossad doesn't think so."

"So what the fuck does this have to do with me?"

O'Malley gave him a brief summary of the conclusions they'd reached about the manner in which the inhabitants of Massapequod had been burned to death, about the narcotic and how it worked. Then he pulled a copy of the letter out of his pocket and extended it to him. Vituzzo took it, hesitated for a moment, gestured to O'Malley to turn on the light on the side table, and started reading. As he read, his eyes livened up. Midway through the letter he stopped:

"Holy Mary Mother of God. All those children, all those old people... No one's ever done anything like that before."

When he was done reading, he leaned back on his pillow and dropped the letter. He grimaced in pain. He sat thinking.

"It's strange," he said.

"What's strange?"

"It's just strange. It's a strange story. I can't understand it."

"Vituzzo, I need you to help me."

"It makes no sense. What does that mean: 'the families'? It makes no sense."

"Vituzzo, who's behind this letter?"

"What did they tell you? That unless you do what they ask, they're going to kill a few more?"

"That's right."

"Who told you that?"

"Hankemann."

"Hankemann? How strange. Hankemann."

"Even he was a little baffled by the thing," O'Malley noted. Then he went on: "Vituzzo, you have to help me. I have to find out who's behind this letter. Who's gotten their hands on the narcotic, before it's too late."

"How would I know? Do you think anyone told me about this?"

"No, no. It's just that you know them all so well, you must have an idea about it."

"What are you saying, that you want me to try to guess?"

"I've been trying to guess for days now."

Vituzzo waved his hand wearily.

"I have to think it over," he said. "I'm tired now. Come back tomorrow. I'll be feeling better."

"Tomorrow."

"Tomorrow."

"But I can't leave the letter with you. I don't need to tell you why."

"The letter was written by some old fool. I don't need it."

Port Jefferson, Long Island, NY, Friday, November 1, afternoon

After he got off the ferry, Matterre-Faquet walked for a long time through the streets of Port Jefferson. In a little shop run by a Pakistani, he bought a cheap pair of sunglasses, just a size or two too big for him. Reassured by the fact that the hotel clerk hadn't recognized him at all, and protected by the new screen over his eyes, Matterre-Faquet entered a bar, ordered a glass of beer, and went over to a phone booth in the corner. He wanted to give Julie a call to see if he could go to her house any earlier. She told him that there was no chance of that. She was still on the fishing boat, in open waters. Matterre-Faquet nagged her for a couple of minutes, then told her not to worry about it. The last thing he needed to do was to arouse her suspicions.

When he hung up the phone, he realized that the bar had suddenly emptied out. Even the bartender was at the door, looking out into the street. All the other customers were standing on the sidewalk.

They weren't the only ones. There were people who had poured out onto the sidewalks from the shops on Thompson Street and Main Street and others who had simply come to a halt as they were out walking. Everyone was looking in the same direction. There was a woman who was pointing her finger at a young boy holding a plastic bag, demanding: "What do you have in there?"

He was a skinny boy, no more than fourteen or fifteen. He was wearing a filthy greasy baseball cap sideways on his head, a pair of jeans several sizes too big for him, down-at-the-heels shoes, and a tattered baseball jacket. Matterre-Faquet remembered seeing him, half an hour earlier, on his way to the bar. The kid had been rummaging through trash cans, muttering to himself, and was probably just looking for a scrap to eat. Now, he was looking around at the people surrounding him, bewildered. The woman kept asking:

"What's in that bag you're holding?" Matterre-Faquet could see that the boy's lips were moving, but no words were coming out.

A muscular man who had just come out of a health club took a step forward and, as if by some signal, the whole mob moved toward the boy. He started moving slowly, walking backward. He moved strangely. Maybe he was drunk, thought Matterre-Faquet, or, more likely, on drugs. Or else he was just a little retarded. The crowd moved in closer still. He turned and started to run, with an ungainly, wobbly gait. The crowd sped up its pace too. Unable to tear his eyes away from the unfolding scene, Matterre-Faquet followed them.

Despite the boy's attempts to get away, the crowd could have caught him without even breaking into a run. But he soon reached the edge of Broadway. The traffic was intense. The crowd too reached the corner of Main Street and Broadway. The young boy stepped uncertainly into the middle of the road. Now the people were waiting at the edge of the street and the boy was in the middle of the street. He looked back at the mob. Matterre-Faquet could see his lips still moving, and yet no words emerged. He realized that the boy was crying.

He heard the deep sound of a truck horn. The boy looked up the street, then back at the crowd, and then at the oncoming truck again. He took a step toward the sidewalk, where the crowd awaited him, but he stopped. He turned to face the truck again. The only sound was the screech of brakes, jammed down hard in a desperate attempt to bring the long semitrailer to a halt.

The impact was tremendous. A *thump* that echoed across the sidewalk. The boy flew into the air and then hit a lamppost, a good twenty feet away. Another *thump* was heard, and the boy's body seemed to be glued to the lamppost for a few seconds, only to slither to the sidewalk.

The truck had finally come to a halt. The crowd gathered around the corpse. Matterre-Faquet stared at the body crumpled on the ground, in an unnatural pose. The boy's spine was certainly broken. He looked at the face: his eyelids were squeezed shut, as if at the end, he'd been dreading the impact. His cheeks were bathed with tears.

Pierre-André sensed that his eyes too were filling with tears. He looked around. A woman stepped forward, pulled a scarf out of her purse, and covered the boy's face. But that was the sole act of mercy and pity. The people standing around were saying that the best thing would be to wait for the police, to see what that little bastard had in his plastic bag.

In just a couple of minutes, they heard the sirens of an approaching police car. Matterre-Faquet decided that was a good time to disappear.

He found himself wandering aimlessly once again through the streets of Port Jefferson. Massapequod was like an avalanche that was roaring through the heart of American society. How could he have failed to realize that his sedative was actually a terrifying weapon? Apparently, everyone else had seen it at first blush. Even Albert.

That evening, when he first saw Hancock, at Pierre's Restaurant, on Main Street in Bridgehampton, possibly one of the finest restaurants on Long Island, a couple of bottles of Gevrey-Chambertin had finally helped him to suppress the embarrassment of his wounded pride. He had told Albert all about his invention and the seminar. The applause had been encouraging, the lecturer had been witty and insightful, the idea of a sedative that you spread on your skin was original, the findings appeared to point out new directions for further research, and, like all serious scientific research, it even left room for a margin of doubt. However, he added, maybe not everyone had understood the scope, the true significance of the results presented. "Maybe not even the lecturer himself," he had added.

Albert hadn't missed the opportunity for a wisecrack. "Perhaps, devoted as he was to the comprehension of the scientific significance, caught up in his egocentricity, rapt in his determined intellectual ambition, even the lecturer failed to understand what he was talking about."

"That's right," Pierre-André replied. "That sedative can be a narcotic. A powerful narcotic. That even the Pentagon is interested in, apparently."

At that point, Albert stared at him for a moment, wide-eyed in astonishment: "Come on! Don't tell me that you held that seminar without the slightest idea of the military importance of your discovery!"

Pierre-André stood up. They'd settled their check and left. On the way back to the boat, he'd told Albert the rest. And Albert had invited him to spend the night aboard the *Sexy Diode*.

Pierre-André shook himself out of his reverie. Darkness had fallen and for a while, he realized, he had been wandering around in circles, down the same streets. He thought that he noticed a few suspicious glances leveled in his direction. In a flash, there surfaced in his mind an image of the boy's face as he was hit by the truck and the muttered comments of the crowd. With his general appearance of a vagabond without visible means of support and a rucksack on his back, he suddenly felt very vulnerable. How ironic it would be for him to wind up lynched by a deranged mob driven by the fear of the sedative he had invented! He had to get out of there. He understood that the fear of the mob would focus on everything that smacked of being out of place, on outsiders.

He headed for the train station parking lot. He needed to go somewhere where misfits and dropout were the rule, not the exception, where no one paid any attention to anyone else. He headed for Brooklyn.

Saturday, November 2

The pharmacist in La Prairie, Vermont, didn't watch television. He had studied neuropharmacology at Brandeis University, but he'd been expelled on charges of extracting and distributing psychedelic substances from mushrooms and plant roots. In reality, the accusations were completely unfounded, and they'd been the result of false statements by a fellow student who had gone on to use his work in her own PhD dissertation. From that day on, Frank La Crosse had lived in seclusion and isolation. He had taken a job as a pharmacist in a small town back in the mountains. There he could work on pharmacognosy, his favorite line of pursuit. He had practically introduced the art of European witches in America. European witchcraft, the product of centuries upon centuries of discovery and tradition, had been able to identify and distinguish between poisonous and edible roots and berries and mushrooms. The inhabitants of that small town considered him to be an odd duck, but basically harmless.

That morning a little old lady came into the pharmacy to ask what he could do to help free up her respiratory system. Frank La Crosse was particularly happy because this would be an opportunity to show off one of the most recent discoveries of medical science. He set about preparing a concoction that released a dense odorless smoke. "Miss Parkinsons," Frank said, "now all you have to do is put your nose above it and breathe in deeply."

"Hold on a minute, what's all this breathe in deeply and inhale an odorless perfume?" said a customer who was waiting his turn. "Just what is that junk?"

"I see the word catatonic, on the label!" a lady read in a loud voice from the box out of which Frank had taken the powder to make the concoction.

"Is this one more of those things that put people into a cataleptic trance?" shouted the post office clerk. "Janet, run and get William, the town cop, and tell him to come on down immediately."

The crowd began vandalizing the shop, hurling objects selected at random from the shelves at Frank: bottles of syrup, jars, big jars of vitamins...

Mossad offices, Tel Aviv, Saturday, November 2, morning

"I don't like this," said the Owl. In the middle of the large room with bare white walls wicker chairs and sofas were scattered randomly. Set against the walls were four or five low coffee tables, upon which sat a number of large teapots, surrounded by stacks of paper cups. By now, the tea was cold. For more than two hours, the highest ranking officers of Mossad were discussing the narcotic that had been invented by a French scientist, the Mossad agent who had stolen a sample of it, and the use to which it could be put. Chairs and sofas were all occupied, but the discussion had finally boiled down to an exchange between just two men: the Owl and a younger man, dressed in a khaki uniform without insignia or collar badges, sitting across from him.

"I don't like this," the Owl repeated, shaking his head. He had a mass of frizzy, iron-gray hair, perched above a pair of bushy eyebrows, likewise iron gray. It was in fact those eyebrows, which made his eyes seem much larger than normal, that had given him his nickname— absolutely not official—of the Owl. The rapidity with which he was capable of making decisions and organizing blitzes and incursions, as effective as they were discreet, had only reinforced the nickname.

"I keep finding it impossible to understand why," said the younger man. "We have in our possession a weapon which would allow us to get wherever we want, quickly and without casualties, and hit anyone we want, in complete safety. No terrorist can escape us. The problem is reduced to obtaining the necessary intelligence to identify the objective. Putting the operation together is just child's play, once we have that."

"That's not the point," the Owl insisted.

"Why not? It means eliminating entirely all uncertainties in terms of security in our handling of the Palestinian problem."

"Eliminating covers a lot of territory."

"Agreed, eliminating is overstating the case. Still, you have to admit that the risk that a terrorist offensive might change the balance of powers at play is greatly diminished. Moreover, we would also be capable, by carefully selecting the right targets, of influencing the balance of power in their leadership. Isn't that enough for you?"

"No, it's certainly a major consideration. Everything you say is true. But instinct tells me to be wary. Have you thought about collateral effects?"

"Collateral effects? Oh, that's the last thing I would have expected to hear from you of all people. I mean, you don't think twice about firing missiles into a home, killing women, children, old men, and nanny goats, with only a 60 percent probability that the target is really in there."

The Owl smirked. "A missile is a missile. It's something we know, it's nothing new. You can do a better or a worse job of firing missiles. But we use them the way that they use them. This is something different. And the collateral effects are different."

"Look, with this stuff, there are no collateral effects. You put everyone to sleep and then you kill your man, sparing the lives of old men, women, children, and nanny goats. A precise and, most importantly, a clean operation. I bet that even the UN would like it."

"I wouldn't count on that. But I'm talking about other collateral effects."

"For instance?"

"This stuff has been used once before, right?"

"Of course, in America."

"Where?"

"At Massapequod."

"And what were the results? I'll tell you: 160 people dead, men, women, children, and old people burnt to death in their sleep. Only the dogs survived."

"What does that have to do with anything! There it was the Mafia."

"Even worse! You see the connection, the collateral effect? For the mass media, for international public opinion, that is the 'Massapequod bomb.' If we use it, everyone will start saying: the Israeli oppressors are like the Mafia, they're imitating Massapequod, where 160 people died, including women and children and so on."

"For the moment, no one has even made any public mention of the Mafia."

"Sooner or later that detail will come out."

"But the Pentagon wants it too!"

"I'd prefer to let them use it first."

"Anyway, international public opinion has never scared us."

"That's not true. Let's just say that we have always judiciously weighed costs and benefits." The Owl stopped. He ran a hand over his face, wearily. "Anyway, all I'm doing is bringing up doubts and concerns. I'm perfectly clear that this stuff can be very useful indeed. In fact, perhaps, it may be entirely necessary. However reluctantly, I'm ready to make use of it. I only wanted to make it clear that the decision to make use of this narcotic is not a responsibility that we can assume all by ourselves. This is a decision that must come from the government."

No one in the room spoke a word.

"But the problem is," the Owl resumed, "for the moment, we can't approach the government." He paused. "Because of Silberzahn," he added, running his gaze around all the faces in the room. He leaned back into his chair, looking up at the ceiling. "You see," he said, "just how insidious this thing has become? Look at what is happening in the United States. The way things are going, before long they'll be shooting each other in the streets. It's just too easy to use, damn it. A missile is a missile, you can't carry it around in your backpack, it takes special preparation, and lots of logistics. With this stuff, all you need is a vial. It's so damned easy that it gives you an illusion of omnipotence. Which brings us back to this crucial problem: he's got the narcotic, and we don't. Where is Silberzahn?"

A tall man, with a black yarmulke with white embroidery on his head, cleared his throat, shifting uncomfortably on his chair. "We don't know, like I told you," he finally said.

"I heard he was in Beirut."

"That was his mission," the man with the black yarmulke replied.

"A mission that he decided to perform when he chose and pleased."

"That's the way he's always worked."

"But this time he allowed himself to be distracted by something else. Which has nothing to do with his mission."

The man with the yarmulke shrugged his shoulders. "If you want to initiate a disciplinary proceeding..." he said.

"That's exactly what I want to initiate!" said the Owl, slapping his leg. "I want Silberzahn here, behind bars, for insubordination. Immediately. Find him, clean him up, and bring him home. With the narcotic."

The meeting was over.

Long Island, NY, Saturday, November 2, daylight

At dawn he left Brooklyn and headed back to East Long Island. He told himself that in America the safest way to avoid being identified or tracked down by the police, the FBI, the CIA, or the Pentagon, was to drive without breaking any traffic regulations or speed limits. So he got into the Chevy that Albert had rented for him and drove the length of the island, from west to east, from Brooklyn to Patchogue, then north to West Yaphank, then west through the territories of Medford, Ronkonkoma, Hauppauge, and Syosset as far as Shelter Rock, then north to Manhasset, then east again, along the north shore, through Port Washington, Oyster Bay, and Muttontown. He even dared to drive through Cold Spring Harbor, where his house was, and then on through Huntington, Fort Salonga, Kings Park, Smithtown, Rocky Point, Wading Point, and Roanoke, until he reached Peconic and Greenport. Greenport was a lovely little town, he knew, but for that very reason, there were too many people there. He made a U-turn and went west again, passing through Greenport West, Southhold, and Cutchogue, and then Mattituk and Jamesport until he reached Aquebogue.

At Aquebogue he stopped to admire the famous duck farms of Long Island. Sitting on a fence, he gazed for more than an hour at the big quacking, fluttering, veering water birds. It was a monotonous spectacle, repeating itself indefinitely. None of the feathered avians seemed to be aware that their ultimate fate was to wind up in a frying pan. Well, they're not the only ones, Matterre-Faquet pointed out to himself. He'd driven by there a thousand times and never once had it occurred to him that one day he'd spend a couple of hours sitting there, watching ducks, to kill time. He sat down on a low wall.

The death of the boy in Port Jefferson had left a deep psychic mark. Should he just surrender, hand himself over to the American authorities, make it clear once and for all that he hadn't had anything to do with Massapequod? That was the simplest, easiest solution. But it also meant handing himself over to the Pentagon, and become a scientist working for the interests of the war machine. It meant renouncing himself and everything he'd ever believed in. Admitting, after all these years, that his father had been right.

So what else could he do? Leave this immense mess behind him and go back to France, as Annick and even Albert were advising him to do? But this too meant giving up his very essence, turning the direction of his life around, and watching everything he'd fought so hard to achieve vanish into thin air, the dream that he'd cherished for so long.

Those ducks were beginning to look to him like symbols of America. He'd been unable to explain to Annick exactly what America meant for him and what France, on the other hand, symbolized. He'd gone astray and gotten bogged down in vague discourses of idealism. The reality was much simpler and much deeper in his heart. That evening with Albert, with the mood set by the excellent Pierre's Restaurant in Bridgehampton, he had spoken with a calmer state of mind and that reality had emerged more clearly.

Albert had started peppering him with comments about Susan— "the black Venus with fiery eyes who's gotten under your skin," he had described her—and suggested that she was the real reason he'd moved to America. But Pierre-André just shook his head. No, it was much more basic than that, starting with everyday life.

"I run a couple miles every day," he'd explained to him. "I've stopped smoking, and you know that I hate golf, but for an Ivy League snob like you, there are the finest golf courses east of the Mississippi River... Here on Long Island, you really would have the time of your life...if it wasn't for those lunatics with their SUVs and their red, white, and green decals, who drive with their car horns instead of their brains... Plus, I've started riding horses. You know, I take lessons at the Belmont Lake State Park riding school. No, you really can't imagine, I spent a week in the Adirondacks, battling swarms of mosquitoes, following mule tracks or galloping across green valleys. Next year I'm going to Monument Valley, where I'll ride on horseback with a Navajo guide... At last I'll have the feeling that I'm in a Western..."

Most of all, of course, there was nourishment for his restless mind. "Here I use my brain instead of pretending that I've discovered things that I learned from others. I have friends here that I'd never have met in France. One is a doctoral candidate who's working on the conservation of Long Island plant species. He teaches me lots of things about American flora, and how the Indians used them when the English first arrived. And he's not afraid to work for the money he needs for his studies. That's a normal thing here, but in France it would be pure blasphemy. He's a ranger at Caleb Smith State Park, near Smithtown. He keeps an eye on the wild animals, he cares for diseased trees. When I want a little fresh air, a bit of intellectual diversion, I go see him in the afternoon, and we take a hike in the park, we talk about this work, and from time to time I even manage to give him some intelligent advice."

He stood up from the low wall reluctantly. From Aquebogue, he drove southwest, toward Riverhead. He wanted to take a closer look at the vineyards that were producing the renowned wines of Long Island. He drove around the vineyards, stopping here and there to evaluate the grape vines with expert eyes. He was comparing them with the rows of vines in his own vineyards near Bordeaux. For a little while, he managed to think about nothing but sunshine, fertilizers, pesticides, musty grapes, and barrels. That didn't last long.

The vineyards coaxed his thoughts back to France, to which the lure of Annick was calling him. It was an intellectual inferno, for someone like him. "You know what the French are like," he had explained to Albert. "The French scientific world follows fashions instead of creating them. They hate innovation. New things terrify them. If someone discovers something new, their academic power is threatened. And the entire industrial sector, which would only stand to benefit from true innovation, follows these same fashions. If you could just imagine the battles I fought in my attempts to persuade the world of French perfume makers to work on the psychological effects of scents! I was ultimately unsuccessful, but the ones who sabotaged and undermined me most in my efforts were my colleagues, in the universities and the major and minor manufacturers... I am personally convinced that an understanding of the way that the sense of smell functions is the newest field of development in the areas of biochemistry, cellular biology, and molecular biology, but try explaining that to the people who hold onto power by constantly repeating the same things, relentlessly conducting their experiments in the same manner, and discovering that the molecular mechanism of *Saccharomyces pombe*, which their doctoral thesis was based on forty years ago, also exists in *Scedosporium apiospermium*, instead of blazing new paths of research. They'll never admit it. And if I asked the University of Paris to let me use one of their laboratories at my own expense, the way I'm doing here, they'd never agree! Not only because they're terrified at the mere idea of true innovation, but also because their laws are antiquated. They simply don't accept the possibility of such an innovative approach. Let's not even talk about the perfume monopoly in France, eager to lynch me if I make a mistake, and determined to exploit any of my discoveries if I do happen to discover something useful and interesting."

No, he could never turn himself over to their control. But he couldn't stay where he was, either. In the small towns of Long Island, he was in constant danger of being identified as an outside element and subjected to a pitiless manhunt, like the one he had seen. But in big cities, the police were everywhere: he had seen policemen in the subway stations, at the entrances to shopping centers, patrolling the most crowded intersections. These were hard-eyed people, perfectly capable of recognizing the features of a face, even if everything framing that face was different from what was expected. So on the one hand, the frying pan; on the other, the fire. In Brooklyn he would be just as vulnerable as at Huntington or Bridgehampton, though in a completely different way. He was caught between two equally intolerable risks.

He took the East Moriches-Riverhead Expressway to the Sunrise Highway, and then followed it all the way through Bohemia, Islip, and West Babylon. There he caught Route 110 south and sought refuge in the Sayonara Motor Inn, at Amityville.

He'd driven at least six hundred miles. He fell asleep, tired and hungry.

He woke up in the middle of the night.

He picked up the phone from the side table. It was late and Julie's voice was tired. But she told him what he'd been hoping to hear.

Mount Gerizim Saturday, November 2, afternoon

The gusts kicked up small whirlwinds, flinging dust into the air that was as ancient as the half dozen civilizations that had succeeded one another on this ground, taking root and then being swept away over the course of the last two or three millennia.

Scattered stones, which might originally have belonged to a Roman temple or a building demolished during the revolt of the Samaritans, serve as mute testimony to the clash between the ephemeral present and the eternal elements of the human condition.

Every stone on the arid northern slopes of Mount Gerizim might have once been part of the structure of a Corinthian column, or the construction of the apse of a church, or the walls of a mosque. Every heap of rocks might be the product of a convergence of random geological phenomena, or it might have been intentionally piled up to protect manuscripts buried beneath, to conceal a trove of gold, to distract attention from packages of heroin, or as a convenient cache for automatic weapons and ammunition.

Three men, clad in the distinctive garments of the Negev desert Bedouin, were sitting in the shadow cast by another large rock, which screened them from the harsh sunlight. Their camels were stretched out on the ground nearby, placidly munching straw. They could have been herdsmen, like most of the Bedouin, except they had no other camels, aside from the ones they were riding. They could have been smugglers, like many of the Bedouin, but there was no sign that they were transporting goods of any kind.

What they actually were, instead, was just one more of the nodes in the close-knit meshwork of control and intervention that closely monitors Lebanese warlords, Palestinian terrorists, detachments of the Syrian army, and traffickers of drugs, women, and migrants in this corner of the eastern Mediterranean.

One of the three men had his head almost entirely wedged under a low shelter, created by a length of waterproof canvas, draped over a folding camp chair. His glasses reflected the purplish light of a number of computer screens. Suddenly, he pulled his head out and glanced at his two comrades.

"Hey," he said in a loud voice, "Uriel's resurfaced."

"About time. Where?"

"Beirut. Yesterday."

"Why Beirut? Ah, of course, Batik. Uriel never gives up, does he?"

"Wait, there's more." The first man plunged his head back under the cloth. In front of him, on the glowing screen of a small smartphone, apparently meaningless sequences of numbers, letters, and typographic characters were streaming by rapidly. A wire ran from the smartphone to a black box, and from the box a USB cord ran to a laptop. The man placed the pad of his thumb onto the sensor on the top of the box, to begin the process of conversion. And on the screen of laptop words and phrases began to appear, and then vanished once and for all into the ether.

"He's wounded."

"A gunshot wound?"

"Not at all. He's been badly beaten and kicked around."

"You're kidding! The great Uriel?"

"Well, from what I heard, someone caught him with his pants down."

The two other men laughed.

"He was trying to rape someone from Batik's group. A woman, just to be clear."

"What do they want to call that? Excessive zeal? Anyway, he blew his cover, right?"

"Of course. He was seen, hobbling in pain, clearly badly beaten, but the report says that he refused the contact and vanished."

"I'll bet the dickheads in Tel Aviv had a succession of heart attacks."

The three men had a few more hours to wait until sundown, when they would be able to resume their march toward the Samaritan village of Kiryat Luza. They smoked, they ate something, they smoked some more. At last, a stuttering sequence of flashes under the canvas alerted them to another incoming communication. "Uhmm," said the nearest man, as he stuck his head under the canvas, "a point-to-point communication. It's addressed to us."

"Well would you look at that," he went on. "Who do you think? It's from Uriel."

"Send him our regards."

"Tell him our thoughts are with him. How is he?"

"He seems to be fine."

"Where is he?"

"He says that's none of our business."

"As usual."

A few seconds passed, as the man with his head under the canvas read the monitor. "He wants to know," he finally said, "about this morning's meeting in Tel Aviv."

"Well," said the man to the left of the cloth, "he can be told just as we were told, no? They want him to bring the loot back to home base."

"Wait a minute," said the other man, "I talked to our guys in Tel Aviv about that earlier. What does he want to know?"

A few seconds went by. "He wants to know what they plan to do with the narcotic."

"They haven't made a final decison."

"But Uriel wants to know whether, in our opinion, they're going to use it."

"That's a decision for those ass-kissing politicians."

A few more seconds past. "He cut off the contact," said the man under the cloth.

Wadi el Arish, Saturday, November 2, sunset

In the thin desert air, in the blue bowl of the sky still illuminated from the west by the sinking sun, the first stars were already flickering into view. A man was sitting on a rock, his legs crossed under his heavy cloak. His camel was placidly chewing straw, as he held a cell phone between his ear and the turban that protected him from sun by day and the night chill. Other camels had descended into the dry bed of the *Wadi el Arish*, in search of the occasional blade of grass that still sprang up even here, in the wake of the rains far from the arid soil of the Sinai. Their precious cargo was stacked in orderly piles next to the fire. The man was listening, rather than talking: his eyes were staring southward, looking at the scattered lights of the village of Bir Lahfan, glittering in the clean desert air, but without really seeing them. Three other men, apparently half-asleep, were taking advantage of the cool breeze that sunset was ushering in off the Mediterranean; they were facing in three different directions. At dawn, they would resume their brief journey toward the village of El Arish and the sea, then they'd continue along the coast as far as Port Said, where they would deliver their shipment of heroin, fruit of the poppy plants of the Afghan highlands. Then they'd receive a shipment of weapons to transport back east, once again to El Arish and from there to Gaza, following the eternal cycle of smuggling. They'd follow an age-old track, possibly a route dating back over the millennia. There are those who believe that it was the original track of Exodus, the one followed by the people of Israel when they fled from Egypt, to cross the desert and reach the Promised Land. There are others who suggest that this was the path followed by the Holy Family as they fled into Egypt, to carry Baby Jesus to safety, far from King Herod's reach. Certainly it was the path taken by the Israeli in 1948 and again in 1967, to rout their Egyptian enemy. These issues however were of no concern to the four camel drivers, who would remain in their position until dawn, three of them at the tips of an almost equilateral triangle: in their hands, in the dim light of the moon, they held sticks that, examined more carefully, would prove to be rifles. They were standing sentinel around the man who sat at the center of that imaginary triangle.

The phone call came to an end. The man folded his cell phone and slipped it back into his cloak. He stood there thinking for a moment. Then he spoke in a loud voice.

"That was Uriel Silberzahn," he said to the three other men.

"The one from Mossad?" one of them asked, without turning his head.

"That's the only Silberzahn we know."

"He's also the only one who has ever helped us."

"True. May Allah preserve and protect him."

"And we helped him."

"Yes. We gave him information that he needed and gave us information that we needed. Our information was good, and so was his."

"Favor for favor, the way it's meant to be."

"Yes." The chief's voice had become doubtful, as if he were reluctant to draw an inevitable conclusion.

"Now what does he want?" asked another of the three men forming the triangle.

"Refuge," answered the chief.

"Refuge?"

"Yes. Refuge and a boat."

"And why should one from Mossad seek refuge among us?"

"I don't know, I didn't ask him, and I don't want to know."

"What does he need the boat for?"

"I don't know, I didn't ask him, and I think it's better for us not to know."

"Did you say yes?"

"Yes. Tomorrow we meet at El Arish. Unload a camel. We'll take him with us as far as Port Said and then, on the way back, we'll get him a boat at El Arish."

There were a few minutes of silence.

"We have a debt with him," went on one of the men in the triangle.

"Debts belong to the past. The future is more important," replied the chief.

"What did he promise in exchange?"

"That he will know how to repay us, just as he has before."

"I would have preferred something more specific."

"Yes, that would have been preferable."

"Then why did you accept?"

"Because I think that, without meaning to, he's doing us a favor. I even think he knows that's what's happening, but that he's so desperate that he has no other options. And that makes it an even greater favor that he's doing us. Our only concern is how to cash in on it."

Miami, Saturday, November 2, noon

O'Malley was sitting by the side of the bed again. Vituzzo's eyes were a little more alive than the day before.

"All right then, do you want me to start guessing?" Vituzzo said.

"Yes."

"Well, let's start with the strange things."

"Well, first of all, the negotiation. Don't you find it odd that the Mafia should think of negotiating with the state?"

"Less strange than you might think. They tried something like that in Italy at the beginning of the Nineties. Of course, it takes guts and imagination to think of anything of the sort here in America. But that's one of the clues that might help to unravel the riddle. No, the strangest thing is the massacre. Women, children, old men all murdered ruthlessly, without any apparent reason. The organization has never done anything of the sort. In fact, that's exactly the kind of thing they've always avoided. It makes me think that someone was operating on their own initiative, to force the organization's hand. That they simply presented the others with it after the fact. That's something we can't know for sure. But then there's another odd aspect. The signature."

"Well?"

"*The families*. What does that supposed to mean, how does it fit in? Have you ever seen a ransom letter or an extortion letter with a signature? Normally they just send the letter, unsigned, and they wait for the recipient to try to find them. And of course, they let themselves be found. Period. If you ask me, that signature, in the plural, is designed to show that all the families are in agreement. And if someone is trying to make it look that way, it must mean that they aren't in agreement, or that the person who wrote the letter isn't that sure it's a solid agreement."

"So?"

"You're looking for an identikit, aren't you? So if I was going to make a guess, I'd have to say that this is a letter that wasn't really agreed upon and signed by everyone. This is an individual initiative on the part of one operator who managed to get a tentative agreement out of all the others and he wants to remind them of the fact. This isn't a guy from one of the big families either, he'd not from Miami, Los Angeles, or New York. He's still a small operator."

"Well, then, who is it?"

"Hold on. He's small, but he's smart, like I said. He's got guts and imagination. None of the old bosses would have sniffed out this opportunity with the narcotic, none of them would have figured out how to make use of it. It takes a fresh, well-prepared, educated mind. What's more, look at the demands. Frankly, you could havecome up with something much better if you tried. So..."

Vituzzo broke off with a grimace. He shook his head, as if to chase away the pain.

"You can never get it out of your head," he said ruefully.

"Wait a minute. Maybe I have it," said O'Malley. "Let me try and guess for a minute. So, if the individual demands aren't what matters, the objective is something else. A more general objective. To make the Mafia a force to be reckoned with, a respected power that can demand face-to-face negotiations. Maybe in the shadows, but with respect."

"That's right, with respect. I think that's the idea. All right, so we're trying to put together a composite sketch of this guy. Small time, young, ambitious—very, very ambitious. Modern. Educated. Capable of thinking big. You get it yet?"

"Cal Salina."

"Don Calogero Salina, that's right."

"Boston. He went to college, he never felt inferior to anyone else. He makes money, just like everyone else, on gambling, casinos, and prostitution. Not old-school whore houses, protection for luxury escort services. He deal drugs, but without going overboard. Most important of all, though, is the fact that he controls a nice business in Internet pharmaceuticals, he has a finger in more than a dozen different laboratories. Right?"

"Maybe. I told you that I couldn't do any better than guessing."

Now O'Malley was in a hurry.

"Thanks, Vituzzo. You're the best. See you again soon."

"Yeah, at my funeral. But do me a favor and don't come."

"Don't come where?"

"To my funeral. It wouldn't make me look very good."

New York City, Upper East Side, Saturday, November 2, afternoon

Calogero Salina turned off his computer, pulled a comb out of his jacket breast pocket, and carefully swept back his hair. He was very proud of this thick head of hair. His father had died practically bald and in order to escape that fate, young Calogero brushed his hair vigorously, for many long minutes, every morning, in the belief that by stimulating the blood flow to the follicles in his scalp he was underwriting the best possible anti-hair-loss policy.

He studied his hair in the blank screen of the computer he'd just turned off. This new betting website seemed to have real potential. He should talk about it to his computer guru Jeff to figure out if there was a way to make some more money off it. If there was a way of getting free access to the servers, he could work miracles. But with the Feds constantly on his tail, he was forced to work cautiously and make use of commercial servers. But all that could change in a hurry. A smile of satisfaction spread across his face: things were going pretty well. In fact, he never expected such spectacular results. It had all worked out beautifully, far better than his wildest expectations. Now, the important thing was to keep cool and do what needed to be done, and pay no attention to the guys who were wetting their pants. Soon, they'd all line up on his side.

Calogero Salina—though he preferred to be called Cal—had gone into business with the small inheritance his father had left him. A couple of casinos and a bordello or two, and a modest drug-trafficking network. But he was smart, clever, and always looking ahead. He had insisted on going to college where, to everyone's surprise, he had taken a degree in biology. Without any real distinction, truth be told. In fact, he had struggled. But at college he'd understood where the frontier of the future was, even for people like him, who belonged to the Mafia. For four years, like everyone, he'd practically lived on the Internet. And as soon as he went back to work, that had been his chief focus. Thanks to his father's Canadian contacts, he had picked up a considerable share of the traffic in counterfeit medicines online. Then he got two gambling websites in the Caribbean. He ran a bit of prostitution on the web, too, but you couldn't make that much money on whores and they were a troublesome and undisciplined group of people to work with.

But the winning card, he felt sure of it, was his initial instinct. He sensed a slight movement on his right, on the far end of the large room, near the window. That was Saro. Saro always managed to move his considerable and imposing body mass in perfect silence. He was tall, massive, of indeterminate age, with a mass of strong, thick hair, which Calogero envied deeply. Saro was now in front of the large window that covered nearly the entire wall and inundated a row of cactus, neatly arranged in a line of vases, with sunshine. He was holding a small watering can and was watering some of the vases.

"Be careful not to use too much water," Calogero said. "Remember, they're succulents." Saro said nothing. He almost never spoke. Calogero, on the other hand, was euphoric, and felt like talking. He pointed to the far wall, with four blowups.

"Do you remember the time we went to the villa of the Cerasa family, to see Don Pino?" He was a friend of his father's, and was much older than him. "Photos everywhere, right? Don Pino with Lucky Luciano and Don Pino with Carlo Gambino, and Don Pino with Aniello Dellacroce, with John Gotti. *Mamma mia!*" He snorted with a sneer of contempt. Those weren't his heroes, those weren't the people he wanted to emulate.

"The whole place reeked of mold, right, Saro?" Saro didn't answer.

Cal Salina walked over to the wall with the gigantic photographs.

"These don't reek of mold, do they, Saro?" The blowup on the left was of Sergei Brin, the man who had made Google possible. The one on the far right was Mark Zuckerberg, the founder of Facebook. He could have put up others, but Zuckerberg and Brin gave a good idea of what he meant by people capable of changing the parameters by which other people thought and lived, of turning over a new leaf and writing much of what filled that page. After Zuckerberg and Brin, the world was no longer the same. The world, he thought, will never be the same after Cal Salina has attained his objectives and manages to take the organization to an entirely new level. Actually, there were Mafiosi in the other two blowups. But they were pretend Mafiosi: Marlon Brando in *The Godfather* and a poster of *The Sopranos*. Actors, movies, but actually proof that the Mafia could become mainstream.

"Those guys got the Mafia into people's minds, eh, Saro?" Saro, actually, had finished watering the plants and had already left. Calogero went over to inspect the vases under the window. He cautiously caressed the thorns of a cactus. His intuition—which would allow the qualitative leap forward—was to cultivate, as he liked to say, science. What they wouldn't be able to do soon with genetics, trafficking under the table with forbidden genes! He had a series of new college graduates who were keeping track for him of the newest discoveries announced in journals and online. But he also had a more discreet network, scattered across the landscape, in contact with the most important laboratories and in public agencies, from NASA and the Pentagon to the NIH and, naturally, the FBI.

It was Mariuzza, an old classmate who now worked at the Bureau's office of reports, who had told him about the French scientist's research into "Extracts That Put People to Sleep." He had seen her again after all these years at the feast of the parish church where they'd grown up and where he was something on the order of a hero, because of his generous donations. Mariuzza came over to say hello, they had talked, she had told him what she was doing for a living these days, and it hadn't taken him more than a second to understand that he'd just found a treasure. They met once a week for dinner, and she told him everything that had passed through her hands. This stuff wasn't top secret, they were just scientific reports, and he had easily persuaded her that what she was doing wasn't all that scandalous after all. In exchange, he paid the tuition at the expensive private school her daughter attended. A fair trade, he told himself. Mariuzza had the right kind of ambitions. And when she had told him about those extracts, he had immediately under-stood what he could do with them. And good old Mariuzza, who had even agreed to sandbag that report!

His personal cell phone rang. There was no calling number on dis-play.

"Hello?"

"Calogero, this is Mariuzza."

"Maria, what in the world made you think it was a good idea to call me on my cell phone! I told you to always call me on Skype only. Any-way, aren't we having dinner tomorrow evening?"

"I'm sorry, Calogero, but I couldn't call from the office and I didn't want to wait until I got home."

"Listen, hang up the phone!"

"Calogero, I'm afraid they're onto something."

"Maria! Where are you calling from?"

"From a pizz..."

Calogero had turned off his cell phone.

He said in a low voice: "Saro?"

"I'm right here." Saro wasn't very visible, but he was always right there.

"Saro, Mariuzza has just become a problem."

"A clean job?"

"Make it look like she did it herself."

"When?"

"Now."

Maria looked at the receiver that was buzzing busy now. She looked around. She was in a shop selling pizza by the slice. No one was paying the slightest attention to her. But it was quickly becoming clear to her that she'd made a mistake. A fatal mistake.

As she was heading back to the office, she furiously tried to think it through. She had figured out that someone—that is, certainly, O'Malley—suspected that she had buried the report about that scientist in the wrong archive. And she thought she should talk to Calogero to get his advice, to warn him, just to vent her worries. She had thought of Calogero as a friend. But he wasn't her friend. Now she was afraid.

When she got back to the Bureau, instead of going up to the fifth floor, where she worked, she went up to the seventh floor, where O'Malley had his office. She poked her head into his section. "Is Agent O'Malley here?"

Meg answered:

"Sorry, sweetie. Jamie isn't in."

"When could I find him?"

"Tomorrow. He's coming back from a mission tonight."

Maria had a moment's hesitation. But she wanted to talk to O'Malley and no one else. "Thanks," she said. And she left.

It wasn't very hard for her to get his cell phone number. When he answered, she could sense he had other things on his mind. He was remote. But when he understood who was calling him, she sensed a flash of interest.

"Exactly who I was thinking about. Maria, right? I need to talk to you."

"No, I need to talk to you. As soon as possible."

"Well, I'm boarding a plane right now. Can we meet tomorrow in the office?"

"No, it has to be tonight."

O'Malley seemed a little surprised.

"All right," he said all the same. "I'll land at La Guardia at seven o'clock. I'll be at your house by eight. Give me the address."

New York City, Saturday, November 2, evening.

The airplane landed with the usual fifteen-minute delay. When he turned his cell phone back on, O'Malley was still thinking about what Vituzzo had told him, a few hours earlier. There was a message on his cell phone, from just a few minutes earlier. All it said was: "Help." O'Malley had no doubt about who it was from. He ran to the taxi stand, jumped to the head of the line waving his FBI badge, and told the cabbie to take him to Maria's address, running lights and honking his horn all the way. He called the office and told Meg to rush over to Maria's apartment.

He wasn't surprised to see a knot of rubberneckers outside the apartment building, an ambulance, and two or three cops. He ducked under the yellow crime scene tape, showing his badge again, and went over to the corpse. "She jumped off the eleventh-floor balcony," the cop informed him.

O'Malley bent over Maria's body. She was crumpled up face down on the sidewalk. He gripped her shoulder and turned her over partway: her face was a bloodied shapeless mask of flesh and bone.

"Odd," he said.

"Odd how?" shot back the policeman. "This time of year they kill themselves like moths around a campfire. We get at least one a day."

"Strange that she fell on her face," O'Malley went on. "Usually, when someone jumps out a window, they turn their head at the last second."

He looked up.

"She jumped off that balcony on the eleventh floor," the policeman informed him helpfully, for the second time. O'Malley gauged the distance between the wall and Mariuzza's dead body. If you jump off a balcony, in most cases, you're going to jump out and land a yard or two from the plumb line of the edge of the balcony. But if you're thrown off a balcony, you fall like a dead weight, even if you're still alive while you're falling. Mariuzza was pretty much on a line with the edge of the balcony.

The medical examiner had arrived. O'Malley showed his badge. "Could you do me a favor?" he asked. "Check to make sure that there's no signs of violence."

"What do you mean? Like rape?" The medical examiner was incredulous.

"No, that's not what I meant at all. I'm thinking fists to the face, that sort of thing."

Out of the corner of his eye, he saw Meg and Jill arrive. Meg was bundled in her usual combat jacket and a pair of baggy jeans. Jill, under her Burberry, was wearing a cashmere cardigan and a pair of close-fitting black pants.

"Quite the lady killer you are. So she couldn't resist your fatal charms?" said Meg.

"Meg, you're disgusting. You can't be willing to do anything just to get off a one-liner."

"Well, this afternoon she came looking for you."

"I know. But this time, I was the one who didn't think fast enough. When I called you this afternoon, I should have told you to come here and wait with her until I got here."

"Do you think she killed herself?"

"I'd be very surprised."

"Is it serious?"

"I would say that we've lost our one chance to nail down what, for right now, is doomed to remain nothing but an idea. I was an idiot. I didn't realize that she was the evidence that we needed to pin this on the man who's behind it all. And that I wasn't the only one to know it."

"Can you explain what you mean?"

"Have you spoken to Personnel?"

"I talked to them," said Jill. "They pretty much confirm your suspicions. It didn't take much, to tell the truth. They were quite embarrassed. They kept saying that Maria only had a low-level security clearance."

"Because they're stupid. They're the ones who gave it to her. Anyway, what did they say?"

Jill stood up straight, the way she always did when she was about to report something.

"Maria has...had a daughter. Georgina. Age thirteen. She goes to the Cloisters Academy."

"Cloisters?" O'Malley whistled silently. "Wow, that's one of the most exclusive schools in all New York."

"That's right," Jill agreed.

"It's a highway straight to Harvard, Yale, or Princeton, for wherever you want to go, right?"

"Exactly."

"But it cost a lot of money, right?" O'Malley looked at Jill, with an amused gaze. Jill was blushing slightly.

"When I went, it cost twenty thousand dollars a year. It's gone up to thirty-five thousand dollars by now."

"That's a lot for a low-level secretary. What do the people in Personnel have to say?"

"Yeah, it's a lot of money. But there could be an explanation."

"Wait a minute. Is the girl upstairs?" O'Malley looked up at the eleventh-story balcony.

"No. Cloisters Academy is in Westchester County, right?"

"Right. Of course. Obviously."

"Georgina lives with her grandmother, who has a place pretty near there. She saw her mother on the weekends."

"Okay, let's get back to the money."

"Maria got divorced eight years ago. Her ex-husband is Michael Di Donato. He has a wine business."

"Di Donato? Sure. He has wine stores everywhere."

"Right. He's a big operator. Big enough to be able to make a few sacrifices and pay the tuition at Cloisters. That's what they figured in Personnel. Maria, aside from the alimony for her daughter, deposited 2,000 dollars in the bank every month."

"Checks?"

"Cash. That's not so odd for someone who must take in that much cash every day in his stores."

"But it turns out instead that…"

"Well, in Personnel no one ever thought of talking directly to Di Donato."

"So when they did?"

"So when they finally called him, he explained that he had nothing to do with the 2,000 dollars. When Maria had mentioned Cloisters to him, he'd refused to listen. He said that he'd turned out just fine with CUNY and that a woman should worry about getting married, not studying."

"I can just imagine. So Maria had to get busy to find that money. I think I can guess who was giving it to her. Too bad that she can't tell us herself."

O'Malley stood up.

"All right. Call everyone. We'll meet in the office in an hour. I have some things to tell you."

"From Florida?" asked Meg.

"Right. Come on, let's get out of here."

He too a last look at Maria's body, still crumpled on the street, like a doll tortured by a hysterical child. "Sorry, beautiful," O'Malley murmured, "but you know what you were getting into."

Sunday, November 3

These were probably not the best few days to have a treasure hunt on the beach. But Sammy hadn't drawn a link between the things he was seeing on television and the risks that he and his friends might be running. And they had taken special care not to mention it to their parents, who would probably have thought it through more clearly. He had hidden the treasure in question, the latest edition of the videogame Grand Theft Auto, wrapped carefully in a double layer of plastic sandwich bags and further protected inside a rigid injection-molded plastic case that looked like a pirate's wooden treasure chest, on the preceding Sunday afternoon, which was the last opportunity he'd had to get away from school. For the rest of the following week, he had challenged Jim, who sat next to him in class, Carl, the tall boy with whom he played basketball, and the other three boys, who were all one year ahead of him at Church Street Junior High School, between Freeport and Merrick Bay, to find the treasure.

Maximum time limit: two hours.

That was why they were all standing around now, eager and excited, having finished their breakfasts. They were about to undertake a treasure hunt in the deserted area between Jones Beach and the swamps further inland, in the nature reserves around Cow Meadow and Pettit Marsh, where Sammy said he had concealed the treasure. Sammy noted down the exact time and then gave the signal: the five young boys took off at a dead run, spreading out in all directions. Each of them slowed almost immediately to a careful walk, scanning the ground intently for tracks of where Sammy had passed the week before or signs of recently excavated soil. They moved the branches of bushes and hedges, pushed rocks aside, lifted pieces of wood or small logs, bending down and standing back up again frequently.

On one of the beaches, Joe Orton, a Winchester rifle cradled on his knees, and a small pair of binoculars glued to his eyes, was pretty much fed up. For an hour now, he'd been perched high atop a lifeguard's lookout chair in the bitter winter cold, scanning the sea in search of potential unidentified boats that might be attempting to affect an unfriendly landing. The binoculars didn't actually work very well, or perhaps he just didn't know how to adjust them. Whatever the case, he saw numerous images that were simply black shadows, darker than the waves of the chilly sea. So far he'd failed to spot any watercraft.

His umpteenth yawn was stifled at the arrival of Kyle Morrison. Kyle was the other member of the vigilante squad that had been assigned to keep a watchful eye on that stretch of inland sea. They'd taken 90-minute shifts sitting on the lifeguard's chair, but by now Joe was starting to think that shorter shifts might be more effective. Now Kyle was frantically moving around underneath on the lifeguard's chair, pounding his feet into the sand and waving his arms. Joe could see that he was moving his lips. "Could you speak up a little?" he said loudly.

Kyle made a gesture of irritation and put a finger to the tip of his nose in an exaggerated signal for silence. After a moment's hesitation, he climbed up a few rungs of the tall chair to bring himself a little closer to Joe's ears. The lifeguard's chair wobbled slightly. "There's something moving," Kyle whispered. "Where?" asked Joe, jerking around and grabbing the binoculars to scan the waves, in vain. "No, not that way! Behind you!"

Joe half-turned on the lifeguard's chair and pointed his binoculars toward the marshes behind him. Damn, it was true! There were figures moving furtively among the bushes. The sun was glaring off the lenses, creating a dance of dizzying reflections, but he had no doubt: someone was there.

"You see them?" Kyle asked anxiously.

"Hell, yes! There's three of them, no, wait, four of them."

"What are they doing?"

"They're walking. Now one of them is kneeling down and digging in the dirt or something, but I can't see him very clearly. Another one is hiding behind a log lying on the ground. No, there, he just stood up again. It looks as if they're burying something."

"Or else they're unearthing something," Kyle replied thoughtfully. "Let me go see," he added, on impulse, putting his hand on the revolver that he had stuck into the back pocket of his jeans.

"Why on earth would you do that?! I can get them from here." He raised the Winchester rifle and braced it against his shoulder. "Get down," he told Kyle. "You're rocking this damned thing."

In order to lift the rifle into firing position, he'd been forced to put down the binoculars. In any case, now that he'd picked them out, he should have no trouble finding them again. He zeroed in on one of the moving figures: it looked like a short, skinny man. He took careful aim and squeezed the trigger. The rifled cracked and the skinny little man crumpled to the ground. The others, instead of scattering or diving for cover, stood up and stared in his direction. "Better than a herd of deer!" Joe snickered. He took careful aim and dropped another man. Now, the others hit the ground. After a few seconds, Joe saw a white handkerchief flutter in the air.

"They're waving a white flag," he told Kyle with some bafflement.

"Hold on, let me go see."

That evening, *Long Island News* reported that Jim Prescott, age fifteen, had suffered a flesh wound to one leg. Lonnie Donegan, age fourteen, was injured more seriously, in the shoulder. Both of them, in any case, were out of serious danger. Joe Orton and Kyle Morrison would have to stand trial, but for now the sheriff had released them on their own recognizance because they had acted in an emergency situation.

Mineola, Long Island, NY, Sunday, November 3, morning

A vicious winter wind was blowing, tearing the last autumn leaves off the skeletal trees. Pierre-André left the Sayonara Motel in Amityville well before sunrise and headed for Mineola in the pre-dawn darkness. When he reached Mineola, he parked the Chevrolet that Albert had rented in the vast shopping mall lot and walked away. His main objective was to avoid capture by the FBI or the military, but with his head shaved bald and a combat jacket, and what's worse, on foot, he realized that he was a prime target for the vigilantes who were now running roughshod over the entire island. Just yesterday, they had fired on a group of kids, seriously wounding two of them, somewhere between Freeport and Merrick.

Pierre-André was worried. He was afraid he'd be taken for a narcotic-dispersing terrorist. He walked the long way around, zigging and zagging to avoid notice, and finally made his way to Julie's house. When he got there, a little after ten in the morning, he was terrorized, exhausted, and chilled to the bone.

When Pierre-André walked into the apartment, the warm air in the living room made him feel better. The music washed away the sense of insecurity that had been dogging his steps. The half-darkness that shrouded the apartment almost made him forget that it was morning and that he was a hunted man, or at least felt like he was, pursued by forces so much bigger than him. Julie was dressed like a little girl celebrating Halloween. Only much sexier.

She saw that he was shaved bald and her mouth twisted in a grimace of astonishment.

He walked toward her and she remained motionless.

Silence reigned in the room.

She let the costume slip off her body. He felt an incredible wave of chemistry pass between their bodies. That same wave of attraction that brought him back to her week after week, sometimes day after day.

He told her: "I want to spend quite a few days with you."

Still, she sensed his insecurity. She picked up the costume, wrapped it around her shoulders, and repressed the shiver of desire that was sweeping over her.

She wasn't looking at the usual self-satisfied Frenchman. For the moment, it struck her that Pierre-André needed a warm hug more than frantic hot sex.

He reached out, touched her, and sought her mouth. She turned her face up to him, but they only brushed lips.

He stuck his face into her hair and inhaled, then he nibbled at her ear and dropped his hand. She took his hand and led him to an armchair. She asked him if he'd like a glass of champagne. He shuddered and asked for a cup of coffee instead.

She brewed him a cup and then sat in his lap, curled up like a kitten, and told him all about her trip to Cabo San Lucas, the week before, all alone, without a man, a genuine vacation, between the sea and the vultures, with whales going by less than half a mile from the coast. Whales that could knock over a sailboat with a single smack of their enormous flukes. Pierre-André thought of the curse of Captain Ahab, compared himself to him, and smiled in ironic self-deprecation. The woman told him that she had played squash with wealthy women whose hair was tinted light blue, and she'd played poker with rich Texans who wore their cowboy boots to the beach. There were cactus plants as tall as three-story buildings, there were birds of prey, pelicans, cormorants, and black-necked stilts.

He sipped his coffee. He was warming up, he felt a little less afraid of the future. He moved his hand up over her belly, she smiled at him, she blew him a tiny kiss onto his bald head, picked up the coffee pot again, poured herself a small cup of coffee, and took just a small sip of it.

She got up and turned off the television set. She looked at Pierre-André with an enigmatic smile and suggested:

"Cold as it is out, why don't you take a nice hot shower?" and went into the bathroom to run the water for him.

Pierre-André stood up, swallowed the last of the coffee, took off his shoes... and thought about Susan.

Susan, a woman he had to reconquer each time... while with Julie there was a fantastic chemistry that demanded no mental elaboration. Perhaps Matterre-Faquet no longer had the time, the will, or the ability to be spiritually creative every time. And maybe that's what drove him to ask himself whether Susan was the right woman for him, and especially to ask himself that question right there, in that living room, a few feet away from the tits of a white call girl with red hair.

What if it was Yale that made Susan so attractive? But then why had he had all those tender yearning feelings in the truck when he was escaping from the service plaza and on the ferryboat on Long Island Sound? When he explored his feelings toward Susan, both the ones from last year and the ones from last week, leaving aside the joys of sex, Pierre-André wondered whether his new excitement over Susan might not have been prompted by the possibility of a professorship at Yale. And, in a brief moment of intellectual honesty he wondered: "Am I or am I not a son of a bitch? Does Susan have a right to doubt whether I'm really in love with her, or does she not?"

Washington, Pentagon, Sunday, November 3, evening

The cardboard boxes taken from the offices and the laboratory of Dr. Matterre-Faquet were occupying much of the floor space in the office of Midshipman Marmaduke Kendrew, whose forebears had served in the British Royal Navy for generations. In his family, there were still those who claimed that a great-grandfather had fought with Nelson at Trafalgar. There were also those who did everything possible to forget that, one hundred thirty years later, a great-uncle had left many soldiers behind in the drink at Dunkirk. Marmaduke bore the name of a younger son of that family, the youngest brother of the great-uncle who had moved to the New World in pursuit of the nurse who had tended to the wounds he'd received after a fight with an Italian Navy cruiser off Pantelleria during the Second World War. Young Marmaduke had followed in his family's military footsteps, but he had also pursued his passionate interest in biology. After high school, therefore, he had enlisted in the US Navy and taken a college degree in biology and biochemistry thanks to financial aid from the Department of Defense. That was why he'd wound up in the Navy's center for scientific studies and now had twelve large boxes cluttering up his office.

He had spent the past few days leafing through scientific journals, hoping to find something that might guide him along the path and allow him to guess what he should be looking for, but the briefing given him by his superior officers had been fairly vague. Matterre-Faquet was not someone who scribbled comments in books or journals. After a desultory search through the contents of the other boxes, he was confronted by the correspondence. He felt the stirring instinct of a voyeur and dug into the correspondence with the eager curiosity of someone who loves peep shows.

Naturally he found nothing compromising or unseemly. Matterre-Faquet was the rigid, nonconformist son of a rigidly militaristic father, but he did find some indications of what Matterre-Faquet's objectives had been for his cataleptic extract. In a couple of letters to two colleagues who worked for different pharmaceutical houses, Matterre-Faquet asked whether there would be interest in a bland sedative that left no aftereffects upon reawakening.

It was getting late and he was tired. He decided to read another dozen or so documents. He went to the coffee machine where he ran into Commander Ralph Randall, who asked him how he was doing with his research into the documents.

"Nothing in particular, Sir. That Frenchman doesn't make notes on his documents. He doesn't write anything compromising or embarrassing. You'd think he'd taken a course in security tradecraft."

"What do you have here?"

" Nothing special, Sir. A couple of bills for refrigerator repairs, and a receipt for the purchase of a laminar flow and exhaust fume hood... oh, yes, there's an estimate for a toxicological analysis..."

"Hell's bells," thundered Ralph Randall, "a toxicological analysis? What are you talking about? Are you trying to tell me that... Who was supposed to carry out this toxicological analysis? What's the date of the estimate? Let me have that. Good job! At ease," and he tore the sheet of paper out of Midshipman Kendrew's hand and rushed back to his office, slamming the door behind him.

Monday, November 4

The Steward's next door neighbors had a son whose slight mental retardation did not keep him from performing fairly simple tasks. When he was little, Harvey Gehdehawn had been a lovely child, but at school it had become clear that he had a learning disability. His face was slightly misshapen, he never moved very fast, he sometimes drooled, and he scared the other children. As he got older, he became a teenager who could help carry groceries from the trunk of the car to the kitchen table. He could also water the plants and play ball, but the Stewards never seemed very interested in having their little boy Daniel play with Harvey. That morning, Harvey's dad had put the leaf blower on his back and had told him to blow the leaves off the grass in the backyard. Harvey was pleased with that job and he happily cleared away the withered leaves. Then he noticed that he could blow the ball away too, and he did that for a while until it rolled into the Steward's backyard. Harvey stepped through the hydrangea hedge that separated the two properties and went on pushing the ball. The ball got caught in the window well of the cellar, where the Stewards had their central heating system. Harvey went on blowing air into the cellar. Daniel saw him, took fright, and started shouting: "What are you doing? What are you doing? Go away!"

In his upstairs bedroom, Daniel's older brother Jeff, a fifteen year old, was watching TV and had just heard the anchorman with suspenders and eyeglasses repeat for the umpteenth time: "We're under attack from a cruel and wily enemy, both treacherous and invisible. This enemy will stoop to any method to disseminate his horrifying message of death. He could even use your next door neighbors."

When Jeff heard Daniel shouting, he grabbed his baseball bat, galloped downstairs, ran out into the yard, and saw Harvey blowing dust and leaves into the cellar window. He lunged at him, shouting: "Oh, you think you're going to put my family to sleep and burn down our house, do you? Are you blowing poison into our basement?" and he began hitting the boy hard on his ankles. Harvey burst into tears, his father came running out of the house, tore the baseball bat out of the teenager's hands, and waited to have a serious talk with Mr. Steward.

Tel Aviv beachfront, Monday, November 4, noon

The two men were strolling along the Tel Aviv beachfront, surrounded by young women going to sunbathe and office workers relaxing on their lunch hour. One of the two men was in his early sixties, with a pair of bushy eyebrows, black trousers and short legs, and a white short-sleeved shirt covering his massive torso. The other was in his early forties: tall, sunglasses, khaki trousers and shirt, and a classic black yarmulke on his head, held in place by a black bobby pin. They could easily have been two bank executives, caught between the end of lunch and the return to the office. In fact they were the chief of operations of Mossad and the section chief to whom Uriel Silberzahn reported. They were meeting on the beachfront because the chief of operations, whom many called the Owl, wanted to eliminate any of the sense of bureaucratic formality that would have been inevitable in the office. This was a face-to-face discussion, cards-on-the-table time. But he'd been careful not to give the other man any sense of that. He had pretended to run into him by chance, at the front door of a café where he knew the younger man liked to eat a light lunch.

"It's singular, to say the least," said the Owl, gazing out to sea, "that Silberzahn should have gone to America, come back, and then gone to Beirut, without you knowing a thing about it."

"You know how he works."

"Yes, I do. It's not the first time I've mentioned it to you. What's truly singular, however, is that after Beirut he just vanished into thin air."

"He's good at hiding."

"He's good at hiding *from others*, you mean to say. Not from us. Why on earth can't you find him?"

The man with dark glasses shrugged his shoulders uneasily.

"Uriel knows how we work. He's one of our best spy-catchers. He'll be able to anticipate whatever moves we make. And block them."

"But we know how he works too, don't we? Shouldn't we be able to block his moves as well?"

"Sure we can. Trust me. We'll catch him soon enough."

The shorter man wrinkled his face in annoyance. Then he went on:

"I'd like to be sure that you understand clearly, especially after yesterday's meeting, that the decision whether or not we should make use of the narcotic has to be made here, and in particular by the government. You do understand that Silberzahn *has* to bring the material back to Tel Aviv, don't you?"

"Of course I do."

"Really? Sometimes I'm not so sure." He paused. "By the way, it strikes me that you're in favor of making use of this narcotic."

"Yes. And I'm not alone, as you've seen. It seems like an exceptional weapon."

"Oh, I think it is too. But I think that it should only be used with the greatest possible caution."

"I heard you, yesterday. But... speaking theoretically... I'm not sure how far I'd take this issue of caution."

"What are you trying to say?"

"Well, like we were saying yesterday, what matters are results. You, more than anybody else, have always said that what matters most are results. And in this case, I think it's safe to say that the results could be extraordinary."

The man in dark glasses stopped, spread both arms, and concluded emphatically:

"Well then, let's take a look at these results! I believe that we'd only need one example to change the strategic picture entirely in terms of power relationships. To kick the terrorists back into their lair! To make the Palestinians understand once and for all that we have them by the short hairs, that we can hit them whenever we want! Then we can see what kind of negotiations come out of that!"

"I see," said the Owl, resuming his stroll. "Then, Uriel, for instance..."

"Hold on a second! Say that Uriel goes into action, releases the narcotic, and kills one or two ball-busters in Gaza or Ramallah, the kind of guys we can't hit with missiles..."

"Is that what he wants to do?"

"Well, I certainly don't know that. But that's what you or I would do, isn't it? That why we want the narcotic in the first place."

"I'm not sure if that's exactly what Uriel wants."

"Sure it is. Uriel has always been faithful to the missions he's been assigned. Now, let's imagine that he goes into action. We could finally be rid of people like Batik and a few others. We could cash in that result. And then, even if we stopped there, it would be an excellent result. And we could always just say that Uriel had gone rogue, was acting on his own initiative, then we could dump him and put him on trial..."

"Ah, so that's what you have in mind!"

The older man had stopped and was staring the other man in the eye.

"The Massapequod bomb? Show everyone in the world that we aren't capable of reining in our own men? That they're wildcat operators? Don't you think we'd come out of that with a black eye and a broken arm?"

With his gaze fixed firmly on his interlocutor, the Owl heaved a deep sigh.

"So," he said, "it's true: you are covering for Uriel."

The other man's shoulders sagged, as if he had just realized that this wasn't a chance encounter. He took off his sunglasses, ran a hand over his eyes, and looked out at the sun-dazzling sea.

"No, that's not true."

"Do you know where he is?"

"No, I swear it, we don't know."

He had put his sunglasses back on and stuck both hands into his pocket.

"Still, you're in contact with him."

"No, I'm afraid not. I'm not in contact with him." The Owl noticed that he'd shifted from the first person plural to the first person singular.

"But you know what he intends to do."

"Well, let's just say that he's in contact with us. He got in touch this morning. I would have told you."

"What did he say?"

The man with the sunglasses heaved a deep, prolonged sigh.

"That Operation Morpheus..."

"Operation Morpheus?"

"That's what he's calling it. After the God of Sleep. Of course, a second-class god. I think that he wanted to give it a profane name in order to keep the details secret. If he had chosen a sacred name, he might have given away too much information, especially to us... Anyway, the operation has begun and can no longer be stopped."

The Owl tensed his hands into fists, until the knuckles turned white.

"All right, then," he finally said. "Listen to me carefully. From this moment on, Uriel Silberzahn is no longer an agent returning late from a mission. He's a wanted fugitive. Do you hear me? A wanted fugitive. Which means two things: A) we use all means available to stop and capture wanted fugitives, even the most extreme. If we have to shoot him, we're going to shoot him; B) as a wanted fugitive, Silberzahn is no longer under your jurisdiction. He's my business from now on."

"But..."

"The service order was issued while we were down here on the beach having this conversation. And I," he went on, "have all the elements I need to catch him, whether he likes it or not. So I'd be grateful if you could let him know—how you do it is up to you—that I'm giving him twenty-four hours to get back in the ranks. After that, hunting season is open."

Brickell Key, Miami, FL, Monday, November 4, dawn

Jill looked at Urlacher. Urlacher looked at his watch. It was a few minutes before five in the morning. They had been sitting for the past quarter hour in the parking lot of the elegant gray apartment building in Brickell Key, one of the chic neighborhoods of South Miami. With Urlacher were a dozen or so men and women from the SWAT team, in black jumpsuits with an enormous yellow FBI written on chest and back. She had the FBI logos too, but only on a black jacket that she wore over her tailored suit. Instead of wearing combat boots, she'd kept her high heels. When Urlacher saw that, he'd glared at her in disapproval.

"We're going to be moving fast, you're going to have a hard time keeping up," he'd told her.

"I'm used to running in these," she had told him in a relaxed tone of voice. Urlacher had snorted in disgust, but he had nothing else to say. The operation—as he had said repeatedly on the afternoon of the day before, during the meeting at the central headquarters in Fort Lauderdale—wasn't something he particularly liked, and Jill's clothing was just one more unimportant detail that didn't fit in.

Urlacher gave the signal. Everyone surged into the apartment building. Behind the plate glass window, the doorman stared big-eyed and then shrank behind his desk. They piled up the stairs. Jill took off her shoes and ran up after them, six flights up, until she reached the top floor. In front of apartment 6B, no one seemed to have to stop and catch their breath. They knocked open the door and burst into a large living room, where the furniture was all white and a large picture window offered a view of the ocean. On the table was a two-foot-tall humidor: inside were thirty or so Cuban cigars, mostly giant Cohibas. In front of the enormous plasma-screen television set was a miniature Sicilian cart. On the table by the front door were two Sicilian "coppola" caps: one dark brown and the other beige. Next to them were the keys to an Audi Quattro and a Mini Cooper.

Through the wide-open bedroom door, Jill could see that the officers had already handcuffed the master of the house. He had a powerful physique, a bouncer's shoulders, a bald head, and the eyeglasses of a man who was no longer young. Renato Quagliata, Sicilian by birth, was impeccably dressed in a white T-shirt and boxer shorts. Jill heard a woman's piercing scream. She stuck her head in the door. The girl was completely naked. Pressed against the wall, she was frantically trying to cover herself with a bath towel that was far too small to do the job. She refused to drop the towel so that the agents could handcuff her.

"I'm a respectable citizen," Quagliata was saying. "There was no need to break down the door. I would have opened up if you'd just knocked."

"We didn't want you to have to waste time looking around for the keys," Urlacher replied dryly. His men had started searching the apartment. Quagliata watched them.

"I deal in wines and liquors," he said. "You already know that. I'm not what you think I am." Now the girl had walked into the living room too. She was handcuffed, but they'd found a bathrobe for her to wear.

"Who's she?" Urlacher asked the officer closest to him.

"She says her name is Lola Osorio. She says she's a friend." Urlacher turned away without interest. Jill, on the other hand, looked at her curiously. She would have expected to find a young girl with Quagliatab and, considering his type, probably a very young girl, maybe underage. Lola, on the other hand, couldn't have been much under thirty. And just a minute ago, the parts of her that weren't covered with the towel had astonished Jill. The glistening mass of raven black hair was noteworthy, but there was plenty of cellulite on her hips and thighs. Quagliata could certainly have afforded better, much better. Was he in love with her? That might be Quagliata's weak point. Jill went over to the girl, pretended to trip, and brought her heel down hard on her bare foot. Lola let go with a piercing scream. Everyone turned to look at her for a second, including Quagliata, though his face remained impassive. If the spin cycle of the washing machine had been slightly off kilter, he would have shown greater concern. Obviously, he wasn't in love: he just liked women that looked like her, that was all.

Quagliata turned back to Urlacher and gave him a quizzical look.

"The charge is money laundering," Urlacher finally said. "Under cover of your wine importation business from Sicily, in fact."

"But that's the same charge as last time!" Quagliata shot back. "And you couldn't prove anything then either."

"The last time was the last time."

"So do you have new evidence?"

"You'll see when the time comes."

Urlacher didn't look particularly pleased. He seemed uneasy. He turned toward the picture window to put an end to the conversation.

"I want my lawyer," said Quagliata. He almost looked amused.

"That's your right," Urlacher replied without turning around.

"Just a minute," Jill broke in. She turned to Urlacher. "Can I speak with him for a minute or two?"

Urlacher shrugged his shoulders. Jill took Quagliata by the arm and led him over to a corner. The man looked at her curiously. Obviously, this wasn't the first time he'd had the Bureau in his house, and it wasn't going according to the standard script.

"Money laundering is a pretty serious charge," Jill said.

"My lawyer will get rid of this problem in no time at all," Quagliata replied confidently.

"I wouldn't be so sure of that. This is a very odd time." Jill took a long pause, looking Quagliata in the eye the whole time.

"They're taking their time on everything. Get ready for a long and exhausting wrestling match this go-round."

The man raised his eyebrows, but said nothing.

"So that's why I'd recommend," Jill resumed, "well, this thing with the lawyer...."

"Yes?"

"I'd think twice about calling him."

"Why?"

"Because, possibly, there are things that you might want to say that, you know, it'd be better for no one else to hear. Not even your lawyer."

"What the hell are you talking about?" Quagliata's voice was tense.

"What did you and your friends talk about last night at Masaccio?" Quagliata laughed.

"What do you think we talked about? Women, of course."

"Women from Maine?"

"From Maine? That's a little far away, don't you think?"

"What about Massapequod?"

Quagliata looked at her with bewilderment.

"What the hell do I have to do with Massapequod?"

Jill enunciated her response very clearly.

"Massapequod is what we *really* care about. Do I make myself clear, Quagliata? We're so interested in Massapequod that we don't have time to think about anything else. Anything at all."

A shadow passed over Quagliata's face. Followed by a frank and open burst of laughter.

"I already told you that I'm not what you think. But even if I was, I wouldn't be that high up."

Mineola, Long Island, NY, Monday, November 4, early morning

She had fallen under the blows of Pierre-André's violent sensuality. She could sense his allure, his power, his anguish, and she'd yielded to him, abandoning her body, repeatedly, to the liberating orgasms caused by his force, his imagination, and his ability to take care of her.

Julie was sleeping on the bed, her body partly covered by the sheets, her long mane of red hair spread out on the pillows.

Pierre-André was finally rested. The excess of testosterone had washed away his anguish. His male pride was soothed by the prowess he had shown that afternoon and night.

Now the only thing he could do was wait patiently.

Miami, Florida, FBI field office, Monday, November 4, evening

"It was your idea."

"I thought we had all agreed."

O'Malley adjusted his suspenders and let himself fall back, with a sigh, into the chair behind the desk. He was in Miami to organize the sweeps and roundups and the interrogations that the FBI had decided to launch against the Mafia. Gillespie had decided to call him up on a video conference, and now he was scrutinizing him from behind his eye-glasses, with a worried expression. All you had to do was take one look at his face on the screen, O'Malley mused, to see that trouble was on the way.

"Well, that's true," Gillespie replied, "but you know how these things go."

"No, I'm not sure I do. Why don't you explain it to me?"

"Don't be a troublemaker, Jamie. You know I spend my days defending you."

"So what are we going to do now? Nothing? I don't think I heard anyone suggesting any alternate strategies."

Gillespie grunted, but he said nothing. A shadow passed over his face. Uh oh, O'Malley thought to himself.

"If it would at least help us to nail Salina," Gillespie went on.

"Salina vanished, and you know it. If I were in his shoes, I'd do the same thing."

"Where is he?"

"Probably in Canada. He's got lots of contacts there and it's not far away."

"And we can't bust his balls in Canada."

"No, we can't. We don't have any solid evidence against him."

"Nothing at all?"

"Nothing. We all, including the Canadians, know that he's a Mafia boss, but we wouldn't be able to make a serious case against him in court."

"All we've got in this case is deductions, inferences, and theories."

"That's right. I'd be willing to bet my right hand on these deductions, I'm positive that he had the narcotic and he directed the game, but I don't have a shred of proof."

"No proof about the woman who fell to her death, either."

"No, damn it. That's probably my fault, too, and you know it. On that point, at least, you can kick me in the ass all you like. This Maria was the one who buried the report on the narcotic, she practically told me so. But she never actually named Salina. She wasn't fast enough. He killed her, I have no doubt about it. He had her thrown off the eleventh-story balcony by his henchman, Saro, I have no doubts about that either. But I also have no proof. Officially, her death is listed as a suicide."

"Well, we can't go telling the Canadians why we want Salina."

"Exactly."

Gillespie looked at the ceiling.

"We've stirred up a nice shit storm, with nothing to show for it," he observed.

"What do you mean, nothing to show for it?! What about the letter from the families? We're showing him that the state exists and that it can strike back. Hard, damn it!"

Gillespie waved vaguely with one hand.

"Of course, sure. We're keeping principles in place. But I've got half the Bureau on the warpath."

O'Malley scowled. But Gillespie talked over him.

"All the agents are furious, because they're not doing anything useful, you realize that?"

"We've confiscated a fair amount of drugs..."

"Oh, sure. We've confiscated some drugs, shut down some casinos, saved some girls from a life of prostitution, arrested a nobody or two. But that's not the point. The intelligence operatives tell us that we're just tickling them. All of these operations are leading us nowhere. The Mafiosi are laughing at us, to our faces. We put them in jail in the morning and they're out by noon, free as a bird, happy as a clam, and confident that we can't really touch them on any of these charges. If we were to decide to go ahead and use everything we have on them, whether it's solid or not, just to come down on their heads, we'd be forced to try to nail them down with a bunch of half-baked investigations, full of ifs, ands, and maybes. They'd get out of it in a second, with a smile on their lips. We couldn't even take them to court. We're just destroying years of investigations and hard work, Jamie."

"Who gives a damn, Bob? We have a much bigger problem to solve. The idea wasn't to destroy the Mafia at one fell blow. The idea was to make them see that we don't exactly wet our pants when they threaten us."

"You already said that."

"Well, there's nothing wrong with saying it again. But above all, the idea was to put pressure on them. Which would put someone in the condition to see an advantage to talking with us..."

"That hasn't happened yet."

"There's no guarantee that it will happen, Bob. But above all, the objective of his wave of sweeps, round-ups, searches, and arrests is to put pressure on them, Bob. Pressure. Pound them and hit them. Pound them and hit them, day after day, without letting up. Making life impossible for the Mafioso, the average Mafioso, that is to say. They're used to our periodic offensives. They know how to live with them. They know they'll come to an end. But this one should paralyze them, cut off all their business, paint them into a corner. We want to choke the life out of them."

"But at least if we were concentrating on Salina's business affairs, the agents would understand it better."

"Wrong, Bob. At best, we could leave Salina alone entirely, with his online poker websites and his whores. Because Salina is riding the tiger no matter what, and he's going to go on riding it. There's nothing we can do to scare him. But we can come down hard on the others. The others might decide that it's not worth the cost and the risk, and jump off the tiger's back. These are the cracks in the structure that we're waiting to see."

"So far, we haven't seen any."

"No, you're right, we haven't."

Gillespie drummed his fingers on the desk.

"That's not all, Jamie." I knew it, O'Malley thought to himself, Bob wouldn't have called me into his office just to tell me that the agents aren't happy.

"Someone in Washington is worried that Salina is ready to raise the ante," Gillespie began. "He could raise the stakes with another Massapequod, on a bigger scale. Have you thought about that?"

"I think about it all the time. So? We can't be ostriches, sticking our heads in the sand and waiting for someone to come along and shoot us in the ass."

"Sure, but they have elections in this country, Jamie. And in Washington they're well aware of the fact. America is slipping into chaos: roadblocks, civil unrest, lynch mobs chasing strangers, militia groups out of control. Can you imagine what would happen if there was another Massapequod?"

"Yes. And what we're doing is designed to prevent one."

"I hope so. But there are too many cards that we can't control in this game."

"Do you think that Salina could decide to make the extortion demands public?"

Gillespie hesitated for a moment.

"No," he concluded. "That'd be too risky. In the light of day, that demand wouldn't hold up." He hesitated again. "Though, as I've already said, this is a country where people vote. I don't know how public opinion would react to another Massapequod."

"Bob, are you telling me that they're thinking of negotiating in Washington?"

Gillespie shifted uneasily in his chair.

"How high up, Bob?"

"Not that high up," Gillespie replied. "But it's better for you to know that the idea's starting to circulate."

"But that's absurd. It's crazy. We can't sell the country to the Mafia," O'Malley blurted out.

"I'd have to agree with you," Gillespie replied.

Only you couldn't say for how much longer, O'Malley thought. He went back on the offensive.

"Listen, Bob. You have to track down Matterre-Faquet, so we can figure out where that narcotic might have gotten to. And we have to get our hands on Salina's supply."

"That's right, Jamie. We need to find Matterre-Faquet and get our hands on Salina's stock of the narcotic. But we have to do it immediately. This is an intolerable situation. I mean within days, within hours. Not weeks."

"I get you. Anyway, we go on conducting raids and sweeps, right?"

"Sure," Gillespie agreed gloomily. "As you say, it seems to be the only thing we can do. They like it on TV, if nothing else. We don't have much else to show them.

"But, remember," he added, "what we need is results. Now."

O'Malley watched grimly as the screen went blank. Actually, he was about to get a result, though he didn't know it. Meg was about to bring him one. When he had planned his offensive against the Mafia, it was the last thing he would have expected. But it was a big win all the same.

Soho, New York City, Monday, November 4, evening

When she needed to, Meg could cut quite an attractive figure. If she had had any doubts on the matter, she need only have noticed the glances she collected in the half hour she spent behind the plate glass window of a Starbuck's in Soho, spying on the entrance of a building across the street through the pounding rain. She'd carefully combed her blonde pageboy haircut and put on an impeccable array of makeup, making abundant use of all the resources in her medicine chest. Under her open raincoat, it was possible to glimpse a skirt that she'd always considered a bit too risqué, because the flimsy material clung to her wide hips and her powerful thighs. The blouse, too, was made of a thin silk, with one button too many left undone, to make it clear that she neither wore a bra nor needed one. All for Vinnie Piccata.

Piccata was a pimp. In fact, he ran an entire prostitution ring. At the Bureau they were pretty sure that he ran Salina's entire stable of hookers, in New York City and on Long Island. O'Malley didn't want to confront him openly, for fear of throwing Salina into a high state of alert. But he decided that Piccata might turn out to be useful: he must be close enough to the top to have information about his boss and his movements and, possibly, even about the narcotic. And so, he had decided to assign Meg to the case. She would have to figure out how to get close to him, study him carefully, strike up an acquaintance, and figure out whether it was worth running the risk of squeezing him for information, which could easily get back to Salina.

She hadn't seen anyone come out of the front door, but she was also keeping an eye on the BMW coupe, which she knew was Piccata's car. The car was pulling away from the sidewalk, with a man at the wheel. Maybe the pimp had already been out and about and had just come back to get the car. In any case, she hoped he'd stay out for at least a couple of hours, so she'd have a chance to search the apartment. She buttoned up her raincoat, opened her umbrella, and walked across the street. Just to be safe, she rang Piccata's buzzer, but no one answered. She went in search of the super. The door to the basement was open. She slipped inside. She closed her umbrella, opened her raincoat, tucked in her blouse to make it a little tighter and a little more revealing, and started down the hallway, swaying on her stiletto heels.

She found him a few doors down, moving around the washing machines. A bent old man, more than seventy years old, with a pair of overalls, a baseball hat, and tufts of white hairs protruding from his nostrils. Meg knew that she didn't have the slender physique of a young girl from the country just come to town, with a few addresses of people who could help her in the big city. She was more like a *Playboy* foldout, perfect for playing the part of the girl who'd been around the block more than once, the kind of girl you were likely to find moving in Piccata's circle. She put on a hoarse voice.

"I'm looking for Vinnie."

The man looked her up and down, without a hint of embarrassment.

"If you rang his buzzer and he doesn't answer, that means he's not in," he finally said.

"But I can't wait for him outside, with all this rain. My hair will get flattened to my head."

The man pulled back his lips to reveal his dentures in all their glory.

"You can wait in here."

"As if. The minute I turn around in here, I'm going to get grease all over my skirt. I'll wait for him in his apartment. You've got his door key, don't you?"

The man smiled shrewdly.

"Maybe I do," he said. "But that doesn't mean I can give it to anyone who asks for it."

"Look, Vinnie is expecting me. I've been here before, up in his apartment. I just must be here a little early."

The old man shrugged his shoulders. Meg insisted.

"Come on, give me the key."

"What's in it for me? You know what they say: you scratch my back and I'll scratch yours."

Meg rummaged around in her clutch and pulled out a ten dollar bill. But the old man shook his head.

"No, I don't want your money. If you don't want to wait here or out on the street, you can come up to my place. I'll make you a cup of coffee."

That's not what Meg had expected from that old man. But it could still turn out to be useful. Meg gave him a broad, provocative smile.

"Hey, what kind of idea have you got into your head?"

The man smirked.

"It seems like a fair offer," he said. "Anyway, Vinnie just left and you'll have plenty of time to kill."

Meg flashed the same smile at him, but shook her head.

"Listen, it took me hours this morning to get all pretty to come see Vinnie. You think I'm going to start over or even show up looking like a mess?" She pretended to think it over. "Listen, maybe when I'm done with Vinnie, I'll come down and find you."

The man looked at her hungrily.

"All right," he finally said. "You can just knock on the door by the stairs."

He walked ahead of her toward the elevator. To Meg's relief, he didn't try to grab himself a little sample in advance in the cabin of the elevator. He walked her to the door of Vinnie's apartment, he picked out a key from the bunch in his hand, and he opened the door. Meg quickly slid inside and firmly closed the door in the super's face.

She looked around. The apartment was tastefully decorated. There were plants at the windows, flowers in vases on the tables, and lots of bric-a-brac that suggested an almost feminine touch. Maybe Vinnie lived with a woman: the FBI dossier on the pimp was pretty thin, she thought to herself. One wall, though, was devoted to business. In front of a comfortable armchair was a long table with five computer screens.

Under the table was a battery of electronic equipment, some of which was big enough to suggest a full-fledged server. The screens were turned on. Meg noticed that four of the screens featured websites in which individual girls were self-promoting and entertaining potential customers. As she watched, one of the screens changed its site and featured the home page of another girl. Evidently, a timer switched the computers through all the websites of the girls that Piccata controlled. The fifth monitor, on the other hand, was a gray page with a list of names and a column of numbers beside them. Meg figured out imme-diately that this was a registry of the number of hits each girl was getting: a real-time popularity ranking.

She sat down and started fooling around with the mouse, trying to find Piccata's email. This alone was worth the trip, she thought to herself. The first message in the queue had two heavy video attachments. It was from someone named Kylie. Meg opened it. "Hi, Vinnie," it said.

"Here are the videos we talked about. The first one is me alone. It's 8 minutes 33 seconds, I figured I'd drag it out a little. The second one is 25 minutes 47 seconds, but it's obviously a bunch of different sections, which can be broken up if you want. I made it with a black guy I met in a bar. Well, this guy is incredible. Really. I've never seen anything like his junk. When you see it you won't believe it. You're gonna like this one. We found a very nice position for the video camera. As for the money, you and me're going to have to talk, because he wants money too. So call me." She didn't need to open the videos to know what she was talking about. Obviously, the girls made a little extra money, by producing videos for Salina's porn websites.

She would never be able to read all the email before Piccata got home. She had to find a way to compress the incoming mail and forward it to the Bureau. Vinnie would never even notice. While she was figuring out how to do it, the phone rang. After five rings, the answering machine clicked on. There was a brief greeting from Vinnie and then a shrill doleful little voice: "Vinnie, this is Annie. I'm sorry, please forgive me, but I can't work today either. The doctor says... he says that I need to go to the hospital and do some tests for this pain in my belly. This isn't an excuse, Vinnie, I swear it. I'm really sick. Don't worry, I'll make up for it." Being a pimp must be more or less like running a girl's boarding school, Meg mused. But the answering machine had aroused her curiosity. Before trying to compress the emails, she decided to listen to the other messages. There couldn't have been many since Vinnie went out.

In fact, there were just two messages. The first, from a girl named Chris, informed Vinnie that she would never as long as she lived agree to see that pig from Commack again: he was filthy, he was smelly, he drank too much, and he had certain tastes that, well, she was a serious professional and she didn't want to have anything more to do with him. Vinnie couldn't expect that of her. But the second message left Meg breathless.

"Hello? Vinnie? This is Julie. Everything's fine, don't worry. But there's something a little... odd. The guy who was here last night wants to spend the whole week with me. I mean, he's paying every penny, don't worry about that. If you think it's okay, I might give him a discount.

He's a nice guy, you know, he's my foreign customer, the one who always comes to see me. But this time he's just... strange. It's as if he was hiding out. He doesn't want to go out for dinner or to the bar to get a drink. He doesn't even want to go out to buy champagne. I'm afraid of him. He's never been like this. Do you know who I mean? The Frenchman, the professor. Now he's in the other room, sleeping.

"Don't you think you ought to check and see if he's done something wrong? Maybe there's something about it in the newspapers? He doesn't even want me to watch TV. I took his driver's license. Let me tell you what his name is. It's: M-A-T-T-E-R *beep.*" The answering machine had cut off the message. But Meg had heard enough. She stared at the phone wide-eyed. A professor. A Frenchman. Matterre-Faquet. They'd found him.

Meg started wandering around in the apartment. She had forgotten about the emails. She was looking for a directory or a ledger, in the computers or in some drawer. Who was Julie? Where did she live? How long would it take that bastard Vinnie to get home?

She was lucky. She heard a key turn in the door. Vinnie was home early.

"Well, well, I hear we have visitors," piped a high, unworried voice, as the door swung open.

"And who do we have here?"

Meg was stunned. She'd seen Vinnie's mug shots, dressed in prison garb. She'd noted that he was skinny and small and he had a delicate, symmetrical face. But the man she was looking at now was a completely different Vinnie. She had assumed that pimps were all former hunks and jocks, rough and slightly violent. Vinnie was quite another category. He was wearing skin-tight purple pants, boots with exaggeratedly high heels, a bright flower-print shirt open to the chest, a fur coat, iPod earbuds in his ears, and a flashy pair of white sunglasses. If she wanted any confirmation, she only needed the gaze with which he was methodically studying her. Meg was accustomed to being mentally undressed by the men who looked at her and, sometimes, she didn't even mind it all that much. But this was a chilly gaze, the same look a horse breeder might give a mare he planned to take to his stables to be serviced. Not even the most remote flicker of male interest.

Well, that explained all the bric-a-brac. Vinnie was a homosexual. On the other hand, there's no rule written down anywhere that a pimp has to sample the merchandise he sells to his customers. Well, that was better. He was so effeminate that, if he wasn't armed, he'd be less dangerous.

"FBI, Vinnie," she said, pulling her badge out of her purse.

Vinnie's mouth gaped open, without uttering a sound, as if he were a fish. "What? Wha— what do you mean, FBI?" he finally managed to get out.

"Vinnie, who's Julie?"

"What are you talking about, FBI? What right do you have to come in here? Where's your warrant?"

"Vinnie, don't waste my time. Tell me who Julie is and where she lives. Where does she work?

"Just think about that, the FBI." Vinnie's voice shifted from a querulous whine to something flatter, harder. "Get out of here! Get out of here! You don't have a warrant." He pointed toward the door.

"Julie, Vinnie." Meg walked toward the man.

"No Julie, no Annie, no anybody else! If you want to talk to me, send me a letter and I'll come in with my lawyer."

Now Meg was close to him.

"Julie," she repeated in a hard voice. But she didn't give him time to answer. With all her strength she hit him with a left hook to the liver and, immediately afterward, kneed him in the groin. For a long handful of seconds, Vinnie seemed to be trying to catch his breath, then he collapsed to the floor, twisting and writhing, his hands reaching for Meg. He seemed unable to breathe, then he started moaning:

"Help! Help! You're a monster! A monster!"

Meg gave him a kick to turn him on his side and then planted one of her shoes right in front of his eyes.

"You see this heel, Vinnie? Unless you talk to me about Julie, I'm going to stick where you can't even imagine." She paused. "No, Vinnie." Another pause. "In your ear, Vinnie. If you ever want to hear music again, you'll have to learn to read the singer's lips."

Vinnie shot her a glare of hatred, and continued to clamp his hands between his legs.

"I'll make you pay for this," he hissed. Meg just lifted her foot and carefully set the stiletto heel down on his ear.

"Julie Baxter" Vinnie wheezed. "32-2 Juniper Avenue, in Mineola. On the buzzer it says Beecham. The telephone number is..."

"I don't need the telephone number." Meg picked up her purse and headed for the door. At the threshold she turned around and said:

"You should probably put some ice on that."

FBI field office, Miami, FL, Monday, November 4, night

"Hello, Klara?"

"Hi, Jamie, what can I do for you?" Klara's voice sounded annoyed.

"How are things going?"

"You know perfectly well how things are going."

"Well, yeah, I have head that this Matterre-Faquet is still at large."

"Right, exactly, he's still at large. We came close to getting him once or twice, him and a friend of his, but he slipped through our fingers."

"That French devil!"

"But as far as I can tell, you haven't made a lot of progress either. You've kicked up a hell of a ruckus, though. You're in Miami, right?"

"Yes. And unfortunately you're dead right. Things have kind of run aground. But not entirely. I have some hopes."

"Jamie, if you don't mind, I've got things to do. Maybe we could talk some other time, what do you say?"

"Wait a minute, just wait! I wanted to understand one thing. Didn't you tell me that you guys in the CIA know how to work a case, that you have a reliable trail, and so on?"

"Jamie, I told you that I'm busy."

"Maybe you should have followed the trail of his personal tastes."

"What do you mean?"

"What do people like him say? *Cherchez la femme*, that's right."

"Jamie, we've been tailing and staking out his girlfriend, 24/7."

"What an American you've become! That's just *one* girlfriend. He likes *women*. Not just one woman."

"Jamie, do you know something?"

"And, if necessary, he's probably willing to pay for them, A call girl, for instance."

"Jamie, what do you know?"

"Matterre-Faquet has been employing the services of a call girl on a regular basis. And I'll bet she's cute and sweet."

"Who is she?"

"So cute and sweet that he feels perfectly at home over at her house."

"You mean..."

"That's right, Matterre-Faquet slipped through your fingers and now he's holed up with a call girl."

"Where is he? Goddamn it, Jamie, where is he?"

"Calm down, Klara. I'll give you the information. Julie Baxter, in Mineola. 32-2 Juniper Avenue. The name on the buzzer is Beecham."

He could hear Klara barking orders at someone.

"Don't get exited, sweetheart," he said in a soothing voice. "You can take your time. The situation is completely under control. We've got the whole neighborhood staked out. We work hard for our money, you know that right?"

O'Malley folded his cell phone. That had been a real satisfaction.

Tuesday, November 5

Jesus Ruiz went past the watchman at the door with a wave and headed for the elevator. It was an old office building, in the middle of Sacramento, and the elevator was a ramshackle old cabin that rose up the middle of the stairwell, inside a metal cage. He pushed the button for the top floor. On each floor, he saw people moving on the landings.

Jesus Ruiz rose past the last floor with office doors and reached the top floor, just below the roof. He stepped out of the elevator, atop the last flight of stairs, closed the door behind him, and headed for a small door. He opened it and pushed a button. This was the control room for the HVAC system. Four large aluminum ducts came in from outside, running through a series of machines and then running down to the floors below. He put his toolbag down on the floor, opened it, pulled out a large screwdriver, and went over to a large metal panel on the wall. "Let's see if it's the same problem as last time."

He was fooling around with the screwdriver when he heard the door slam open behind him, hitting the wall violently. A small crowd of angry office-workers filled the doorway. Jesus Ruiz blinked at them, in astonishment. "Hello, people," he said.

"There he is," said the man who had thrown the door open. "Look at him, he was about to put it into the air conditioning system!" shrieked a woman. The crowd poured into the small room. Jesus Ruiz put the screwdriver down on a shelf, but they were already on him. Two men grabbed his arms and held him still, while a third man hit him hard with a straight punch to the stomach. He folded over forward, feeling a sudden urge to throw up. He felt a sharp woman's shoe jab him in the ankle. Another fist hit him, this time near the ear, and almost knocked him unconscious. "He's one of the those bastard Spics," said a woman. "Look what he has in his bag!" he heard a voice say. Then another voice: "Let's throw him off the edge." "Right, let's make this son of a bitch fly straight down to hell!" An enormous black man appeared right in front of him, grabbed him by the straps of his jump-suit, and started dragging him toward the window.

"Stop, you idiots! He's the HVAC maintenance guy!" There was a uniformed watchman standing at the door. Jesus Ruiz fainted.

Mineola, Long Island, NY, Tuesday, November 5, after midnight

They didn't even bother to knock. They'd politely awakened and forcefully persuaded the night watchman at the Hamlet, a cluster of three-story apartment buildings, with lots of small apartments scattered over a large green meadow, to use his passkey to open the door of Julie Baxter's apartment. Once the lock clicked open, they walked into the living room as if they were venturing up against an enemy machine gun nest.

Matterre-Faquet and the woman with red hair were sleeping, naked, at opposite ends of the giant bed. They were immobilized in their sleep by policemen and policewomen armed to the teeth.

All of this was embarrassing, even for a Frenchman. Despite what certain old-school puritans might say, the French don't spend all their time with cops and hookers, as people might think who know nothing about France but what they see in Hollywood movies.

Pierre-André did his best to get dressed. The young woman ran for the bathroom, but she was pulled out by two muscular policemen, who handcuffed her before wrapping her in a blanket and shoving her outside to the cars with the flashing lightbars.

Matterre-Faquet started arguing, and the policemen let him get dressed.

"What do you want with me?"

"You are under arrest for mass murder and criminal arson. Anything you say can and will be used against you in a court of law."

"Then why are you taking away the only witness who could establish my innocence?" Pierre-André was bluffing. "I spent the last three days here with her."

That was almost true but in the specific case, of no real value, since Massapequod had taken place a full week earlier. In fact, his words seemed to bounce off a rubber wall.

Very politely, a policeman asked him:

"So are you saying you'd rather be charged with incitement, exploitation, and patronizing the services of a prostitute? We're going down the stairs. Behave yourself and we won't handcuff you."

"Gentlemen, gentlemen, I don't know what the devil you're talking about. This whole thing strikes me as a gross travesty of justice. I do have the right to call a lawyer."

In this case too, the phrase worked like magic. Everyone stopped and Matterre-Faquet was given back Hancock's cell phone. He punched in a number and told the sleepy lawyer who answered where he was, and most important, that he should contact Konstantinos Papadopoulos, Susan Sheffield, and the officers of the US Navy who had detained him in Connecticut and make sure that they all showed up, next morning, at the police station of Mineola, where the FBI, the CIA, and the Nassau County Police Department had all agreed to meet.

Tuesday, November 5, the waters off An Nazlah (Gaza), sunset

Uriel Silberzahn confidently steered the old, filthy, reeking fishing trawler as it glided through the water. Concealed beneath a tarp stained with oil and fish blood, the silent 500 horsepower Norton engine had been shut off the minute Uriel sighted the lights of Gaza. He had continued chugging north, with the boat powered only by the old engine that was visible on deck. Its wheezing mutter, like that of dozens of fishing trawlers, wouldn't attract any attention. He had come even with Al Nazlah, where the houses along the coast became fewer and farther between and the lights that began to switch on in the lowering sunset were dim and scattered. The old, filthy, reeking fishing trawler made a half turn and came to a drifting halt.

Uriel, his face still marked by the evening in Beirut, looked around. That stretch of sea was deserted. In his binoculars he tried to scan the heaving waves to see if there was anything moving. He saw practically nothing. Only an elegant skiff hired by tourists was pitching and yawing, half a mile away. They must be tourists who did sport fishing while free diving. Through his binoculars he had seen diving fins and harpoon guns, but no airtanks or other equipment for prolonged underwater immersions.

While Uriel was turning to look back toward the land, the skiff drifted to a halt, too. Uriel scrutinized the coast, peered into the windows of the houses, carefully examining the buildings one by one. His gaze lingered on the minaret. He made a mental count of the people. Two of the three young men aboard the skiff wore diving masks and fins, as they let themselves slide into the salt water. All that broke the darkening surface of the sea now was a pair of snorkels. They swam straight to the hull of the old, filthy, reeking fishing trawler. One of them hit the keel. Uriel looked down in surprise, and was shoved into the water by the second diver, who had silently clambered over the far side of the trawler. A white circle of foam emerged on the surface of the water, where Silberzahn and the first diver were engaged in a short, violent struggle.

The fins allowed the diver with whom he was fighting to move faster through the water, but they also slowed down his movements. Uriel took advantage of that fact to knee him hard and viciously in the belly. As soon as he felt the grip of the other man's hands begin to loosen on his arms, he turned slightly in the water and hit his temple with his elbow. The diver slumped. Two quick strokes took Uriel back to the boat. The second diver was easier to polish off than the first. Uriel had no doubts about their mission, or for that matter about their provenance. The second Mossad agent was completely absorbed in his search for the metal bottle full of narcotic, and he had no time to look overboard.

But Uriel knew that old, filthy, reeking fishing trawler better than the two divers did. There was a hatch, barely visible, just below the waterline in the port hull. That was where he had hidden the bottle, in a cork jacket that would ensure it would float, so that he could easily transport it to shore. He pulled open the hatch and grabbed the cork-jacketed metal bottle. Inside the compartment, there was also a boathook. He used it to yank open the hatch that led to the engine compartment. Now the old boat was taking on water.

Silberzahn swam away, stroking vigorously toward the tourists' skiff. He knew the Mossad agent still on board wouldn't follow him because he was frantically trying to find the bottle of narcotic before the boat sank. He surfaced in the lee of the skiff's hull. He knew there had to be a third agent on board. No more than one, because a second agent would have been redundant, and Mossad never did anything superfluous. He called out: "Hey, recruit!" That's the term that Mossad agents used to address the junior member of a team and it made perfect sense that they'd leave the least experienced one behind on the skiff. The young agent should have remembered that they were dealing with another Mossad agent and therefore he should have been cautious and mistrustful. But he hadn't been in service long enough to be sufficiently skeptical: the mission had looked simple and straightforward when they set out. The young man leaned out over the edge of the skiff. What filled his field of vision was the metal narcotic bottle, which Silberzahn was holding straight up out of the water. He reached out both hands to take it. Uriel dropped the bottle, grabbed one of the young agent's hands, and jerked him down into the water. As soon as surfaced to breathe, he hit him over the head with the metal bottle. Luckily for the young man, he had complied with instructions and was wearing his life-jacket. He floated unconscious in the water, as the sun sank below the horizon.

Uriel climbed aboard the skiff just in time to watch the old, filthy, reeking fishing trawler sink under the waves. He noted the spray of the diver swimming as hard as he could away from the boat, to escape the suction as the boat went down; the conscious diver was further weighed down by his comrade, still dazed from Uriel's elbow to his head.

Uriel was satisfied. He had saved his mission. He smiled to himself, started the engine of the skiff, and set his course northward.

The police station in Mineola, Long Island, NY, Tuesday, November 5, late morning

A helicopter and two police squad cars arrived in Mineola. Commander Ralph Randall stepped out of the Navy helicopter, while Susan was let out of the squad car of the Nassau County Police Department by a tall policeman who resembled Denzel Washington. The tall policeman gallantly opened the door and extended his arm. When the door of the Suffolk County squad car was opened, Professor Papadopulos got out and, to Matterre-Faquet's surprise, so did Benjamin Safar.

Dr. Papadopoulos confirmed that he had allowed Matterre-Faquet to make use of his lab refrigerator to store his samples. He further stated that he had seen the samples in the refrigerator as late as the afternoon of Friday, October 25th. But the crucial testimony came from Benjamin Safar. Papadopoulos had told the head of the department why he was going to Mineola and Safar jumped into the police car with him. Safar had an important piece of evidence to contribute; it allowed Matterre-Faquet to solve a mystery to his satisfaction. In fact, Safar explained that an electronic manipulation of the locks had allowed someone to open the doors of the department of plant physiology between the night of Friday the 25th and the morning of Saturday October 26th, more than twenty-four hours before Matterre-Faquet entered the building, on the following Sunday morning.

Next it was Commander Ralph Randall's turn. He testified that he had met Doctor Matterre-Faquet in Connecticut on the morning of Saturday, October 26th and that he had taken him to the Pentagon to discuss a research project of great military importance, which remained top secret. At the end of the morning, a deeply embarrassed Susan Sheffield persuaded a detective to discreetly accept her written statement that, on the night of Friday, October 25th, Matterre-Faquet could not have been at Stony Brook because he had been with her in Connecticut.

Therefore, as the police lieutenant in charge of the investigation pointed out thoughtfully, Doctor Matterre-Faquet had left for Connecticut without the bottles, and it could not have been him who broke into the university facility in order to steal them on Friday night because, in fact, he had been in Connecticut. The CIA, however, decided that this still meant nothing. Klara Siebers, who up till now had done no more than to listen to the series of questions and answers with growing irritation, slowly stood up: "What does all this mean? Nothing! Matterre-Faquet could be the mastermind, and he could have put this whole theft together with the assistance of accomplices.

"And in any case," she went on, "it's not so much October 25th that interests us, as the evening of Monday October 28th. Just where was Matterre-Faquet that night? I seem to understand," she added, addressing Randall, "that he... ahem... broke off contact with the Pentagon."

The officer coughed in embarrassment. He had no intention of recounting the unpleasant incident that had occurred at the service plaza, even if the evening news had amply covered it, and it was no longer a secret from anyone. In any case, he pointed out, the Pentagon had lost track of Doctor Matterre-Faquet on the evening of Saturday, October 26th. "Saturday, October 26th. Exactly," Klara immediately emphasized. "Then, the following morning, Doctor Matterre-Faquet reappeared in Stony Brook. From there, he vanishes. He had all the time he needed to get to Maine by Monday. What were you doing in Maine, Doctor?"

Now it was Matterre-Faquet's to get histrionically to his feet.

"At last a specific date! So you're accusing me of having gone to Maine to burn a village there? Has everyone lost their mind? On the evening of the 28th I was... Well, certainly, I was with Albert Hancock, aboard his boat, the *Sexy Diode*, in the Hamptons..."

Klara looked him dead in the eye.

"The marina log book says that the *Sexy Diode* wasn't tied up at the pier on the night of October 28th."

Klara was bluffing. She hadn't consulted the log book of the marina, but if by some chance the scientist was unable to reconstruct with precision exactly where he had been at any given point over the course of a frantic escape, she would be able to trip him up in a contradiction. And she might even have succeeded. But Matterre-Faquet remembered Annick. Just then, he felt absolutely no embarrassment about that very strange night. He reacted confidently.

"That's false! The boat was most certainly there. And to think that I might have had a hand in the massacre of so many innocent people is an outrage, *Madame*. You may phone Albert Hancock. He's competing in the regattas right now. Send whoever you like to the marina. There are plenty of eyewitnesses who can confirm that we were at the marina club house that night." After a moment, he regained his chilly equipoise and added, running his hand over his head: "Naturally, my hair was long then."

The lieutenant broke in. "Are you able to produce this log book?" he asked Klara. "And therefore to prove that the boat wasn't moored at the pier on the night October 28th?"

Klara snorted in embarrassment. "I'd have to check the registrations to make certain," she admitted. But she recovered promptly. "But one thing is certain: he's not there now. And he hasn't been there since November 1st, that much I know. The regattas began, but Mr. Hancock, despite the fact that the regattas are the official reason he came to Long Island and the fact that he is registered to compete, does not actually appear to be participating in the races.

"We're looking for him, with helicopters among other means, but with the huge number of boats, belonging both to participants in the regattas and simple onlookers, that are present around the Hamptons in this period, we have not yet managed to track him down," she concluded with a gesture of frustration.

But she wasn't done. "Mr. Hancock's disappearance makes him potentially complicit with Doctor Matterre-Faquet," Klara went on. "And the presence or absence of the *Sexy Diode* at the wharf, on the night of Monday, October 28th, does not not prove in any dispositive manner that Doctor Matterre-Faquet, whether in cahoots with Mr. Hancock or otherwise, did not entrust to other accomplices the task of stealing the narcotic, on Friday, October 25th and burning the town of Massapequod, on Monday, October 28th."

The lieutenant was fairly irritated with Klara's bluff about the marina log book. "That doesn't prove that he did it either, does it?" he noted.

"He could have done it." Klara insisted. "He had the opportunity."

"And he could have just as easily not done it," the lieutenant insisted. "Do you have any other evidence tying Doctor Matterre-Faquet to an involvement in the burning of Massapequod?"

Klara shook her head with a grunt.

"Fine. Then we can't do anything until we've had a chance to talk to this Hancock and the staff at the marina."

Pierre-André was not particularly surprised that Albert had chosen to disappear, in order to avoid being questioned and to give Pierre-André more time to escape. Now, however, his testimony would be decisive. Luck was on his side. The hearing had only ended a few minutes earlier when CIA agents contacted Klara to inform her that they had finally tracked down Hancock. His boat was tied up in a small harbor town in Connecticut. When questioned, on instructions from Klara and the lieutenant, by those CIA agents, Albert confirmed that he had given Matterre-Faquet accommodations on his boat and that he had spent the night of October 28th, aboard the boat, moored at the wharf of the Bridgehampton marina. When compared with the statements given by the marina staff, that testimony ruled out any direct and conscious involvement on Matterre-Faquet's part in the fire in Massapequod and therefore made his continued detention pointless, according to the lieutenant.

Klara didn't think there was any point in insisting. She had fought to keep Matterre-Faquet behind bars, not because she considered him to be guilty of what happened at Massapequod, but because it looked like the easiest way to keep an eye on him, make sure he supplied the Pentagon with the necessary information about the narcotic and its specifications, and prevent him from coming into contact with foreign intelligence agencies or even, perhaps, the Mafia. In Washington, in any case, they hadn't seemed quite so worried about it. In fact, they had pointed out to her, as a free man, Matterre-Faquet could give himself away or even become a variable in a larger equation that might help move the investigation along. "You need to tail him like you were his shadow," they had told her.

Two hours later, Pierre-André was given the keys to his Acura, which a policeman had gone to fetch, on instructions from Hancock, from the parking lot of a shopping mall. It was in excellent condition, aside from a few spots of seagull shit on the roof and windshield, evidence of its prolonged stay in the open air not far from the ocean. Matterre-Faquet couldn't believe he'd been let off so easy. Is this why he'd been on the run for days and days, with his heart in his mouth? Actually, he had gotten the impression that the CIA and the FBI hadn't exercised all the pressure on the police that was certainly available to them. As if he were really a secondary concern, and no longer the key element in the tragedy of Massapequod. As if they had more important things to worry about.

To some extent, that impression was confirmed by Klara herself. "For the moment, Doctor," she had said to him, looking at him with her ice-blue eyes, "that's how things stand. We have no evidence that would allow us to jail you. But even if you had nothing at all to do with what happened in Massapequod, you still possess an important secret. We'll be talking to you again. The technicians at the Pentagon are completing a number of tests. Tomorrow they'll come to see you. In the meanwhile, we'd be grateful if you could stick around your house and the university." She went on to clarify that last point: "By grateful, we mean that we're perfectly willing to drag you back home, if you decide to leave. We're going to be putting you under constant surveillance, naturally, effective immediately."

Pierre-André walked outside. Susan ran after him. She'd been waiting for him.

"Would you take me home?"

"I'd be honored to do so," he replied.

And he gave her a smile.

In the waters off Ziqim, Tuesday, November 5, night time

He had fled northward, and by now the skiff had left the Gaza strip behind it, along with the security checkpoints. He was now off the coast of Israel. Uriel stopped the boat. It was obvious that the smugglers had sold him out to Mossad, the minute they had a chance, and had revealed everything he had done so far. That was a risk he had had to take into account from the very beginning, but he'd hoped they would give him a little more time. Now he'd have to delay his plan. But the situation had changed completely. Maybe that plan was too small, pathetic, and insignificant after all. Maybe he needed to think bigger.

A few hours of nighttime navigation with the running lights turned off, and the motor just above idle, had allowed him to give the situation some calm reflection and to draw some conclusions. He had gone to New York and returned home with the idea that the narcotic was a brilliant solution to the problem that had been troubling Mossad for years. You could put a whole building to sleep, or even an entire neighborhood and then, taking your time and operating carefully, proceed to eliminate the terrorist cells that, by normal means, had proven to be out of reach. He had chosen not to go back to Tel Aviv, clutching at the pretext of the mission in Beirut, because he was afraid that the narcotic would be held hostage to the scruples and nitpicking of the highest ranking officers in the intelligence service and the country's politicians, always too timid and fearful to seize the opportunities that Uriel offered to them. Events had proven him right. From what he had gleaned of the discussions in Tel Aviv, it was clear that the narcotic was destined to remain locked away in a refrigerator somewhere, only to be used someday in the uncertain future. Uriel, on the other hand, was determined not to waste time, because he believed that there was no time to be wasted in the mortal combat between Israelis and Palestinians. And so had decided to carry out, on his own, the mission with which he felt Mossad should have entrusted him. There were many who were ready to applaud his actions: in all likelihood, he would become a hero. Or possibly not. Still, what Uriel cared about was the immediate outcome, the elimination of the enemies of his people. None of the rest mattered to him.

But now everything had changed. By attacking him on the fishing trawler, Mossad had made it clear that they no longer considered him a member of the intelligence agency. In fact, they thought of him as an enemy. Most important of all, after the close combat with his own colleagues that he had just experienced, he had shattered any sense of psychological dependency he felt toward Mossad. The fact that he hadn't just killed one or two of his colleagues was due to pure chance. It hadn't been necessary. If it had, he would have felt no remorse. He was no longer an agent of the intelligence agency. He was a free man. He could do what he wanted, without restraint. He could answer a higher calling.

Uriel knew that his colleagues and acquaintances whispered about him behind his back, murmuring that he thought he was some kind of twenty-first-century Joshua. He'd never really minded it: they were right, actually. That's exactly how he saw himself. But now that his mind was clear, he could see that it was no longer enough. The idea of eliminating a couple of terrorist leaders struck him as nothing more than a footnote in the great book of Israel's history. He wasn't Joshua, he had another name. This was a decisive moment: surrounded by enemies who denied their right to exist, the people of Israel needed to put an end to the siege, let their claim to that right ring out loud and clear, crush their enemies once and for all, and make clear the power of their God. "I am the Lord your God!" the Almighty had proclaimed, when He saw the Jews enslaved by Pharaoh. That had been the moment when, with the survival of His people dangling by a thread, the Lord God had intervened, firm and ruthless, to save them.

That moment, Uriel said to himself, had returned.

Of course, when the Assyrians destroyed the Northern Kingdom, the Lord sent Jonas to Nineveh to convert the enemy, but Jonas detested the Assyrians and instead of going to the east he had gone to the west, as far west as possible, to Tarshish, Tartessos, among the Carthaginians of Spain, and he had been swallowed by a huge fish, which took him back to Nineveh. And in fact, the clash with the three agents from the skiff was a latter-day allegory of Jonas's adventure. The Lord had taken pity on Nineveh. But Jonas had refused to be placated, he wanted the destruction of the city, and so he rebelled against the Lord. And in any case, the Lord had taken pity on Nineveh, but had not taken pity on the Egyptians.

At the supreme moment, what counts is to smite the enemy, without hesitation, without scruples, once and for all. The Lord had done so, with determination, and without false pieties, when He unleashed the ten plagues on the people of Egypt. The fact that there was no link between the Egyptians and the Palestinians was of no concern whatsoever to Uriel. But the water transformed into blood, the rain of frogs, the plagues of flies and lice, the pestilence among the live-stock, the plague of boils, the hail, the infestation of locusts, and the plague of darkness, Uriel recalled, had had no effect. To those who pointed out that the Lord had toyed with keeping success just out of reach, because even as He was visiting the plagues upon the people of Egypt he was also hardening the Pharaoh's heart, so that he refused to let the children of Israel go, Uriel would have answered that it took the tenth plague to bend the Pharaoh's will. The tenth plague had shown the falseness of the Egyptians and the truth of the Lord, the tenth plague had made the objections of the Egyptians null and void, affirming the point of view of the Hebrews. Another tenth plague was needed, in order to confirm the rights of Israel in the face of the claims of the Palestinians. This was his divine mission.

The angel of the Lord had passed over the houses of the Egypt, killing the first born of every family. Uriel would do the same. Like an archangel, he would put an entire Palestinian city to sleep—Ramallah, Gaza, Hebron, or Nablus—and then he would go through the houses and cut the throats of the first born of every house. As many as he could, even more than he could. But only the first born, so that the meaning of that sacrifice should be made clear to one and all.

He looked toward land. He must be off Ziqim, he reckoned. He needed to land and seek understanding, solidarity, and aid. He knew just where to look for them.

Between Mineola and Oyster Bay, Tuesday, November 5, afternoon

"Susan, forgive me."

"For what?"

The car was whizzing northward. They had left the Long Island Expressway and were now on State Route 106, heading for Oyster Bay. Pierre-André was unshaven but that's not why he was asking forgiveness.

"Susan, when we saw each other again last week, I have to confess that I couldn't resist the attraction I felt for you..."

Under her layer of melanine, Susan blushed.

"Well, I certainly noticed that..."

"No, what I'm trying to say, Susan... much more than... I mean, you know what I'm trying to say. I felt engaged, of course, it was a pleasure to hear you talk, as a headhunter for Yale, perhaps... but try to understand, I really was a piece of shit, when you called me, the other day, and I practically didn't speak to you on the phone, well, I was terrified."

"Pierre-André..." she said, and she caressed his neck. "Pierre-André, I'm not someone who wets her pants at the slightest fright, but I was worried, and afraid for you. I'm not a fraidy-cat, but I know very well that, on the one hand the military tends to bulldoze the opposition of a civilian, and that on the other hand, if you refuse money from the Army, well Yale might be... a little less interested in your work..."

"I should have figured it out, I should have gone to your house and taken you away with me, instead of taking the car and running away like a thief. But I was worried about the prank I had pulled on the Navy in the service plaza. I was afraid they'd come and get me and confiscate all my lab notebooks. So I took that chance to burn them. But what I am asking you to forgive me for isn't that. It's what happened today."

"Today?"

"Of course, Susan, you came with the police to provide testimony and get me out of a terrible mess. And you did it because..." and then he blushed.

"Because I like you? Of course! And also because I don't like the way the military uses science."

"You came to help me, and you found me in the arms of a woman that... well, certainly not a woman of your class, Susan...."

Susan decided that not only was he an incredible male chauvinistic pig, he was also an adorable male chauvinistic pig. She laid her index finger across his lips, as if to shush him up, then she brought her lips close to his right cheek and licked his ear gently with her tongue.

He felt a shiver run down his spinal cord. The two CIA men following only a short distance behind them in a black Ford Explorer noticed, to their astonishment, that the driver of the Acura seemed to jerk out of his lane and almost lose control of his vehicle. An adroit straightening of the wheel put the car back into the center of the lane. Pierre-André felt a cold sweat beading up on his brow, but deep down he felt reassured, and the last few miles to Oyster Bay slid by uneventfully. Susan and Pierre-André played a little driving game, trying to guess what the Navy and FBI's next moves would be... it didn't require a lot of imagination to predict what the CIA would do, since two men from the CIA were actually shadowing them... but they didn't have all the necessary information and they pretty much came up with foolish nonsense. Pierre-André took care not to mention the French Direction Générale de la Securité Extérieure and especially its representative, Annick Delaporte. When they reached Oyster Bay, Susan suggested they have a cup of tea. Pierre-André asked if he could use her computer to take a look at all the email he'd missed.

While she got busy in the kitchen, he took off his fatigue jacket and his combat boots, threw away the black watch cap, put his running shoes back on and got comfortable in front of the computer. Parked out on the street, the two men from the CIA were watching Susan's house and dedicating themselves to peaceful and monotonous activities, such as cleaning the seagull droppings off their windshield. They had already taken care of the most important thing, fastening a GPS chip beneath the chassis of Matterre-Faquet's Acura. In the meanwhile, the scientist had logged into his server and he had opened his email. First thing, he double clicked on an email from the Center for Toxicology in Palo Alto, California.

"Dear Dr. Matterre-Faquet, we have finished with our experiments. Our executive summary is attached. You will receive the hard copy of the complete report via FedEx. For any other information, please contact us by phone, and be sure to have your password available."

He opened the executive summary and felt as if a hara kiri sword had just pierced his heart.

"Sample PAMF 36-4 is not cytotoxic at any of the concentrations utilized. It is cataleptic in rats at femtomolar concentrations and greater. The lethal dose when administered orally to rodents is superior to 10 g/kg. It is mutagenic in the Ames test at concentrations above 10 *parts-per-million* and is teratogenic in mice at concentrations below 1 *part-per-billion*." Matterre-Faquet's face went pale. That meant that if a pregnant mouse were to drink just a few drops of that material diluted at a ratio of one microgram per liter, when she gave birth to her litter of baby mice, they'd have three legs instead of four, or else spina bifida, or they'd be born blind, or without ears, or with their liver on the left side, or with some other monstrous deformity. In other words, his molecule was teratogenic.

With a sob he closed the email and grabbed Susan's phone.

Susan was relaxed and the tea was ready.

Pierre-André was as pale as Banquo's ghost and as uneasy as Macbeth.

He looked at her, as if he was in a trance, and asked her: "Can I make a phone call?"

He muttered into the phone: "Listen, excuse me, yes, can you do me a favor? Could you come to Stony Brook, outside my laboratory, in forty-five minutes? Thanks, you're a life saver, okay, bye." And then:

"Susan, I have to run. I'll call you tonight."

Susan didn't have time to emerge from her dream state and return to reality by the time the Acura had already torn out of there, heading east, with the roar of the engine and the screeching of tires.

Without turning a hair, the two men from the CIA spit out their chewing gum, finished drinking their coffee, and started after him in their black Ford Explorer. They wanted to let Matterre-Faquet believe that he had shaken them off his tail, while they were actually following him with extreme precision on their onboard computer screen.

FBI field office, Miami, FL, Tuesday, November 5, afternoon

The phone on his desk began ringing.

It was Gillespie. Since they'd caught Matterre-Faquet, the pressure from the highest levels of the FBI had relaxed somewhat. But he was never happy to talk with Gillespie.

"Make sure you're sitting down, Jamie. I've got something for you."

"Nobody told me that my request for a temporary assistant had been approved."

"Don't make jokes, it's really not appropriate. I got a call from our Palo Alto office."

"What does Palo Alto have to do with anything?"

"The Pentagon has discovered that Matterre-Faquet had some doubts about how harmless the narcotic extract was and contacted a laboratory in Palo Alto. They told our people in California about it and they obtained a warrant from a judge and then went to the laboratory. The results were there, they had already sent them to Matterre-Faquet as well. Well, the laboratory says that the extract is teratogenic."

"Teratogenic? What's that mean?"

"That it can cause problems with pregnancies. The fetus will develop badly and deformed babies are born."

"What do you mean?"

"No one survived at Massapequod, but if a pregnant woman had survived, she would certainly have given birth to a monstrously deformed child."

"Oh, my God. This is no bomb. This is the ultimate weapon."

"Exactly. If Salina still has two drops of the stuff and he finds this out, he's going to ramp up the extortion, Jamie. You can understand that. We can't let him use it again."

Stony Brook, Long Island, NY, Tuesday, November 5, afternoon

As he was driving toward Stony Brook, Pierre-André was torn by a thousand jumbled thoughts.

"Teratogenic! Teratogenic! Of all the problems imaginable, this was the worst. A monstrous extract, in the hands of bandits and the military. He had to destroy it, he had to find some way to destroy it, sure, but damn it, he'd made ten gallons, there was forty liters of the stuff, it would take days and days, with the equipment we have at Stony Brook, to destroy it without causing more problems, and the way things were going lately… better not even think about that solution! If I leave it where it is, it wouldn't be safe. The military might decide to come back and go over the entire building with a fine-tooth comb. Then they'd have it. They wouldn't give a damn that it was teratogenic. Look what they did with napalm and Agent Orange in Vietnam." But that wasn't the only thought that was spinning around in his head. "I put two years of blood, sweat, and tears into extracting that forty liters of material. And who knew? Maybe with a minor chemical modification, a methylation, an alkylation, a dehydrogenation, or with an enzyme, a deaminase, or a kinase, it might be possible to remove its teratogenic traits and leave it the same cataleptic and narcotizing properties. Who could say? It wouldn't be the first time that a substance lost its negative connotation while preserving its positive pharmacological properties! Look at aspirin! Or methanol as opposed to ethanol! Add an extra methyl and you're good to go!"

Pierre-André was, by his very nature, a man accustomed to making rapid and definitive decisions. This time, though, torn between his anxiety about ensuring a future for his most important scientific discovery and the fear of its possible use by the military, he understood that the best thing would be to gain a little extra time and make the final decision later. He met his friend the park ranger in the parking lot behind the laboratory. He got into his jeep and told him that they would have to hurry now.

Watched by a refrigerator of a man wearing a white-and-blue checked tie at the wheel of a beat-up old car concealed behind the shrubbery that surrounds the parking lot for university maintenance trucks, Pierre-André and the park ranger hurried into the cellar of the hangar of the Stony Brook biology laboratories and loaded the four drums onto the jeep that was property of Caleb Smith State Park. Then the Acura and the jeep headed west, in a frantic attempt to win their race against the setting sun.

Parking lot of the Hicksville train station, Tuesday, November 5, sunset

Curled up in a rental car, a young woman with a black pageboy haircut, wearing a pair of ass-hugging skinny jeans, her bosom nicely filling her sweater, was moving her beestung lips rapidly in front of a computer, as if she needed to help her words crowd into the microphone above the screen to get to their destination. The bits that she was sending via Skype, connected to an ordinary wi-fi, went to a phone number, which retransmitted them to another phone number, and so on, as many as were necessary to elude any unwanted eavesdroppers or phone tappers. The destination was far away: Paris, France, and even though her interlocutor wasn't deaf, he certainly refused to understand.

The woman looked around in concern. She was alone in that dark empty parking lot. She was used to bad situations and she was certainly not given to unreasonable fears, but she also knew how to evaluate risks. At that time of night, there were groups of vigilantes roaming the empty streets everywhere, ready to pounce on anyone who might arouse suspicions of any kind. And a woman, in an empty parking lot, talking via Skype and, moreover, now that 9-11 had put Paris into the category of treacherous allies, in French, was certainly a suspicious individual. Morover, with those puritans, she couldn't even count on the factor of surprise and a naughty invitation or two.

"In other words," Annick was saying loudly and clearly into the computer, "I told you that Matterre-Faquet is as stubborn as a mule from northern Corsica... no, he absolutely does not want to come home... well, yes, I did exactly what you told me to do, *mon Général*... if we can't give him glory, then money is the last ditch effort.....*oui, mon Général*, I tried, *mon Général*, ...no, his heart and his... how to put this... his testosterone, are entirely devoted to a...black woman."

Annick stopped for a moment to listen. "Well, I can't help it if this story with the black woman disappoints you. Tell your *Docteur* all about it."

"What? A sample? But..."

Annick listened again, this time a little longer. In the end, she shook her pageboy affirmatively: "*Oui, mon Général.*" She closed the phone and exited the parking lot with a sigh of relief, and headed for her hotel in Uniondale.

Between Smithtown and Plainview, Long Island, NY, Tuesday, November 5, evening

After covering the hole in which he had buried the four metal drums containing the ten gallons of cataleptic and teratogenic extract with plenty of loose soil, mulch, and dried leaves, a man with a shaven head drove the government issue jeep of Caleb Smith Park to the entrance of the park and left it there, in its reserved parking place.

The sun had set, the chilly autumn breeze was blowing, toying with the multicolored leaves in the bushes and at the foot of the trees. Sunset was creating magic reflections on the water of Willow Pond. In complete silence, a white-tailed stag waded across the stream. The man with the shaven head opened the door of an Acura with a manual transmission, got in behind the wheel, started the engine, and headed for the Jericho Turnpike.

As always when he was tense or uneasy, Pierre-André was talking to himself aloud.

"God damn it to hell, I've shaken those guys from the CIA off my tail, but I still have the impression that someone's following me."

He was always very careful when he pulled out of the parking lot at Caleb Smith State Park, because on that stretch of the Jericho Turnpike no one obeys the speed limits. And yet, out of the corner of his eye, he had noticed something move behind him in the parking lot.

"If someone's following me now, that same someone must have followed me earlier. So that someone knows where I buried the perfume. And if this someone is still following me even now, it's not because they want to play me a madrigal with mandolin accompaniment. It's because they want to keep me from digging up what I buried... They want to get me. But since I shook the CIA off my tail, who the hell is this?"

In his rearview mirror, he saw the running lights of a car leaving the park and turning onto the turnpike.

"Well, let's find out what happens if, instead of heading home, I give this guy a wild ride," and he turned left onto Old Willets Path. The car followed Old Willets Path, and managed to slip through the backup that always develops when the traffic light turns red there. Another car, a black Ford Explorer, ran the red light and turned into Old Willets Path.

At the intersection with the Veterans Highway, Pierre-André lurched to the right, and in his rear view mirror he saw that the car was following him.

"Now I'll try riding along at exactly 55 mph, let's see what happens," and as he did, he got in the left lane, blocking the way of the maniacs zipping along at 75 mph on the four-lane highway. The suspicious car followed him at the same speed.

"Well?" Matterre-Faquet asked himself questions and answered them himself.

"I'm acting like somebody who's just been given a hefty fine for speeding and doesn't want to find a state trooper in his rear view mirror, and maybe that guy really did just get a ticket..."

But he couldn't bring himself to believe the lie he had just told himself.

He needed to get over his doubts. He veered to the left onto the Northern Parkway, heading for New York. He talked to himself and to the driver of the car that was following him.

"Okay, okay, but in order to take you where you want to go, let's see if I can trick you into a complete ergonomic fuck-up," and he left the Northern Parkway at the intersection with the Sagtikos Parkway, taking the exit ramp as if he meant to head south but then heading up the next on-ramp and returning to the Northern Parkway, heading east. The other car kept following him.

"Oh, now I understand! All right, let's have a little fun!"

This was something that he'd always dreamed of doing, when he was a teenager watching Hollywood movies and even when he was a post-doc in California: driving like a madman on American highways, skidding through on-ramps and exit ramps, tires screeching, swerving out of control, and now he was happy to have a stick shift, so had perfect control of the Acura's performance. But it turned out to be no fun at all.

He took the next ramp, tires screeching, and wound up heading north on the Sunken Meadow Parkway, but then he took the next off-ramp. Darkness kept him from seeing the blue smoke that his tires released into the air from the brutal friction against the asphalt, but the smell of burnt rubber filled his nostrils. Again, he took the next on-ramp, with a roar. In his rear view mirror he could see the headlights of his pursuer. In the rear view mirror he could also see the four headlights of a slightly clumsy SUV, which could barely make it through the line of the curve, up on two wheels for several seconds until it returned to earth. But Matterre-Faquet had his eyes glued to the headlights of the mysterious sedan. He took the next ramp and found himself heading south on the Sagtikos Parkway.

Seized by panic, Matterre-Faquet had no hair left to stand up on the top of his head, but he could feel the *arrector pili* muscles going into action all over his body, raising what hackles he possessed. He could also feel his sweat glands kicking into action, and he smelled the rank scent of his fear. But his brain was still working clearly.

"Who the fuck could that be? It's not the Pentagon and it's not the FBI. However poor their manners, they weren't threatening and they didn't shoot without asking questions first. Annick had mentioned Mossad and the Mafia. What if this really was the Mafia? And what if I, idiot that I am, actually arranged to shake off my guardian angels from the CIA... But why would the Mafia want to get me? Do they want to force me to make more narcotic for them? Damn: I tell the military I won't do it and the next thing I know the Mafia is forcing me to make it for them?"

The night was becoming darker and darker. He was driving at a speed that was just under what would be considered a crawl in Europe, but that was already well over the acceptable limits in the state of New York, and yet there wasn't a sheriff or a policeman in sight willing to stop him and liberate him from that anguish.

He zigzagged to get onto the Southern Parkway without being trapped on the exit ramp that led over to the Robert Moses Causeway.

With his eyes glued to his rear view mirror, he saw the mysterious sedan skid to the left, and behind it he saw some very bright headlamps swerving around. He was heading west at ridiculous speeds, taking advantage of the fact that, at that time of night, most traffic was heading east and there were no obstacles to his headlong flight.

Fifty yards behind him, the headlights of the mysterious sedan stubbornly stuck to their route.

For ten minutes or so, he felt as if he was driving underwater and holding his breath. Then he resumed his soliloquy.

"All right, now, take the exit, that's right, this one here, now take Route 135 north, okay, that's it, and now turn off your lights, now switch them back on, now drop the hammer, squeeze every cubic inch of power out of this car, as if the devil were biting your hindquarters."

With a roar, the Acura accelerated in no time to 80 mph, and in his rear view mirror he saw the headlights of his pursuer turning onto Route 135 and draw menacingly closer, while other cars zigzagged in the wake of the mysterious sedan.

"Okay, now pass that truck, get back on the right and turn off your headlights, and if the truck gets impatient... sure enough, it's impatient, goddamn it, get back in the left lane and stay there, now turn on your lights again, good boy..."

The mysterious car behind him was still accelerating, it passed the truck on its right, and suddenly blinking colored lights and a grim piercing howl told the world that a cop car had been lurking in ambush on Route 135 and had noticed a vehicle speeding. Now the police car was right behind the license plate of the mysterious sedan which by now was traveling at more than 85 mph.

"Yeah!" Pierre-André exulted.

"The dutiful policeman on Route 135!!"

Snickering, he said, "The cops always hide there! Now he has a cop car glued to his ass, with the siren on and the lights flashing, hahaha, I can go back to driving at a normal speed."

But now a flash of light and the pop of a champagne cork came from the black sedan. The truck began drifting to one side. Something bad was happening, more flashes of light, more champagne-cork pops. They were shooting at him. But if they were shooting, now he was certain that they couldn't be from the Pentagon of the FBI. He veered as far to the right as possible. Now the policeman was shooting back. Behind him were the four headlights of a black SUV, clearly veering out of control, unbalanced by the high speeds. The minivan behind the Acura fishtailed to the left, smashed against the guard rail in a hail of sparks, and bounced back into the center lane. Now the Acura was starting to drift to the left, as if the front left tire was going flat, and then it suddenly whipped around back-to-front, now heading on a collision course with the minivan. But the black SUV—to be specific, a black Ford Explorer—lost control as it tried desperately to brake, hit the minivan, and began spinning furiously as if it has lost its mind.

The police car rammed the mysterious black sedan, twisting it brutally and forcing the rear wheels up off the pavement. The cop knew how to drive, that much was clear. He accelerated, pushing the sedan a little harder, and then jammed on his brakes: his car slid to a halt in a light-blue cloud of foul-smelling burnt rubber, while the dark sedan went into a series of uncontrolled spins on the Plainview exit ramp, weaving and lurching like a drunken cockroach, sliding across asphalt and grass and finally hitting the barrier until it came to a halt, blocking the Plainview exit.

One door opened and a man slithered out, running straight for the woods, with his blue-and-white checked tie flapping in the wind. The state trooper shouted words that sounded something like: "Police, freeze!" but the thug was too fast on his feet and he vanished rapidly into the night.

The state trooper barked a few words into his radio and then turned around to see the gathering disaster on Route 135 North.

The minivan flipped over onto its right side. The truck driver's head hit the right hand window, the left hand door swung open, and the windshield exploded into a thousand pieces of glass.

Piere-André swerved and jammed down the accelerator to get back onto the road heading north, but his front left tire was already in shredded tatters and the bare metal rim glittered on the asphalt without any intention of cooperating with that attempt. Beads of clammy sweat dripped down his forehead. Pierre-André saw that the minivan had hit something. Actually, it had been hit by the black Ford Explorer that was spinning like a top. The minivanveered several degrees to one side, missed the Acura by inches, and slammed into the guard rail three hundred feet further on: a tire snapped off, bounced into the middle of the highway, and crashed into the Ford Explorer's windshield, shattering it and lodging with determination in the cockpit. Paralyzed in his seat, Pierre-André could do nothing more than watch, in slow motion, as his car span around while the guard rail drew menacingly closer, the impact of his left headlight against the metal of the guard rail, the hood crumpling and folding, the bumper breaking away, the air bag filling rapidly, the headlights going out, the impact of the left side of the vehicle against the guard rail, the way his skull slammed violently against the driver side door jamb, the way his left shoulder hit something terribly hard, the sound of dry wood snapping, the way the car skidded the length of the guard rail, the horrible pain in his collarbone, the warm liquid running down the side of his face, the sudden silence, the total black darkness that covered the scene.

Even though he was wearing a safety belt and there was an air bag, Pierre-André had the painful sensation that he had broken something. He touched his left cheek with his right hand, spat out a few curse words, and told himself that he needed to wait for someone to come help him.

In just a few minutes, four ambulances, two fire trucks, four tow trucks, and eight squad cars were in Plainview, to assist the injured, to direct traffic around the scene of the accidents, to clear away the wreckage of the minivan, the Acura, the mysterious sedan, and the Ford Explorer. The injured were taken, one by one, to the hospital in Plainview, and admitted separately.

Miami, FL, Ocean Drive, Tuesday, November 5, evening

O'Malley was massaging his numb, aching knees. For the third night in a row, he was squatting down behind the low wall around the church, keeping an eye on the entrance of Masaccio, a hundred yards or so away. The restaurant was one of Miami's most famous eating places, on the ground floor of a luxury shopping mall, with shops featuring the most exclusive brand names, Neiman Marcus, Brooks Brothers, jewelers like Cartier, De Beers, Van Cleef & Arpels, right on Ocean Drive, across from the Sheraton, the Westin, and the other big-chain hotels. The first night that he and his men raided the place, there had been a long line of people waiting for tables. The line snaked out the front door. This evening, O'Malley noticed with grim satisfaction, there was no one there: the place must be half empty.

He gave the signal and, with his men, left the church enclosure through the main gate and headed across the street to the restaurant. It was an absolutely routine operation. He had spent his days organizing interventions designed to destabilize the world of organized crime throughout the Miami area and then, at night, he would come here to Masaccio and implement the stupidest intervention of them all. He knew that it was also the most spectacular, however. Masaccio was not just any restaurant. It had taken the Mafia and made it its brand name, its chief marketing tool, its top resource in terms of publicity. O'Malley knew that, from time to time, meetings were held there but, primarily, it was a place for the big crime bosses to gather and show off, to see and be seen. People were attracted to the restaurant as an opportunity to rub shoulders with what they assumed were dangerous criminals. For the underworld, Masaccio was a glittering runway on which they could parade like lethal peacocks, in front of an appreciative audience. And O'Malley was all too eager to put himself right in the middle of all that.

He walked in and looked around. Above the heavy Venetian red curtains covering the walls hung posters for *The Godfather* and *The Sopranos*, but in front of them, mostly, there were empty tables. O'Malley smiled with satisfaction. The proprietor, Steve Busacca, was sitting at a table near a column. When he saw O'Malley and his little black-jumpsuit brigade, he stood up with an exasperated expression on his face and drove his fist into the column. O'Malley walked over. "Quiet as a grave-yard around here, isn't it?" he said.

"What do you guys want now?" Busacca hissed. "You were in here yesterday and the day before that, and you left empty-handed, didn't you?"

"We're pretty sure we just didn't look hard enough. Or maybe we didn't look at the right time," O'Malley replied seraphically. He told his men to start searching the place and taking the names of everyone present. Busacca turned angrily on his heel and walked over to the bar, where he poured himself a whiskey. O'Malley caught up with him.

"I told my people not to take any orders from you guys," Busacca explained brusquely.

"That's very kind of you, but I don't want anything," O'Malley replied.

Busacca drained his whiskey.

"I had three wedding receptions and two funerals scheduled for next week," he said, after a brief pause. "All of them canceled. And no new reservations."

O'Malley rummaged around in his jumpsuit and pulled out a cigarette.

"This is a public facility. You can't smoke in here," said Busacca. O'Malley calmly went ahead and lit his cigarette, taking a deep drag and slowly exhaling the smoke toward the ceiling.

"I know that," he said. "You might get fined for this, you know. Or else you could try calling the cops yourself, if you have any friends over there." Busacca glared at him angrily.

O'Malley took another drag on his cigarette.

"So, how's business? Not so good recently?"

"You trying to make me shut down?"

"You're the owner, that's up to you," said O'Malley. "Anyway," he went on, "we like you, Steve. If you do start back up, we'll be there on opening day."

"What are you up to, O'Malley? Why are you busting my balls?"

"That's an easy one, Steve. You guys are busting our balls. A lot. So, in return, we're going to bust yours. I thought you understood that kind of thing."

The two men looked each other in the eye for a long time. Busacca—O'Malley knew—was nobody's fool. But he said nothing. In the end, O'Malley turned and headed for the door.

"See you soon, Steve," he waved as he left.

A hotel room, Uniondale, Long Island, NY, Tuesday, November 5, evening

Stretched out on the bed in her hotel room, wrapped in a white terrycloth bath towel, and reinvigorated by a steaming hot shower and a sip of cognac from the minibar, she had watched the movements of the red dot and the blue dot on the screen of her computer, which was logged on to the mainframe of the Direction Générale de la Securité Extérieure. The red dot gave the location of the rear bumper of Matterre-Faquet's Acura, while the blue dot marked the position of the same person's right shoe. Up to a certain point, they had moved in tandem, sailing along together at insane speeds down the highways and turnpikes of Long Island. Then they'd come to a sudden halt somewhere around Plainview, remained there for a solid fifteen to twenty minutes, whereupon the blue dot had moved less than two miles, and stopped there definitively, while the red dot moved north at an exasperatingly slow rate.

The woman pursed her fleshy lips in a satisfied smirk. The GPS chips that she had planted the night of their first meeting aboard Hancock's yacht had proved useful. Now she just needed to figure out where Matterre-Faquet was hiding out, get dressed, and go have a chat with him.

Plainview Hospital, Long Island, NY, Floor B, Room 29, Tuesday, November 5, before midnight

Pierre-André Matterre-Faquet had been transported to a hospital less than two miles from the site of the accident. The hospital of Plainview was well equipped and efficient, and by now Pierre-André was wrapped in a plaster cast that protected his chest and shoulders. His cranium was covered with a turban of sterile gauze bandages to protect the wound and the many stitches that the doctors had inflicted upon him. He was breathing through an oxygen mask, and the rich mixture left him dizzy, instilling a sense of euphoria that alternated with moments of extreme fatique.

A car driven by a young woman with a black pageboy haircut, wearing a pair of ass-hugging skinny jeans, her bosom nicely filling her sweater, parked in the appropriate space in front of the hospital doors, around midnight.

The young woman was surprised, accustomed as she was to the disorganized disorder that was inherent in the logistics of major Parisian hospitals. She was even more surprised to discover that there were no restrictions on visiting hours. As for her, the nurse whom she asked for directions to the the room in which Dr. Pierre-André Matterre-Faquet was resting, stared at her tits and her mouth, and felt a surge of intense jealousy for the man whom the girl was coming to visit. She told herself that if all French women looked like this one, she needed to take a trip to Paris in the near future.

Because of the shock, the oxygen, and the sedatives, Pierre-André was not capable of thinking as clearly as he would have liked. The thought that kept surfacing obsessively in his mind was that there were four drums of a preparation that could kill and had in fact killed more than a hundred people, an extract that could cause devastating birth defects, and that the people who had followed him could get their hands on it at any time. Now he understood that it had been his ill-considered pride as a scientist that had led him to protect the narcotic at all costs. He should have been working tirelessly to destroy it. Or at least to steel himself to the task and hand it over to the authorities, even if he found the idea revolting. Better for it to be in the hands of the Pentagon or the CIA than to have it fall to the people who were following him. Certainly, the driver of the machine that had crashed in front of him was not on the payroll of the US government.

He opened his eyes and saw Annick. He thought: the French! So puffed up, arrogant, and incompetent that in all likelihood, unlike the Americans, they might simply sit on him, gloating. He clutched at that possibility.

Annick didn't even need to speak. "Go to Caleb Smith State Park," Matterre-Faquet mumbled, "take the north entrance, the one on Gardiner Road. Head south, along the paved lane. When you reach the third fire hydrant, turn left onto the gravel lane through the woods. You'll reach a clearing, with benches, chairs, and a pole with arrows listing the distances to various cities... There's a mound of dirt, leaves, and mulch. Dig there and you'll find four metal drums. They contain the narcotic. You need to destroy it, is that clear? Destroy it. Get Papadopoulos to help you, or anyone else, you can figure that out yourself. Even the Pentagon, if necessary. But it has to be destroyed. Understood? Destroyed. It cannot be used. It's... teratogenic. Even you guys can't use it."

Exhausted by the effort of speaking, Matterre-Faquet shut his eyes and lost consciousness.

Wednesday, November 6

Nate Chambers had slipped into the alley between two apartment buildings, to take a look at the garbage. It's unbelievable the things that white folk are capable of throwing out, even the ones in a neighborhood like that one. Small screen TVs, perfectly good computers... a couple of weeks ago he had found a very nice fur coat, which he had sold to Lev, the Jew who never asked question. He'd made a nice chunk of change on it. This sure beat panhandling.

As he made his way through the dim light of the alleyway, Nate bumped into a trash can, knocking the lid to the cement pavement with a tremendous clatter. Overhead, a light flicked on and a window was yanked open. "Hey, what the hell are you doing down there?" called a voice. Another window opened: "There's someone in the alley!" shouted another voice. The alarm spread from window to window. Nate decided that it was time to beat it.

But it was already too late. The mouth of the alley was blocked off by an angry crowd of boys and men. "We've got you now, you son of a bitch." Nate didn't have time to explain. They were on him immediately and they knocked him to the pavement. "See if he's carrying anything," called an authoritative voice. They searched his pockets. They found a half-empty flask. He tried to explain that it was just a bottle of gin, which he'd bought with the last few dollars from the fur coat, but he was too scared to articulate the words.

"Now we'll give you a taste of the same medicine you wanted to give us," said the man who had the flask in his hand. He waved to the others, who pinned Nate to the cement by his arms and legs. The man opened the flask and poured the contents onto his chest and belly. "What are you trying to do, put him to sleep?" a voice

asked. *"I have another idea,"* said the first man, pulling out his lighter. Nate watched him wide-eyed. *"But that's a sedative." "Well, we'll see."*

He held the lighter up to the gin-drenched shirt, leaping back, along with the four men who had been holding Nate's arms and legs, when a tall bluish flame rose from Nate's chest. The screams echoed through the night.

Plainview Hospital, Long Island, NY, Floor B, Room 29, Wednesday, November 6, just after midnight

They had extracted twenty or so shards of glass from his cheeks and forehead. He'd been given thirty stitches on the forearm he had thrown up to ward off the wheel of the minivan when it came crashing through his windshield: the hub of the shattered semi axle had ripped open his flesh all the way down to the ulna, but it hadn't broken any bones. Now he was bandaged all over, his arm hung helplessly from a sling around his neck, and he was dazed by a heavy dose of anesthetic. The doctor had forbidden him to get up and had ordered him held over-night in the hospital for care and observation. He had looked around for the laptop that was perched on his knees to follow the movements of Matterre-Faquet down to the last inch. But the computer must have flown out the side window that had broken when the Ford Explorer hit the guard rail, after the impact with the flying minivan wheel and when it flipped over in a shower of noise and sparks. The nurse told him that his colleague was still in the O.R.: when the car hit the guard rail, the heavy tire that had shattered the windshield and hurtled into the cockpit had kept the air bag from deploying. The driver's chest had been smashed violently against the steering wheel, and half a dozen ribs had broken on impact. They were removing a fair number of bone frag-ments from his ribs before wrapping his colleague in a rigid body cast that would allow him to breathe. The bandaged man with his arm hanging from his neck asked the nurse to punch in a number on his cell phone.

"Klara?" mumbled the man. "Sorry, I know it's late, we're both at the hospital in Plainview...no, no one's sick... it was a mess, a car opened fire on Matterre-Faquet.... there was a car crash...one dead.... no... Matterre-Faquet? No, I have no idea where he is...our computer disappeared or was taken...yeah, he's still in surgery...why don't you send someone?"

Caleb Smith State Park, Wednesday, November 6, shortly after midnight

The car slowed down, and rolled silently with the engine and head-lights turned off for some five hundred feet down Gardiner Road. A young woman with a dark pageboy haircut slipped out of the car and slipped into the park through one of those gaps in the chain-link fence that exist either because the perimeter of the park was calculated in-accurately, or else to give animals a way out of the park in case of forest fires or earthquakes, or else for less noble reasons.

Those gaps in the fence are usually used by people who want to take their dogs for a walk without going through the main entrance because, in theory at least, household pets aren't allowed in the park.

The night sky was clear. There was a strong breeze that had swept away the recent rain. Stars twinkled overhead. The young woman was running as if she were wearing night-vision goggles. Actually, she was. Of all the things that Pierre-André had said to her, she had memorized only the directions to where the narcotic was buried. She had no idea what teratogenic even meant. She'd worry about that when she got back to Paris. She had absolutely no intention of destroying the narcotic. The general would be beside himself with joy if she brought back four whole drums to him. And he would have forgotten all about the black woman.

She ran along the narrow lane, counted the fire hydrants, turned left, ran up the gravel lane that zigzagged among the trees, reached the clearing, crossed it, and stopped by the pole with the arrows indicating the distance from various cities around the world, looked down at the mound of dirt, mulch, and leaves...and realized that there was a freshly dug hole in the middle of it.

"*Et merde!*" she uttered, barely moving her fleshy pink lips. "Some-one's already taken Matterre-Faquet's drums!"

She clicked on her flashlight, pointed it at the ground, and swung it to the dirt trail:

"Those prints look very fresh," she said to herself, "let's follow them."

In the silence of the night, a woman in blue jeans could run faster than a man pushing a wheelbarrow containing ten gallons of liquid in four drums.

The tracks of the wheelbarrow were heading east, as if the person who was pushing it was trying to reach the northeast corner of the park, where Old Northport Road turns into the Jericho Turnpike, near the big intersection with the monument to Caleb Smith's bull.

A long route, but reasonably accessible and concealed from view.

Despite her transatlantic origins, the young woman ran faster and more silently than one of the Iroquois warriors described by James Fenimore Cooper. In less than twenty minutes she had run a mile and a half, and she had noticed that the footsteps of whoever was pushing the wheelbarrow were growing shorter and shorter and sinking deeper and deeper into the mud, a sign that the man was beginning to grow tired.

Smithtown, Jericho Turnpike, parking lot of The Oasis, a Gentlemen's Club, Wednesday, November 6, shortly after midnight

A dark silhouette moved inside the black minivan. A cigarette butt flew out the window, which then buzzed shut.

With a cell phone glued to his ear, the driver started the engine and said:

"Keep cool, *paisa'*...I'm coming...I'm on my way, capeesh? Three minutes, tops, just give me three minutes."

Caleb Smith State Park, Smithtown, Long Island, NY, Wednesday, November 6, after midnight

The silence of the night was broken from time to time by the whoosh of cars sailing past along the wet asphalt of the Jericho Turnpike, but there was another noise, more continuous and sustained than the intermittent noise of the major thoroughfare. The low-frequency wheeze of the engine of a minivan created an undertone that would have gone unnoticed in a traffic jam, but which could not be ignored by the ears of the young woman tracking a human prey in the wet mud of the trail leading through the woods.

She had noticed a black minivan and two men who were busy transporting four heavy drums. She accelerated to a sprint for the last hundred feet or so, until she reached the minivan. As the first man was getting behind the wheel, she lunged at the second man before he could get the passenger-side door open.

There was a moment of panic and the minivan peeled out, tires screeching, leaving the passenger behind.

The woman grabbed him by the balls and pounded his nose repeatedly with punch after punch, until the blood was flowing. Then she hooked one leg with her foot and shoved him hard, so that he sprawled face-first onto the ground.

Then she grabbed him by his blue-and-white check tie, pulled hard until he was on the verge of suffocating, and hissed:

"Your friends will be back in two minutes. I have plenty of time to kill you. Tell me where you guys are taking that stuff."

"Fuhgeddaboudit," was the response. "*Non mi scassare la minchia*," he wheezed.

So Annick pulled a box of Swedish matches out of her pocket. Each match was an inch long and had a phosphorus tip. She lit one and jammed it into his ear. *Phosphorus fumes and the smell of burning flesh blended in the* night, along with an inhuman scream that seemed to emerge from the bowels of hell.

In the meanwhile, the minivan had reconsidered. It made a U-turn in front of the bull of Smithtown and came back to the place it had just left. The driver opened fire with a loud but inaccurate old rifle.

Annick placed a foot on the shinbone of the man on the ground and then brought her boot down with violent abruptness. She heard the sound of cracking bone and the cry of *"Madonna santissima!"* So the pair of them would have other things to worry about, and would be unlikely to follow her. The young woman vanished into the woods while the blue-and-white check tie fluttered along the ground in the evening breeze.

Annick Delaporte had failed in her second mission as well.

Plainview Hospital, Long Island, NY, Floor B, Room 29, Wednesday, November 6, afternoon

Surrounded by a dozen or so FBI and CIA agents, wedged in between a grim-faced Klara Siebers and a furious Jamie O'Malley, the man with the arm in a cast and the bandage-swathed head was tossing and turning fitfully in his hospital bed.

"They're not there anymore, eh?" Matterre-Faquet asked.

"There's nothing there but a hole in the ground," O'Malley confirmed. He had gone to see, together with Klara.

"Are you absolutely sure how much there was?" O'Malley insisted.

"Yes, four drums, each holding two-and-a-half gallons," Matterre-Faquet repeated. "They were in the fermenter hangar at Stony Brook and I buried them there myself, last night.

"If they aren't there anymore, then whoever followed me and caused the crash must have taken them."

Even then, despite the fact that he felt he was under suspicion again, the scientist couldn't bring himself to tell the whole truth and reveal the role that Annick had played. He hoped that the girl was arranging to destroy the drums at that very moment, even though he didn't feel very sure of it.

"But why in hell did you hide them? Couldn't you have come to us and let us destroy them?" Klara asked.

"Come to you? That would have meant handing them over to the Pentagon! Knowing that it's a far more dangerous weapon than you ever dreamed of?" He stopped and looked around. He swallowed once or twice. "The molecule," he said, "is teratogenic. Do you know that that means? Teratogenic. And you're saying I should have handed it over to the military?

"I wanted to have the time to destroy it," he said, lying to them and to himself as well.

"You're getting a little too worked up," Klara said coldly. "We know perfectly well what teratogenic means. And we also already knew that the molecule was teratogenic. The lab in Palo Alto told us that. And we also know that the Pentagon, for that very reason, has already given the order to destroy immediately any narcotic we manage to find. Destroy it, you understand? We don't fool around with birth defects. Who do you take us for?"

Matterre-Faquet's smirk said: "We'll see."

Just then, Klara's cell phone rang. She looked at the phone number on the display and left the room. She returned a few minutes later. She called O'Malley over to a corner of the room and the two of them spoke in low voices for a while. O'Malley glared at Matterre-Faquet and pulled his cell phone out of his pocket: then it was his turn to leave the room.

When he came back in the room, he went straight to Matterre-Faquet's bed.

"Matterre-Faquet, you are nothing but a piece of shit, a total son of a bitch. I hope that, before we're done with you, I can pay you back in full. Go ahead and tell him, Klara."

Klara pointed her index finger straight at the scientist.

"You lied to us once again. Last night, you told an agent of the French DGSE where she could find those drums."

"I wanted her to destroy them," Matterre-Faquet weakly tried to defend himself.

"Ah, the French yes but us, no? That's not very consistent, is it?" She didn't give him time to answer. "Luckily, sometimes the word 'ally' still has meaning. The French agent was unable to find the drums, but she saw who took them. She reported back to Paris and they were kind enough to let us know."

She leaned over Matterre-Faquet: "And now do you want to know who has ten gallons of a very dangerous, no wait, teratogenic substance, right now?"

"The Mafia, you stupid asshole," O'Malley broke in. "Get it? The Mafia. After last night's car chase, I had some pretty strong suspicions. But now, goddamn it, I'm sure of it. Now we know that a band of assassins that has already terrorized the country and is eager and willing to blackmail us has enough of the narcotic to put the entire United States to sleep and then just burn the whole place down!"

O'Malley started pacing up and down the room, with long strides.

"The alarm has been sounded," he said to himself, to Klara, and to all the others. "But this time, our ass really is bare and up in the air."

Matterre-Faquet was disconcerted and frightened by what he had heard, but he couldn't think of anything to say. For a few minutes, absolute silence reigned in the room. The silence was broken by Stefan Pierkowski, the archivist in O'Malley's team, who liked for things to add up. "Well, professor, let's reckon up. There are four two-and-a-half gallon drums that were buried in Caleb Smith Park and, that are now in the hands of the Mafia. Then, there's the narcotic that was used in Massapequod." He pulled a transparent plastic bag out of his duffel bag; in it was a half-gallon metal bottle, with a SUNY label, on which was written PAMF 36-4. "And this?" Stefan asked.

"Yes," Matterre-Faquet confirmed, "that's the bottle that was in Papadopoulos's refrigerator, the one that was stolen that Friday night, while I was spending the weekend in Connecticut...where did you find it?"

"The police found it in the car of the gangster who shot at you last night."

"So," Stefan resumed, "four two-and-a-half gallon drums and this bottle. That's all the narcotic that you prepared, right?"

Matterre-Faquet's face was ashen.

"I'm afraid not," he stammered. "I had *two* bottles like that one in Papadopoulos's refrigerator."

There was a moment of silence.

"Why didn't you tell us about it yesterday, in Mineola?" Klara blurted out.

"You never asked me. And frankly I had other things to worry about," Matterre-Faquet replied. "Unless I'm mistaken, Papadopoulos started talking about 'samples' that were in his refrigerator and we all went on talking about 'samples.' I assumed that he had told you about the second bottle. Until we can find it, we certainly can't say whether all the material is 'accounted for,' as you like to say."

"Oh, shit," said Klara. "There really is no end to these nasty surprises around here."

O'Malley was thinking. "All right, then, we have one bottle. The Mafia used it. And ten more gallons, which the Mafia also has. But there's another bottle in circulation. It was in the refrigerator too, and it was stolen on that Friday night, too, right?"

"Yes," said Matterre-Faquet. "The Mafia must have taken them both, right?"

"It's possible. But I don't think so," O'Malley replied. "I have the impression that we would have heard about it much earlier."

"Do you think that someone else came in that night?" Klara asked. "Why don't we review the footage of the university's closed-circuit security camera? Maybe we missed something."

O'Malley emitted a grunt of reluctant assent.

"I've got it right here," Stefan said happily. He started his computer.

After a short wait, images of Stony Brook began to flow across the screen. Despite his broken collarbone, Matterre-Faquet was craning his neck to see the video.

"There," said O'Malley, "let's see what's happening... at midnight, a light colored sedan, two men talking, a bottle is handed from one to the other... after midnight... fast forward, Stefan, everything's calm here... now it's one o'clock, nothing... two o'clock, nothing.... hey, look at that, hold it, hold it, go forward slowly... here comes a car... yes, at three o'clock in themorning, what a weird-looking car..."

"It looks like the car that that ball-buster Rachel Goldstein drives!" Pierre-André exclaimed.

"And look here, a man gets out and heads for the front door, and... oh, look, end of broadcast, in keeping with what Safar told us, electronic manipulation of the doorway monitoring system... practically the second this guy gets there... at three in the morning... I think we can rule out the possibility of this being mere coincidence."

Klara looked at Matterre-Faquet. "Who is Rachel Goldstein?"

Stefan beat him to it: "She's the secretary of Benjamin Safar, head of the department di plant physiology."

"I can't wait to talk to her," said Klara.

Thursday, November 7

The sound of a rock hitting the wooden wall, just a few inches from the window, echoed through the office. That was the noise that finally forced Sheriff Hook to admit to himself just how bad things had gotten. He'd never seen anything like this. He'd never even imagined that it was possible. It was a quiet little town: the last thing anyone had gotten worked up about was the decision to eliminate one of the two pedestrian crosswalks in front of city hall. "They're furious," the mayor had told him over the phone. Well, he could see they were furious! He could certainly understand that Russ Freeman and his truck-driver friends would be in the yelling crowd that had gathered in the parking lot across from the office. Or the good-for-nothings from Colucci's bar, who spent the day playing pool and gambling away their welfare money. But what was Mr. Morton doing there? Morton was a respected and respectable citizen, a pillar of the community, always in the front row at charity benefits, the leading real estate broker in the district. And there he was, at the front of the mob, in shirtsleeves and a pinstripe vest, red-faced, apparently apoplectic, shouting as loud as anybody. The one who was shouting right along with him, louder than him or anyone else in fact, the one who was leading the mob in its shouts, was none other than Ms. Jenkins, the principal of the elementary school. The only time anyone had ever heard her raise her voice before was during a school meeting about the menu in the cafeteria. Even now, he could hear her screechy voice, one octave higher than anybody else's: "Bring them out, Sheriff, bring them out."

"Where the hell do they think they are? Has everyone gone crazy?" shouted the sheriff. "No one has ever been lynched here, not in the past two hundred years!" Another rock hit the window, but not hard enough to break the glass. "Maybe you should go talk with them," said his deputy, Abe. Until now, the sheriff had done his best to convince himself that it wasn't necessary, that they might all get tired and go home. But now he had to admit that Abe was right. He walked out onto the front porch with a resolute air, but he stopped at the edge of the porch, three steps up from the parking lot.

"There he is, at last," said a voice. "Give him up, Sheriff," three or four of them shouted.

The sheriff clapped his hat down on his head. "What is all this?"

Morton was the first to step forward. "Sheriff, a community has the right to defend itself. When the danger is extreme, then extreme steps can be taken in self-defense. Our children have the right to sleep safely. But none of us can be confident of their safety as long as two dangerous individuals are on the loose!"

"Why do you think they're dangerous? A couple of young men had too much to drink and they were out walking off the alcohol."

"Sticking their noses everywhere? Stopping at every door?" asked a voice. The sheriff shrugged: "That's what I said. They were out walking. The city is what it is. There aren't many places for them to go."

"Do you think it's normal that they should have gone from house to house, all night long?" It was Miss Jenkins who spoke up.

"And just how do you know that, Miss Jenkins? I thought you were at home sleeping at night," shot back Sheriff Hook, immediately regretting having used the words "home" and "sleep." In fact, the crowd began to murmur after he spoke. "Anyway, everything's okay," he felt it was his duty to add.

"Everything's okay?" That was Russ Freeman. "Everything's okay, because *they're under your protection?"*

"When the situation got a little overheated last night, Abe, here...ahem...thought it might be better to intervene."

"Sheriff, we want to speak to these young men ourselves," said Morton.

"Why do you want to talk to them? These are two former auto workers. They lost their job at the GM plant because of the slowdown. They were heading south to see if they could get work at one of those Japanese car factories. They had a little too much to drink and they were waiting to sober up before starting off again. We verified their identities, checked out their stories, searched them and searched their car. We found nothing suspicious. Let me repeat that: we found nothing suspicious."

Russ Freeman had walked right up to him and put his foot on the first step. "Bring them out here," he said with clenched teeth. "Bring them out, Sheriff, bring them out," the chant struck up again

"I couldn't do that even if I wanted to. We checked everything and double-checked it and this morning we let them go, to avoid new... disorders"

There was a shout of rage. "You let them get away," shouted a voice. "What if they come back tonight?" called another voice. "Traitor!" Morton shouted at him. Russ Freeman turned to the mob: "It's not true. They're right inside."

Sheriff Hook watched several men go to the construction site across the way and come back with clubs and bricks. The crowd pressed closer and closer. A hail of rocks rattled down onto the office behind him. The men with clubs had launched themselves against the windows and were shattering glass. "Let's get them," he heard someone shout. Then they lunged at him. Mr. Morton was hysterically pounding his fists on the sheriff's chest. Out of the corner of his eye he saw Abe at the door, rifle leveled. "Abe, don't do anything stupid," were the last words he managed to shout. But his voice was throttled in his throat: someone was hauling on the collar of his uniform shirt. He felt himself being lifted into the air. They were dragging him to the wall that separated the parking lot from Mrs. Bent's house.

When they got to the wall, they tossed him over into Mrs. Bent's yard. He would probably have broken a leg or a shoulder in any case. But, on the other side of the wall, Mrs. Bent had installed a handsome stone table with two stone benches. He landed on his chest, against a sharp corner of the table, crushing his chest cavity. The last sign of life that Sheriff Hook gave was the spurt of flood that flowed out of his mouth.

It took the fire department with fire hoses to disperse the mob. The office had been destroyed, along with the small, empty jail. It was Abe, from the hospital, who told them where they could find the sheriff.

Stony Brook, NY, Thursday, November 7, morning

Rachel Goldstein had sipped her latte while she listened to the terrible reports on the TV news, then she had made her rounds delivering mail. When she got back to her office to drink an espresso in peace and quiet, the place was full of people. Benjamin Safar was as pale as if he'd just seen the Anti-Christ, Matterre-Faquet, bandaged, in a cast, and as red as a beet, as if he'd just had an apoplectic fit, Konstantinos Papdopoulos as serious as Zeus, intently weighing the destiny of the world, some guy from the FBI, who was introduced to her as Jamie O'Malley, as sallow and glum as if he had an ulcer, and Klara Siebers, an icy and arrogant CIA agent, who scared her even more than O'Malley. Plus a young man, also FBI, whose name she didn't catch.

"Sit down," said Safar.

Rachel Goldstein turned pale. She had never seen Benjamin Safar look so serious.

Stefan Pierkowski turned on a laptop, and on the screen a horrible black squared-off Japanese car appeared and went to park under the closed-circuit security cameras that were installed in front of the biology labs at Stony Brook. A male figure emerged from the car and headed for the building. Three minutes later, the screen went dark. White letters and numbers in the corner of the screen marked the time and date: Saturday, October 26th, 3:12 AM.

Stefan turned off his laptop.

"Well?" asked Safar.

Silence.

"Well?" Safar's voice grew louder.

"That looks like my car," Rachel mumbled.

"That doesn't 'look like your car,' Rachel, that *is* your car." Klara was tense. "Pierkowski, enlarge and zoom in, please, that's right, on the license plate. That's right, those three numbers. Pierkowski, how many cars are registered with the New York state DMV, of that make, model, and color, and with those three numbers on the license plate?"

"Just one, Ms. Siebers, just one. It belongs to Rachel Goldstein."

"I told you," Matterre-Faquet muttered, but no one listened to him.

The girl who was too skinny, with hair that was too long and a mouth that was too big was unable to flash her usual mousey smile.

"What were you doing, at three in the morning, with a man getting out of your car?"

Safar was tense, but he insisted on remaining courteous.

"Nothing... nothing illegal, and nothing obscene, I swear it."

"That's not the problem, I can assure you of that," said Klara in a chilly tone of voice. "And who is that man?"

"A... a friend of mine..."

"So you," O'Malley broke in, "show up here at three in the morning with a friend of yours, with whom you weren't doing anything illegal, naturally, and five minutes after this... this... friend of yours gets out of the car, the laboratory's entire electronic security system goes haywire? Stefan, have you had a chance to take a look at who this young lady— who is so reluctant to speak with us here—talked to on the phone over the past few days?"

"Well, there are a couple of phone calls to an unlisted foreign number. One was an outgoing call, on Monday, October 21st in the evening, but the same unlisted foreign number placed a call to Miss Goldstein on Friday, October 25th, and both calls were relayed through the cell phone tower of Huntington."

"Stefan, this is not the moment for your brainteasers," O'Malley rapped out.

"It took me hours, but I tracked it down, chief." He paused for effect, for the benefit of Safar, Papadopulos, and Matterre-Faquet. Klara and O'Malley already knew everything. "It's a Mossad number."

Benjamin Safar lost what little color remained in his face. His fragile assistant hadn't been involved in a tasteless prank...

"Rachel, what were you doing on the phone with a foreign secret agent?"

"Well, here's how it was. I phoned him after Professor Matterre-Faquet's seminar... the things that people say in a seminar are in the public domain, aren't they? Then he came to spend the weekend with me, last week..." Rachel stammered, trying to hide her face behind her long hair.

"A foreign agent, Rachel?" Safar's voice was icy.

"Well, I mean," and her embarrassment was starting to make the young woman lash out, and forget her customary shyness and reserve, "my Uriel is no foreign agent. We're allies, aren't we? We're their closest allies, aren't we?"

Safar was enraged. "Do you understand what you've done, Rachel? You handed over information of strategic importance to a secret agent working for a foreign power! This isn't a matter of trespassing and burglary anymore. You're looking at charges of espionage and high treason!"

Klara took two steps toward the door. An FBI agent walked in, with a pair of handcuffs in his hand.

O'Malley leaned rapidly down and spoke to Rachel. "I'll come with you too," he told her. "Tell me everything you know and maybe," he added, nodding in Klara's direction, "I can rip you free of the clutches of that bloodthirsty she-wolf."

Mossad offices, Tel Aviv, Thursday, November 7, night

The meeting was held in the same room as the last one, with bare white walls, and tables and chairs scattered randomly. This time, however, there were no teapots and most of the chairs were empty. Only five people were present, sitting in a circle in the middle of the room. Until now, four of them had mostly listened to the only one there who was wearing a dress jacket: a man in his early fifties, with thick glasses, his tie loosened. The prime minister's security adviser. He was just coming to a conclusion:

"So all I can tell you is that we are getting intense pressure from Washington. They want that narcotic back. And I can certainly understand why. This is not the first time that Washington has put pressure, and powerful pressure, on our government. We have shown more than once that we are willing and able to resist this pressure. This time, however, I can assure you that the note of urgency is unmistakable. The prime minister sees no reason to refuse if that would result in a sharp deterioration in relations between our two countries. We have to give them back that narcotic."

"You know, naturally," one of the men in the room broke in, "that right now, actually, we don't have it."

"Yes, I know about the agent. Uriel Silberzahn, right?"

"We intercepted Silberzahn in the past few days," another man explained. "Unfortunately, however, he got away."

"That's your problem," said the government adviser, holding up both hands. "But I imagine you can solve it yourself."

"No doubt," replied the most senior officer present, a man in his early sixties, with a pair of bushy eyebrows. "I just want to make it clear that, here and now, this is strictly a theoretical discussion."

"Indeed, speaking of theories," a small skinny man dressed in a safari jacket that was a size too big for him broke in, "there's something I'd like to understand more clearly. Teratogenic means that this narcotic produces devastating modifications if breathed in by a woman who is expecting a child. These modifications are potentially—and I'd like to insist on that term, potentially—dangerous. Are we sure of this?"

"Washington sent us the scientific report on the tests that have been conducted," the adviser replied. "The report has been studied, we ran tests of our own, and there is no reason to question their conclusions."

"But these modifications," the man in the safari jacket went on insistently," come about later. That is to say, they become evident at birth. Months after inhalation. The link with the narcotic might not be so evident."

"Why do you ask?" the adviser interrupted him with an irritated voice. "Do you think that the effects of this narcotic will really remain secret for very long?"

"I wouldn't know. In any case, I meant the link between our operations and the effects on pregnant women."

The man with the jacket leaned forward.

"Are you saying that you think this is an acceptable risk that we can run? Deformed fetuses, children with three legs or two heads? What would the rest of the world conclude? Let me remind you that this people, our own people, were subjected to genetic experiments by Doctor Mengele, not the other way around. Which side of that equation do you want to be on?"

The man in the safari jacket said nothing. It was a fat woman, with unusually thinning hair, who finally spoke up.

"You're starting off from the supposition that we might actually deploy the narcotic. I don't even believe that that would be necessary. The very fact that they know that we have it would exercise a powerful deterrent effect on our enemies."

"That is to say, instead of becoming Mengele, we would just be a nation that from one moment to the next, might just become Mengele?" said the adviser with a smirk of contempt. "Explain the difference to me."

"If you don't see the difference, most people do, I'm willing to bet," went on the man in the safari jacket. "They could certainly see the benefits of this deterrent effect. Up till now, you've spoken on behalf of the prime minister. Should I assume that the entire administration is informed about this matter?"

The adviser's gaze turned chilly.

"Are you trying to say that some of the coalition parties making up the government might actually consider the option of rejecting Washington's request, in spite of everything I've said here?"

"All I want to know is whether they've been informed and, if so, whether we are dealing with a unanimous decision on the government's part."

"What are you suggesting? A public debate on the subject in the Knesset?" The adviser's eyes had narrowed to two slits, his lips were compressed and white, his jaws were clenched.

The man in the safari jacket shrugged his shoulders.

"I think that, in the interests of the country, having a broad debate is important. We could have a popular referendum, for instance..."

"May the Lord preserve us from such a referendum!" the adviser interrupted. "In any case, this matter falls under the prime minister's jurisdiction." He paused. "Let me urge you not to trespass on territory that is not your domain, the territory of politics. In any case," he concluded, "the prime minister has made his decision. He knows," and here he gave a look around the circle that was meant to be significant," that he has the majority of the Knesset behind him. This Knesset or the next one. What I am saying is that he is not afraid to call for a vote of confidence and to dissolve this government." He got to his feet:

"You," he concluded, "just take care of getting the narcotic back here."

Seen from this side of the Hudson, the Manhattan skyline looked off-kilter, as if a capricious child had shoved the chess pieces off to one side of the board. Larramee stopped looking up at the bright lights of the skyscrapers and focused his attention on the skyline of warehouses, cranes, freight, and containers through which they were moving. They were next to the Hoboken Terminal and they were moving in single file toward a warehouse built of metal piers, panels, and bulkheads, all held together with nuts and bolts, like a giant Erector Set. The FBI had been conducting its offensive for five days now, and this was the third evening that Larramee had come here, with Delgado's team. They knew that the warehouse was one of the bases that Frankie Lampredi operated out of. They also knew that a substantial share of the cocaine traffic of the state of New Jersey came through there. Till now, however, they hadn't been able to pin down any of that traffic. Delgado, however, seemed confident that sooner or later they'd hit the target.

The moon was out tonight and Delgado gave the order to move along the perimeter of one of the buildings in single file, in order to remain in the shelter of darkness. The moonlight was still sufficiently bright to keep them from tripping over scraps of metal or old tubs with an ensuing clattering noise. Still, Larramee knew that the minute they started up the metal steps of the warehouse, it would become impossible to preserve operational silence. They emerged from the shadows of the building across the passageway and plunged into the shadows of the warehouse itself, and began climbing the steel steps cautiously. Larramee saw a flash of light out of the corner of his eye and then heard a bullet clip a steel pole not a yard away from his head. They all lunged into the shelter of the steps as a hail of bullets began pelting down around them. Theoretically, crouching down on the steps, they were out of the line of fire, but in that environment of steel, the bullets ricocheted along unpredictable trajectories.

Larramee heard a smothered moan behind him. He saw Delgado whip around.

"It's nothing, boss," said a gasping voice. "It's just a flesh wound."

"Where, Freddie?"

"Leg."

"Shanahan, tie a rope around the wound and stay here with him." A man slithered back beyond Larramee and stopped a few steps further down.

"Now," said Delgado, moving quickly away from the steps and into the lee of the closest upright pier. All the others moved out behind him, shooting furiously straight up. From above, gunfire could be heard—handguns and at least one submachine gun. But no one else was hit. In any case, they were now under a steel covering. Half of the agents moved a short distance forward and resumed firing upward.

"To get down," Delgado said, "they have to come past us.

"They've put themselves in the trap with their own hands," he went on, slightly baffled. He slicked back his glossy black hair.

"Strange," he added. "And there's not many of them. From the way they're shooting, no more than three or four."

Actually, they'd now almost completely stopped firing from up above, except for the occasional warning shot, in order to pin them down where they were. For the next few minutes, nothing else happened. Then something fell from above, landing on the cement with a tremendous metallic clatter. By the light of the moon, it looked like a bag of garbage. The gunfire from above fell silent. After a couple of minutes, Delgado stood up, emerged from their shelter, and walked slowly toward the bag. He picked it up and came back at the same unhurried pace.

Back in the safety of the shelter, he flicked on a flashlight and looked into the bag, rummaging around intently. Larramee leaned forward to see for himself. There were two .38 caliber handguns, an Uzi, four quarter-kilo packages of cocaine, and a large pile of bills. Delgado broke out laughing:

"Good old Frankie! The last of the old school Mafiosi! We're in the presence of greatness!" He tossed a couple of the bundles of cash, held together by rubber bands, into Larramee's: "Count it." They were hundred-dollar bills. Larramee counted the bills in one bundle: there were 50.

"Just from a quick glance," Larramee said, "I'd have to guess there's a hundred, maybe a hundred thirty thousand dollars in the bag."

"Well, not bad at all," Delgado smiled. "Frankie must have have a big shipment up there, if he decides to toss us this little gift."

Larramee was baffled.

"I don't get it. Is he trying to bribe us?"

"Well, yes and no," Delgado snickered. He ran a finger over his upper lip, as if to smooth a mustache that wasn't there.

"Or, let's put it this way, he's trying to bribe us, but with class."

"What do you mean?"

"Well, you see, Frankie knows perfectly well that this is a drug raid. So he's courteous enough to provide us with the reasonable take from a successful raid, without obliging us to fire another shot. We can go back to our base with a tidy kilo of cocaine, a few weapons we confiscated, and all the cash we decide to hand over to Uncle Sam, instead of just pocketing it for ourselves. Let's say thirty thousand dollars. The other hundred thousand dollars or whatever it is, we split up. Then we report that the bad guys managed to get away, but they were forced to leave the coke behind them. Of course, a kilo isn't all that much. Probably, if we take the bag and go, they'll toss another bag after us, with another four or five kilos. Conclusion: it's a fair take in terms of coke, weapons, and dirty money. A solid success. We could even get a citation. He's probably seen it work before with the local police."

"So what do we do?"

"We're going to go up and catch the big-time drug trafficker Frankie Lampredi. There must be fifty kilos of coke up there."

Delgado waved to two agents, pointing up to the roof. The two began climbing, each one on a lateral steel column of the building.

"Take my advice, slither across that damned roof," he ordered in a low voice. A few seconds later, two more agents went up. Delgado, Larramee, and the others waited under the iron roof. A few minutes crept by, then they heard a muffled cry and a burst of submachine gun fire. A few pistol shots and a second burst of submachine gun fire. Then, silence.

Delgado had already pounded up the stairs, followed by Larramee and all the others. He threw open the door of the room at the top of the stairs and looked around for a light switch. A ceiling light glared on. There were four FBI agents standing in position, their submachine guns at the ready. On the floor, the corpses of two young men, guns still in their hands. In the middle of the room lay a dozen or trash bags, piled neatly. In a corner, his back to the wall and his legs stretched out on the floor, was a bald man with a large paintbrush mustache, wearing a plumber's overalls and a checkered shirt.

"There he is, our Frankie boy," said Delgado.

"Son of a bitch, wasn't the money I tossed you enough?" Frankie panted.

"I was just pretty sure there was more up here," Delgado replied. Frankie had dropped his Luger by his leg. Both his hands were clutching his belly. Blood glittered between his fingers. Larramee walked over to him, kicked the Luger far away, and knelt down next to the man. He gingerly moved the fingers aside and took a look at the wound.

"I think he's going to make it," said Larramee, turning to Delgado.

"Tell your black mule to keep his filthy hands off me," Frankie wheezed. "Tell him not to give me the evil eye."

"What do you mean, evil eye?" Larramee asked, still kneeling beside him.

"Because I'm hoping to die right here, rather than spend the rest of my life in Sing Sing," said Frankie.

Larramee snorted, as he got to his feet.

"Well, you should have thought of that earlier, shouldn't you?" Delgado observed philosophically. He was checking the bags. "Oh, I'd say a lot more than fifty kilos."

"It was a big deal, you bastards. One of the biggest deals I've ever been in on," said Frankie. "Ruined by a band of government faggots who can't see a golden opportunity when it falls out of the sky and lands at their feet." He grimaced with pain. "What the fuck were you doing here, tonight of all nights? You'd already checked the place out, what were you doing coming back a second time? I was sure you'd left, you mokes. Otherwise I'd have been ready for you. Who ratted me out?"

"Nobody ratted you out, Frankie," Delgado replied. "We just wanted to double-check."

"Are you telling me you didn't fucking know anything about it?" Frankie seemed incredulous. He coughed again twice, and moaned in agony. "That was just pure luck, you coming back again?"

"Let's just call it persistence," said Larramee

"Go fuck yourself," Frankie swore. "Persistence, my ass! In thirty years, I've never seen anything like it. A guy can't work in these conditions," he said.

In the distance, an ambulance siren grew closer.

Friday November 8

Knees bent, one hand flat on the grass, Ladashaun Mitchell, number 59, puffed, moving his massive bulk, and tried to concentrate again. The fact that his team was the Redskins and his opponents were the Cowboys was just a fluke of destiny, adding a little spice to a rivalry that was already legendary in the NFL. The two teams hated each other. Not just because one was from Washington and the other was from Dallas: politics, the mutual mistrust between the nation's capital and the deep heartland, was of no interest to anyone, neither fans nor players. But the two teams were in the same division. They played regularly, at least once a year: the Cowboys, loaded down with trophies, and the Redskins, who hadn't made it to the playoffs in a lifetime. To beat the Cowboys here, in their home stadium, could be enough to give some meaning to the season for the Redskins. Now, with six minutes to the end of the third quarter, to their own surprise they were leading, 20-13. But it was the Cowboys' ball: third down, on the 30 yard line. Their quarterback was an arrogant piece of shit, but he was talented enough to invent a touchdown in practically any situation.

Ladashaun had already seen that they were using the shotgun formation. The quarterback, with that bastard of a running back at his side, was several yards behind the line of scrimmage, directly behind the center, from whom he would receive the snap. Time was ticking, play would resume in a couple of seconds, no more. By rights, there ought be a deafening roar from the home crowd, a thunderous ovation from the grandstand to urge the Cowboys on. Instead, there was only a barely audible hum. The stadium was practically empty, the spectators were scattered through the bleachers in small groups, distant from one another. People had chosen to stay home and watch the game on TV. And Ladashaun couldn't really say he blamed them.

Suddenly, he heard shouts from the grandstand on his right. He glanced at the man on the opposing team, directly in front of him, but he was watching the bleachers too. A man in a red jacket was running along a tier of seats, pursued by a small crowd of spectators. Other spectators were converging on him, from above and below. He'd never make it to the exit. He looked at the quarterback. He had the ball in his hand. In theory this was when he, Ladashaun, was supposed to lunge forward, tackle the quarterback, and knock him to the ground. But the quarterback was motionless: he was looking up into the stands as well. The man with the red jacket tossed what looked a coffee cup far away from him, one of those containers made of metal and black plastic. He heard a gunshot. The quarterback dropped the ball. In the stands, the crowd had caught and submerged the man in the red jacket and now they were shoving each other aside in their fury to beat and kick him. Out of nowhere, groups of policemen appeared and waded into the fray.

Ladashaun dropped to the ground. He took off his helmet and cradled his head in his hands. The man across from him, kneeling, shook his head and touched his shoulder, as if to comfort him.

Jerusalem, Friday, November 8, shortly after dawn

The Silberzahn question was becoming not only dangerous but unmanageable. He hadn't needed yesterday's meeting to remind him of the fact. Skillful though he might be, Uriel would not have been able to go on hiding without protection from powerful figures. The Owl had a pretty good idea of who they might be. And so, shortly after dawn, his car braked to a halt behind a rabbinical school in a part of Jerusalem that he normally tried to visit as seldom as possible. The rabbi he was going to see was not a famous person, but Mossad knew very well that he was one of the most influential figures in the movement of the most extremist settlers.

The room, brightly illuminated by the morning sunlight, was stacked high with books, as was fitting for a religious man, but also with topographic maps of the various regions of Israel, which might seem better suited to a military leader. The rabbi was sitting at a small desk. He had cleared a space for the Owl on a wooden bench that faced the large window. The result, the Owl noticed, and he couldn't say whether it was intentional, was that his face was left in the shadows, while the rabbi's face was inundated with light.

The two man exchanged a chilly glance.

"Amos Benn, we don't see much of you around here," said the rabbi. His name was no secret, but using it so openly was a kind of challenge, thought the Owl. It was as if to say that, in that room, Mossad had no special standing and Amos Benn was a person no different than anybody else. This meeting wasn't beginning well, decidedly.

"I've come to tell you about a crisis," the Owl began. He started telling him the story of Massapequod, the narcotic, Silberzahn's role. This information of course was top secret, but the rabbi showed no sign of surprise, and the hint of a grin of contempt hovered around the corner of his mouth. It was clear that he knew all about it, and that just confirmed the Owl's suspicions about the rabbi's contacts with Uriel.

The Mossad man stopped talking.

"So you're telling me you've spoken with Silberzahn?" he said.

"That's right," the rabbi replied. "There's no reason to deny it."

"You know where he is." It was a statement, not a question.

The rabbi's hands waved vaguely in the air.

"It's not important whether or not I know. I can tell you that he's with trusted people."

"You do realize that Silberzahn can unleash a very grave crisis for our country?"

"A crisis is just another test to which our Lord puts us. Israel has faced countless crises. Israel has always overcome them."

"Never for free."

The rabbi shrugged his shoulders. "The Lord never puts us to the test without demanding a cost."

"But Silberzahn's plan of putting an entire section of a town, or a whole city, to sleep in order to kill one or two terrorist leaders, is not only dangerous. It's pointless. We can attain the same objective in at least ten other ways."

Now the little smile of superiority on the rabbi's mouth was unmistakable.

"That is not the mission on which the Lord has summoned Uriel," he said.

"What do you mean, this isn't the mission?" The Owl's face turned gray.

"Makot Mitzrayim."

"The plagues of Egypt? What do the plagues of Egypt have to do with anything?"

"Do you remember the tenth plague, Amos Benn?"

The Owl's brain was whirling around. He realized that he knew the answer, but he refused to convey it to his conscious mind.

"Toward midnight I will go forth among the Egyptians - the rabbi began to quote - and every first-born in the land of Egypt shall die, from the first-born of Pharaoh who sits on his throne to the first-born of the slave girl who is behind the millstone; and all the first-born of the cattle."

"But that's madness!"

"Often the Lord's plans strike us as madness. How can we judge Him?"

"It's a senseless massacre!"

"Senseless, Amos Benn? Don't you remember the other words?: But I will harden Pharaoh's heart, that I may multiply My signs and marvels in the land of Egypt....And the Egyptians shall know that I am the LORD."

That is the meaning and the worth of Uriel's mission. To demonstrate and prove that their gods are false. Their words and their will are as dust. The Lord our God is one, and He is not Palestinian."

"Just a minute, just a minute," the Owl spoke hastily. "Maybe you don't know this, but the narcotic has other effects. Terrible effects. Tremendous effects. It causes birth defects. The unborn would pay. It creates deformed fetuses."

The rabbi smiled.

"I know that. Uriel knows that. They told him. To stop him. But nothing will stop Uriel. Deformed babies in the wombs of Palestinian women? That will be the eleventh plague, is what Uriel said."

"I didn't know that Uriel thought he could outdo the Lord our God," said the Owl.

But sarcasm wasn't about to stop Silberzahn or the rabbi.

"Man is weak, but he can contribute to the works of the Lord," he said.

"Let's come back to earth, if you don't mind. You have to stop Silberzahn."

"I have no such intention. I certainly don't mean to stay the armed hand of the Lord. And anyway," he added with satisfaction, "it's too late. Otherwise I would never have talked so openly with you."

"Why is it too late?"

"Uriel is ready to complete his mission."

"Where?"

"Now that I don't know. It is up to him to listen to the words of the Lord and understand where He directs him to smite the enemy. I imagine it could be anywhere."

"When?"

"Soon, very soon," said the rabbi with a smile of anticipation. "Do you remember the tenth plague? After sunset."

Amos Benn stood up, turned his back on the rabbi, and left the room. He was thinking furiously.

Jerusalem, Friday, November 8, early morning

Forty years of working for Mossad had taught the Owl to think clearly, even when it seemed as if the world was collapsing around him. His heart was torn with anger and anguish, at the idea of Uriel intently cutting the throat of sleeping Palestinian children. But in the car taking him to the government office building, his brain was coolly evaluating the situation.

The rabbi's cockiness as he was revealing Uriel's plans to him meant that by now everything was ready for him to spring into action and the moment of the attack must be imminent. "Soon, very soon," the rabbi hadsaid. And then, enigmatically, "Do you remember the tenth plague? After sunset." If it was sunset this evening, why hadn't he said, very simply, this evening? The Owl sat thinking for a while. If the sunset in question was this evening's, then there really was nothing left that he could do. He looked at his watch: it would mean he hadn't even got ten hours left to stop Silberzahn. Even if he focused on the places where the extremist settlers might have helped to hide him, short of an incredible piece of luck, he would never be able to catch him in such a short time. Moreover, the rabbi had been very vague about the site of the attack. Was he doing to have to declare martial law in the entire country, as well as in Gaza and the occupied territories?

But instinct told the Owl something else. Today was Friday. At nightfall, when the third star appeared in the sky, more or less at sunset, Sabbath would begin, the Sabbath of meditation and rest. If Uriel went into action after sunset, he would carry out a massacre on the night of the Sabbath. The Owl frantically tried to remember the thirty-nine *melakhot*, the activities prohibited on the Sabbath. One of them was definitely reaping. Another one was slaughtering. He wasn't sure that either of those two terms could be properly applied to what Uriel intended to do. In any case, the prohibitions in this category were fairly vague and complicated. Moreover, while in everyday Hebrew the word *melakhot* meant "work," the original meaning was actually "deliberate activities," something undertaken with the specific intention of attaining a given result. And Uriel's mass murder certain fell into that category. Now, the Owl reasoned with himself, was it possible that the pious Uriel would complete the mission of the Lord in a bloodbath, a mission that he certainly perceived as holy and yet, at the same time, as challenging and exhausting, on the holiest of days, the day that the Almighty had solemnly dedicated to peace and to rest? He was willing to bet that the answer was no.

That meant that the first feasible sunset was the one that followed, when the third star that rose would put an end to the Sabbath. He had little more than thirty hours to stop Silberzahn. It was more than he had before, but still too little time.

He walked into the office of the prime minister's security adviser. The man must just have arrived. He still had his jacket in one hand. He'd switched on his monitor and was about to sit down in front of his computer. He looked up at the Owl and asked:

"Silberzahn?"

"Yes."

"Did you catch him?"

"No."

"Pity."

"It's much worse than that." He started telling him about his meeting with the rabbi and the tenth plague of Egypt. As he went on with his story, the incredulity on the adviser's face made way for a sense of revolt.

"But this is insanity!" he blurted out when the Owl was done.

"Insanity is not one of the categories of Uriel Silberzahn's world."

"We absolutely have to stop him!"

"And I'm absolutely in agreement. The problem is: how?"

"You can't catch him?"

"Of course we can. And I'm certain we will."

"So?"

The Owl heaved a deep sigh.

"You're confusing two different operational levels," he said. "I'm absolutely sure that I can capture Silberzahn and I'm sure that I will. But I'm not sure exactly when. If my calculations are correct, however, I have to catch him within the next thirty hours. I'm not absolutely certain that I can capture Silberzahn in the next thirty hours."

"So what do we do? Do you have any ideas?"

"Yes, I do. We have to ask for help."

"From who? The CIA? The British?" He hesitated. "The Russians?" he added doubtfully.

"None of them can be of any help to us."

"Then who?"

"Listen," the Owl said slowly, "the only people who follow and monitor our agents, especially important agents like Uriel, I mean, beside us are... the Palestinians."

"The Palestinians? Wait a second, have you gone insane too?"

"Well, it's their children we're talking about here."

"But we can't ask the Palestinians to work with us to capture one of our own agents!"

"Then you give me another solution or else, tomorrow evening, resign yourself to giving an official count of the children whose throats have been cut."

The adviser stopped to think.

"So who can guarantee that this will work?" he finally asked.

"No one," the Mossad officer replied. "But it might work. None of the other possibilities has a chance."

The adviser thought again. This time, it was a longer reflection, his eyes peering into the middle distance, his chin resting on both hands. Suddenly, his eyes swiveled to stare at the Owl directly:

"Hamas or Fatah?"

"Hamas would be preferable, but it would also be pointless. They would spend at least thirty hours just dressing us down about the fact that Uriel is an Israeli. I'd try Fatah."

The adviser looked at him. Then he stood up:

"I need to talk to the prime minister," he said. And he walked out a side door.

He came back almost half an hour later. He stopped and stood in the doorway.

"Are you going to call them or am I going to call them?" he asked.

"Neither of us are going to call them," the Owl replied. "No matter how we put it, it's going to be tough to persuade them that this isn't a boobytrap of some kind. There've been too many like this in the past. Here, they've got to take our word for it, immediately. We need someone they can trust, politically as well as in operational terms."

"Then that rules out the Americans."

"The French."

"Paris…I'll call them," said the adviser.

He looked at the man from Mossad: "The only consolation," he said, "is that we can think of someone who might be able to track down Silberzahn."

"That doesn't really make me all that happy," said the Owl. "If they know where Silberzahn is, then they know where all the others are."

DGSE headquarters, Paris, Friday, November 8, morning

Madame set down the receiver of the phone, smiled faintly, and admired the tips of her fingers with some complacency. The smile remained on her face. This was the double *en plein* win of her life, really the sweepstakes win she'd been waiting her entire career. She'd finally be done with the withering sarcasm about French *grandeur*, the witticisms about the country that "wants to speak with a voice that's much bigger than its fists." Here she had not only the arrogant Israelis, but even the bullying Americans crawling at her feet, begging for help that only she— in other words, that only *la France*—could give. She indulged in a smothered laugh. She gave a gleeful slap at the telephone, she got to her feet, and she went over to the liquor cabinet. She opened the cabinet door, thought for a moment, and decided that, in spite of the hour, just a finger of cognac was in order. She stopped to think whether she ought to inform the general. He was traveling with their cabinet minister and by now, she had developed the habit of consulting him only when she needed political cover. This time, from Le Pen to the wild-eyed kids of

Lutte Révolutionnaire, no one in France could do a thing but applaud, that is, if they ever learned about it all. She would tell the general when the job was complete. He was on the road with the minister, there was no time to waste, and in any case, the immense satisfaction over this French success would cover over any disgruntlement. She toasted silently, put the glass away in the little cabinet, and then called out:

"Claude."

The officer appeared immediately in the doorway.

"Exactly where is Dufresne right now?"

"Jaffa."

"Have him call in immediately. Then come back into this office. I want you to listen to the phone call.

The officer returned about a minute later, just as the phone on her desk was ringing. Madamespoke briefly with the chief operative of French agents in the Middle East. Dufresne was an accomplished veteran of the region, and he had assured her that the mission was feasible. Perhaps with Hamas, he had told her, but certainly, it would be much easier with Fatah.

Claude looked excitedly at her.

"This is a momentous day," he said.

"Let's hope so."

"The general will be pleased."

"You can count on that. Now, get me Annick."

"Annick?"

"Yes. She's still in the United States, isn't she?"

"Yes, of course. But what does Annick have to do with any of this?"

"A CIA jet is waiting for her. They guaranteed me the use of their aircraft, but that jet's not going to wait forever. She has to go to Gaza, with one of their agents, Klara Siebers, to oversee this operation."

"But Annick doesn't know anything about the Middle East. She's never even been there."

"I don't care what she knows or doesn't know. She doesn't have to say a thing. She just needs to be present."

"But why?"

Madame slowly shook her head.

"Claude, you are a soldier and an excellent officer but in order to do this job, you need to have a political brain and diplomatic sensibility as well." She relaxed into the back of her chair.

"As you know, even if we are—almost always—present at the moments that really count, on an international level we don't really cut such a spectacular figure. We cast a fairly small shadow, as it were. In this case, if the operation comes off successfully, it's only because we were there—France, our foreign policy, our presence in the region. It must have cost the Israelis, and the Americans too, a great deal of pride and political capital to call this number." And with one hand she pointed to the phone on her desk. "I have no intention of letting them forget it anytime soon. Dufresne will be waiting with the Israelis and the Palestinians at the airport to greet Annick who will be arriving on the same plane with the Americans. From beginning to end, we will not only be clearly visible, in the front row, but we will be the ones without whom nothing could have happened, the ones who led everyone else, by hand, to the solution. It's not the same as catching Silberzahn ourself but, perhaps, it's even better."

New York, NY, Friday, November 8, morning

The sunlight pounding through the blinds woke him up. O'Malley sat there for a short while with his eyes closed, then he threw off the blanket, sat up, and finally put his feet down on the ground. He sat there for a few seconds, to prepare his back, before getting up. Finally he moved, barefoot, across the floor and into the kitchen. It was neater in the kitchen than he had feared. For that matter, he almost never used it. He turned on the coffeemaker and went back into his bedroom. He pulled open the blinds and squinted, dazzled by the sudden burst of light. Probably, there had been bright sunshine the past few days as well, but he hadn't had time to notice it. He took a look at himself. His pajamas were spattered with coffee stains, of varying intensity and color, marks that had accumulated over time. He snorted in disgust and irritation, took off his pajamas, and tossed them into the laundry hamper. Naked, he went back to the kitchen, and poured himself a cup of coffee. Moving slowly to avoid spilling his coffee, he went back to the living room. He turned on the TV and cautiously sat down in his armchair. He squirmed around a little, because the leather upholstery was sticking to his bare buttocks, but then he stopped because his attention had been caught by the television news broadcast.

Apparently something completely unprecedented had happened. The game between the Cowboys and the Redskins, yesterday evening, had been interrupted and then suspended entirely because of disorderly behavior by the fans in the bleachers.

"Petra Wonacott has our story," said the anchorman. "Petra?" A disagreeable looking, square-jawed woman appeared on the screen, against the background of an empty stadium. She described how, according to the version of events that the police had come up with, a number of spectators had noticed, during the third quarter of the game, that a man was doing something suspicious with what looked like a coffee carry-cup. What does "something suspicious with what looked like a coffee carry-cup" even mean, O'Malley wondered? Was the man trying to drink his coffee? Anyway, the spectators had started shouting at him, the man had jumped to his feet and started to run, and a mob had chased after him. Someone had fired a shot and wounded him. The police had immediately intervened and had stopped the shooter but before the policemen were able to identify him, the crowd had attacked the police, pulled the man away from them, and allowed him to escape. "We know what he looks like, and we'll catch him soon," the chief of police assured the journalists. That doesn't strike me as the main problem, thought O'Malley. And now, standing next to Petra Wonacott was the star of the Cowboys, the quarterback. "It's a sad and incredible story," said the football player. "I don't know what we ought to do. Maybe, with everything that's going on in our country, we shouldn't go on playing as if these were normal times. Or maybe, on the other hand, we should play to remind everyone that normal times exist." Intelligent young man, O'Malley thought to himself. Answering the next question, the quarterback said that he didn't know whether the game against the Redskins would be replayed from the beginning or if it would take up where it had been suspended.

He changed channels. On the next channel, they must have already talked about the game. The anchorwoman was listing a series of news stories that painted a picture of a country on the brink of collapse. In

Alabama, they'd closed the schools; nationwide, air travel had become an excruciating ordeal because of security checks; the number of communities that had organized impromptu vigilante groups were proliferating; road blocks managed directly by citizens were popping up everywhere. O'Malley shuddered. Public rage was rising against the government and the White House. A White House press conference appeared on the screen. As he got comfortable in his armchair, he carelessly spilled a little coffee onto his stomach. He swore softly: the coffee was still hot. In the meanwhile, the overburdened White House press secretary was doing his best to answer the hail of questions pelting down on him from all directions. But he really had very little to say. The only thing that could buoy the country's optimism were the many "no comments" concerning the progress of the investigation, which might suggest, as the news anchorwoman commented, that there actually were developments in the manhunt. The truth is, O'Malley grimly told himself, that people only know half of the story, and what people knew wasn't the worst half. He knew that there had been discreet contacts made, in prison between the men from Salina's gang and people close to the administration. Whether that was just a way of stalling for time and preventing the Mafia from reprising the experience of Massapequod or whether, instead, especially now that they had learned that the damned narcotic caused birth defects, someone was seriously considering negotiations, he could not say. And maybe, it was better not to think about it. He noticed that, where the White House press secretary was particularly generous with details, it involved the number of men and women and the sheer volume of resources that were being devoted to the hunt for the narcotic.

"The real point is that we're not achieving a thing," O'Malley pointed out to himself, speaking aloud. "And when they figure that part out, we're done for."

He'd finished his coffee. He looked around for his cigarettes. He heard his cell phone ring.

"This is Hankemann."

That was the last thing O'Malley expected.

"Good morning Counselor, how are you doing? Did your conscience get the better of you?"

"Forget about that, O'Malley. Getting involved in this matter in the first place was a mistake, and one mistake leads to another. This is a phone call that, as a lawyer, I should not be making."

"Well, it's too late to fix that now. You've already made the phone call."

"All right, let's keep it short. There's somebody who wants to talk to you. And I think that you're going to be interested in hearing what they have to say."

"Who is it? Or are you going to play hide and seek?"

"I'm going to play hide and seek. You'll find out who it is on your own. Let me repeat, this person has some very interesting things to tell you."

"And when is he going to tell me these things?"

"Tonight, at 3 am, you will be waiting outside Mandy's bar, on Sixth Avenue."

"At that hour, the bar will be closed."

"That's right."

"Doesn't it strike you as an odd hour for a meeting?"

"Everything about this whole story is odd."

Hankemann hung up without saying goodbye.

Ramallah, Saturday, November 9, morning

They raced into a narrow lane in the center of Ramallah. Klara and Annick were in a nondescript black sedan. In front of them, in a military jeep, rode Dufresne with a young Mossad agent named Zach. He and Dufresne had come together to the airport to pick the two of them up and then they had driven them here. The presence of Zach had allowed both cars to pass through all the checkpoints between Jerusalem and Ramallah without stopping. The sun was already high in the sky, but the day was gray and damp anyway. They had stopped in a square in the middle of the narrow lane, in front of a building that looked like a school. Behind a wall, in fact, you could hear the cries of children playing.

A door swung open and a man with a submachine gun on a strap around his neck appeared in the doorway. He gestured for them to come in. Klara, Annick, and Dufresne walked past the man single file and into a long hallway. At the end of the corridor, they could see an open door. The man with the submachine gun stayed in the door watching Zach, who was standing in the middle of the square, with his cell phone pressed to his ear. This was his last opportunity to see whether Mossad had managed to track down Silberzahn, thought Annick.

In the office, behind a ramshackle desk, and in front of a wall that bore an unmistakable array of bulletholes, a man was sitting. He was in his early forties. He was in shirtsleeves: bald, short, a little chubby, with a wispy mustache.

"Hello, Latif," said Dufresne. Latif replied with a nod of the head. Then he got to his feet. "Miss Siebers, Miss Delarue," he said, leaning forward to shake hands with the two women, showing no difficulty in distinguishing between the Frenchwoman and the American. He showed no sign of concern over the fact that Zach was not there.

Klara gave him an unmistakable questioning look. Without speaking, Latif answered with a broad smile and a reassuring nod of the head. Klara heaved a sigh of relief: at least they knew where Silberzahn was hiding. Just then, Zach walked in. Latif seemed to stiffen for a moment, then he relaxed in his chair. The two men looked at one aother without saying hello. Latif was the first to speak:

"Until yesterday, I never would have dreamed that we would be obliged to help get Mossad out of hot water."

Zach hesitated for just a moment:

"Well, actually," he said, "you're the ones who are in hot water. You're the designated victims."

"The front-line victims, you mean to say," Latif shot back. "Afterwards, of course…"

He let the unfinished phrase hang in the air, accompanying it with a vague gesture of one hand. He seemed to think for a moment, as if he was deciding whether or not to utter the words he had on the tip of his tongue. "I don't think that I'm revealing a closely held secret," he resumed, "if I tell you that many believe that our people could withstand yet another sacrifice, if it was a way of making sure you were stuck in this pool of shit of your own making." He looked Zach right in the eye:

"To show the world," he added, "the true nature of the state of Israel."

"I wonder just what you would have done," Zach replied, "if the children in danger were in Gaza and, therefore, likely to vote for Hamas someday."

Latif looked at him with a scowl.

"As you said earlier, I'm Palestinian and nothing more," he hissed.

"However," Zach went on with a challenging note in his voice, "I'm still curious. What would you have decided to do if Uriel's plan had been to do what everyone thought at first? That is, to assassinate a few Hamas leaders? Maybe you wouldn't have been quite so concerned."

"Uriel is one of your own men, don't forget it," the Arab replied.

Klara was about to step in, and Zach was about to reply, but Latif beat them both to the punch. He had slumped back in his chair: "In any case, I was in favor of leaving you to flounder around in your own shit, too. But the politicians made another decision."

"And the decision to get you involved in this matter was made by the politicians, too," Zach replied.

"And that goes for all those people who say that there's never a time to say a good word in favor of politicians," Klara finally broke in.

The two men stood staring at one another for a few seconds. Then Latif got to his feet. "Let's get busy," he said. He stood up and went to the door.

"Wait here," he said as he walked out the door.

Klara spoke to Zach.

"What's this guy Silberzahn like?"

"A very skillful and efficient agent," the Israeli replied. "Or perhaps I should say effective. Possibly the best agent that we have. Some people think of him as a hero. Actually, though, he's a cruel and unscrupulous bastard, convinced he is the depository of a mission from God. Impossible to control. Someone like him, you take him as he is. Or you leave him. I personally would have left him. He's a genuine son of a bitch... But, of course, he's *our* son of a bitch," he resumed after a moment's pause. "So I would have preferred that it be us settling matters with him. Here, we're just contracting debts. Latif," he concluded, "is right."

"What about Latif?"

"Latif is a capable operator. Very capable indeed. Otherwise he wouldn't be here, he'd be in prison."

"Over there," he explained, with a nod of his head toward Jerusalem. In the meanwhile, Latif was back. With him was a young woman, her head and shoulders covered with a dark-colored scarf, over a loose pair of military trousers. She had a pistol on her belt.

"This," Latif said," is Fatimah."

"She's been on Silberzahn's trail for a while now," he added, with a rapid glance at Zach.

Annick noticed that Latif treated Fatimah with great respect. And the woman certainly did not have a submissive, timorous demeanor. She must be more than just an ordinary militant. Still, she had a very strange attitude. Her large dark eyes were sad and dull.

Fatimah began speaking.

"We've been following Silberzahn since he left..." and here she hesitated for a moment, closing her eyes, "...Beirut." Her voice was slow and neutral, as if she wanted to maintain the greatest possible distance between herself and the man she was talking about.

"He moved around a great deal and very quickly. That forced us to follow him."

"Without ever getting very close to him," she added immediately. "Then he moved into the Negev Desert. There, we lost track of him."

"You lost him!" Klara broke in. Fatimah shook her head no.

"In that area there are three kibbutzes... fundamentalist kibbutzes."

It seemed like a strange word to Klara, coming from a woman with her head covered in keeping with Muslim custom, but Fatimah didn't seem to see it that way.

"And he was in one of the three kibbutzes," she resumed, "But for us, it was dangerous to get near those kibbutzes. Then," she went on, looking at Klara directly for the first time, "you told us about the narcotic and how it could be used. That's when we understood which of the three kibbutzes he had gone to."

"Which kibbutz is it?" asked Klara.

"The one with the helicopter."

"The helicopter?"

Fatimah held up her hand, telling her to wait.

"We went to check and we saw him."

"He's there?"

"Yes. He's there."

Fatimah stood in silence. Latif broke in.

"The kibbutz," he explained, "makes use of the helicopter, an old piece of combat equipment long since taken out of active service, in order to spray fertilizer onto the fields. It's clear exactly what use Silberzahn plans to make of that equipment. Gaza is just a few minutes away by air."

"Then the target is Gaza," said Klara

"From there," Fatimah explained, "it's the only credible hypothesis. All the other cities are too far away."

Klara glanced over at Zach, but luckily the agent wasn't saying a word.

"Is it so easy to enter Gaza's airspace?" she asked him.

"Theoretically, it's not," replied the agent. "But from the southeast, they're certainly controlling the airspace less carefully. And a helicopter from a kibbutz, of course, doesn't arouse a lot of suspicion. Probably that helicopter is constantlyin flight in that area. Plus, all Silberzahn needs is a few minutes in the air. Then, in all likelihood, even the Israeli soldiers will be fast asleep. Then he can land and do... what he's planning to do."

"But what about the people on the kibbutz?" Annick asked.

"They certainly know him and admire him," Zach replied. "It's probably not the first time he's used this place as a base. They hide him and they protect him."

"Will they let him take the helicopter?" Annick went on to ask.

"They might not give it to him ," Zach replied. "But that doesn't mean they'll keep him from stealing it."

"He's already been there for a day and a half," Latif broke in. "He can't hide out there for much longer. We assume that he'll act this evening, probably immediately before sundown."

"We think the same thing," Zach said with a nod. "More or less when the muezzin calls the faithful to prayer."

"How can we stop him?" Klara asked.

"I'll call out the army," Zach replied.

"Hold on a second!" said Klara, raising both hands and holding them up flat. She knew that most of the narcotic was in America and that the decisive battle would be fought there. But that was Jamie's problem. Her one objective was Uriel's bottle and she wanted to make sure she got her hands on it. "Remember that Silberzahn is important but, far more important, we have to get the narcotic back. I want to be there too."

Zach was expecting that.

"All right," he said. He glanced at his watch.

"If we get moving immediately, we can get there by helicopter by mid afternoon."

"Before the evening prayer," said Latif.

"Before the muezzin's call and before the end of the Sabbath," Zach agreed.

"Let's go." He headed for the door.

Latif's voice stopped him.

"Fatimah is coming with you," he said.

Zach turned and looked at Dufresne, more surprised than annoyed.

"That," he said, "wasn't part of the arrangement."

"Fatimah is going with you," Latif repeated, in a firm voice.

Zach looked first at Latif, then at Fatimah, and then back at Latif. He leaned over to the Arab. "Was Fatimah," he whispered, "in...Beirut?"

Latif nodded yes, as he gaze steadily into the Israeli's eyes.

Zach thought it over. "So be it, then. We'll make room for her."

New York, NY, Saturday, November 9, before dawn

At 3 am, O'Malley was standing in front of the dark picture windows of Mandy's bar. A long black sedan pulled to a halt front of him. As he expected, there was one man driving and another man in the back seat. The rear door swung open. He got in. There were no greetings and no introductions. No one said a word. The car pulled away from the curb immediately. It had gone just a short distance when the man seated next to him pulled out a black handkerchief and tied it around his eyes. O'Malley let him do it.

They drove around for half an hour. When they stopped and the man removed the handkerchief, he saw that they were in a narrow alley separating two blocks. A small door opened. The man pushed him through it with a gentle shove. He walked in. Immediately inside the door, a narrow metal staircase led upstairs. He climbed up one flight of stairs. Behind the walls he heard the sound of machinery operating and a few voices. The smell was unmistakable.

At the top of the flight of stairs was a door. He opened it and found himself in a small office, with a desk covered with papers and filing cabinets against the walls. Behind the desk was a man in his early seventies, with a spectacular white mustache. He was laboriously lighting a cigar, but even so he nodded his head, inviting him to take a seat in the chair in front of the desk. Seated on another chair, in a corner, outside of the cone of light cast by the lamp on the desk, was another man, dressed in an overcoat and hat.

O'Malley sat down, pulled a pack out of his jacket pocket, and lit a cigarette. The other man was still engaged in his complicated endeavor. He finally drew a deep puff of smoke and, in the blue haze of tobacco that surrounded him, said:

"Surprised to see me, O'Malley?"

"No. When Hankemann called me, I figured that there might be two or three people in question, and one of them was you, Don Vincenzo."

"I like you, O'Malley. You're a quick thinker."

"Still, I didn't expect to see you here."

Don Vincenzo laughed with pleasure.

"Good one, O'Malley. I said you were a quick thinker. You're right. We shouldn't be here, should we?"

"This is your wife's dry cleaners, in the Bronx. It's neutral..."

"That's right. It's neutral territory. No men's business done on the premises. This evening, however, we're going to make an exception. Because this is an exceptional occasion."

"Which is to say?"

Don Vincenzo paused for a long time.

"So many things have happened, recently."

"Yes."

"Unpleasant things."

"I'd be tempted to use a stronger word."

"Okay, then let's say horrible things."

"And you didn't expect these things to happen?"

"Well, yes and no. Let's say that we expected something a little less, shall we say, dramatic?"

"But there was a meeting of all the top bosses and you voted in favor."

Don Vincenzo gave him a penetrating glance.

"Is that something you got from Meg or is it from Larramee?"

"Let's just say that we work as a team and we work hard."

Don Vincenzo seemed to think that over. O'Malley took advantage of the opportunity to pull out another cigarette and light it with the stub of the one he'd been smoking. Don Vincenzo took another drag on his cigar.

"We voted, it's true. But that's not the U.S. Congress, you know. You'd have to think about it pretty carefully before voting for a minority view."

"I understand," said O'Malley. "Well?"

"So I've thought it over. Right now, what is the one thing you care about most?"

"Finding the narcotic," O'Malley said, without hesitation.

Don Vincenzo nodeed.

"Do you know who has it?"

"Cal Salina."

"Calogero Salina, that's right. Young Don Calogero, the man with a thousand plans. You work hard, there's no doubt about it."

The boss suddenly sat bolt upright in his chair, set his lit cigar down on his desk, and leaned forward.

"Baddington, Massachussetts. The industrial park. People work there 24-7. Warehouse 56. Near the perimeter fence."

O'Malley stood up, dropped the cigarette on the floor and crushed it with his heel. "Thanks," he said. And he turned to go.

"Hold it, O'Malley," Don Vincenzo raised one hand. "Where do you think you're going?"

"To Baddington."

"There's no hurry. For the moment, I can guarantee you that nothing's going to happen. You have all the time you need. Let's talk. Do you understand clearly why I'm breaking my oath of omertà?"

"No. And I don't give a damn. I have other things to worry about."

"Always in a hurry, aren't you, O'Malley? This time, though, you're going have to hear me out. You see, even I'm not sure why I just told you what I did. Around here," and he gestured to the man sitting in the corner, his face shrouded in darkness, "it's not like I have anyone I can talk to about it. I think that talking it over with you will help me clear my head."

O'Malley sat back down. He lit another cigarette.

"I'm all ears," he said.

"One hundred sixty dead, right?" the old man began. "One hundred sixty people—women, children, old men—who had nothing to do with us and who we had nothing against. Nothing like that's ever happened before. We'd never done anything like it before. If you're going to do something like that, you'd better have some pretty good reasons, right, O'Malley? Strong reasons. What do you think, do we have good reasons for doing this thing?"

"Well, why don't you tell me?"

"Well, Salina says we do. But let's take a look at the demands in the letter. One by one. The casinos. Six new casinos, formally belonging to Indian tribes, but actually run and controlled by us. Two for the family in Miami, one for the family in Dallas, one for the people in Los Angeles, one for Chicago, and one up in New York state. So one for me, too, right? Salina was very careful. But was this really the only way of getting this? How many casinos have we set up in all these years, without all this mess?"

Don Vincenzo stopped talking. He took a puff on the stub of his cigar which had gone out in the meanwhile. He tossed it into the trashcan next to the desk.

"Then," he resumed, "there is the prison. I'm delighted, as you can imagine, for Calogero Urzì, Frank Lamorte, and all the others who will be moving from hard time cells to those lovely country club prisons where they'll be serving cheek by jowl with the lords of Wall Street, where they can order meals catered by a restaurant and, of course, go on tending to family matters. We are all happy as can be about that. But prison is one of the risks of our line of business, and even worthier and more respected people than Calogero, Frank, and even me have wound up there. It's not the end of the world. In fact," he snickered, "it tends to bring in new blood and accelerate promotion through the ranks. Last of all, the money. For half a day, we can move our money anywhere we want around the world. Well, that's fine, especially for someone like Salina, who is constantly dealing with the stock exchange. But come on, we've always moved our money around exactly as we pleased, okay, with the occasional legal hassle, but still..."

Don Vincenzo stopped. He smacked his lips a couple of times.

"Santuzzo, a glass of water, please."

The man in the corner stood up and opened a door. He came back from the adjoining room with a bottle of San Pellegrino and two glasses. He set them down in the desk.

"Look at the water I have to drink. Low in minerals. For my stomach," said Don Vincenzo. "Care for a glass, O'Malley?"

O'Malley shook his head. "Maybe," he said, "the demands are really only a pretext. The point of the letter is to begin negotiations. A formal, institutional exchange. Between two equal counterparts."

Don Vincenzo finished drinking his glass of water, in a series of long sips. "That's what Salina says," he answered. "The qualitative leap. That's how we'll show them, he says, that from now on they have to sit down at the table with us and talk." He stopped and looked hard at O'Malley. "Bullshit," he decreed. "Salina talks that way because he is an arrogant bastard. And he has no respect for the state." He paused, running a finger over his mustache. "I have a great deal of respect for the state," he resumed. "I don't believe for a second that you're all a bunch of puppets that we can make dance to whatever tune we like. You are an enormous, unstoppable power. We can stay a length or a neck ahead of you, we often manage to do it, but we always feel your breath hot on our backs. What does Salina think is going to happen? Does he think Congress is going to pass a law in our favor? Even if the letter was accepted, two or three years from now, there are going to be new faces in power. What does he think, they're going to renew negotiations? Does he think that the state will be willing to deal with the Mafia?"

O'Malley was careful not to interrupt him.

"Of course," Don Vincenzo resumed, "there's this poison. Which has made him even more arrogant, still blinder. How long does he think he'll be able to hold onto it, before you get your hands on it, or find an antidote, or something else I can't imagine? Six months? A year? Time isn't on his, or our, side."

"He could strike again."

"Which is exactly what I'm most afraid of. Already you're on our asses for what happened. What could you unleash against us if we kill another five hundred or a thousand people? I'll tell you. A relentless manhunt. It would spell the end for us."

Don Vincenzo shook his head.

"No," he went on, "the demands, the negotiations, it's all bullshit. Trinkets, just so much garbage. Salina has something else in mind. He's thinking about us. Salina wants to gain sufficient advantage to become the *capo di tutti capi*, and rule over the rest of us. That's a perfectly legitimate ambition but he's not the first one to think of it. Usually, though, the one who tries to gain that position pays for the right himself, he doesn't ask everyone else to pay for him."

The old man paused to pour himself another glass of mineral water.

"It seems perfectly clear to me," O'Malley said.

"No, it isn't," Don Vincenzo answered him. "Those are all perfectly good reasons, but none of them, taken alone, is enough to justify a betrayal. Think about it, O'Malley. In my world, honor and self-respect come before freedom. Now here's my problem: are all of them, taken together, enough to justify this act in my conscience?"

"If you're asking me, just one of them is plenty. Take your pick."

"It's enough to start a gang war with Salina, sure. But it's not enough to hand him over to the Feds. Do you understand what a difference there is, for me?"

O'Malley opened his mouth to reply, but he wasn't fast enough. Don Vincenzo spoke first, and caught him off guard.

"My son is doing well in school," he said.

O'Malley fell silent.

"Very well, in fact," Don Vincenzo went on. "He got a full scholarship. To Princeton. He's not the first of our people to go to Princeton. But he's the first one to go with a full scholarship. He did it all on his own." Don Vincenzo stopped to catch his breath and looked at his hands, which lay flat on the desk. O'Malley had lit another cigarette.

"You see, O'Malley, my wife, Concettina, was an outstanding

woman, but we never had children. So when she died, as much grief as I felt, still, I remarried."

"With a Korean woman."

"That's right, with a Korean woman. A lot of people thought it was kind of funny. I took some criticism. From their point of view, they might even have a point. She wanted something all her own, this dry cleaners, and she always kept our boy far away from… from our world, I guess. And now he wants to go to Princeton, get his MBA, and get a job on Wall Street. I can understand him. This is a tough life. I wouldn't wish it on him."

Don Vincenzo heaved a sigh.

"Don't get me wrong, O'Malley. I don't regret a thing. You've tried, a million times, to nail me, and you never did it. If you ask me, you won't in the future either. But let's just say that I've done lots of things in my life. Including some pretty… heavy things. Well, I'd do them all over again. Because that's what my life has been. On the other hand, if I hadn't done those things, the Mexicans or the Jamaicans would have done them instead. Well, you know what I say? Let them do those things for a while. Maybe it's time for us to look ahead. Time for my son to look ahead. I don't want him to have to drag the weight and the burden of hundreds of deaths that he had nothing to do with for the rest of his life." Don Vincenzo stopped. "Now that's a good reason to do something," he added.

The two men sat looking one another in the eye for a few seconds.

"I understand, Don Vincenzo."

He got to his feet, but he didn't shake hands with him.

"I understand completely." A stab of pain in his hip reminded him that he had been sitting down for too long.

"Now I'm going to Baddington," he added. "Wish me good luck."

"Good luck?" Don Vincenzo pounded his fist on the desktop. "What the fuck kind of good luck are you talking about? You take me for a fool? Listen, tonight I turned down a one-way street. No exit. I'm betting everything on you. I can't afford to lose that bet, because if I do, everyone will turn on me. I need to get that poison, just as much as you need it."

Don Vincenzo got to his feet vigorously. He spoke quickly now.

"Today, you're going to Baddington, but you're not going alone. One of my men will be waiting for you there. There are certain things you'll need to know about that that warehouse." He gestured to the man in the corner, who jumped to his feet and accompanied O'Malley to the door and then down the metal staircase, to the car. Inside, the two men were waiting. He got in and sat in the back seat again. The man sitting beside him was about to wrap the black handkerchief around his head again. But the man who had sat in on the meeting with Don Vincenzo leaned in and said a few words to him in Italian. The other man dropped the handkerchief on his knee.

O'Malley relaxed in the car seat. It was dawn by now. The pantomime with Don Vincenzo had gone on far too long. If what he wanted was to protect his son, he had only to ask. He could have set his conditions and then told him about the warehouse. But maybe the old boss really did want to confess his sins. The Mafia in the new millennium had many faces.

The Negev Desert, Saturday, November 9, afternoon

Out of concern that Silberzahn might disappear with the narcotic once again, Klara had asked Zach to make sure that the units of soldiers that he had mobilized should only arrive at the kibbutz once they were already in the area. As they flew over the Negev, in fact, they had spotted a small column of Tsahal trucks, on the march toward their destination. Klara also wanted to be sure that their helicopter didn't alarm Silberzahn. And so they landed about a dozen kilometers from the kibbutz and continued from there with two jeeps.

Zach and Klara and Annick were in one jeep, Fatimah and Dufresne were in the other.

When they got there, the sun was still high in the sky. A strong wind was kicking up windfunnels of dust. The kibbutz was in a hollow and in order to get a glimpse of it, they had to get closer than they had expected. It was a series of agricultural buildings, silos, residential structures, and isolated houses, surrounded by an enclosure wall marking the perimeter. On the right, there was an open space, occupied only by a single helicopter.

"It's an old army helicopter, reconfigured. You see the tank underneath it, added for spraying fertilizers?" asked Zach. Everyone could see it and everyone knew what it contained now. Through the dust, they could see a figure moving around the helicopter.

"It's still early!" Klara exclaimed. "Wasn't he supposed to wait for sundown to get moving?"

"I'm afraid somebody must have seen the army trucks and warned him," Zach replied. "Even though I don't think he wants to take action before the end of the Sabbath. Probably, he decided just to get out of there and go hide somewhere, where he can wait for sunset."

The hilltop from which they were looking out was too close to the kibbutz. The figure standing next to the helicopter stopped and turned to look at them.

"*Merde*! He saw us!" Annick cried.

In the meanwhile, Silberzahn had jumped into the helicopter and the blades were beginning to rotate. Zach made a beeline for the jeep.

"Damn it," he yelled, "he's too close to use the Stinger; it wouldn't have time to range in on the heat source in the engine." He came back with a high-precision rifle. "Before he can get the bastard in the air," he muttered. He knelt down on one knee and took careful aim. Too late. The helicopter was rising into the air. Zach squeezed the trigger. A shot rang out. Immediately afterward, a second shot. But with a reckless and apparently impossible piece of piloting, the aged helicopter, just a few yards from the ground, veered away at a 45-degree angle and shot off sideways. Silberzahn knew what he was doing. The bullets bit the dust.

The helicopter made a wide loop and now it was heading straight for them.

"He's got the wind at his back!" Klara shouted. "He wants to spray us with the narcotic and keep us from launching the alarm!"

She realized that suddenly Fatimah had appeared beside her. She had the Stinger on her right shoulder. The weapon weighed thirty pounds, the missile was five feet long, but the woman was handling it with no apparent effort, moving lightly, as if she were dancing. Zach watched her.

"He was stupid enough to veer off to that distance," Fatimah cut him off before he could speak. "I know exactly what to do," she added. Then she knelt down. The chattering, roaring noise of the helicopter had become a lacerating howl. Silberzahn was heading straight for them. That meant he couldn't change course—he couldn't take evasive action. At the same time, it meant he was offering them the smallest possible target. A risky bet: typical Silberzahn.

"He's mine now," said Fatimah in a low voice. She pulled the trigger. With a puff of smoke and a whoosh of pneumatic suction, the missile took off at a velocity that seemed inconceivable. It fishtailed for a moment, then the infrared system locked on to the target. A fraction of a second later, it bullseyed into the helicopter. First there was a flash of yellow flame, then a second, larger blast of red fire. Then the fireball was shrouded in black smoke, as the helicopter disintegrated in midair. The flight of the archangel was over.

Baddington, MA, Saturday, November 9, afternoon

They were standing on top of a crane, a few hundred yards away from Salina's warehouse. Next to O'Malley were Williamson, a tall guy with a buzz cut, who would lead the operation, and an Italian who spoke unaccented English. Williamson was watching the warehouse through a pair of binoculars.

"It's an old warehouse. The pillars and the terrace are made of reinforced concrete, but all the rest is iron and plate steel," the Italian was explaining. "It's on two floors, a ground floor and a second floor, with a freight elevator connecting them. The second story has a door leading out to the terrace. The warehouse adjoins an enclosure wall, but there are no openings there. Instead," he pointed at the hill sloping gently down toward the wall, "look at the hump, among the trees, halfway down the slope." There was a rise in the side of the hill, about a hundred feet from the road running over the top of the hill. "That's important. That is where you'll find the mouth of the underground tunnel that runs out of the basement of the warehouse. It's big enough for two men to walk in it side by side and it ends in a flight of stairs and a landing right in front of the door." O'Malley looked at him quizzically.

"Ten years ago or so, we used that warehouse ourselves and the tunnel proved to be...ah...useful." O'Malley grunted:

"Is that how they're planning to get away?"

"Not necessarily," Williamson broke in. "If they have armored vehicles they could try and run the roadblock. In any case, we need to keep the tunnel in mind."

Baddington, MA, Saturday, November 9, sunset

The sun was setting. Soon, it would be dark, dank, and chilly. O'Malley was hiding behind a bush. If there was one thing that could stop the country from sliding into chaos, it was what they were about to do. With him were Meg and Larramee and seven other FBI agents, fanned out radially, around the vegetation-concealed opening of the tunnel. O'Malley was holding pistol, a Beretta 90two 9x21, Meg had a sawed-off shotgun, and Larramee had a Heckler & Koch HK416 assault rifle.

They were all wearing bulletproof vests. Williamson had deployed five other men, as a second line of defense, along the road. The rest of them, with Jill and Stefan, about thirty in all, were arrayed around the warehouse.

"Jill told me that we've lost track of Salina since this morning," said O'Malley.

"I know," Larramee replied.

"I don't like it. Are we sure that they haven't gotten out of here with the narcotic by car and we're just playing soldiers here?"

"Since this morning, only a single car has arrived and it's still inside. Aside from the fast food truck. It was here twice."

"What about the fast food truck?"

"Calm down, chief. That was one of our people driving. They even told him that he was working too hard because he came by for lunch and for dinner."

"So what did he see?"

"He counted at least fifteen of them or so. But he brought enough food for ten more to eat."

"Let's just hope that they're really hungry. Otherwise, I'm afraid Williamson got his numbers wrong."

O'Malley sat down behind a boulder and lit a cigarette. He went on talking with Larramee

"In your opinion, do they know we're here?"

"I don't think so. Williamson told everyone to come one at a time, dressed as construction workers."

The sun had set, and in the gray air, visibility was declining.

Two trucks roared into the open space in front of the warehouse and turned on their spotlights. Williamson's voice echoed through a loudspeaker:

"FBI. Come out with your hands up." O'Malley took one last long furious drag and then crushed out his cigarette.

Naturally, nothing happened. Except that the lights disappeared from the fissures in the walls of the warehouse. The FBI men remained under shelter and silence descended over the open space.

The silence was broken by the rattle of gunfire from what sounded, to O'Malley's untutored ears, like a heavy machine gun. They were shooting from the second floor. Williamson's agents returned the fire. Immediately afterward, submachine guns, handguns, and rifles began shooting from the warehouse.

In the gathering darkness, the muzzles flashed bright flames.

The firefight went on for a few more minutes, with no visible results. The spotlights inundated the warehouse with light, making it possible to see dark silhouettes behind the windows. Two helicopters were cruising overhead. But no one moved. The agents would have had to cross the open space to get inside and, under those conditions, it would have amounted to suicide. Williamson had another idea.

The intensity of the firefight was waning and O'Malley could distinctly hear the sound of a crane moving. The arm of the crane appeared over the terrace. There was a cage hanging from the arm of the crane, with a group of agents riding inside it. Inside the warehouse, they couldn't see it. The cage set down gently on the roof: the agents darted out of it, making for the trapdoor and lowering themselves through it. The cage rose into the air again. Now the battle was being fought inside the warehouse.

"Nice job!" said O'Malley.

The banging of pistols and rifles could be heard inside the building. The agents in the open space began to converge on the entrance. But the doors suddenly flew open and two cars barreled out at top speed. The headlights blinded the agents who were cut in their rays. The cars were armor-plated and the bullets ricocheted off them. The only possibility was to hit the tires, but there were only seconds to go. "Damn it," Meg murmured under her breath.

The agent driving the crane had the idea. He spun the huge machine around at top speed, at the risk of tipping it over, and dropped the heavy metal cage about thirty feet in front of the first car. The driver jammed on his brakes, but he was too close and he ran into the basket with a screech of bending steel. The other car managed to brake to a halt and the car doors flew open, but the men inside the car were riddled with bullets before they could set foot outside.

O'Malley hoped that the vehicles were nothing more than a diversion and that the narcotic wasn't in there. He wanted it intact and he wanted it all. But he was convinced that the answer would come from the tunnel.

The firefight seemed to have been going on for hours and, at the same time, it seemed to have just begun. By now it was pitch dark. O'Malley looked at his watch. They'd been shooting for more than twenty minutes. Why were Salina's men taking so long? Just then, he heard a sound in the underbrush. The three spotlights around the exit from the tunnel switched on: behind the branches of the shrubbery, the door had opened.

"Hold it. Hold it!! FBI, *eff-bee-eye*, FBI Freeze!! Come out with your hands up," said a voice, as per regulation. The only response that O'Malley could see were a couple of objects tossed out of the door. They landed near the spotlights. And they exploded.

"Hand grenades!" he heard someone swear nearby.

The hand grenades had put two of the spotlights out of operation and they'd grazed the third, which now pointed straight up into the air. In the spectral light that ensued, O'Malley saw six men carrying a heavy metal case. Around them, eight others were firing furiously, covering their escape route to the top of the hill.

O'Malley heard the screech of brakes from the road on top of the hill and then a series of furious bursts of automatic weapons fire. That's why they'd taken so long. They were waiting for reinforcements.

Williamson had made a mistake by putting so few men on the hill. Salina's soon outshot them and they started running down the slope, firing as they went.

An agent next to him had already called in the helicopters. But from the street, they saw the fiery trail of a Stinger heat-seeking missile. The missile missed its target but the two helicopters were forced to fly away in a broad curve.

O' Malley, Meg, and Larramee were caught in the crossfire between the group with the case and the Mafiosi who were coming down the hill. O' Malley only had a few seconds to make up his mind, before the case vanished into the darkness. If they managed to make it to the cars, they would have at least a two- or three-minute headstart, before he could put together a serious pursuit. He did the only thing he could think of. He took aim and fired. He missed the target. The shooting pains in his hip were tormenting him, but he fired a second time and missed again. A dull thud slammed into his shoulder and knocked him to the ground. He felt a terrible burning sensation where he'd been hit, but he managed to turn around and speak to Meg.

"Meg, get their legs!" he shouted.

Meg always won the sharpshooting contests, back at the office. He saw her drop to one knee and stay there, as if frozen solid, in the midst of the noise of shooting. He didn't see her pull the trigger. He had twisted his head around as far as he could and he could see the men running away with the case. Suddenly one of them seemed to stumble and he let go of his grip on the case, which in turn seemed to become much heavier. Another shot was fired and another man stumbled, then a third shot hit him right in the other leg. The man slipped to the ground, the others lost their balance and fell to the ground alongside him, along with the case, slithering down the slope they had been trying to climb. The momentum of their escape was halted. Williamson's men had taken control of the warehouse, and now they climbed the wall and were clambering up the hill, spraying submachine gun fire at the men who had been carrying the case just a short while before.

Meg bent over Jamie. He embraced her hard with his unhurt arm and held her close to him.

"You're still the best shot," he murmured to her.

"Always such a gentleman," she replied, freeing herself from his grip. O'Malley didn't get a chance to hear her. He had already passed out, with a smile on his face.

A Hospital in Baddington, Sunday, November 10, early morning

He woke up, with a struggle, in a hospital room. A nurse was busily tending to his bed. When she realized that he had opened his eyes, she immediately said: "They're just outside in the hall."

Meg, Jill, Larramee, and Stefan trooped in in single file and gathered around the bed.

"Everything's fine," said Stefan with a smile.

"What's fine?" he managed to mumble.

"Your shoulder, The doctors says it's only a flesh wound. You'll be on your feet again in a couple of days. But they do say you have a bad case of arthritis of the hip."

"Fuck you. Well?" He looked at Larramee.

"Everything's under control, chief," smiled the man who, without his realizing it, had become his de facto deputy. "The narcotic was in the case. Four drums, two-and-a-half gallons each, full to the brim."

"Well, I guess that's good news," O'Malley mumbled.

"But...?"

He looked at Larramee. And Larramee was a smart young man.

"Salina's dead," he said. "He was one of the guys who were carrying the case."

"But ..." O'Malley murmured. They must have given him a heavy dose of sedatives, because he fell right back to sleep.

Saint Mary Hospital, Baddington, MA, Wednesday November 13, afternoon

O'Malley was packing his few possessions into a bag. His arm was still numb, the bandages were a little too tight, but he was ready to leave the hospital. He turned when he heard the door opening, even though it might only be the nurse. But he was accustomed to not wanting anyone behind him unless he knew exactly who it was. Instead his eyes were greeted with a surprise. Framed in the doorway was Meg, sheathed in an overcoat with a belt and wide lapels over which her slightly messy hair tumbled luxuriantly. For once, the coat was short enough to reveal her shapely legs. She smiled, and in her arms she held two bottles of wine.

"Meg?" He was happy to see it was her, instead of Jill or Larramee.

"Jamie, I'm glad to see you on your feet." Meg walked quickly over to the table and set down the two bottles, next to O'Malley's bag.

"I ran into Matterre-Faquet, downstairs. He understands how much trouble he's caused, the risks that he forced us to run. He had them bring him by here to say goodbye, but then he was afraid to come up to see you in your room. He gave me these bottles and told me to tell you not to forget them. He says this is the wine he makes and that it comes from near Bordeaux. Without any false modesty he insists it's first rate. Apparently you can't buy it in a wine store, on this side of the Atlantic. When you feel like toasting to the happy conclusion of this unhappy story, he says that this is the wine you should use to fill up the right glass."

O'Malley looked at Meg, as if he were thinking about other things, not wine. She noticed and went on: "He says that it's one of the few red wines that you can drink with Camembert."

"Well, that was nice of him," O'Malley mumbled, "but I think that wine should go into your glass, Meg."

An FBI agent never blushes, but Meg's cheeks flushed to a color suspiciously close to a reddish pink. She looked down and went on:

"That poor bastard Matterre-Faquet," she smiled. "He got himself into a hell of a mess and it took a lot of people to get him out of it. But you, Jamie, you're the one who did the most decisive thing, by getting Salina's narcotic back and getting us out of that nightmare."

"Thanks, Meg, but don't forget that you all worked hard, and risked your lives, to stop this fucked-up perfume-sedative-narcotic." He patted her on the back, so gently that it could have seemed like a caress.

"Listen, Meg, one more question. Tell me the truth, like you always do," O'Malley added immediately, "are we sure that there isn't anymore of this stuff around?"

Meg smiled.

"You know, I asked that frog-eater what he thought. You know what he told me? He said, 'Well, you saw it for yourself on TV, didn't you? The whole ceremony that the Pentagon put on to show everyone, live, the destruction of the narcotic, to eliminate all doubts once and for all.' Then he said, with that attitude of the cynical bastard that he is: 'Of course, I can't exclude that they set aside a vial of the stuff.'"

O'Malley laughed.

"What a son of a bitch he is! He hasn't figured out anything about the way things work here. We Americans are careful, precise people. The journalists have probably checked out ten times, coming and going, that the quantity that was destroyed corresponds exactly to the quantity that was declared. If we wanted to set a vial aside, we should have thought of that earlier, right, Meg? That is, before we announced how much we recovered from Salina. But since Larramee made that statement, no one can come and shift things around. As for the material that wound up in Israel, another person that I trust, my ex-wife Klara, saw it blown up in midair, when Silberzahn's helicopter exploded, and we have no reason to doubt her word. No," he went on, "when I was asking if there's anymore of this stuff around, I was talking about something else."

"What, exactly?"

"His head, Meg. The formula for the narcotic is still in there, isn't it? He could make it again, together with the French intelligence service."

"Him? No, Jamie, I really don't think so. Someone like him, stubborn enough to refuse to help the Pentagon, where they pay in dollars, is just as likely to refuse to help the French intelligence service, who pay in glory and nothing more. On the other hand, he left France especially to be free to do his own science. Isn't that what he was saying?"

"Still..."

"Still?" asked Meg, curiously.

"Meg, science is strong and it's resilient."

"What do you mean?"

"I mean, science never goes backwards and it never forgets. Once it's been established that something can be done, you can't go back, you can't pretend it never happened. Many scientists will try to reproduce it, maybe eliminating the negative effects in the process, rendering it non-teratogenic. In the end, someone will succeed."

"You think this has occurred to the people at the Pentagon or in France or Mossad?"

"I wouldn't be surprised," O'Malley replied. "Though I hope it hasn't. I hope that this molecule doesn't persecute him for the rest of his life, and that Matterre-Faquet really is able to forget everything that's happened."

"Do you mean that he's been through enough to make him want to forget about that molecule for the rest of his life?"

"Well, he thought of it as a bland sedative. When he understood what it could be used for, he no longer recognized it as his own creation, so to speak. At least, that's what he told me."

"In any case," Meg added, "he's about to begin a new life."

"What do you mean?"

"He's going away. He's leaving America."

"He's leaving America? Where is he going?"

"He's going back to France. For him it's a burning defeat, and the real truth is that he was practically forced to go back. Here in America, after what happened, no one wants him around anymore. Even at Stony Brook, he says, they avoid him with some considerable embarrassment. So the only place left for him is France. From what he told me just now, downstairs in the lobby, though, it seemed to me that what the French chiefly want is to get him out of circulation. He's an explosive personality, he's uncontrollable, he's an insubordinate...they found a second-class university for him, near his castle and his family's vineyards, where he can study wines and perfumes. In any case, he seems resigned to it. He says that he wants a quietlife now," Meg giggled. "A quiet life, someone as arrogant as him? He wants to be on the front page of the major newspapers! Poor bastard, he really took a kick in the teeth!"

"Well, at least he always has that Jamaican girlfriend of his, and she's not too bad to look at, right? What's to become of Mrs. Sheffield?"

"You know, I asked him about her," Meg replied with a mischievous grin. "He says that she'll decide what she wants to do when she feels ready. My opinion is that a talent scout for Yale whose candidate rejects money from the Pentagon must lose a certain amount of human warmth for her candidate ..."

"In other words, he's going to look after his vineyards."

Meg shook her hair and smiled, as if to dismiss all serious thoughts.

"By the way, speaking of wine... Is your offer to see together if the wine was worth it still valid? I mean, that is, if it's worth all this trouble to see if the wine is still good. That is, is it any good?"